THE INSURMOUNTABLE EDGE

Thomas H. Goodfellow

THE INSURMOUNTABLE EDGE

A Story in Three Books
BOOK ONE

SPENSER PUBLISHING HOUSE

Spenser Publishing House, LLC
11661 San Vicente Boulevard, Suite 220
Los Angeles, CA 90049
www.spenserpublishinghouse.com

ISBN 978-1-7346130-0-1 (hardcover)
ISBN 978-1-7346130-3-2 (paperback)
ISBN 978-1-7346130-6-3 (e-book)

Library of Congress Control Number: 2020902684

Cover and interior design by Lisa Ham at spaceechoes.com
Image by peterschreiber.media

FOR J.A.G.

What is a fair lifespan for a human being? And if that life be taken by another before its natural end, what debt shall be owed?

Inscription on a stone tablet found on the island of Mykonos. Author unknown, circa 1200 B.C. Translated from the Greek.

PROLOGUE

The men said it was just a game but the boy knew better. The boy was eight years old and his name was Sam. The men had taken him and his sister from his home early in the morning and they stood over him then. There were three men and they all looked alike. They were tall and very thin with dark, lined faces and black hair and beards. The men smelled bad and wore baggy clothes unlike any Sam had ever seen before. Sam believed they were from a foreign country. He thought they might be brothers.

"Keep digging," said one of the men to Sam. "We will start the game as soon as you are done."

Then the man laughed and the other two men laughed with him.

Sam's sister was digging next to him. Her name was Lizzy and she was seven. Both Sam and Lizzy had shovels.

"Sam, I'm scared," Lizzy said.

"Don't be scared Lizzy," Sam said. "We will play the game and then go home."

But Sam knew better. Sam also knew they were somewhere in the desert. He had been to the desert before but this was not the same one. The sun was directly over his head and it was very hot. Sweat had gathered on Sam's brow and some of it dripped into Sam's eyes, stinging them. Sam wiped the sweat away with the back of his hand. Big birds were circling around the sun and Sam recognized them as vultures. He thought he could hear the vultures making a low whining sound but could not be sure. The ground he and Lizzy were digging in was sandy, and the brown hills in the distance were blurry and without trees or bushes. Sam thought he saw water near the hills but he did not think it was real. Sam had learned about mirages in school and that is what he thought the water was. There were houses surrounding him but their windows were all broken. It looked like there had been some grass in front of the houses but the grass was all dead now and the air was full of its smell. He decided no one lived here anymore.

"Dig faster," said the man who had spoken before. "We do not want to be late."

The man laughed and the other two men laughed with him.

Lizzy looked questioningly at Sam. Sam gave a nearly imperceptible shake of his head. Lizzy understood. She kept digging.

Sam tried to think what his father would do. His father had been a soldier but was dead now. Sam wanted to be a soldier too one day. What would a soldier do, he wondered.

The hole was then three feet deep and about four feet wide. Sam dug a shovel-full of earth and tossed it out the side of the hole. As he did so, he snuck a look over his shoulder with his eyes only. He did not want the men to see where he was looking. Sam saw that the man in the dark suit and yellow socks was still there watching them about thirty yards away. Sam thought the man in the suit was Asian. The Asian man leaned against the small black bus they had all come in. The bus had darkened windows. The two white men, the ones who seemed to be the Asian man's friends, were still inside the bus, behind the windows.

Sam knew the Asian man was the boss because the other men listened to him. The Asian man said his brother had known Sam's father but something had told Sam not to ask how, so he did not. Sam tried to memorize the Asian man's face so he could tell the police what he looked like later.

Sam threw another shovel-full of earth out of the hole. He knew if the hole got much deeper his sister, even with his help, might not be able to climb out. Sam decided he knew what a soldier would do. A soldier would fight. A soldier would not give up.

Sam waited until the man nearest him looked away. Then, wielding his shovel like a baseball bat, Sam took his batter's stance like he had been taught in Little League and swung as hard as he could, hitting the man in the knee with the shovel's blade. The man bent over clutching his knee and screamed in agony.

"Run Lizzy!" Sam screamed.

Lizzy froze for a moment, but then dropped her shovel and tried to scramble up the side of the hole. She was too small to get out on her own. Sam bent down and gave her a lift. Lizzy cleared the edge and took off running. Sam clawed the side of the hole, lifted himself out, and sprinted after her.

The other two men, who had been laughing at the one that Sam had hit with the shovel, stopped laughing. Sam could hear their footsteps running behind him. Sam caught up with Lizzy and took her hand.

"Faster, Lizzy," Sam said. "Faster."

Sam and Lizzy ran as fast as they could but it was only a few seconds later when the men caught them. One man grabbed Lizzy by the scruff of her neck and the other did the same to Sam. The men carried Sam and Lizzy back to the hole and threw them in. The man Sam had hit in the knees leaned over, grabbed Sam's hair, pulled back his head, and spit in Sam's face. Then the man stood up, pulled a gun out of his pocket, and pointed it at Sam.

"If you do that again," the man said, "I will kill you. Both of you face me, put your hands at your side, and do not move."

The man turned to the other men and said, "The hole is deep enough. Place the stakes."

One of the other men reached down, took the shovels out of the hole, handed one of the shovels to the man who did not have a gun, and kept the other for himself. The two men quickly used the shovel blades to hammer some green metal fence stakes into the ground on the outside of the hole. They pulled Sam and Lizzy out of the grave and tied them to the stakes with rope. The ropes cut into Sam's and Lizzy's bodies and the children were unable to move. Lizzy was crying.

"We have to be brave," Sam said to her. "Someone will come for us."

The three men walked about sixty feet away. The man who had pointed the gun at Sam put the gun into his waistband. He then used one of the shovels to build up a small pile of earth while the other two men gathered stones. The stones the two men were gathering were the shape and size of small balls, like baseballs or tennis balls.

Sam tried as hard as he could not to, but he started to cry. He wished his mother would come for him and Lizzy.

The two men finished gathering stones about the same time as the other man finished building up the small pile of earth. Sam thought the pile looked like a pitcher's mound. The two men dropped the stones near the mound.

Lizzy was crying uncontrollably then. Sam kept trying to stop crying but could not. His arms and chest hurt where the tight rope was cutting into them. Sam did not know why, but he turned again to look at the Asian man. The Asian man had left the bus and was walking toward them. He had put a mask on his head. The mask looked like a dragon.

Sam turned back to look at the men near the mound. The man who had built the mound picked up a rock and seemed to weigh it in his hand and study its shape. The man stepped onto the mound, peered at Sam as if he was looking for a sign from a catcher, then wound up and threw the stone as hard as he could. The stone hit the ground between Lizzy's and Sam's bodies and skirted off into the brush behind them. Lizzy was wailing then.

The man threw three more stones and each of them missed. The other men were laughing at him. The man seemed to get very angry. He picked up another stone and looked like he was concentrating very hard. He wound up and threw it. The stone hit Lizzy right between her eyes and there was a sickening crunch. Lizzy stopped crying and her head fell to the side. Blood spurted out over her face. The two men who were laughing before then started clapping. The one who was pitching took a bow.

Sam shut his eyes very tight and tried to block out all sounds. All he could hear was his own breathing and his heart beating. In his mind he saw the two strongest men he knew about. The men had played football in college with his father and then later fought with his father in the Army. His father said they were the best soldiers who had ever lived and that he had always tried to be just like them. Sam had photographs of the men on his bedroom wall at home. He had memorized their names. One was named Jack Wilder. The other was Jeff Bradshaw. They were both Army generals.

Sam knew that General Bradshaw and General Wilder could destroy the man in the dragon mask and the men on the pitcher's mound. The generals could save him and Lizzy if only they knew that he and Lizzy were tied up and they had enough time to get to them. Sam prayed for the two generals to come and help him before it was too late.

But it was already too late.

Sam felt a sudden quick pain at the front of his skull and then everything went dark for him forever.

PART I

GENERAL JACK WILDER'S RANCH

CHAPTER 1

I first spotted the big blue Maybach at about 7:00 a.m. on a Monday morning when the car was approximately a mile away from my position and trundling slowly towards me along the narrow, tortuous confines of my ranch's main dirt road. At that time I had no idea who the Maybach's occupants were, and as far as I was concerned, those occupants were uninvited and unwelcome.

The sun had risen two hours prior to the Maybach's approach. At first light, the fierce star in the center of our solar system had glowed bright orange in the eastern Sierra skies, but seemed to have been off duty ever since. The air was bitterly cold and full of the smell of snow.

That freezing Monday morning also happened to fall on the 5th of June. I remember the date well, because not only did that mysterious blue Maybach's visit augur the loss of a legion of innocent lives, and forever change my own life, but also because that particular June 5th was the fourth anniversary of my beloved wife Grace's death.

In the four years since my wife Grace had died, the number of visitors I'd had at the ranch was exactly two. Which averages out to half a visitor a year. Grace was a more polite and social being than I am and when she was alive our yearly visitor rate was probably twenty-five times higher than that. Those dozen or so visitors a year had always been invited, however, and were therefore welcomed by Grace and me with open arms.

It was possible that if Grace had been alive that day she would have counseled me to keep an open mind with respect to the Maybach's unknown occupants. She may have even suggested we give them a well-mannered reception, at least until they proved they deserved otherwise.

Entertaining visitors without Grace, however, was not my cup of tea. That morning I didn't care how far the Maybach's passengers might have come, nor how difficult it had most likely been for them to find me or my ranch. I considered the passengers' intrusion as trespassing, plain and simple.

Since my ranch's main road was over three miles long and the

Maybach couldn't have been moving faster than five miles per hour, that meant the passengers' trespassing had been going on for at least twenty minutes. Twenty minutes of trespassing is more than enough time to win my ranch's trespassing gold medal. It's not a gold medal anyone in their right mind would ever want to win.

It wasn't only the Maybach's trespassing passengers with which I had a problem, however. I also had a problem with the Maybach itself. Back then, I happened to have a strong and abiding dislike for all things Maybach. Indeed, my enmity for Maybachs was so intense, that whenever I saw a Maybach, my stomach would start to churn and I'd get an acrid taste in my mouth. I was experiencing both - the churning stomach and the acrid taste - as I watched the Maybach's approach along the ranch's road.

It would be a grievous mistake, however, to think that my aversion to Maybachs was based on some half-baked, lame-brained, fancy-ass presumption. Because it wasn't. My aversion was grounded in hard fought, mostly bitter, experience.

During my service in the special forces of the United States military over the previous two decades, my commanders had assigned me the task of blowing up a Maybach, and the passengers inside it - bad people all - more than a dozen times. Those demolition assignments had always entailed placing my men and myself in situations far more tricky and dangerous than I would have preferred. I'd never lost any men, but it had been a close call on many an occasion.

All because Maybachs, in my opinion, far and above any other car in the world, were just too damn hard to blow up.

In theory, that big blue Maybach heading my way that morning also never should have been able to find me in the first place. My ranch, which has been my home since the day I was born, is hidden amidst the California High Sierras in an isolated and extremely remote area that lies about 350 miles north of Los Angeles. The ranch encompasses over three thousand secluded acres of low, rolling hills and sits on the floor of a wide valley ringed by the granite-peaked mountains that lie east of Yosemite. The hills are covered with pumice and studded with hundreds of trees. The trees are mainly Jeffrey and lodgepole pines, red firs, and western junipers.

The ranch has been in my family since my great-great-grandfather, the great warrior General Tristram Wilder, decamped from the Union Army shortly after the Civil War, headed west, and, courtesy of the Homestead Act, made the ranch's land his own. I'd been lucky enough to follow in Tristram's footsteps and had also risen to the rank of general in the U.S. Army. I'd been on leave for the two years prior to the morning the Maybach showed up, and I'd spent almost all that leave on the ranch.

I'd actually been in a rather pleasant mood up until the Maybach's vexatious appearance. I'd awakened before sunrise and grabbed the shirt I had carefully laid out on the dresser next to my bed the night before. The shirt, a black Grateful Dead t-shirt that had been given to me by Grace, was the one I always wore on the anniversary of her death. Over fifteen years had elapsed since Grace, who loved the 'Dead, had bought the t-shirt for me at one of the band's Oakland Coliseum concerts. We had attended that concert when Grace and I were both still in our early twenties.

Though the t-shirt was precious to me, some might have considered it not to have been the most romantic of items. The front of the shirt depicted a human skull. The top of the skull had been split open into two jagged halves of splintered cranial bone, one half fire-engine red, and one half cobalt blue. Between the skull's bony halves lay the surface of a naked, pulsating brain. The words 'Steal Your Face' had been written beneath the skull.

"You know why I bought this t-shirt for you, don't you, my darling?" Grace had said as she handed the shirt to me.

"Because it reminds you of my brain?" I had said.

"No," Grace had said. "Because if I could, I'd steal your face and keep it safe and warm by my side every time you go away."

I was already in the Army back then, and Grace had been referring to my military missions, which could take me away from home for many months at a time. I was only a captain at that time, however. My promotion to the rank of general wouldn't come until many years later.

"You'd give my face back to me when I came home though, right?" I had said.

"That depends," Grace had said.

"Depends on what?" I had said.

"On whatever I decide it depends on," Grace had said. Then she had wrapped her arms around my neck, pulled my face close to hers, and kissed me long and passionately on my lips.

With the memory of that too, too, long ago kiss from my dearly departed wife still lingering in my mind - and the Maybach's trespass still hours away - I had continued to prepare to meet the day. I slipped my arms into the 'Dead t-shirt's sleeves, poked my head through its crew neck collar, pulled on a pair of blue jeans, and laced up my tan leather hiking boots. I put my iPhone, a sniper spotter scope, a humidity tester, and some match grade bullets into the pockets of my jeans, then washed my face, brushed my teeth, and made my way to the kitchen. In the kitchen, I prepared and ate a breakfast of bacon, orange juice, pancakes, scrambled eggs, toast, and coffee. As soon as I'd finished eating, I'd thrown on a windbreaker, exited my house, and went into my front yard. In the yard, I picked some purple Sierra lupine wildflowers. The lupines were Grace's favorite wildflowers when she was alive.

Cradling the lupines in my arms, my nose full of their sweet grapelike fragrance - a fragrance Grace adored - I had climbed the small hill on top of which Grace's grave lay. Arriving at her grave, I had carefully laid out the flowers beside her headstone, taken a seat on the pine bench next to the stone, and begun a nice long talk with Grace.

Over the previous four years a number of people had said, "Jack Wilder, you talk to your wife too much. You need to stop." I had never listened to what those people said. I loved Grace and I missed her. She was a beautiful, intelligent, vibrant woman. Grace was only thirty-three years old when she died. I was thirty-seven the year the Maybach showed up. Grace and I had been the same age when she died.

I should note that no matter how long, or how many times, I had talked to Grace, she hadn't talked back. If Grace had, it would have meant my sanity would have been just as questionable as the sanity of the other two human inhabitants then sharing the ranch with me. Those two inhabitants were General Jeff Bradshaw, my best friend, longtime comrade in arms, and true American war hero, and Adelaide Monroe, Grace's seventeen year old juvenile delinquent niece. Adelaide was staying on the ranch with Jeff and me until she fulfilled the terms of her probation.

I should also note that Jeff and Adelaide were the two visitors to which I had earlier alluded - the only two visitors to the ranch I'd had in the four years since Grace's death. Two visitors who had arrived, each with their own special troubles, and never left.

Grace's grave, and the pine bench next to it upon which I was sitting, were near the center of the ranch and also at the ranch's highest point. From that high point there was a clear view of the land surrounding the ranch for miles and miles and also the granite peaks that abut Yosemite's eastern border. The point had been Grace's and my favorite place to view the world when Grace was alive and it was where Grace had chosen to rest in death.

I had been talking to Grace about the view when the Maybach first encroached on my consciousness that morning. As soon as I had seen the Maybach, I knew I wasn't going to be able to avoid dealing with it. I had, however, estimated that the Maybach was then far enough away so that I could indulge myself in the luxury of spending at least another ten to fifteen minutes with Grace before I would have to tear myself away from her and begin thinking in earnest about how to handle the car's intrusion.

Still, it would have gone against both my instincts and military training not to have at least intermittently checked on the Maybach's progress during even that small window of time. And so, I occasionally stole a glance at the approaching car while I continued to talk to Grace.

'Talk', however, may have been something of a misnomer. Distracted as I was by the presence of the Maybach, what I did could probably be more properly described as rambling. I flitted from topic to topic during those precious remaining minutes, saying things like -

"I'm sure you can see I'm wearing the 'Dead t-shirt you gave me, Grace. I know it's illustrated with a split open brain, but I still find it very romantic..."

"I've been thinking about how wonderful our children would have been if only fate hadn't taken away our chance to have them..."

"I know you're probably upset I haven't found someone new, but I just can't bring myself to look, let alone be with anyone but you..."

What I spent the most time discussing with Grace, however, was the day, as it was a day Grace would have cherished -

"We had a really hard rain last night, Grace, and there was a light snow early this morning. Most people might think the snow is unusual, but you and I know we can get snow up here in the Sierras even in late spring. It's cold too, just the way you like it, and my breath is misting right before my eyes. The sun is a gorgeous orange-yellow. It's climbing in the east right now, and it's especially beautiful since it's framed by a brilliant cerulean - you like that word? I looked it up just for you - sky above and snow-dusted silvery granite peaks below. The sun may not be doing much for the cold air, but it's warming the earth just enough to give the snow a push towards melting. The seagulls are circling over-head, riding the rising thermals. The gulls are making a lot of noise too, cawing in that language of theirs that's clear to them, but certainly not to me. A little breeze just kicked up and it's knocking some of the snow-flakes out of the pines' green needles and stirring up some of the pines' scent. It's actually a pretty pungent smell. Oh, look at that! A couple of golden-mantled ground squirrels are racing down the trunk of a pine tree. Now they're running across the snow...and...there they go, scram-bling up another trunk..."

And then, just like that, my time with Grace was up. The Maybach, though it had been slowed by the mud created by the nighttime rain and morning snowmelt, and also by having to contend with the manzanita, scrub brush, and occasional boulder clinging hard to the side of the narrow ranch road, had kept coming and needed to be dealt with.

I got up off the bench, wincing as pain shot through my left knee and half the other joints in my body. I stayed fit, but my body was a mess compared to most thirty-seven year olds. Too much shrapnel and too many bullets and hard landings. My left knee only worked at all because it had been completely reconstructed with pieces of my ham-string and patella tendons, the operation a gift from Uncle Sam. Neither the knee nor my other less than perfect joints appreciated rapid changes in weather.

"I'll be back soon, my love," I said to Grace.

I kissed Grace's headstone and set off towards the Maybach.

CHAPTER 2

The best place to observe the Maybach's approach was going to be from a bluff along the western edge of the plateau in the middle of my ranch. The plateau's upper surface is at an altitude of slightly over 8,000 feet. The plateau itself is about one hundred feet above the rest of the ranch, a little more than two hundred acres in size and, like the ranch's land that surrounds it, is covered with tall trees, the aforementioned red firs predominating.

Grace's gravesite and the ranch's main buildings sit atop the plateau. The western bluff was about five hundred yards away from Grace's grave and it would take me about five minutes to get there. As I walked, my hiking boots made crunching sounds in the snow, leaving a trail of footprints behind me. My feet were cold, but the sun had begun to grow stronger and it warmed my upper body. I unbuttoned my windbreaker.

I hadn't gone far when a glimmer of movement in the snow caught my eye. A seagull flailed about, flapping its wings, snapping its beak, and stumbling in a small erratic circle on its spindly legs. Its neck and left leg were entangled in a plastic six-pack soft drink holder, the kind with six interconnected rings.

Adelaide, Jeff, and I don't generally leave trash lying around the ranch. The gull probably had become ensnared somewhere in the outside world and then traveled as far as it could until it finally got so tangled up in the plastic rings that it could no longer fly. I picked up the gull and felt its ribcage gently flex beneath its soft feathers. I carefully extricated the bird from the offending plastic, then set it back down on the ground. The gull shook the snow off his wings and upper legs and flew away.

I continued toward the bluff. Two hundred yards later, the firs thinned out and I came to the clearing in which I lived. Jeff, Adelaide, and my dog, Ashley, were in the clearing and already well into their morning activities.

Jeff was perched atop his thoroughbred racehorse, Eclipse. Eclipse was moving in a fast gallop around the ranch's dirt training track. Jeff had built the track himself with the use of an ancient bulldozer I owned.

Eclipse was a former champion who had been forced to stop racing due to injury and was then Jeff's rehabilitation project. Jeff, who suffered mightily from post-traumatic stress syndrome, could also have been said to be a former champion in need of rehabilitation. I believed Jeff thought that if he could fix Eclipse, he could fix himself.

Adelaide was climbing the ladder of the thirty-four-foot parachute jump tower that lay just beyond the northern edge of the training track. Adelaide, whose dream was to be a special forces soldier, was using the tower to practice parachute jumps. The tower, which Jeff and I had built for Adelaide, was a near duplicate of the tower from which the two of us, as young special forces soldiers, had taken our own first training jumps at Fort Benning. The purpose of the tower was to train the proper way to exit a plane for a parachute jump and then land safely on the ground.

Ashley, a black Newfoundland, was chasing some late migrating mallard ducks in the large pond that took up most of the track's infield. The mallards had iridescent green heads and yellow beaks. The ducks vigorously kicked their webbed feet, leaving tiny wakes on the pond's surface as they managed to stay, as always, just out of Ashley's grasp. The small Zodiac boat with which I sometimes accompanied Ashley on her quixotic quests laid tied up to the pond's dock.

Watching Ashley, Adelaide, and Jeff merrily gamboling made me momentarily feel like some outcast child who had been banished from the playground. Such banishment was, of course, entirely the fault of my having to deal with the Maybach, and my resentment of the interloping car grew by leaps and bounds.

I reached the edge of the plateau's bluff and took cover behind a brace of densely leaved green chinquapin bushes so that I could observe the Maybach unseen. The Maybach had continued to make slow going as it had slogged through the deep mud, and at that moment, was still a half-mile out. At the rate the car was traveling, it would be about five minutes before it arrived at the stream that borders the plateau.

The stream comes in from the north end of the plateau where it then splits into two sections. Each section flows around either side of the plateau until they join together again at the plateau's south end. The stream thus forms what is, in effect, a moat around the plateau.

Normally, the section of the stream that was below me was about four feet deep and twenty feet wide. Due to the rains, however, the stream was flowing much higher than normal, the water rushing loudly in foam cascades around the moss covered boulders that protruded above the stream's surface.

The only way to cross the moat-like stream was to make use of the steel drawbridge which joined the ranch's main road to the road that climbed up the bluff to the top of the plateau. The drawbridge, which was on my side of the stream, was up and locked with a chain and padlock. When the Maybach reached the stream, it wasn't going to be able to come any further unless I put the drawbridge down, which, of course, was something I was never going to do. If I'd been in a better mood, I might have even congratulated myself on being so prescient as to have built the drawbridge in the first place, but I wasn't, so I didn't.

I took the sniper spotter scope out of my pants pocket. I had intended to use it for the sniper lesson Adelaide had requested I give her later that day, but the scope would also work just fine to get a closer look at the Maybach. I placed the scope's leather lanyard around my neck, and lifted the scope up to my right eye.

Thanks to the scope's magnification, I confirmed the Maybach was a high security Maybach. High security Maybachs are expensive. This one probably had set its owner back close to a million dollars. The car's armored steel exterior was coated in brightly polished blue metallic paint. Its solid black rubber tires were airless and blowout proof. All the windows were bulletproof and composed of thick, layered polycarbonate resin that would repel large caliber rounds. The windows were also heavily tinted so that I could not make out who was inside.

Just then, my iPhone rang. I took the phone out and checked the screen. I was surprised by who the caller was, but the caller was also someone whose call I could never refuse to take. I pushed answer, placed the phone to my ear, and keeping one eye on the Maybach, spoke into the phone.

CHAPTER 3

"General Martinez," I said.

"How did you know it was me, Jack?" said the voice in my ear. The voice belonged to Lt. General John Martinez. Martinez was a good man with whom I had shared many a battlefield over the course of my career, but I hadn't talked to him in over two years.

"Your name came up on my cell phone," I said.

My cell phone was a specially modified iPhone that I had used when I was on active duty. I had retained it even though I was on leave. One of the things the phone could do was identify any caller calling on a United States military line.

"Oh, right," Martinez said. "I suppose you know why I'm calling?"

"Well, John, if it has something to do with the fact we're about to go to war with China over Saudi Arabia, then yes," I said. "I may be on leave, but that doesn't mean I don't follow the news. I also saw you were just promoted to deputy commander of CENTCOM. Congratulations."

CENTCOM is the United States Central Command and oversees combatant command for the central part of the globe. The entire Middle East is within that central area.

"Thanks," Martinez said. "You're correct, we are about to go to war with China. We could really use you out here, brother."

"That's kind of you to say," I said. "But my brain's been slowly turning to mush due to lack of use for the last two years. Not sure I'd be of any good to anybody."

"General Jack Wilder at fifty percent, no, strike that, at ten percent, is worth anyone else at a hundred," Martinez said.

"Ten percent is probably the right number," I said.

"Perfect," Martinez said. "Get on out here."

"Flattery will get you everywhere," I said. "Now, why did you really call?"

"We've got a situation we'd like your input on," Martinez said.

"What is it?" I said.

"The Chinese have a million troops camped out on the Iraqi side of the Iraq-Saudi border," Martinez said. "They also have two thousand tanks fronting their infantry with new ones arriving by the hour. In the last week alone, they added fifty more bomber and fighter aircraft to the five hundred they already had stationed in and around Baghdad. Another supercarrier just joined the one they've had hanging around within striking range in the Indian Ocean."

"Big numbers," I said. "Guess the Chinese figure those billion plus people they got are gonna need a lot more oil than they currently have."

"Yeah, more oil than they're already pulling out of Iraq anyway," Martinez said.

"It's always been unfathomable to me why the politicos didn't let us stop the Chinese from taking over Iraq in the first place last year," I said.

"Nearly everything the politicos do is unfathomable, Jack," Martinez said. "You know that."

"I do," I said. "I suppose the reason they've drawn a line in the sand when it comes to China invading Saudi Arabia is equally unfathomable?"

"To all of us at CENTCOM it is, yes," Martinez said.

"You actually believe the Chinese are going to start shooting at us anytime soon?" I said.

"We do," Martinez said. "The problem is it doesn't make any sense."

"Sense as in all war is senseless?" I said. "Or we've got them hopelessly outclassed so what are they thinking?"

"The latter," Martinez said.

Through the spotter scope I watched as the Maybach took too much speed into one of the tight turns on the ranch's road. The car barely missed crunching a fender against a boulder. I cringed involuntarily, even though nothing would have made me happier than to see the Maybach wound itself.

"The Chinese aren't stupid, John," I said. "They must believe they have some kind of advantage."

"From the chatter we've picked up, that is exactly what they believe," Martinez said. "They're calling that advantage 'The Insurmountable Edge.'"

I took the spotter scope away from my eye and gave Martinez my full attention.

"Do you guys know what the 'The Insurmountable Edge' is?" I said.

"No," Martinez said. "We're pretty convinced we're not vulnerable to any kind of cyberattack, and we don't think they'd be crazy enough to use chemical, germ, or nuclear weapons."

"Chemical, germ, or nuclear would be suicidal on their part," I said. "We'd just retaliate in kind. What's your best guess then on what else could be 'insurmountable'?"

"That's why I'm calling you," Martinez said.

"What does that mean?" I said.

"We all know what great instincts you have," Martinez said. "We thought maybe you might be able to come up with something, because, frankly, we're stumped."

"That can't be possible," I said. "You've got nothing but geniuses over at CENTCOM."

"We're missing the one that's hiding on some goddamn ranch out in the middle of nowhere," Martinez said. He paused. "Actually two. I don't suppose you could bring Jeff onto this call as well, could you?"

"Jeff's doing better," I said. "But I don't think that'd be a good idea."

"I'll have to trust your judgment on that," Martinez said. "Give Jeff my best, please though. Now, back to my original question. What's the edge?"

"I suppose you've also already ruled out death ray satellites and giant Japanese robots?" I said.

"I'm glad to see you haven't lost your sense of humor," Martinez said. "Seriously, though, what do you think?"

"Jesus, John," I said. "I have no idea. It sounds to me like you've already hit on everything it could possibly be."

"I was afraid of that," Martinez said. "Do me a favor and give it some thought, okay? Call me if you come up with anything."

"I'll do that," I said. "What's your estimate of when the Chinese will launch their attack?"

"Four weeks from today," Martinez said.

A loud thunderclap reverberated across the ranch's pumice plain. I looked over my shoulder. Another storm was moving in from the east, its huge, black, roiling clouds seeming to extend from the earth to the sky. High above me, a jet was traveling west toward the Pacific Ocean, its contrails dissipating rapidly in the storm's winds.

"I'll be in touch well before then," I said.

"Well before would be highly appreciated," Martinez said.

We both clicked off the call.

I put the spotter scope to my eye again and checked on the Maybach. It was stuck in some mud. Tires spinning, clumps of dirt and snow spattering its rear bumper and fenders, the Maybach rocked back and forth as whoever was behind the wheel tried to free it. After several tries, the car gained traction. It lurched forward, dodged a boulder on one side of the road, but then scraped up against a manzanita bush on the other side. The scope's optics were strong enough so that I could make out newly minted granular abrasions in the Maybach's blue paint. I allowed myself a small smile.

I heard a soft thump behind me and turned around. Jeff and Eclipse were approaching.

CHAPTER 4

Eclipse was taking long, powerful strides, and with each of them his hooves punched down through the thin, crusty snow to the mud below. The hoof prints filled rapidly with snowmelt, forming tiny shimmering pools. Jeff gently tugged Eclipse's reins, guided the horse next to me behind the chinquapin bush, then jumped out of the saddle, landing effortlessly on the ground.

Eclipse, blowing hard, nuzzled my face. I stroked his long nose. At eight years old, Eclipse was still a magnificent animal. He was dark bay, over 17 hands tall, had a classic head, intelligent eyes, and strongly muscled shoulders and hips. As good as he looked, I still thought it would take a miracle for him to ever race again. But seeing Eclipse race again was what Jeff wanted, and if I had learned anything during all my years with Jeff, it was never to count him out. He usually found a way.

General Jeff Bradshaw was African American, six foot three, one hundred and ninety pounds, and was then thirty-seven years old. Jeff kept himself in perfect physical condition and his jaw and cheekbones looked like they were sculpted. His jet black hair was close-cropped and his eyes were like two black pearls. Jeff's ever present special forces ring was on his left hand.

Most women say Jeff is the handsomest man they have ever seen. Jeff says it would be a hundred percent except sometimes I am standing next to him detracting from the vote. I don't ever comment on that.

Jeff had been afflicted with post-traumatic stress disorder - PTSD - two and a half years earlier following a horrifically bad battlefield experience in the Sudan. I normally would have been with Jeff on the mission that set off his disease, but I was in the hospital recuperating from my knee surgery at the time. Even though my absence that day was out of my control, I still felt guilty about not being with him.

Jeff had been severely wounded physically as well during that last battle and he had been taken to Walter Reed National Military Medical Center for treatment. The Army doctors did a good job of patching up Jeff's body, but they had made a mess of his psychological care. I watched Jeff suffer for six months, then decided I could do no worse on my own and brought Jeff back to the ranch with me.

For the previous two years I'd been doing my best to nurse Jeff back to health. We had been cooped up on the ranch since we had returned to it, and neither of us had seen any combat during those two years. Jeff and I had been on active duty for nearly all of the fifteen years before he got sick, so it had been quite a change for both of us.

That June morning Jeff was wearing a t-shirt with a picture of Willie Shoemaker on it, blue jeans, brown leather riding chaps, shiny black riding boots, a blue and white striped jockey helmet, and a bright red English fox hunting jacket with a black velvet collar and brass buttons. There was no question in my mind that Jeff had to be the biggest jockey in America at that time.

Jeff walked up to me and crouched down behind the chinquapin bush. He gestured with his chin towards the Maybach.

"We expecting visitors?" Jeff said.

"No," I said.

"So you don't got no idea who be in that car?" Jeff said.

"I do not," I said.

"Really?" Jeff said.

"Yes, really," I said.

"Bet that don't make you happy," Jeff said.

"No, it doesn't," I said.

"We gonna run them off?" Jeff said.

"I'm hoping they'll turn around when they get to the moat," I said.

Jeff seemed to study the Maybach for a moment. He shook his head.

"My gut say ain't no way they gonna turn around," Jeff said. "Fact, they seem so determined, I believe they swim the moat if need be."

"Thanks," I said. "That makes me feel a lot better."

"Just telling it like it is," Jeff said.

"Of course you are," I said.

I patted Eclipse's nose again.

"How'd he do today?" I said.

"Smoking," Jeff said. "They got a stakes race at Santa Rosa in August I'm gonna enter him in."

"What's with the Shoemaker shirt?" I said. "I thought you were a

Pat Day fan?"

"Shoe better," Jeff said. "Shoe so tiny, he lived in a shoebox when he born."

"Shoe win the Kentucky Derby?" I said.

"Yep," Jeff said. "Four times."

"Four Derbies?" I said. "That's a lot."

"Woulda' been five he don't stand up just before the finish line on Gallant Man in '57," Jeff said. "Bill Hartack blew right on by."

"Gallant Man's owner must have been pissed," I said.

"Suspect so," Jeff said.

Jeff seemed to suddenly notice I was wearing my Grateful Dead Steal Your Face t-shirt. He frowned.

"Sorry," Jeff said. "Just realized."

"Realized what?" I said.

"Today is the anniversary of Grace's passing, isn't it?" Jeff said.

"Yes, it is," I said.

"My condolences," Jeff said. "I'll bring some flowers up to her grave later, pay my respects."

"Thank you," I said.

"You already been up there talking with her?" Jeff said.

"I have," I said.

"Grace talk back?" Jeff said.

"No," I said.

"Good," Jeff said.

Jeff stared at my shirt for another moment.

"Huh," Jeff said. "Never noticed that before."

"Noticed what?" I said

"Those lines on that brain cortex," Jeff said. "They all intersecting and interconnecting in little boxes and shit."

I should note that Jeff spoke in the way he did by choice. Jeff was the son of two investment banking graduates of Harvard Business School and was raised in a fifteen thousand square foot mansion on twenty heavily forested, lush green acres in Greenwich, Connecticut. His diction and grammar were better than anyone I had ever met. He had stopped using that diction and grammar, however, at least most of the time, when he got to West Point, which is where we met. Jeff wanted to fit in, and he believed, rightly or wrongly, that the other mostly middle-class cadets would resent a rich black kid, especially one who spoke as elegantly as he did. Jeff, thus, had changed the way he spoke.

"I know the lines you're talking about," I said.

"Good, because then you'll understand why I got to tell you something," Jeff said.

"Not sure I like where this is heading, Jeff," I said.

"Understandable," Jeff said. "But you know how Grace said she got you that shirt because she wanted to steal your face and keep it close to her?"

"That's what Grace said," I said. "I found it very romantic at the time."

"If I'd given it to you, it woulda been for a different reason," Jeff said.

"What reason would that be, Jeff?" I said.

"Reason be those lines remind me of your brain," Jeff said. "They look like the bottom of a bone dry lake bed, like you know in Morocco or something, all those cracks and such."

"So you're saying my brain is cracked?" I said.

"Well, you certainly ain't no paragon of compos mentis, now is you?" Jeff said.

Jeff laughed.

"I appreciate how sensitive you're being on the anniversary of my loss," I said.

"I'm being sensitive," Jeff said. "Just not to you."

"What does that mean?" I said.

"Before she died, Grace told me it was my job to get you to move on," Jeff said. "Been four years. Seem like there been very little moving on to me."

"Yeah, well as far as I'm concerned I'm right on schedule in that regard," I said.

"Uh huh," Jeff said. "You care to share that schedule?"

"Not with you, I don't," I said.

The truth was I had originally had a very precise schedule for moving on after Grace died. The schedule called for me to move on after exactly one year, which was the amount of time Grace had told me was all I was allowed to mourn for her. But I'd long ago thrown that schedule out. I was still mourning for Grace and my current schedule, which I was quite happy with, was to mourn for her the rest of my life.

Jeff, who seemed to have been studying my face for any sign of weakness that would allow him to further upbraid me about my schedule, apparently reached the conclusion that such an endeavor would bear little fruit at that moment, and it was thus time for him to move on to other things.

Jeff extended his hand to me.

I knew what that hand meant.

Jeff's and my fifteen years of combat together in nearly every hot spot on earth had pretty much made it so that both of us knew what the other was thinking, or wanted, without a word needing to be spoken out loud. In this case what Jeff wanted was the sniper spotter scope. I took Eclipse's reins away from Jeff and gave him the scope. Jeff adjusted the scope's focus and pointed the scope at the Maybach.

"Windows got a nice tint job," Jeff said. "Can't see nothing inside, but I say it be two Normans and a package."

"The Normans are big, close to three-fifty," I said. "The package is small, maybe one ten."

Jeff and I prided ourselves on possessing a lot of knowledge that others might find of questionable value. One of the things we knew how to do was to predict the contents of a vehicle by the way it moved and sat on its suspension. Normans are bodyguards. The package is what the Normans are protecting.

"Normans in front," Jeff said. "Package in back."

"Package could be a jockey," I said. "Or a baby."

Jeff glared me as if I'd committed a venial sin.

"Ain't fun if you don't take this serious," Jeff said.

"Sorry," I said. "I'm still hoping they just turn around and hightail it back to wherever the hell they came from. I was having a nice day until they showed up."

"I understand," Jeff said. "Still ain't no excuse. What it be?"

"Package is a woman," I said.

"Correct. Package be a woman," Jeff said. "And she's hot."

"That's a rather large leap," I said.

"From Beverly Hills, California," Jeff said.

"Not impressed," I said. "I read the license plate holder too."

"Hoping you missed that," Jeff said. "Suppose they coulda just bought the damn thing in Beverly Hills. Maybe they from Bel Air, Brentwood, Malibu, or some other such nonsense."

"Wherever they're from, they just need to turn around," I said.

"You already say that," Jeff said. "Tires solid rubber, can't shoot them out. Might get a few rounds through the windshield. But that could get messy."

He paused.

"I know what you're thinking," Jeff said.

"Do you now?" I said.

"Maybachs hard to blow up," Jeff said. "Banja Luka for instance."

"Caracas, Herat, Johannesburg, the list is endless," I said.

"Bad guys got the same bad taste all over the world," Jeff said.

The Maybach kept inching toward us. It would reach the stream soon.

"Think this got something to do with the Chinese?" Jeff said.

"Why on earth would a Maybach slogging through the mud and snow of a beaten up old road on a ranch in the middle of nowhere have anything to do with the Chinese, Jeff?" I said.

"Not my fault your mind isn't big enough to grasp the concept," Jeff said.

"Uh huh," I said.

"Big boys at CENTCOM worried about the Chinese," Jeff said. "Guess you know better than they do."

"How do you know what CENTCOM is thinking?" I said.

"I spoke with them," Jeff said.

"You spoke with CENTCOM?" I said.

"You deaf?" Jeff said. "What'd I just say?"

"When did you speak with them?" I said.

"This morning," Jeff said. "5:00 a.m. Of course that was 3 p.m. Saudi Arabia time, in case you didn't know."

"Who'd you speak to?" I said.

"Little Stevie Kent," Jeff said.

Little Stevie Kent was General Steve Kent, the CENTCOM commander. Kent, as CENTCOM commander, was General John Martinez's superior officer. Little Stevie was also anything but little. He was six feet, eight inches tall and weighed 275 pounds.

"Guess you rate higher than me," I said.

"What's that mean?" Jeff said.

"I just got off the phone with John Martinez," I said.

"He tell you I talk to Stevie?" Jeff said.

"No," I said. "Steve tell you John was going to call me?"

"No," Jeff said.

"That's weird," I said.

"They both probably stressing," Jeff said. "Maybe they don't even know what the other one is doing."

"Steve tell you about the Chinese insurmountable edge?" I said.

"Yep," Jeff said. "He wants to know what I think it could be."

"What'd you tell him?" I said.

"Told him I'd have to give it some further consideration and get back to him," Jeff said.

"I said the same thing to John," I said. "Have you given it any further consideration?"

"Yep," Jeff said.

"What'd you come up with?" I said.

"I think they in deep shit," Jeff said.

The Maybach brushed another manzanita bush on the side of the road and flushed a brace of pheasants. The sunlight flashed off the pheasants' golden chests, and the pheasants' squawks, along with the low-pitched staccato rumble of their rapidly flapping wings, echoed below us.

"We should be going there," Jeff said.

"Going there where?" I said.

"Saudi Arabia, fool," Jeff said. "Show them Chinese a thing or two."

"Sounds like you already have a plan?" I said.

"I do," Jeff said. "We drive to Beale, catch a ride to Moody. Moody got nonstops to Riyadh twice a day."

Beale is a U.S. Air Force base in Marysville, California - a few hours away from my ranch by car - and Moody is an Air Force base in Valdosta, Georgia. The one thing Jeff wanted to do, above all other things, was return to soldiering. In my opinion, however, he was nowhere near ready. Just the night before, at 2:00 a.m., Jeff had been up screaming about IED's - improvised explosive devices.

"We taking your twin with us?" I said.

Jeff's expression told me he wasn't sure where I was going with that. He seemed to think it over for a moment.

"Might," Jeff said warily. "You seen him?"

"Think so," I said. "Last night guy who looked exactly like you was running around the house in his underwear. Screaming something about an IED under his bed."

"Damn," Jeff said. "Thought he was still back in Connecticut with the folks."

"Maybe we should stick around 'til he calms down," I said.

Jeff studied me for a moment, his eyes seeming to become slightly unfocused.

"Yeah, maybe," Jeff said. "Now might not be a good time to leave him on his own."

The Maybach stopped at the edge of the stream, a spot about seventy five yards from where we stood. The driver's door opened.

A giant got out.

CHAPTER 5

Jeff, who still had the sniper scope I had given him, appeared to study the giant through the scope. Thirty seconds passed and I decided it was my turn to take a look. I tapped Jeff on the shoulder.

"What is it?" Jeff said, without turning away from the giant. "Can't you see I'm busy here?"

"You've been looking long enough," I said. "It's my turn."

"Five more seconds," Jeff said.

"Five more seconds?" I said. "What difference is five more seconds going to make?"

"Lotta difference," Jeff said. "It just the right amount of time to get you pissed off since it makes no sense."

"Jesus, what are you two years old?" I said.

"Two, two and a half," Jeff said. "Somewhere around there."

Jeff laughed and took the scope away from his eye. He turned around, grabbed Eclipse's reins from me, and slapped the sniper scope into my right palm. I put the scope to my eye, trained it on the giant man who had gotten out of the car, and took a close look at him.

The man appeared to be in his late twenties. He was about six feet, six inches tall, and over three hundred and fifty pounds. He was muscular and carried his weight well, moving with an almost surprising nimbleness, as if he had once been an athlete. Maybe he still was. The man's arms hung out at wide angles from his chest, pushed there by the bulk of his lat muscles. Even for the man's size, his head was much bigger than normal. His bronze-colored face was broad, large jawed, with a flat nose, and big round nostrils. Thick, dark, stringy hair, worn parted in the middle of his big skull, fell over his ears and halfway down his neck. He wore a black suit with a white dress shirt and a thin black tie. The suit was two sizes too small for him and bulged at the seams. The skin of his forearms was exposed at the ends of his too short sleeves, and white socks showed at the bottom of his too short pant legs. The muddy ground soaked and stained his black leather dress shoes.

I handed the scope back to Jeff.

"Samoan," Jeff said softly.

"Bet he played ball," I said.

"Wouldn't wanna get in front of that train once it got rolling," Jeff said.

"Me either," I said.

The Samoan reached the stream's edge. He looked upstream, then downstream, seemingly trying to find a way across. Not finding one, he rubbed his chin, apparently thinking it over. The drawbridge, standing on its end and in its upright position, was directly across the stream in front of him, but he seemed not to notice it. Maybe he didn't know what a drawbridge was. It wouldn't have mattered if he did know what a drawbridge was, however, because he wasn't going to be able to do anything with it. Unless he'd brought something with him in the Maybach to cut off the bridge's chain and padlock that is.

"Might not be the sharpest tool in the shed," Jeff said.

"Probably tackled with his head," I said.

"Samoans that way," Jeff said.

The Maybach's right front passenger door opened. Another man got out. It was hard to tell without the scope, but the man seemed to have the same face, same body, same hair, and same suit as the other man. Definitely the same walk. Not just the same, but exactly the same.

"Twins?" I said.

"Uh huh," Jeff said.

"Never seen twin Samoans get out of a Maybach before," I said.

"Tweedledee and Tweedledum," Jeff said.

"Which one's which?" I said.

"Nobody knows," Jeff said.

"Not even their mom?" I said.

"Nope," Jeff said.

The second twin joined his brother by the stream. They appeared to confer. Before long, they were both rubbing their chins. A five pound rainbow trout suddenly broke through the stream's surface and rocketed skywards to catch a fly. The trout left a trail of water droplets in its path and its skin glittered red, green, and gold in the sunlight. It could have been the trout's sudden appearance, its sheer size, the sound it made slapping back into the water, or some combination of the three, but whatever it was, the trout startled the Samoans and they jerked backwards in fright.

The rear right passenger door of the Maybach opened. A woman got out. As with the Samoans before her, the woman was too far away for me to get a good look without the scope.

I put out my hand.

Jeff ignored it.

"Didn't we just go over this?" I said. "It's share and share alike."

"Hold on," Jeff said. "You get your turn."

Jeff trained the spotter scope on the woman.

"Shit," Jeff said.

"What?" I said.

"You ain't gonna believe this," Jeff said.

"Let me see," I said.

Jeff ignored me. I grabbed for the scope. Jeff, without taking his eyes off the woman, whipped his shoulder around and blocked my arm.

"Fine, be that way," I said.

Jeff said nothing, just kept looking at the woman.

"She's not hot is she?" I said. "You're embarrassed you got it wrong."

"Be careful what you say," Jeff said.

"What's that supposed to mean?" I said.

"Means I gotta prepare you before you look," Jeff said. "Otherwise your heart might stop and you'll die right here."

"Looking at a woman's not gonna make my heart stop," I said.

"This ain't no ordinary woman," Jeff said.

He paused.

"You know Grace is dead right?" Jeff said.

I thought maybe Jeff was having a hallucination like the one he had had the night before. The thing was, though he had hallucinations nearly every night, he rarely had them during the day. The day ones, when they came, however, were worse.

"Yes, I know that Jeff," I said. "We just talked about that. You said you were going to bring Grace some flowers."

Jeff took the scope away from his face and turned to me.

"You also know there's no such thing as ghosts, right?" Jeff said.

Great. A crazy man was lecturing me about ghosts.

"Yes, I know there are no such things as ghosts, Jeff," I said.

"Okay, here," Jeff said.

He handed me the scope. I put it to my face and trained it on the woman. My heart nearly stopped and I almost died right there.

"She's not a ghost," Jeff said. "You know that, right?"

She might as well have been. The woman was a near carbon copy of Grace.

CHAPTER 6

The sight of the woman sent my head swimming in a sea of strange and surging emotions. One part of me knew the woman was not Grace, but the other part was desperately trying to convince me that she was. I found myself frozen in place, unable to do anything but stare transfixed as the woman joined the Samoans at the side of the stream. I watched as she pointed at the drawbridge and appeared to patiently explain to the Samoans what it was.

The woman was beautiful, just as beautiful as Grace had been. An aura of intelligence, dignity, and class surrounded her. She was tall, maybe five feet, nine inches, strong yet slender, and she carried herself with a lissome agility. Her lustrous skin was the color of light honey, and her smooth, golden hair, worn swept off her face, gently wafted down to her mid-back. Her lively, luminous eyes were almond-shaped and framed by dark lashes, her irises the turquoise blue of the Caribbean Sea. Her nose was straight, her smiling mouth wide and dazzling, her lips gentle, and covered with just the barest amount of pink lipstick. She had perfectly sized and shaped gleaming white teeth. Her cheek-bones, jaw, and chin were flawless, her neck long and graceful with just the slightest hint of freckles where it met her upper chest. She wore an expensive-looking white short sleeve linen shirt, a light brown leather vest, and tailored sun-washed blue jeans that were skin tight around her fit rear end and long legs. Her delicate ears had tiny sparkling diamond studs in them, and a heart shaped gold and diamond pendant hung around her neck. Her arms were tan and supple, and a gold bracelet hung loosely on her left wrist. Her fingernails were painted a bright scarlet. Soft blue leather ankle-high hiking boots were on her feet. She seemed to be in her late twenties or early thirties.

"Looks just like her, doesn't she?" Jeff said.

I almost didn't hear Jeff, so intent had I been on absorbing every detail of the woman's seemingly half-real, half-phantasmagorical presence.

"Who?" I said.

"Don't screw with me dude," Jeff said. "Grace. You know it too. Your jugular pounding."

"Grace's hair was darker," I said, "and her eyes were green."

"And this one's breasts are bigger," Jeff said.

"Hey," I said.

"Hey what," Jeff said. "I saw you looking."

I didn't say anything.

"I think it a sign," Jeff said. "I think Grace sent her here for you."

"It's good I already know you're crazy, otherwise what you just said might have come as a shock," I said.

"Been four years to the day, bro," Jeff said. "Grace wanted you to find somebody new. Looks like this be the one."

Down below, one of Samoans began to wade across the stream. He stepped carefully from rock to rock and appeared to be doing his best to keep from falling into the water. The woman and the Samoan's twin looked on.

"Think he can swim?" I said.

"Samoans an island people," Jeff said. "Of course he can swim. Don't be changing the subject."

"I don't need another woman right now," I said.

"Yes, you do," Jeff said. "You lonely."

"How could I possibly be lonely?" I said. "You and Adelaide are such fine company."

Suddenly, a voice behind us said, "If I were you Jack, Jeff is the last person I'd take spiritual advice from."

Jeff and I turned around. Adelaide stood behind us, covered in mud from head to toe. The mud even covered the black and forest green camouflage paint she had slathered on her face. Since Adelaide had snuck up without us hearing her, I took it as a sign her combat skills were improving.

Then again, maybe Jeff and mine were withering away.

Adelaide gave Eclipse a kiss on the nose, then refocused her attention on Jeff and me.

"What's got you two cowards so spooked you hidin' behind this bush?" Adelaide said.

Because Adelaide had pretty much taken to wearing the same clothes every day, I knew beneath the mud there was a baggy pair of green combat fatigue pants, an equally baggy Viet Nam-era combat jungle coat, a tight fitting black t-shirt with the word 'Ranger' scrawled across the chest in yellow block letters and encased by a yellow rectangle, a British special services floppy camo hat, a camouflage belt, and lace-up black leather Army Ranger boots. The camouflage belt, besides holding up her pants, supported a sheathed SOG tactical knife.

Though Adelaide was rarely clean, she cleaned up well. She was a fresh faced, willowy beauty with long fine brown hair, blue eyes, and a shapely mouth that could have landed her a job as a model in a teen magazine if her interests had trended on a more genteel line than her then current career choice. She had been Grace's niece through Grace's sister, and she was five feet, eleven inches tall, quick as a cheetah and defiant as a hellcat. Adelaide had been an All-American high school volleyball player as a freshman before the death of her parents two years ago. Her subsequent run-ins with the law had landed her on the ranch with me, and she was my ward. Beneath the fatigue pants, an ankle monitor was strapped to her left leg.

Adelaide noticed Jeff's red hunting jacket. Frowning, she grabbed the jacket's velvet lapel and ran her fingers across it.

"What's with the jacket, Jeff?" Adelaide said. "You a royal now? Aiming to be the first African American king of England? Wouldn't hold my breath if I were you."

"You got a good imagination, girl, you got all that from this little ol' jacket," Jeff said.

"Whatever," Adelaide said.

She turned to me.

"You'll be happy to know I've already taken ten jumps from the tower and completed the obstacle course twice this morning," Adelaide said.

Along with the parachute jump training tower, Jeff and I had built an obstacle course for Adelaide. The obstacle course was a duplicate of the Malvesti course at Ranger school. Our course had a rope climb, monkey bars, vertical ladder, and a nasty twenty-five yard mud crawl under low barbed wire. The mud crawl was responsible for Adelaide's state of sartorial splendor.

Jeff and I had been training Adelaide's mental skills as well as her physical skills. We'd taught her about such topics as battlefield tactics, assisting or confronting counterinsurgencies, hostage situations, unconventional warfare, and how vital careful planning and maintaining operational secrecy were to the success of any mission. Adelaide is a very good student and soaks up everything like a sponge.

"Nice workout, Adelaide," Jeff said. "I can see why you didn't have time for a shower."

"So sorry I'm offending your sissy sensibilities Jeff," Adelaide said. "Back to my original question. What's got you two spooked?"

Neither Jeff nor I said anything.

Adelaide rolled her eyes, pushed her way between us, and moved closer to the edge of the bluff. She peered through a gap in the chinquapin bush and took a closer look at what had caught our attention.

"That's what you two old fogeys are afraid of?" Adelaide said. "Those two butterballs and the bimbo? Well, have no fear, Adelaide is here."

"Thirty-seven isn't old Adelaide," Jeff said. "Also, we aren't afraid, and we can take care of ourselves, thank you."

"We'll see," Adelaide said. "Who are those clowns?"

I said, "We don't know."

Jeff said, "Jack was hoping they turn around and go home. Until he saw the woman, that is."

I shook my head.

"Woman doesn't change a thing," I said.

"Hell she don't," Jeff said.

Adelaide extended her hand to me. I gave her the scope.

"She's pretty," Adelaide said. "Looks sorta like Aunt Grace. Maybe she's not a bimbo after all."

The Samoan crossing the stream fell when he was at the halfway point. The spot was surrounded by boulders that slowed the stream down into a relatively calm four foot deep pool. If the Samoan had kept his wits about him he could have easily stood up. Instead, he thrashed wildly in an inept display seriously lacking in water skills. He repeatedly sank below the surface, then burst out like a Polaris missile, only to sink back down again. Each re-surfacing was accompanied by an explosive expulsion of spray from his gaping mouth that closely resembled the eruption emitted by the blowhole of a breaching whale. Every expulsion was followed immediately by the loud gasping sounds of a man desperately sucking in air.

"Huh," Jeff said. "Maybe he isn't an island Samoan. Maybe he's from Carson."

"Where's Carson?" I said.

"Carson be south of L.A.," Jeff said.

"On the beach?" I said.

"On the freeway," Jeff said.

"Not good," I said.

The other Samoan twin, who I assumed was worried his brother might drown, began to wade across the stream by stepping from stone to stone.

Adelaide appeared to have had enough of the water show. She turned away from the bluff's edge, and arms akimbo, gave Jeff and me a challenging look.

"So," Adelaide said, "am I getting my sniper lesson or we gonna waste time watching these fatboys drown?"

"What do you think?" I said to Jeff.

"They ain't gonna drown," Jeff said.

I didn't think so either. And while my initial feelings about the Maybach's intrusion had been mainly ones of annoyance, Jeff had been right about the woman. She had aroused my curiosity and maybe even more than that. Right then, all I wanted to do was keep looking at her.

But I wasn't about to admit that to Adelaide or Jeff.

"Sniping it is," I said.

Adelaide said, "And when we're done with that, how about we use that Maybach for a little demolition practice? Maybachs can't be as hard to blow up as you two pussies say they are."

CHAPTER 7

Adelaide led the way as she, Jeff, Eclipse, and I walked along the bluff toward the ranch's shooting range. Adelaide had a natural roll to her hips when she walked. At some point I was going to have to help her get rid of that roll. If she didn't, Adelaide would risk attracting the wrong kind of attention at Ranger school. Which would mean someone might get hurt. Someone other than Adelaide, of course.

Using the spotter scope, I intermittently kept an eye on the proceedings at the stream as we walked. The second Samoan had suffered the same fate as the first, and both twins were thrashing in the cold, rushing water. The woman calmly took off her blue leather hiking boots and socks, shoved the socks into the boots, hurled the boots across the stream onto the bank on the other side, rolled up her pant legs, and went in after the Samoans. I caught a glimpse of her feet just before she stepped in the water. They were delicately shaped and her toenails were painted with scarlet polish. Her ankles were tan and a thin gold ankle bracelet dangled around the right one.

Adelaide, Jeff, and I kept moving. We turned a corner that blocked my view of the stream, so I lost track of what the woman and the Samoans were doing. By the time we reached the shooting range, the air had warmed up considerably, most of the night snowfall had melted, and sunlight gleamed on the wet granite of the distant mountain peaks. A soft breeze whistled through the pine needles. More than a dozen gulls circled overhead soaring higher and higher on the thermals, their caws growing harder and harder to hear the more they rose. I took off my windbreaker and tied it around my waist.

A CheyTac M200 sniper rifle, covered by a green canvas tarp, lay on the shooting table where Adelaide had set it up with her other sniping equipment earlier that morning. Adelaide removed the tarp to reveal the CheyTac along with a Bluetooth laser GPS range finder, a Bluetooth barometric pressure, wind, and temperature meter, a pair of Wiley X protective ballistic shooting glasses, three shooting range earmuffs, horse earmuffs for Eclipse, and a Mac computer. The GPS range finder was capable of measuring distance, altitude, azimuth, and inclination. Adelaide needed the meter and rangefinder to quantify, and the computer to process, most of the factors that could affect her bullet's flight.

The CheyTac, resting on its bipod, pointed down range at a target pinned to a thick, upright wood plank jammed into the ground about twelve hundred yards away. The rifle had a range of more than 2500 yards, but it would be a while before Adelaide could manage a shot of that distance. Around the target the land was flat and devoid of life other than a few clumps of grass poking through the pumice at odd intervals. The target was in the shape of a man, and scoring rings numbered seven through ten marked the target's head and chest. The bullseye, centered on the head, was five and one-half inches in diameter. Only bullets to the head would be considered successful shots.

Adelaide, Jeff, and I grabbed a set of muffs and put them around our necks. Jeff draped the horse muffs over Eclipse's ears and tied them on. I knew that only forty feet away from the sniping table there was a spot from which I could again observe the stream, but I stayed put as I also knew that if Adelaide sensed I wasn't giving her my full attention, there would be hell to pay.

Adelaide turned on the computer and took her measurements. She worked quickly and silently.

"Bullet please," Adelaide said when she was done.

I reached into my pocket, removed one of the 419 match grade rounds I had grabbed earlier in the morning, and handed it to Adelaide. All the ammunition on the ranch is kept locked up and I have the only key. Since Jeff back then was mistaking Adelaide and me for enemy combatants at least once a week, it wasn't a policy I felt needed changing.

I turned my attention back to Adelaide. Each of her measurements had transferred wirelessly via Bluetooth into the Mac, which then calculated the CheyTac's aim point relative to the target. Adelaide had written the computer's ballistic program herself and named it 'Sepultura'. Sepultura was both Spanish for burial and the name of a death metal band. It seemed like a fine name to me.

"What did you measure?" I said.

"Distance to target, barometric pressure, windage, temperature, altitude, inclination, and azimuth," Adelaide said.

"Why azimuth?" I said.

"Coriolis effect," Adelaide said.

"Explain," I said.

"The earth's rotation causes clockwise deflection of moving objects in the northern hemisphere, counter-clockwise in the southern, otherwise known as the Coriolis effect," Adelaide said. "Bullets qualify as moving objects, so we need to adjust for the effect."

"Anything else you need to measure?" I said.

Adelaide shook her head.

"Proceed," I said.

Adelaide sighted the CheyTac at the spot Sepultura told her would compensate for all the measurements Adelaide had made so far. The amount a bullet dropped due to gravity at 1200 yards would be more than twenty feet. That drop, coupled with the wind and the other factors, meant Adelaide was aiming at a spot well above, and to the left of, the actual target.

"Target sighted," Adelaide said.

Adelaide, Jeff, and I pulled our earmuffs over our ears. Adelaide put on the Wiley X protective eyewear. I handed the spotter scope to Jeff. He sighted the scope on the target with one hand and held Eclipse's reins with the other. I gave Adelaide a thumbs up.

Adelaide gently put her cheek against the CheyTac's stock, placed her eye behind the sight, and curled her finger around the trigger. She took long, slow, deep breaths which would help her focus on her heartbeat. The human body moves imperceptibly with each heart contraction. A sniper pulls the trigger between beats to keep that movement from affecting his or her shot.

Adelaide took the shot. All three of us pulled our earmuffs back down around our necks. Jeff lowered the spotter scope from his eyes.

"Center chest," Jeff said. "Since we aiming for the head, that be a big fat zero for Adelaide."

"No way," Adelaide said. "Gimme that."

She grabbed the scope and checked for herself.

"Damn," Adelaide said.

I said, "Adelaide, you should have been suspicious when I asked you what else you needed to check. What'd you forget?"

Adelaide appeared to think about what I had said. After a moment, a light seemed to go on in her head.

"Humidity," Adelaide said.

Jeff said, "Humility more like it."

"Shove it, Jeff," Adelaide said.

I handed Adelaide the small digital humidity tester I had also stowed in my pocket that morning.

"At twelve hundred yards, how much can humidity alone affect bullet drop?" I said.

"At least three inches," Adelaide said. "The same as the length of Jeff's dick."

"Since you know nothing about that, I'm not even going to respond," Jeff said.

"You just did respond, turkey," Adelaide said.

Adelaide tested the humidity and redid her calculations. She took five more shots. Each shot hit the head portion of the target, averaging eights and nines each time, but no bullseyes. By the rules of our training session Adelaide had one more chance to hit a bullseye. She began to remeasure her calculations.

Since Adelaide seemed preoccupied with what she was doing, I took a moment to wander off and use the spotter scope to steal a glance at the woman and the Samoans.

The woman had succeeded in getting the Samoans safely to shore on our side of the stream. The Samoans were soaked to the bone, their hair, shoes, and suits dripping with water. The woman's jeans were rolled back down, her socks and boots back on her feet. Everything the woman was wearing was perfectly dry. Unlike the inexperienced Samoans, who had gravitated to the deeper water, she must have managed to not only find the stream's submerged boulders but stay balanced on them as well during her rescue efforts.

The woman appeared to spot the drawbridge. She walked over to it and examined it, lifting the bridge's padlock and chain, then tugging on the padlock. When the padlock didn't release, she upped the ante by bracing her feet at the bridge's base and leaning back to get her whole body into the enterprise. When that didn't work the first time, the woman gave it a few more forceful yanks. When those didn't work either, she gave up, though it appeared she was reluctant to do so.

I felt that it took a certain kind of mind to trespass on a stranger's property and assault his bridge.

It was the kind of mind I found attractive.

The woman seemed to say something to the Samoans and then pointed at the road that led up the bluff to the top of the plateau. Her flaxen hair flowing in the breeze, the woman began walking up the road with purposeful, yet graceful strides. The Samoans, sopping wet, trudged behind her.

My hunch was that the woman had been paying attention to the sound of Adelaide's shots and would find us by estimating where those shots had come from.

Time would tell.

I walked back to the shooting table and gave Adelaide her last bullet.

CHAPTER 8

Adelaide squeezed the trigger. Her seventh and last shot flew towards the target.

"Bullseye," Jeff said.

Adelaide jumped up and did a celebratory dance, rocking her arms over her head and shaking her hips.

"Dead scumbag, twelve hundred yards, bitch!" Adelaide said. "Vultures be feasting tonight."

"One out of seven ain't no call for celebration," Jeff said.

Adelaide glared at him.

"You can do better, huh?" Adelaide said.

"With both eyes closed and banshees screaming in my ears," Jeff said.

Adelaide snorted, pulled a bullet out of the chest pocket of her combat jacket.

I said, "Where'd you get that bullet, Adelaide?"

"I got it," Adelaide said. "That's all you need to know."

"Give it to me," I said.

She ignored me, bent over the rifle, and shoved the bullet in the chamber.

"Adelaide you know better than that," I said. "Take the bullet out and hand it over."

She picked the rifle up and turned to Jeff. Something in the way she was looking at him set little alarm bells off in my head. I moved toward her.

"Put the rifle down, Adelaide," I said.

Before I could stop her, Adelaide threw the rifle at Jeff. Jeff caught it without even a hint of strain in his body. Given a CheyTac weighs more than thirty pounds, that was quite a feat. On both their parts.

"Goddamnit, Adelaide," I said.

I spun on my left leg toward Jeff. A jolt of pain rocked my rebuilt knee.

"Give me the gun, Jeff," I said. "You know the rules."

Jeff backpedaled away from me.

"She know the rules too," Jeff said.

I could have chased Jeff, but with a loaded rifle in his hands, that wouldn't have been a good idea. I felt anger rising in my throat.

"No guns, Jeff," I said.

"Your face getting red, Jack," Jeff said.

"No guns, Jeff," I repeated. "Come on man, you been so good for so long. Now's not the time to blow it."

Jeff pointed the rifle at me. There was something strange going on behind his eyes. As if he was gearing up to fight, or maybe fighting something going on inside him. I couldn't tell which. The muscles in my neck and chest tightened as I saw the last two years of work with him going down the drain. Out of the corner of my eye, I saw a look of worry pass over Adelaide's face. A little late for that, Adelaide, I thought.

"Give me the goddamn gun, Jeff," I said.

"One condition," Jeff said.

"What's that?" I said.

"You take the shot," Jeff said.

"This session isn't about me, Jeff," I said.

"About you now," Jeff said.

"This isn't a negotiation," I said.

"You been out of commission so long you afraid you'll miss," Jeff said.

"You're right," I said. "That's why I won't take the shot."

"Damn," Jeff said. "Reverse psychology never do work on you."

Jeff curled his finger around the trigger, the gun still pointed at my chest.

"Either you take it, or I take it," Jeff said.

I turned to Adelaide.

"You happy now?" I said to her.

Adelaide said nothing.

I turned back to Jeff. I kept my eyes focused on his trigger finger.

"Give me the gun, Jeff," I said. "You're not going to shoot me."

"You don't think so, why you concentrating so hard on my finger?" Jeff said.

"Habit," I said.

"You think you can dodge this big boy if I let it go?" Jeff said.

Jeff's trigger finger twitched ever so slightly. I tensed up, unable to stop my reflexes from acting on their own.

Jeff laughed.

"You haven't lost a thing, have you?" Jeff said. "Didn't think you catch that."

A potent mixture of anger and fear grew inside me, threatening to take over my mind. I did my best to wrestle down my emotions, believing that if I didn't, the situation would get even more out of control than it already was.

"Ooh, that good, Jack," Jeff said. "That real good. I can see you trying to stay calm."

I didn't say anything.

"Too bad all your training be focused on tangos," Jeff said. "You got no idea what to do when your best friend's lined up on you, do you?"

I didn't respond.

"I'm waiting for an answer to my question," Jeff said. "Can you dodge this big boy or not?"

My heart rate continued to shoot up.

"No, Jeff, I can't," I said.

"Right answer," Jeff said.

He re-centered the CheyTac's barrel on my chest.

Adelaide chose that moment to try to intervene.

"Come on, Jeff," Adelaide said. "I was only..."

I shook my head at her. She backed off.

Jeff's eyes were glassy. His nostrils flared, and his teeth bared in a snarl.

"Funny way for us to end," Jeff said.

He braced the CheyTac against his shoulder, put his eye tight to the sight.

"Got any last words?" Jeff said.

"No," I said softly.

"Okay, then," Jeff said.

I was convinced Jeff was going to take the shot. Every neuron in my brain and nerve in my body was in overdrive. My arms and legs felt numb.

Jeff's finger twitched.

I tensed.

But Jeff didn't shoot.

Instead, he raised the CheyTac above his head and threw the gun at me as hard as he could.

"Take the shot!" Jeff screamed.

I watched the rifle flying at me through the air. It moved in slow motion, as if in a dream. I still don't know why I did what I did next. Maybe it was the adrenaline rampaging through my body, anger, fear, reflex, Jeff's ferocious expression, his scream ringing in my ears, or something else, but I caught the gun, jammed it against my shoulder, whipped around, sighted the target, and fired. The sound of the shot boomed across the plain, its reverberations seeming to last forever.

Jeff focused the spotter scope downrange.

"Bullseye!" Jeff said.

Adelaide looked like she was in shock.

Jeff walked up to her, snapped his fingers in front of her eyes.

"Don't be going off on me girl," Jeff said. "Lesson isn't over yet."

Adelaide stared blankly at him. Jeff handed her the spotter scope. She sighted on the target.

"Six holes," Adelaide said almost too softly to be heard. "He missed."

"Think again, sweetheart," Jeff said.

I was so drained, all I could do was put the rifle down at my side. I used it as a crutch to stay upright. I probably would have fallen down if I didn't have it. When I spoke, there seemed to be no energy behind my words and I hardly heard them.

"You have any more bullets, Adelaide?" I said.

She shook her head.

Jeff led Eclipse over to Adelaide, handed her the reins.

"Check that target," Jeff said. "Tell me what you find."

Adelaide looked at me. She seemed unsure of what to do.

I nodded at her.

"Go ahead," I said.

Adelaide put her left foot in the stirrup, swung her right leg over the saddle, and galloped off on Eclipse.

"Sorry about that," Jeff said. "Figured it be the only way you'd take the shot. Someone gotta show her who's boss."

I hung onto the CheyTac, took deep breaths. The feeling started to come back in my arms and legs.

"You can't be pulling that kind of shit, Jeff," I said.

"Said I was sorry, didn't I?" Jeff said. "She's too cocky. Especially for someone without a dick. Gonna get her killed."

"You want to lecture Adelaide on overconfidence, go ahead," I said. "But I suggest you leave the dick part out, or you're the one that's going to get killed."

Adelaide and Eclipse arrived at the target in a little over a minute. Jeff handed me the scope. I watched Adelaide dismount, examine the bullet holes one by one, then unsheathe her combat knife.

Seemingly out of nowhere, a soft, honeyed voice said, "Hello."

I turned around. The woman and the Samoans had come up behind us. Jeff and I had been so focused on Adelaide, we hadn't even realized they'd done that. Earlier, we hadn't realized Adelaide had come up behind us either. Jeff and my skills really had withered.

Up close, the woman looked even more like Grace. For a moment, the woman actually became Grace in my mind, and I stared at her, spellbound. I don't know how long I stared, but it must have been for an embarrassingly long time, because the next thing I knew I was being painfully jolted back to reality by Jeff's elbow in my ribs.

The Samoans snickered. Jeff was instantly inflamed.

Jeff, looking and sounding like an infuriated commanding officer, a role he had once known well, and a role in which he had once made grown men quiver, said, "What you two laughing at?"

It had been such a long time since Jeff had behaved in that manner that I'd almost forgotten he was capable of doing so. The giant Samoan twins appeared to have reacted no differently than the other men exposed to Jeff's wrath. The twins were both wide-eyed and seemingly tongue-tied. I thought they might shit their pants.

"Don't be trying my patience," Jeff said. "Nothing good will come of that. And I mean nothing."

"W...w...we're sorry, sir," stammered the twin on the left.

Jeff narrowed his eyes.

"Apology accepted," Jeff said.

The twin on the right seemed to regain his composure. He said, "Can I ask you a question, sir?"

"You may," Jeff said.

"Well, sir, we were watching you shooting as we were walking here," the twin on the right said. "We're curious why you appeared so focused on what you were doing if you were just shooting at nothing?"

In the twins' defense, it was actually easy to think as they had. Since the target was twelve hundred yards distant out on the pumice field, no one would have had any idea where was it was unless they had been told where to look and probably had a sniper scope as well.

The woman said, "I apologize for Manu and Mosi. It's clear they have never been on a sniper range before."

CHAPTER 9

I did my best to control my emotions as the woman walked up to me and, her blue eyes sparkling, her pretty mouth smiling, extended a hand. I took her hand into my own. Her skin was smooth, soft, and warm, and her grip firm.

We shook.

The heat of her touch traveled up my arm, my shoulder, my neck, and into my skull, finally settling in the middle of my brain where the cells there resident began to melt.

"Sorry for the intrusion," the woman said. "My name is Kate Lennon. General Wilder, I presume?"

My tongue was heavy and my throat suddenly dry and hoarse.

"Yes, ma'am," I croaked.

"So nice to finally meet you," Kate said.

Kate Lennon turned and extended her hand to Jeff.

"And you must be General Bradshaw," Kate said. "I'm honored to meet you as well."

Adelaide and Eclipse suddenly barreled in from the plain and skidded to a screeching halt next to Kate. Eclipse's hooves splattered mud in all directions, the speed of his turn such that it left a wind swirl in its wake.

Adelaide glared at Kate.

"I don't know what you want, lady," Adelaide said, "but you're going to have to wait your turn."

I said, "Adelaide, that's no way to treat our visitors."

Adelaide rolled her eyes. She tossed a small, silvery, metallic ball-like object at Jeff.

"It's some kind of trick you two rigged up, isn't it?" Adelaide said. "No one makes a shot like that free standing."

Jeff said, "Weren't no trick, girl."

Jeff, holding the object between his thumb and forefinger, lifted it up to the sun, where it glinted in the light. The object looked like two separate, tiny, squashed metal pancakes that had been welded together.

Kate peered closely at the object, appeared to understand exactly what the tiny pancakes were.

She turned to Adelaide.

"That must have been an amazing shot!" Kate said. "Congratulations!"

Jeff's eyes narrowed.

"Why you say that?" Jeff said to Kate.

Kate hesitated, seemed to be momentarily unsure of herself.

"She fired two bullets, one right on top of the other, didn't she?" Kate said. "That is what I'm looking at, isn't it?"

Adelaide cut Jeff off before he could answer. It looked as if it pained her to speak, and Adelaide's words carried a decidedly begrudging tone.

"Yeah, that's what you're looking at alright," Adelaide said. "Target's bullseye is only five and a half inches wide. Bottom bullet was dead center. Second round hit exactly on top of it. Means the shooter drilled a quarter-inch hole at twelve hundred yards. But I didn't take it, he did."

Adelaide jerked her thumb at me. I tried to appear humble.

"How'd you know what you were looking at?" Adelaide said to Kate.

Jeff said, "Yeah, and how'd you know this was a sniper range?"

Adelaide's words had been more challenge than question. Jeff's tone had been suspicious bordering on paranoia. Others might have been insulted or intimidated, but Kate appeared to take what they had said in stride.

"My husband was a special forces captain, General Bradshaw," Kate said. "He fought with you and General Wilder. He played football with both of you too."

Adelaide's defiant demeanor softened for a moment. Jeff, however, appeared to withdraw into himself. Maybe Jeff was only trying to recall who Kate's husband was, but more than likely he had gone wherever he goes whenever his diseased mind decides to take him anywhere other than the present moment.

If Kate's husband's first name was Paul, then there was no question that Jeff and I knew Paul Lennon, and knew him well. I was about to ask Kate if Paul was indeed her husband's name, when one of the twins - Manu or Mosi, I didn't know which - suddenly became so excited he could barely contain himself, and he smothered my question with a blurted interruption.

"Oh man, we know you," the Samoan said. "You guys are the Wilder and Bradshaw who tied for the Heisman Trophy almost twenty years ago, aren't you? You played for Navy, right?"

I said, "It was Army, and we tied for second place in the Heisman voting."

"That's still great, man," the Samoan said. "My brother and I played for Southern Cal. We tried to play in the NFL but we were too small."

For a moment, I pondered how six feet six and three hundred and fifty pounds could be too small. I stopped my pondering, and was again about to ask Kate her husband's name, when Jeff returned from the twilight zone and interrupted me.

"What do you know about Herodotus?" Jeff said to Kate.

Adelaide shifted in her saddle, spit on the ground.

"Jesus Jeff, can't you at least pretend you aren't nuts?" Adelaide said.

I was about to reprimand Adelaide for her rudeness, but decided it would only spur her on, and instead kept my mouth shut.

Kate seemed unfazed.

Adelaide said, "I'm gonna cut you some slack lady because of your husband. But you and your tubby clone friends here are trespassing and that's not cool. You're lucky you didn't get yourselves shot."

"You're right," said Kate. "I'm sorry. I'm only here because I need General Wilder's help."

Adelaide sniffed.

"Good luck with that," Adelaide said.

Adelaide tugged Eclipse's head around with the reins, nudged his flanks with her heels, and galloped off.

Kate watched Adelaide go, then turned to Jeff.

"I know a fair amount about Herodotus, General," Kate said. "Is there something specific you would like to discuss?"

"You know why I'm asking about him?" Jeff said.

Kate studied Jeff's face for a moment. When she answered, her voice was surprisingly calm and soothing.

"Yes, I believe I do," Kate said.

Jeff looked closely into her eyes.

"Yes, I believe you do too," Jeff said. He paused. "You know, you remind me of someone."

"Hope it's a nice someone," Kate said.

Jeff gestured at me.

"You remind him of someone too," Jeff said, clearly referring to Grace.

I stepped between them.

"Okay, that's enough of that," I said. "Ms. Lennon, you said you were here because you needed my help?"

"Please call me Kate, General," Kate said. "Both my father, Milton Feynman, and my husband, Paul Lennon, always said that if all hell broke loose, and they were down to one last option, that option would be you."

"That's kind of them," I said. "I know your father and husband well. If you don't mind my asking, why didn't one of them simply call me themselves?"

"My father and my husband are dead, General," Kate said. "They died almost three years ago."

CHAPTER 10

It might have been because it was the anniversary of Grace's death and ripples of grief had been flowing heavily through me all that morning, or it could have been due to the disorienting sensations arising within me from Kate's resemblance to Grace, or it might even have been because Jeff's lining up the CheyTac's barrel on my chest had affected me in ways I didn't understand, but when Kate told me both her father and husband were dead, my mind was flooded by strange and confusing images. I felt lightheaded, and it was all I could do to stay upright. I reached behind me for the shooting table, backed up to it, and sat down. Jeff, Kate, and the Samoans looked at me with concern.

"Must have been something I ate," I said.

"Uh huh," Jeff said.

As I sat on the table trying to regain some semblance of self-assuredness, fragments of buried memory hurtled up at light speed from some seemingly fathomless cavern within my brain. Vaporous chimeras commanded my attention. The kelpies metamorphosed back and forth between two human shapes, both of whom stared at me with black, pupilless eyes. One was a tall, well built, dark haired young man and the other a fit, distinguished looking older gentleman. Each time the younger phantom appeared, he was clothed in either worm-eaten military fatigues or a threadbare Army college football uniform. The younger man's materializations alternated between a mist-shrouded West Point Michie Stadium field and Fort Benning's training grounds, the grounds gray with drizzling rain. At times the younger man's clothing matched his location, but at other times the clothing was the reverse of what one would expect, and the younger man could be seen blowing frosty breath as he dodged unseen tacklers in his military garb at Michie, or left cloudy trails like fantails behind him in the dewy mist as he churned through the Fort Benning obstacle course in his football uniform.

I realized the young phantom was Kate's husband, Paul Lennon. Paul's daunting visage provoked no fear within me. What it did provoke was sorrow at a life lost so young.

The ghostly older gentleman had an even more profound effect on me. In contrast to Paul Lennon, each time the older man coalesced he was immaculately dressed in khaki pants, a plaid work shirt, and hiking boots. He also always corporealized in exactly the same place in the middle of a cool, clear, sun drenched Mojave Desert, the wind blowing through his graying hair, his black eyes unmoving. I recognized the site. It was a weapons testing ground. The distinguished wraith held in his hands a communication device and was explaining how it worked to a young person standing next to him. The man was Kate's father, Milton Feynman, and the person he was explaining to was me, over fifteen years ago.

Kate stepped forward, put a hand on my head, and looked into my eyes.

"You sure you're okay?" Kate said.

"Yes," I said. "Just give me a minute."

Milton Feynman. Businessman, inventor, patriot. Founder of the North American Space and Air Defense Company - known by the acronym NASAD - one of the United States' most important and innovative defense contractors. I first met Milt Feynman seventeen years ago when I was a newly minted special forces lieutenant and working on a new project with him. Starting then, and for the next five years after that, Feynman had been like a father to me, imparting invaluable knowledge about the ways of the military and how modern combat technology could help me do my job. I had never met my own father as he had been killed in combat before I was born. Because my duties had taken me in far flung directions and Feynman's responsibilities weighed heavier and heavier on his time, the apparition before me was the first time I had laid eyes on the great man in over a decade.

Feynman's ghost handed me the communication device. I took it.

"You're not breathing," Kate said.

"I must be," I said.

"That's better," Kate said. "Keep talking."

Kate stepped back but kept a watchful eye on me.

How did I not know of Milton Feynman's passing? Had I really been so distracted by Jeff's condition over the last two and a half years - the most recent two of which having been spent isolated on the ranch - that I had never learned of Milt's death? Was it possible I had heard that Milt had died and suppressed it?

Slowly the specters dissolved until only a murky fog remained. Kate kept peering into my face, but if anything her attention was making it harder for me to regain my bearings. I was seeing not Kate, but Grace. Grace who had finally come back to me.

Jeff leaned his head in close to mine, gently grabbed my left elbow and surreptitiously dug a finger as hard as he could into my ulnar nerve as he whispered in my ear.

"You need to snap out of this dude," Jeff said. "It's gettin' embarrassing."

His words had little effect, but the pain in my elbow certainly did. I suddenly felt a lot less woozy. Somehow I gathered myself and managed to project a reasonably good approximation of a man serenely in control of his faculties.

Employing a hint of a mid-Atlantic accent - an accent I'd picked up from watching too many 1940's movies with Jeff while we were stuck in some hellhole in northern Africa - and my best to-the-manner-born tone, I said, "Jeff, if you don't mind, I think it best if I talk to Kate in private. Would you be so kind as to entertain Manu and Mosi for a while?"

Jeff stared at me. He seemed as if he might have been surprised, and possibly even annoyed, that I'd been able to effect so sudden a transformation. The fact that Jeff hated it when I affected that particular accent - he said I sounded like W. C. Fields in a state of inebriated stupefaction - didn't help things either. Jeff appeared to be struggling to hold his tongue and for a moment I was afraid he might say something unfortunate. In the end, however, all Jeff said was:

"Sure thing, buddy."

CHAPTER 11

Leaving Jeff and the giant Samoan twins behind, I led Kate away from the shooting range and along the narrow path that would bring us to the ranch's living quarters. It was a path Grace and I had walked countless times. I purposely didn't look back at Kate, feeling that, if I did, whatever tenuous connection to Grace she represented to me might be lost forever.

The gently rising path passed through a small aspen grove. A warm breeze had kicked up and the breeze caused the aspen leaves to quake. The quaking leaves made soft rustling sounds as they flashed from dark to light green and back again in the brightening sunlight.

Whiffs of drying pumice mixed with pine scent. The cawing gulls that had been riding the updrafts were gone then, having been scared away by the red-tailed hawks which had taken their place. The hawks - their tail feathers more a translucent orange than red against a silvery blue sky that was filled with white, wispy cirrus clouds - soared higher and higher on the thermals. A lizard darted across the path and disappeared into the snow-dusted, long green forest grasses. An hour had passed since I had first seen the Maybach and it was warm enough then for a small sweat to again break out between my shoulder blades. The exercise slowly worked a kind of magic on my mind, and my emotions began to calm.

Kate was out of breath, most likely from the altitude. Her breath came in soft, rapid ins and outs behind me. As I listened to Kate's breathing, I wondered why I had not known Milton Feynman had a daughter. I made a mental note to ask Kate why her father had never mentioned her.

"Adelaide is a pretty girl beneath all that mud and paint isn't she?" Kate said.

"Very," I said.

"I'll bet she's got a good heart beneath that gruff exterior too," Kate said.

"That's debatable," I said.

"You're a man of few words, aren't you?" Kate said.

I laughed.

"Sometimes," I said.

We passed through another grove of pines and reached the clearing in which the ranch's house sat. The house had started as a small cabin built by my great-great-grandfather Tristram when he first arrived out west and settled the ranch. The house had grown into its present size over the intervening years and then had three one-story wings. The wings spread north, east, and west from a large two story high central structure that resembled a manor hall. The house's walls were built in the style of traditional log cabins everywhere, the logs laid horizontally on each other and sealed with caulk. The roof was a pitched 'A' sheathed in pine shingles and had a tall brick chimney atop it. A covered porch, also made of pine, lined the entire front of the house. Multipaned windows, framed by green-painted wooden crosspieces, were interspersed at regular intervals in the house's exterior walls.

Kate and I climbed the wood plank front steps that led up to the porch and came to the house's big oak front door. I opened the door. We were greeted by the aroma of the coffee I had brewed earlier that morning. The door's hinges creaked softly as I closed it behind us and we entered the high-ceilinged main hall. Outside, the logs that made up the walls of the hall were weathered and nearly gray, but inside the logs were shiny with a pale yellow sheen from coat upon coat of lacquer applied over the years. The hall's floor was ivory colored linoleum, its then current surface much more scratched and scuffed than Grace had ever allowed it to be when she was alive. The breeze outside made whistling noises as it blew in between the few places where the caulk between the logs had dried out and contracted. The windows still had the yellow gingham blinds Grace had chosen many years ago.

"Would you like anything to eat?" I said. "A cup of coffee?"

"Coffee sounds good," Kate said. "Black, please."

"Come with me," I said.

We walked across the room to the long maple wood counter that separated the kitchen from the rest of the main foyer. The coffee maker sat atop the counter's fifty-year-old ceramic tiles, tiles that Grace had kept white but were then more an indeterminate grey. I poured some hot coffee from the coffee maker's glass flask into two mugs and handed one to Kate. We both took a sip.

I studied Kate for a moment, trying to decide if then was a good time to give voice to the question that had occurred to me earlier. I decided it was.

"Kate, in all the years I knew your father, he never mentioned a daughter," I said.

Kate frowned.

"You don't think I am who I say I am?" Kate said.

"I didn't say that," I said.

"My father was a very private man when it came to his family," Kate said. "I don't think he ever shared anything about his personal life with his business associates."

"Fair enough," I said. "Paul never mentioned a wife either."

"When did you last see Paul?" Kate said.

"Must have been eleven or twelve years ago," I said.

"Paul was married to his first wife back then," Kate said. "The marriage was pretty stormy and I think he was embarrassed by how difficult it was for him. He rarely spoke about it to anyone. I'm wife number two."

"Hard to imagine you'd be number two in anything," I said.

Kate smiled. She could, of course, have been lying to me about both Feynman and Lennon, but I didn't think she was.

A soft flapping sound came from behind Kate and me. We both turned and saw that Ashley had just entered through the doggie door that was installed in the lower half of the kitchen door. The kitchen door leads to the area outside the back of the house and Ashley had picked up mud on her paws from the snowmelt. Ashley, tracking the mud on the linoleum, sidled up beside me, stared at me with her big brown eyes, and wagged her tail. I took a cookie from the jar next to the coffee maker and popped it into her mouth. Ashley laid down on her belly, spreading her legs out front and back, and ate the cookie.

Kate bent down and stroked Ashley's head.

"Who's this?" Kate said.

"Ashley, our resident duck hunter," I said.

Kate gave me a quizzical look.

"The ranch's pond gets a lot of migrating ducks," I said. "Ashley never actually catches any of them. She just enjoys the thrill of the chase."

Kate nodded. She pet Ashley again and stood up.

"I want you to know I didn't take coming here to see you lightly," Kate said. "I exhausted every avenue I could think of before I decided you were my last, best hope."

"Good to know I came in last," I said.

"That's not what I meant," Kate said.

"I know," I said. "Why don't you tell me what the problem is?"

Kate hesitated for a moment.

"Is there someplace we can sit?" Kate said. "I've had a rough twenty-four hours. We spent the night in Bishop so we could get here early. I didn't sleep a wink."

"Follow me," I said.

The hall had a large L-shaped extension at one end that served as a den and that's where I took Kate. Grace had furnished the room with big ranch style sofas, easy chairs, brass lamps, sheepskin rugs, gnarled oaken bookshelves, and an ancient giant walnut coffee table. The area smelled of cigars, something it didn't do when Grace was alive, Jeff and I having taken liberties since her passing.

I gestured to an easy chair whose cushions were big, overstuffed, and covered with muted red and green plaid fabric. Kate moved toward the chair, but something caught her eye and she changed direction. She walked over to one of the bookshelves and gently ran her fingers over the glass cover on a boxed display of military medals. The box and its contents were not the kind of thing I would normally have out, but Jeff had put the display there and it seemed to calm him whenever he looked at it. Those days not too many things had that effect on him.

"Four Bronze Stars, five Purple Hearts, six Silver Stars, three Congressional Medals of Honor, more than a dozen rifle and pistol shooter badges," Kate said. "Jeff's and yours?"

"You know a lot about medals," I said.

"Paul taught me," Kate said. "You two have been busy."

She turned away from the medals and faced me. It appeared she hadn't noticed the other two other medal boxes stashed away on the top shelf of the bookcase, and I saw no reason to call her attention to them. One of those two boxes contained my father's medals - a Congressional

Medal of Honor and two Purple Hearts. The other box contained combat medals too various and numerous to list that had been earned by my grandfather, great-grandfather, and great-great-grandfather.

"I guess this gives more credence to what my father and Paul said about you," Kate said.

"What did they say?" I said.

"That you were the greatest warrior they had ever known," Kate said. "Brilliant, resourceful, unnaturally skilled and strong, fearless and…"

"And?" I said.

"Brutal," Kate said.

"Sexy," I said. "They left out sexy."

Kate rolled her eyes.

"Is that a warrior quality?" She said.

"You have a point," I said. "Did they mention Jeff?"

"My father didn't know Jeff," Kate said. "Paul thought Jeff was great too, but not as great as you."

"That's arguable," I said.

"I'm just repeating what they told me," Kate said.

"Might be better if you don't repeat what they told you in front of Jeff," I said.

"Please," Kate said. "I have more sense than that."

Kate walked over to the easy chair and sat down. I sat down in the chair beside her. In front of our chairs was a lacquered redwood tree stump that served as a table. Kate and I placed our coffee cups on the wide oval tree-ringed surface of the stump. Kate seemed about to speak, but again became distracted.

The distraction this time was a photo of Grace in a gold frame that sat atop the table. Grace was perched on a horse, her face turned back over her shoulder and looking at the camera. Grace and the horse were on a narrow trail cut into the side of a sheer granite peak thousands of feet above a pine-covered valley floor, the two of them silhouetted by a Yosemite sunset. Grace looked particularly wonderful in the photo, her blond hair flowing back from her head, her perfect white teeth peering through her lustrous smile, her body still youthful and athletic, the way it had been before she got sick. I had taken the photo while the two of us were alone on a weeklong camping trip.

"Your wife?" Asked Kate.

I nodded.

"Can I meet her?" She asked.

"Nothing would please me more if you could," I said. "Unfortunately, Grace passed away four years ago today."

"I'm so sorry," said Kate.

"Thank you," I said.

She studied me for a moment.

"Now I understand though," Kate said.

"Understand what?" I said.

"Why you were looking at me the way you did today," Kate said. "I look a lot like her, don't I? Of course she's much more beautiful than me."

Part of what Kate had said was true, but part was not. I said nothing, however.

Kate turned away from the photo, looked at me, let out a long breath.

"I don't know where to start," Kate said.

"How about at the beginning?" I said.

"It's hard," Kate said. "I'm afraid you'll think I'm crazy."

"Try me," I said. "If I think you're crazy when you're done, I'll tell you."

Kate seemed unsure of what to make of that. She appeared to study my face again for a moment. I saw the intelligence move behind her pretty eyes.

I smiled.

"I'm kidding," I said.

"No one knows I'm here," Kate said.

"Other than Manu and Mosi," I said.

"Other than Manu and Mosi," Kate said. "I made them turn off their cell phones when we left Malibu. I turned mine off too. I didn't want us tracked. I told my brother, NASAD security, and the FBI I needed to get away and was going to Palm Springs."

"You have a brother?" I said.

"Yes," Kate said. "His name is Freddy."

"Freddy, huh?" I said. "Nice name. How old is he, twelve?"

Kate appeared to study me again. The intelligence danced in her eyes again. She smiled.

"Mentally, yes," Kate said. "Maybe even younger. Chronologically, he's thirty-two."

"So, you're fourteen years apart?" I said.

"What are you talking about?" Kate said.

"You're eighteen, right?" I said.

Kate rolled her eyes, but she also smiled her dazzling smile, her perfect white teeth peeking out between her lovely lips.

"Very funny," Kate said. "I'm a year older than Freddy. The Maybach we came in is his. It's armored. Freddy, the head of NASAD security, and the FBI all insisted I take the Maybach. They also all said I needed to bring Manu and Mosi with me as well."

I took a sip of coffee.

"How'd you get involved with the FBI?" I said.

Kate paused, took another deep breath, let it out slowly. She raised her right hand to the side of her head, swept her beautiful blond hair back away, then rubbed her neck for a moment as if the thought of the FBI was causing her pain. She slowly dropped her hand to her lap where she intertwined it with her left hand and rested both of them atop her attractive jean clad thighs.

"I first became suspicious that something was going on a year ago," Kate said. "As you know, my father founded NASAD. Freddy and I still have control over the company due to the stock my father left us. Freddy is the chairman and CEO, but we're both on the NASAD board of directors. I presented my suspicions to the board. The board decided that, due to the potential national security issues involved, the only entity that could investigate my concerns was the FBI. The FBI came in and found nothing. I didn't want to let it go, but the board told me I had no choice."

"What did you want investigated?" I said.

"NASAD engineers were dying," Kate said. "We lost four in the year before last."

"Four?" I said.

"Yes," Kate said.

"Dying how?" I said.

"A drowning. A fire. A bicycle crash. A fall while hiking," Kate said.

"Accidents," I said.

"I didn't think so," Kate said.

Ashley walked up to me and looked fawningly into my eyes. She wanted me to believe it was a look of love, but what it really was a look that said 'I want another cookie.'

"One's enough," I said to Ashley. "It's for your own good."

Ashley knew she would get no further. She plopped down next to me, resting her head on her front legs. I looked back at Kate.

"NASAD still builds fighter planes, submarines, drones, laser guidance systems, and hundreds, if not thousands, of other things, doesn't it?" I said.

Kate lifted her cup off the table and took a sip of coffee. She put the cup back down.

"Yes," Kate said.

"You must have at least seventy-five thousand employees?" I said.

Kate nodded.

"Four accidental deaths among seventy-five thousand people doesn't seem that out of line with what one might expect over the course of a year," I said.

"I agree," Kate said. "However every one of the engineers was a project manager. They were quality control experts and top-notch troubleshooters with over twenty years' experience. They were some of my father's most trusted people. And they all worked on drones. Drone submarines, to be exact. There were maybe thirty such people in the entire company."

"What kind of subs?" I said.

"Ohio class and Seawolves," Kate said.

"Ohios carry nuclear warheads," I said.

"I know that," Kate said.

"And you're saying you lost almost ten percent of the drone sub engineering project managers?" I said.

"Yes," Kate said.

"What did the FBI say?" I said.

"They said the autopsies were all consistent with accidents," Kate said. "That sometimes things happen despite the odds."

"They actually said that?" I said.

"Yes," Kate said.

A particularly large gust of wind hit the side of the house, whistling loud and shrill through the cracks in the caulking and rattling the windows. I took the gust as a signal the storm I had seen approaching earlier was getting closer.

"You seem like the kind of person who would look up the real odds," I said. "Did you?"

"Yes," Kate said. "They are over ten million to one against NASAD losing four engineers out of thirty in the same division in one year due to accidents."

"Sounds about right," I said. "But yours turned out to be actually one in ten."

"They were," Kate said. "But then the odds got worse."

CHAPTER 12

I truly wished Kate hadn't just used the word 'worse'. From what Kate had described, I had already begun to think something quite bad was going on at NASAD, and, while Kate hadn't yet specifically told me what her visit to the ranch was about, I was pretty convinced she was going to ask me to help her in regard to the deaths of the NASAD engineers.

And helping Kate was the last thing I wanted to do.

Despite Kate's beauty, her resemblance to Grace, and the fact she was Milton Feynman's daughter and Paul Lennon's widow, I was not in a helping mood. Jeff and Adelaide were using up all my help. Helping Kate would also almost certainly involve leaving my ranch, and I was very happy where I was, thank you.

If, however, what Kate said next convinced me that NASAD's situation was even worse than I already feared, my loyalty to her father Milt Feynman and the potential national security issues raised by NASAD's situation - NASAD was, after all, involved in one way or another with almost every key technology used by the U.S. military - would make it very hard for me to turn down Kate's request for help.

I was therefore extremely tempted at that moment to cut Kate off, whisk her out of the house, and send her packing without hearing another word she had to say.

But that is not what I did.

Duty demanded I hear Kate out.

"Worse?" I said, barely forcing the word out of my mouth.

Kate picked up her coffee cup from the redwood table, took a sip, and gently laid the cup back down.

"Over the last twelve months, we lost five more top drone submarine engineering project managers," Kate said. "Then four days ago, on Thursday, we lost another three."

"Three?" I said. "In one day?"

Kate nodded.

"The three on Thursday were attending a convention together in

Las Vegas," Kate said. "They died together too."

"How?" I said.

"From what I was told, their hands were tied behind their backs and they were then forced to kneel down side by side," Kate said. "Once they were kneeling, they were all shot in the head."

"Executions?" I said.

"Yes," Kate said.

"Four drone sub engineers two years ago, and eight so far this year," I said. "That makes twelve out of NASAD's original group of thirty drone sub engineering project managers, correct?"

"Correct," Kate said.

"Twelve out of thirty is forty percent," I said.

Kate nodded.

"I guess you weren't exaggerating when you said things got worse," I said. "A forty percent death rate would probably qualify being a top NA-SAD drone submarine engineer as the most dangerous job in America."

As soon as I had said those words, I realized how insensitive they sounded. The only thing I can say in my defense is that I was probably trying to somehow keep my own emotions in check. What Kate had just told me had made me very angry, and I knew that if I got angry enough, it would make me feel like I had to do something about my anger. Doing something about my anger would mean agreeing to help Kate, and at that moment that was still the last thing I wanted to do.

My comments appeared not to have gone over well with Kate. Kate's eyes narrowed, her brow furrowed, and her upper lip became firm.

"Those engineers were real people with real lives, General," Kate said.

Great. Now we were both angry. Not only that, but I'd succeeded in making Kate angry after knowing her for all of thirty minutes. I felt bad about Kate being angry at me, but I didn't know what to do about it. The only thing I could think to do was to stall.

I took another sip of coffee, and then another, and another. On the third swallow, I felt I'd stalled as long as I could, and decided the best thing I could do was to pretend I had not said what I had said, and just forge ahead.

I put my cup down and nodded.

"I'm very aware of that," I said. "No other NASAD division has death rates out of the normal range?"

Kate's eyes remained narrowed. She seemed like she might be about to lash into me again, but for whatever reason, that's not what she did. Instead, she took some deep breaths, and appeared to be trying to control her emotions.

"No," Kate finally said. "I checked. There is no other division with abnormal death rates."

"Has NASAD provided security for the eighteen NASAD drone sub engineering project managers who are still alive?" I said.

"We have," Kate said. "They are guarded round the clock. We've also increased the security surrounding all our facilities."

"What about the FBI?" I said. "I assume they're back now?"

"Yes," Kate said. "The same fool who ran the investigation a year ago has returned. He's also the same fool who refused to investigate the five new deaths we had this year before the ones in Las Vegas. He said I was paranoid."

"You don't seem the paranoid type," I said.

"I'm not," Kate said.

"Fool's a pretty harsh word, though," I said.

"True," Kate said. "However, I'm sure you'll agree with me that fool is the right word after you've had a chance to meet Special Agent in Charge Burnette."

There it was. My worst fear realized. That was a request for help from Kate as surely as night follows day, wasn't it? How else would I meet this Special Agent in Charge Burnette ⎺whoever he was - unless I signed on to help her? And, as it was highly unlikely Kate would suggest to this Burnette fellow that he come to meet me on the ranch, the clear implication was she expected me to leave the ranch. Well, that wasn't going to happen. No way, no how.

"After I've had a chance to meet him?" I said.

"I don't see how meeting him can be avoided if you decide to help me," Kate said.

As I said, as surely as night follows day.

I was about to tell Kate to go jump in a lake as politely as possible, but before I could, she suddenly transformed again into Grace. Deep down, I suppose that I knew I had to be hallucinating, much as earlier that morning at the shooting range I had hallucinated the presence of Grace, Milt Feynman, and Paul Lennon, but at that moment I fully believed that it was Grace who was sitting in front of me. I was so overcome with longing that I spoke before I knew what I was saying.

"Grace?" I said.

Kate looked confused.

"What did you say?" Kate said.

A crow flew into the window behind Kate/Grace. It was not a hard collision, and the crow, though dazed, seemed none the worse for wear, and quickly flew away. The crow, however, momentarily distracted me, enough so that Grace transformed back into Kate. I tried to get Grace back but couldn't.

I then realized that Kate was staring at me and that I had completely lost track of our conversation. I dimly remembered the conversation had had something to do with some fool FBI Special Agent in Charge named Burnette and accidents and executions.

I took a stab.

"The Agent in Charge," I said.

"What about him?" Kate said.

"He didn't try to pass off the executions as accidents did he?" I said.

"No," Kate said. "He didn't do that."

"Well, that's a plus, isn't it?" I said.

"I just told you he wasted a year of our time," Kate said. "I hold him responsible for the deaths of those eight additional NASAD employees."

"What is Burnette's current theory?" I said.

"A disgruntled employee did it," Kate said.

"The three most recent ones, or all of them?" I said.

"The three most recent," Kate said. "The other nine are still accidents according to him."

"Oooh," I said.

Kate bristled.

"That's your response?" Kate said. "Oooh? Forgive me, but I think Burnette's theory is much worse than just Oooh."

I tried to come up with something intelligent to say, but my mind was still foggy from Grace's materialization and disappearance only a few moments before. I also realized that I was not only foggy, but weak, so weak that I was having trouble staying upright in my chair. I decided that rather than risk embarrassing myself by saying something stupid, it would be best to say nothing at all.

Kate shook her head sadly.

"Maybe I came to the wrong place," Kate said. "Maybe my father and husband were wrong about you."

My mind was so enfeebled at that moment that I was sure Kate was right, that Milt and Paul must have been horribly deluded if they thought that I could ever help anyone with anything.

"Maybe they were," I said, gripping the sides of my chair to keep from falling out of it.

Kate stared at me. At first she seemed baffled, but her bafflement appeared to quickly give way to annoyance.

"Jesus," Kate said. "This can't be happening."

"I'm sorry," I said. "But it looks like it is. I'm not going to be able to help you. If I were you, I'd just get that FBI agent...what's his name again?"

"Burnette," Kate said. "You just said his name thirty seconds ago."

"Did I?" I said.

"You did," Kate said.

"Be that as it may," I said, "I suggest you get Burnette replaced. The FBI has plenty of good agents who should be able to handle something like this."

Kate glared at me. Somehow, in the middle of the enervated, depressed muddle that was then engulfing me, I found myself thinking how attractive her glare was. I also became convinced I was completely losing my mind.

"With all due respect, General Wilder...," Kate said.

"Call me Jack," I interrupted.

"What?" Kate said.

"Call me Jack," I said.

Kate seemed exasperated. She rolled her eyes.

"Fine," Kate said. "With all due respect, *Jack*, trying to replace Burnette is a dumb idea."

"Why?" I said.

"Because it will never happen," Kate said. "The NASAD board was told Burnette was the best and pulled a lot of political strings to get him.

He's not going anywhere."

"Did *you* at least try to replace Burnette, though?" I said.

"What do you think?" Kate said.

I didn't say anything. Kate seemed to study me.

"Alright," Kate said. "I don't know what's going on here, but I refuse to accept that my father and husband could be so wrong about you. I'm going to assume you're having a very bad day for some reason and leave it at that. But no matter how bad a day you're having, you better buck up right now. Because there's another part to the story that I haven't told you yet, and I'd rather shoot myself than trust the FBI with it."

CHAPTER 13

When Kate said there was more to her story and that she'd rather shoot herself than trust the FBI, it was 8:30 a.m., about an hour and a half after I had first spotted the Maybach. Outside, the sun had melted all the snow that had accumulated on the pine needles and the blue jays were more active, hopping from branch to branch, whistling and gurgling. Ashley remained asleep at my feet, her body occasionally twitching as muffled growls escaped from her throat. She must have been chasing ducks in her dreams.

I, on the other hand, felt like I had suddenly been jolted wide awake. I don't know how or why it happened. In fact, I was surprised as hell by the fact that my bout with weakness and mental confusion disappeared even faster than it had come on. I felt quite refreshed, and, despite my overriding goal of sending Kate packing as soon as was humanly possible, I decided it wouldn't hurt if I allowed her a small amount of time to impart to me what it was she didn't want to tell the FBI. Maybe I should have questioned how my mood could have swung so drastically from one extreme to another, but, at the time, I didn't.

Kate seemed to immediately sense the sudden change that had come over me. She also seemed taken aback by the change.

"Jack," Kate said, "may I be blunt?"

"Certainly," I said.

"You're kind of freaking me out here," Kate said.

"I'm sorry about that," I said. "You were right that there was something wrong with me for a moment back there. Honestly, I have no idea what it was. But I'm feeling fine now, so let's proceed."

"You're sure you're fine?" Kate said.

"Absolutely," I said.

To emphasize how fine I was, I took a very slow, very controlled sip of coffee. I then put the cup back on the table with what I hoped appeared as a breezy casualness, and continued, "Now what was this you were saying about there being another part to the story?"

Kate hesitated for a moment, as if she wasn't quite convinced that all was truly fine with me. I don't know how she ultimately came down on that question, but in any event, what she did do was to open her vest, unzip one of its interior pockets, and pull out an iPhone. When she opened her vest, there was no way I could avoid getting a very good look at her chest. I had to admit Jeff had been right about her breasts - they were bigger than Grace's.

"I hope that's a waterproof vest," I said.

"I wouldn't have gone into the stream unless it was," Kate said. "Oh, and thanks for letting down the drawbridge."

"We're a little leery of uninvited guests," I said. "I'm sure you can understand that."

"Wow, an uninvited guest," Kate said. "That's cold."

"Well, I don't feel that way now," I said. "I'm happy you're here."

"Why don't I feel you're being sincere?" Kate said.

"I'm sorry," I said. "It's probably because I wasn't completely honest with you when I said I was fine a moment ago. I'm a little distracted today and I actually do know the reason why."

"Do you want to tell me what the reason is?" Kate said.

"Well, as I told you earlier, today is the fourth anniversary of my wife Grace's death," I said. "Unfortunately, the anniversaries are especially hard on me."

Kate's eyes opened wide. She brought a hand to her mouth.

"Oh my God," Kate said. "I can't believe how selfish I've been. I'm so sorry."

"Don't worry about it," I said.

"I am worried about it," Kate said. "I show up here completely unannounced and commence to tell you about my problems, while all the time being completely insensitive to the fact that maybe you might be suffering with your own."

"Really, don't worry about it," I said. "There's no way you could have known."

"Well, I'm still sorry," Kate said.

"And I'm sorry about the drawbridge," I said. "I didn't mean to offend you. Now, please proceed."

"Okay," Kate said. "I need to turn my phone on, but I'll leave it in airplane mode."

I heard what sounded like two squirrels scampering across the roof. Their feet were moving rapidly, but the usual expected scratchiness of their claws was muffled by the snow still covering the roof.

"Good idea," I said. "It's better if you're not trackable. Nothing you've said leads me to believe you're in direct danger, at least not yet. But you can't be too careful."

Kate seemed surprised.

"What do mean 'not yet'?" Kate said. "You think whoever is behind the murders at NASAD might come for me next?"

"You hadn't considered that?" I said.

"No, I hadn't," Kate said. "When my brother, Freddy, NASAD security, and the FBI insisted I take precautions, I thought they were just overreacting to what happened in Las Vegas. I thought they should be more worried about our engineers, not me."

"But you just said you turned off your phone so you wouldn't be tracked," I said. "Who didn't you want to be tracked by?"

"Freddy," Kate said.

"Freddy?" I said

"I don't want him to have any idea what I'm up to," Kate said.

"Why?" I said.

"Because I don't want to have any more fights with him," Kate said. "Freddy sided with the NASAD board when I tried to replace Agent Burnette. All the board members said I should just butt out and let the FBI do its job. Freddy would be furious if he knew I came to see you."

"Okay," I said. "I get it."

Kate paused for a moment. She appeared to be thinking about something.

"You really think I'm in danger, don't you?" Kate said.

"I think you need to consider that whoever has been conducting the assault on NASAD might change its target," I said.

"Now you're making me worry," Kate said.

"I didn't mean to," I said. "Look, you have your bodyguards Manu and Mosi. You have an armored Maybach. No one knows where you are, and, with the FBI back, someone has to be making plans for your security. You're probably fine for right now."

Kate considered this.

"What about my kids?" Kate said.

"You have children?" I said.

"A boy and a girl," Kate said.

"Where are they?" I said.

"At home," Kate said. "Their nanny is taking care of them."

The squirrels again darted across the roof, this time back in the direction from which they had come. Ashley must have heard them in her sleep as she emitted a low growl.

"You have a security system and security personnel at your house?" I said.

"Yes," Kate said.

"You trust the security personnel?" I said.

"Freddy hired them," Kate said. "They're supposed to be good."

"And you're planning on getting home by tonight?" I said.

"Yes," Kate said.

"I'm sure the kids will be fine until you get back," I said.

"How sure?" Kate said.

"Very sure," I said. "Nothing you said makes me believe things will change in the next few hours. Down the road, maybe. But not right now."

Kate studied my face.

"Okay," Kate said. "I believe you."

"Good," I said. "Show me what you have."

Kate seemed confused, as if she didn't know what I was talking about. I pointed at the iPhone in her hands. She looked down at it, then back up at me.

"You made me so worried I completely forgot what I was doing," Kate said.

She refocused on the cell phone, powered it up, unlocked it, and laid it on the coffee table.

"I received a voicemail on Friday," Kate said.

CHAPTER 14

Kate pushed a few buttons on the phone. A voice came out of the phone's speaker. It was a deep mechanical voice that sounded like Darth Vader on steroids. The voice had clearly been processed by a voice-altering device.

"Dr. Lennon," the voice said, "I am an employee of NASAD. I am turning to you as I do not know who else to trust. I believe I know who is responsible for the recent murders of our fellow employees. I also believe the same entity has put our country at grave risk in the event of war, and that NASAD will be blamed. I will shoulder most of that blame, but you must believe me when I say I was only doing my job. You must find someone high up in the military you can trust. When you do I will explain the file I have given you. I apologize for the enigmatic way in which I have contacted you, but I am fearful that in doing so I have violated my security oath and, unless everything is handled properly, I may spend the rest of my life in prison. Until I am sure you understand the situation, and that I can trust you, I will be using a code name. I apologize for this as well. Please remember it was never supposed to be this way. I will contact you in the next few days and when I do I will use the name Dr. N..."

At that point the recording became garbled and cut off.

"That's all there is?" I said.

"Yes," Kate said.

"Did you catch that last bit?" I said.

"I've listened to it over and over," Kate said. "I think he said Dr. Nemo. Like in 'Twenty Thousand Leagues Under the Sea.'"

"That's what I thought I heard too," I said. "But that was Captain Nemo, wasn't it?"

"Yes, I think you're right," Kate said.

Kate took a sip of coffee.

"Who is Dr. Lennon?" I said.

"Me," Kate said.

"Sorry, I didn't know you were a doctor," I said.

"No way for you to know," Kate said. "I didn't tell you."

"What kind of doctor are you?" I said.

"I'm a pediatric cardiac surgeon," Kate said.

"Whoa," I said. "I understated the situation when I said you were intelligent. Brilliant more like it."

"Thank you," Kate said.

"You're welcome," I said. "So, were you able to trace the call?"

"It came from an internal line at NASAD," Kate said. "But there was no way to tell from what extension."

"NASAD has stringent security protocols, correct?" I said.

"Yes," Kate said.

"Most likely someone with clearance to be on NASAD property, then," I said. "Which would support his or her claim to be an employee."

"His or her?" Kate said.

I took a sip of coffee. A flash of movement caught my eye and I turned to the kitchen window. A rivulet of water created by the roof's melting snow was dripping off the roof and across the window.

"The voice is altered," I said. "Could be a male or a female."

"I hadn't thought of that," Kate said.

"Besides being a doctor, are you also a security consultant?" I said.

"No," Kate said.

"No one would expect you to, then," I said. "I suppose he or she could also have been a visitor with clearance."

"Could be," Kate said. "But the data file Nemo sent me was appended with a top secret identifier. The identifier could have only been known to a NASAD employee."

"More likely an employee then," I said. "Still could have been a visitor who somehow gained access to the identifier. You have the file?"

Kate nodded.

"The file was huge," Kate said. "Dr. Nemo must have compressed it. I still have a copy of the file on my iPhone, but I was only able to open the file on my computer at home. I printed up the first few pages and transferred them to my phone so I could show them to you."

"Did you show the file to anybody else?" I said.

"Yes," Kate said. "Since I couldn't trace the phone call, I thought I might be able to trace the computer the file came from. I showed it to a software engineer at NASAD that I trust."

"Did he get anywhere?" I said.

"No," Kate said. "The engineer said whoever sent it was extremely sophisticated. The data file had been routed through so many different IP addresses, some of them used only once and then destroyed, others masked as having come from false locations, that the original sender was completely untraceable."

"I agree with your software engineer," I said. "Any sender capable of completely covering his or her tracks would have to be extremely sophisticated. Please show me what you have."

Kate leaned back over the coffee table, pushed a few buttons on the iPhone, and handed the phone to me.

The screen showed:

```
TKFJ    PXCM    QHTE    BRZM
UWSL    EDKI    WYZE    IAXT
OQAJ    RMDL    FNSE    PFON
```

I scrolled down. The letters repeated endlessly in the same pattern.

"Jeez," I said. "Just when I was thinking there was some connection between the NASAD drone submarine engineers and the choice of a code name from a Jules Verne undersea story, it turns out Dr. Nemo is actually an ophthalmologist."

"What?" Kate said.

"That's an eye chart isn't it?" I said.

"You're not serious are you?" Kate said. "Because I thought from what you said before, you were going to take this seriously now."

"No, I wasn't being serious," I said. "I'm sorry, but it's an occupational hazard."

"Not being serious?" Kate said.

"Yes," I said. "You live through enough crappy situations, you develop habits to match. Habits like saying inappropriate things to release tension."

"It's called deflecting," Kate said.

I took another sip of coffee.

"If you say so," I said. "But deflecting isn't such a bad thing is it? I mean, I've heard plenty of field surgeons tell jokes laymen would find extremely inappropriate while they're operating on wounds as nasty as a brain falling out of a soldier's skull. Hell, they even made a movie about it."

"M.A.S.H?" Kate said.

I nodded.

Kate smiled.

"I see your point," Kate said.

A sliding sound coming from the roof over the kitchen window caught my attention. I turned just in time to see a chunk of snow falling off the roof and down across the window. The chunk landed outside the house with a thud. Ashley growled again in her sleep.

"Did Nemo give you the key to the letters on your iPhone screen?" I said.

"The key?" Kate said.

"Those letters on your iPhone screen look like code," I said. "You need the key to decipher the code."

"Sorry," Kate said. "Code deciphering wasn't covered in medical school."

"Not even simple alphabetical substitutions?" I said

"What's an alphabetical substitution?" Kate said.

"In an alphabetical substitution you substitute the letter in the coded communication with a different letter," I said. "The key tells you how to perform the substitution. For example, the rule for the key might be to substitute the letter that is three letters later in the alphabet than the one written on the page in front of you. An 'H' would be rewritten as a 'K.' An 'X' would be an 'A,' a "Q' a 'T'. And a 'B' is...?"

"The 'E' at the end of Kate," Kate said.

"You catch on quick," I said. "Captain Midnight Decoder Rings that kids got in the 50's and 60's worked similarly. The ring had two concentric wheels, one within the other, and each with the alphabet written on them. You and the friend you are communicating with agree how the wheels will line up so you can encode and decode messages you send to each other. You get a message with a 'J' you look down at your ring and you know you have to change it to an 'M.'"

"Dr. Nemo didn't give me a Captain Midnight Decoder Ring," Kate said.

I smiled.

"I was pretty sure he didn't," I said. "It would have made deciphering the code on your phone a lot easier if he had, though. Of course, if Nemo really works for NASAD, and is who he says he is, there's no way he would have used such a simple key. These days the keys are very complex algorithms to keep the wrong entities from intercepting and deciphering the messages. One day the algorithms will probably be based on quantum mechanics."

"Can't wait," Kate said. "Why did you say if Nemo is who he says he is?"

"This whole Dr. Nemo thing could be a hoax couldn't it?" I said. "Or someone throwing some misdirection your way."

"It's possible," Kate said. "But I don't think Dr. Nemo is a hoax or a misdirection. I think he's real."

"If you're right, then you probably really do have a pretty nasty problem on your hands," I said.

"Exactly," Kate said. "And the only way I'm ever going to get to the bottom of it is if you help me. Are you going to help me?"

At that moment, what I truly wanted to say to Kate was, 'Sorry, but no, I'm not going to be able to help you. I prefer to stay put on my ranch where things are nice and peaceful and where I can watch over Adelaide and Jeff. You're just going to have to make do without me.'

But I didn't say any of that.

I'm not sure why I didn't.

Perhaps it was because Kate looked like my beloved Grace, or because my sense of duty toward her dead father, Milt Feynman, and her husband, Paul Lennon, kept nagging at me, or because I couldn't get out of my mind that there really was a grave threat to our national security staring me right there in the face. Perhaps it was a combination of all three.

But, while I didn't say no to Kate, I didn't say yes, either.

What I did do was stall again.

"Let me think about it," I said.

CHAPTER 15

Kate sat bent forward in the easy chair, her elbows resting on her elegant thighs, her pretty hands cradling her chin, her intelligent blue eyes watching me closely as I thought things over. I was trying hard to make a case to myself for staying on the ranch. I was finding it difficult to concentrate at that moment, however, because Kate, by leaning over, had caused her breasts to tauten the fabric of her shirt, making them appear more pronounced. I tried to appear as casual as possible and also not to stare. Staring was winning out, so I distracted myself by lifting my coffee cup off the redwood stump where I had left it, taking a sip, and putting it back on the stump. That worked passably well, and I went back to thinking. A minute or so later, I got very close to finalizing what I was going to say to Kate to gently let her down. Kate, however, interrupted me before my speech was perfected.

"I can tell by your face you really don't want to help me, do you?" Kate said.

I surfaced slowly out of my near dream-like state.

"You're a mind reader now?" I said. "I thought you were a doctor."

"You're changing the subject," Kate said.

"You're right," I said. "I didn't really mean to, however."

"Well, whether you meant to or not, please don't," Kate said. "Just be honest and tell me what's keeping you from helping me."

"Lots of things, most of them personal," I said. "But the main thing is I don't believe you've explored all your other options."

"Such as?" Kate said.

"For one, Dr. Nemo said to find someone in the military you could trust," I said. "You could have just as easily gone to NASAD's military liaison instead of me."

"Can't trust the liaison," Kate said.

I raised my eyebrows.

"Things are much different now than when my father was alive," Kate said. "It seems like everyone in the Armed Forces we work with is trying to set up a job in the private sector for when they retire from military service. I'm not sure what they're loyal to."

"Not everyone is like that," I said.

"Everyone we work with now is," Kate said. "My father wouldn't have put up with any of them."

"If everyone you work with now truly is as you describe them," I said, "then I agree, your father absolutely wouldn't have put up with them."

"My husband wasn't anything like the current crop of military officers we have to deal with, either," Kate said.

"I'm sure he wasn't," I said.

"Of course nothing matters about what my father or husband were like, or what they would do, since they're both dead," Kate said. "Nothing except one thing, that is. They both made it clear they would put their lives in your hands, and that's what I'm doing right now."

A blue jay landed on the exterior windowsill of the window directly behind Kate's head. The jay danced on the sill with its spindly legs, rapped the window with its blue crested head a few times, whistled, and flew off.

"Again, that's very kind of you to say," I said. "But this isn't a job for a guy like me, because, frankly, I wouldn't have any idea what to do. I'm a soldier. All I really know how to do is kill bad guys."

Kate looked skeptical.

"That's all?" Kate said.

"That, and sometimes I get good guys out of bad situations," I said. "But that's it."

"Assuming for the moment I believe you," Kate said, "who is this a job for?"

"Like I said, the FBI is perfect," I said. "What you have is a murder investigation. You need detectives, not military guys. FBI is loaded with the best detectives in the world."

"Uh huh," Kate said. "What about Dr. Nemo?"

"If Dr. Nemo's real, the FBI will find him," I said. "Once they find him, if they determine there really is a threat to national security, they'll know how to handle that as well."

"How will they handle it?" Kate said.

"They'll bring in the NSA and Homeland Security who will coordinate with the Defense Department," I said.

"And what will they do?" Kate said.

"I don't know," I said. "Whatever their protocols tell them to do, I suppose."

"You have a lot of faith in those protocols, do you?" Kate said.

I didn't say anything.

"You know as well as I do that all those protocols will do is lead to one big bureaucratic mess," Kate said. "I'll have more dead employees, and, as Dr. Nemo said, our country will be exposed to grave risk if there's a war." She paused. "You get the news up here?"

"I do," I said.

"Then you know we're about to go to war with China," Kate said. "Maybe that's the war Dr. Nemo was warning us about."

Again, I didn't say anything. My left knee hurt from sitting and staying in one position too long. I rubbed it.

Kate lifted her coffee cup off the table, took another sip, put the cup back down. Then she just stared at me. The stare made me feel uncomfortable.

"Why are you looking at me like that?" I said.

"Because you're so full of shit," Kate said. "You don't want to help me, or your country, I get it. But don't make up fake reasons for why you can't do it. My husband Paul told me how things work."

Ouch. Kate essentially saying that I didn't care about my country, and what might happen to it in the event of war, hurt even more than my left knee. I took a deep breath, let it out.

"What did Paul tell you?" I said.

"Paul said he and his special forces teams would get set down in some godforsaken country like Colombia, Somalia, Yemen, or whatever," Kate said. "A lot of times when they got there, they'd find the intel was bad. His team would be on their own then, and they'd have to figure out what was really going on. Who's doing what to who, why they're doing it, how they're doing it, where they're doing it. I know that's what you and General Bradshaw did as well - you figured all that out, and then you took action. And you did that a lot."

"Maybe," I said.

The rubbing hadn't helped my knee. If anything, it hurt more. I put my hands on the arms of my chair, carefully pushed myself up, and tried to walk the pain off.

"What do you mean maybe?" Kate said.

"If what you just said was true, it would be top secret stuff," I said. "If I admitted it to you, I'd have to kill you."

"I have a security clearance because of my position as a director on the board of NASAD," Kate said.

"Not for that kind of thing," I said.

Kate rolled her eyes.

A new searing pain shot through my knee. I stopped in my tracks, bent over, and rubbed it again. The rubbing still didn't help.

"What's wrong?" Kate said.

"Nothing," I said. "My knee's a little out of whack, that's all."

"Anything I can do to help?" Kate said.

"You got a sledgehammer?" I said.

"Sledgehammer?" Kate said.

"Yeah," I said. "You could hit me in the head with it. Look, I understand how unhappy you are with the FBI and that you can't get them to replace this guy...what's his name again?"

"Burnette," Kate said. "Special Agent Burnette."

"Right, Burnette," I said. "But maybe you get someone to come in and work beside him. Like I said, there are plenty of stellar FBI agents."

"If you knew Burnette," Kate said, "you'd know what a bad idea that was."

The pain in my knee began to lessen. I sat back down.

"Why is that?" I said.

"Because no one any good will work with him," Kate said. "One, he's an officious little prick, and two, they wouldn't be able to stand the obnoxious sycophants that Burnette surrounds himself with."

"He doesn't sound that different than other guys I've known in similar positions of responsibility," I said.

"There's also three, four, and five," Kate said.

"Three, four, and five?" I said.

"Yes," Kate said. "Burnette has a potbelly, wears a porkpie hat, and carries a pearl handled, gold-plated Glock."

"Really?" I said. "A pearl handled, gold-plated Glock?"

Kate nodded.

"Okay, you're right," I said. "I'm convinced. No one good would ever work with a guy like that."

"Thank you," Kate said. "There's something else I'd like to convince you of as well."

"What?" I said.

"Despite you repeatedly saying that Dr. Nemo might not be real, I know he is," Kate said. "I am absolutely sure of it."

I didn't ask Kate how she knew Nemo was real, since, contrary to what I'd been saying to Kate, I was pretty sure he was real too. Something about the way Nemo had said he was afraid he might spend the rest of his life in prison had seemed real to me. I couldn't quite put my finger on exactly what that something was, but what he had said didn't feel like anything someone could make up.

"I hate to admit it, but I agree with you," I said. "I think Nemo is real too."

Kate smiled and got out of her chair.

"That was easy," Kate said.

Kate walked over to me and stood directly in front of me. She was so close that the scent of her jasmine perfume filled my nostrils. I breathed in deeply to take in even more of her scent. I felt like I was in heaven. Kate then put both hands on my shoulders and bent forward so that our faces were only inches apart. I went somewhere beyond heaven.

"Nemo said to get someone high up in the military," Kate said. "I'm going with that and that's you."

"Military's not allowed to get involved in domestic issues," I said, my voice hoarse. "There are strict laws about that."

Kate leaned in even closer to me. Her knees touched the inside of my knees.

"Forgive me, General," Kate said. "But I just don't believe you're the kind of man who would let a little thing like the law stop you. Especially when the stakes are so high."

"That's an interesting observation," I croaked. "Do me a favor please, however, and don't go around repeating that to anyone."

Kate smiled again.

"I won't," Kate said. "Besides, no one needs to know what you're doing."

"You have an invisible suit for me to wear while I wander around

NASAD?" I said.

"I'll tell everyone you're a friend of mine," Kate said. "You're just visiting and I'm showing you around."

A friend of Kate's?

Down big boy.

"What about Adelaide and Jeff?" I said. "They need me here. It would look very bad to Adelaide's probation officer if I left Adelaide in Jeff's care."

Kate's knees moved farther inside of my knees. I felt like I was going to faint.

"Probation officer?" Kate said.

"Guess you didn't see the ankle monitor," I said, barely getting the words out.

"What'd she do?" Kate said.

"She got in a fight," I said.

"Anybody hurt?" Kate said.

"You could say that," I said.

Just then the deafening, high-pitched drone of a big gasoline engine springing to life came from an area outside the kitchen. The sound violently rattled the house's windows and shook the floorboards. Ashley instantly woke up, jumped to her feet, and ran out the doggie door. Kate, who appeared startled, pulled away from me. She looked toward the kitchen window.

"What's going on?" Kate said, her voice on edge.

I had been so deeply entranced by the closeness of Kate's beautiful presence, that it took me a moment to compose myself.

"It's nothing to worry about," I said, standing up. "Follow me and I'll show you."

Limping a bit from the pain in my knee, I led Kate to the kitchen window. From the window there was a panoramic view of the scenery outside, a view that had not been visible from where we had been sitting. The view encompassed the surrounding mountains, the plateau's forest of trees, and also, just to the right of the kitchen and in front of the trees, a small clearing. A Piper Super Cub, its propeller spinning in a fast blur, was perched in the clearing about fifty yards away from the tree line. The plane's fuselage was painted a bright yellow and its wings a sparkling crimson. Jeff was in the cockpit in the pilot's seat, and one of the Samoans was next to him in the passenger seat.

"Which twin is that with Jeff?" I said.

"You think I can tell them apart?" Kate said.

I laughed.

Ashley bounded up next to the plane. The pilot side door opened. Ashley jumped in and the door closed behind her. The Cub's engine revved. A mini dust storm flowed from the propeller's wake.

"Is Jeff testing the engine?" Kate said.

"I think he's going to take your man for a ride," I said.

"There's no runway," Kate said.

"Watch," I said.

Jeff must have released the plane's brakes just then, as the plane shot forward on its two huge, black rubber tundra tires. Within fifteen feet, the Cub was airborne. The airplane rose swiftly into the bright blue sky, cleared the treetops, then banked westward to the Yosemite peaks, the sun flashing off its wings.

"I've never seen anything like that," Kate said.

"Wait until you see it land," I said.

"Are you a pilot too?" Kate said.

"No way," I said. "Jeff and I experienced one blown extraction too many. We decided one of us better learn to fly. Jeff drew the short straw."

We both watched as the Piper Cub moved farther and farther away. After a moment, Kate turned from the window. She put both her hands on my shoulders again, looked up into my face, focused her stunning blue eyes directly into mine, and held my gaze. I had a hard time not wobbling.

"So, what's it going to take to get you to help me?" Kate said.

"I just don't see how it can work," I said.

"If you're worried about Adelaide and Jeff, I'll put a NASAD jet at your disposal," Kate said. "You can be back here from NASAD head-quarters in Westlake Village in less than forty-five minutes."

There was no question the jet would make it easy for me to get back to the ranch in an emergency. But the main issue still remained. I didn't want to leave my home and I truly believed there was little I could add to what the FBI was already doing for Kate and NASAD.

"That's a nice offer," I said. "But I'm afraid it's still a no."

Kate didn't say anything. Her eyes narrowed as she appeared to study me. She seemed to have an inspiration.

"I want to show you one last thing," Kate said.

"It won't make any difference," I said.

"Just let me give it a try," Kate said. "Stay right where you are."

Kate strode back to where we had been sitting, picked up her iPhone, made a few strokes on its screen with her fingers, and walked back to me.

She put the screen up to my face.

CHAPTER 16

At first, the screen was a little too close for me to clearly see what was on it. I gently took Kate's wrist and pushed the screen back a bit from my face. I liked holding her wrist. It felt warmer and more full of life than any wrist I had ever held other than Grace's. I continued holding Kate's wrist while I looked at the screen. If Kate had asked why I hadn't let go of her wrist, I had planned to say I needed to keep the screen at a good viewing distance. But Kate didn't ask.

The photo on the screen was of an attractive Latino woman with dark eyes, long silky black hair, and wearing a form-fitting red dress. The woman had a big smile on her face and held in her arms a little boy who had her same eyes, hair and smile. She had lofted the boy about chest height, and he had his arms around the woman's neck.

"Jennifer Moreno," Kate said. "Single mother, served two tours of duty with the Army in Afghanistan, had a Ph.D. in engineering from MIT, in charge of sonar systems on NASAD's drone sub program. Jennifer was thirty-six when she died in a fire in her home. She was barely able to get her son out before she succumbed to the flames. That's her son, Hector, in her arms. He was three years old at the time."

The photo and Kate's words made me feel something I didn't want to feel. I let go of Kate's wrist.

Kate swiped another photo onto her iPhone screen. This one showed a distinguished looking grey-haired African American man in a blue suit and tie. He appeared to have lost both legs above his knees and was sitting in a wheelchair. Fourteen young adults, dozens of small children, and a beautiful woman who looked to be close to his age - all of whom were well-dressed and posing for the camera - surrounded the man.

"Garfield Langhorn," Kate said. "Marine veteran, he lost both legs to a land mine in Viet Nam, had engineering degrees from the University of Tokyo and Harvard, was with NASAD for over thirty years, and headed the navigation program for the drone subs. Those are his children, their spouses, and his grandchildren surrounding him. Dr. Langhorn was an expert scuba diver, and yet died when he got tangled in a kelp bed and ran out of air off the coast of Catalina. He was sixty-five years old when he died."

The feeling I didn't want to feel was only growing stronger.

Kate swiped a new photo on the screen. Two balding, smiling, slightly paunchy, late middle-aged Caucasian men dressed in matching sweaters, khaki pants, and sneakers stood facing the camera. They had their arms around three young Asian children, two boys and one girl. The entire group was standing at the edge of a pier with their backs to a wide blue ocean.

"The man on the right is Frederick Steuben," Kate said. "The man on his left is his partner, Alvin Siegel. The three children are siblings from Sumatra, orphaned in the tsunami of 2004 and adopted by Mr. Steuben and Mr. Siegel. Mr. Steuben was a Navy Seal who got his engineering degree from Caltech and ran the drone subs' weapon systems program. Mr. Steuben died in a fall while hiking a trail in the Grand Canyon by himself. He was fifty-three years old when he died."

Kate paused for a moment then said, "You know who these people are, don't you?"

I didn't say anything.

"I've only shown you three," Kate said. "There are nine more. The NASAD engineers left behind wives, husbands, partners, children, grandchildren, brothers, sisters, parents, friends. All the engineers were innocent. The ones they loved, and who loved them, were innocent. As I understand it, you protect the innocent. And sometimes you avenge them."

My throat had grown tight. I tried to swallow but could not.

"You can take that away now," I said.

Kate pulled the cell phone away from my face and slipped it in her vest pocket. I turned towards the kitchen window, placed my hands on the tile counter next to the sink, and leaned on the counter as I watched Jeff make lazy turns in the sky. Something was nagging at the corners of my consciousness, trying to surface, to make itself known. I closed my eyes and tried to relax. The nagging thing spiraled higher and higher in my mind, felt like it was getting closer to a place where its message could become clear. The spiraling seemed to take forever. When the spiraling ceased, and the nagging thing finally unveiled its message to me, it seemed my conscious mind could have grasped the message's content much earlier, and I wondered why it had not.

"Kate," I said, "did your husband work for NASAD?"

"Yes," Kate said. "Paul's official title was assistant vice president of defense systems, but he was pretty much an overall troubleshooter for my dad."

"What happened to him and your father?" I said.

"You mean how did they die?" Kate said.

I nodded.

"In a plane crash," Kate said. "It happened nearly three years ago. They were on a fishing trip in Alaska. They took a day off to go grizzly viewing at Katmai. Their plane went down at sea. The plane's emergency locator beacon must have malfunctioned, since it worked for only a short time before its signal died. Search and rescue teams looked for days in the area of the beacon's last transmission, but no trace was ever found of my father, my husband, the pilot, or the plane."

I knew the beacon Kate was referring to was an EPIRB - an emergency position indicating radio beacon. It is standard equipment for small planes everywhere but is especially necessary in Alaska, where small planes very often fly across uninhabited and extremely rugged territory.

"An accident," I said.

"Yes," Kate said. "A tragic accident. My life and my children's lives were changed forever."

I turned away from the window and looked at Kate's face. She watched me intently. I was about to ask another question, but something I thought I saw pass over her features made me stop myself. The something I thought I saw was hope, hope that I was going to help her. The more she seemed to study me, the more hopeful she appeared to become. I didn't like that she was becoming more and more hopeful. At that moment, I didn't care that Kate reminded me of Grace, who Kate's father and husband were, what NASAD's problems were, or who Dr. Nemo was. I wanted to stay on my ranch. I wanted Kate and Manu and Mosi to get in their damn Maybach and drive off of my land and never return.

Kate stayed quiet. Her hope seemed to continue to grow. I tried once again to bring myself to ask my newly formed question, but could not. An unexpected change had come over me, a change brought about, perhaps, by the unfathomable workings of my heart. I suddenly found myself wanting that beautiful face to have its hope and didn't want to interfere with that hope or interrupt it. There was no way, however, I could stop hearing the unspoken question in my head, or wondering how strangely the human mind worked at times and how it kept things from us, protected us from hurt and pain. I didn't ask Kate anything further. There was a chance I was wrong after all. But I didn't think I was wrong and I continued to wonder. Before me was a strong, intelligent, forceful, highly educated, beautiful woman, who had struggled for years to get someone to pay attention to a list of NASAD employees she was convinced were dying not in accidents, but being murdered instead.

How on earth had Kate failed to add her father and husband to that list?

CHAPTER 17

I turned away from Kate once more and looked out the kitchen window. Kate stood behind me, not saying a word. I watched as the Super Cub returned from its flight, its big tires bouncing on the ground as it rolled to a stop, the entire landing taking less space than it had used to take off. The Cub's engine shut down and Jeff jumped out of the plane. He was followed in close order by the Samoan twin and Ashley. The three of them disappeared to parts unknown.

Why does anybody do anything? I'm the last person anyone should ask. Oftentimes, I have no idea why I do what I do myself. Those moments I spent gazing out the window was one of those times. I was buffeted by waves of emotion, tossed by anger and sadness, longing and yearning. Angered over the loss of so much innocent life among Kate's employees. Saddened by the deaths of Milt Feynman and Paul Lennon. Longing for my dead wife Grace, while at the same time yearning for Kate to somehow represent Grace's miraculous resurrection.

And I was torn too. Torn between wanting to stay on the ranch, and leaving with Kate. If I went with Kate to pursue the problems at NASAD, that would mean leaving Adelaide and Jeff behind, a leaving that felt to me like an abandonment.

Could I do that?

Should I do that?

What had the poet said?

The past and present wilt. I have fill'd them,
emptied them.
And proceed to fill my next fold of the future.

The wilting part was known to me.

The question was, what was the next fold to be...

In my heart, I knew that the investigation at NASAD was most assuredly being botched and that more innocent life was also likely to be lost, probably sooner rather than later. And, as I believed Dr. Nemo was in all likelihood a real person and not a hoax, I also worried what would happen if his warning of a potential future became a future fulfilled.

Because if that future did become a reality, the lives of hundreds of thousands of American servicemen and women would be at risk and a great many of those servicemen and women would probably die. If I could have prevented those deaths, but failed to do so, how would I ever be able to forgive myself?

In the middle of my questioning, I turned my head from the window and my eyes fell upon a book on one of the den's bookshelves. The book was a battered and oft-repaired first edition of *Infantry Tactics, or Rules for Maneuvers of the United States Infantry*, written by Winfield Scott and published in 1835. It had been my father's book and passed to me upon his death. My father, a special forces soldier, had been killed at the age of twenty-three in combat in Viet Nam before I was born.

My father had been given the book by his father - my grandfather - who in turn had received it from his own father - my great-grandfather - all part of a tradition spanning over 150 years in which the book passed through the Wilder family from generation to generation, from father to firstborn son. All of those Wilder men, including me, had been soldiers. We had fought at the Alamo, Antietam, Gettysburg, San Juan Hill, Meuse-Argonne, Guadalcanal, Iwo Jima, Normandy, the Battle of the Bulge, Inchon, la Drang, Khe San, Khafji, Fallujah, Nasiriyah, and Wanat. Some of the Wilder fighting men made it home alive, some did not - Jeff and I were survivors of Khafji, Fallujah, Nasiriyah, and Wanat.

Despite the book's title, as far as the Wilder men were concerned, the tactics in the book were not the book's most meaningful contents. No, what all those fathers and sons paid attention to, updated, and added to during their lifetimes were the notes their predecessors had scrawled in the margins and on the back pages of the book, new blank pages having been glued in as they were needed. All of us had learned from the book, which included not only our ancestors' thoughts and experiences, but ideas they had gleaned from such far-ranging mythic and real influences as Gilgamesh, Arjuna's adventures in the Bhagavad Gita, Athena, Alexander the Great, Yennenga, the Knights Templar and of the Round Table, Joan of Arc, the Samurai Code, George Washington and Patton, and countless other brave men and women warriors.

I had not yet added my own words to the book. The last words in the book then, the only ones that had been written on the book's most recently added and final page, were my father's. He had been eighteen when he had written them, and there were just three lines. I did not need to open the book to know what the lines said. Their words had been ingrained in my mind since the day when, as a five year old boy, I had first been old enough to read and understand them.

Protect the innocent.

Never run from a fight that needs fighting.

Let no comrade's death go unavenged.

Words from a father to his son. Neither of whom had ever met the other, but knew each other well.

I turned back to face Kate. Kate, this beautiful woman who resembled my beloved Grace, and who had traveled far, and not without risk, to ask for my help when all else had failed her. Kate, the daughter and wife of my dead comrades, comrades who had most likely been murdered, and who had seemingly sent this messenger with their request of me from beyond the grave.

Protect the innocent and stop this slaughter.

Avenge them.

Avenge us.

And so, I really had no choice, did I?

I had to go with Kate.

As to leaving Adelaide and Jeff, I told myself that I wouldn't be gone long and that I wasn't going far. If Adelaide and Jeff needed me, and a phone call would not suffice, Kate's jet could, as she said, get me back to the ranch from Southern California in less than forty-five minutes.

"Okay," I said to Kate, my voice a near whisper.

"I'm sorry, I barely heard you," Kate said. "What did you just say?"

"I'll help you," I said.

Kate's face lit up, her blue eyes moist, shiny, and wide. She raised herself on her tiptoes off the kitchen floor, threw her arms around my neck and held herself suspended there as she gave me a kiss on the cheek.

Her lips felt like Grace's lips.

I almost died.

"Thank you," Kate said.

CHAPTER 18

"You're welcome," I somehow managed to say.

Kate lingered another moment with her arms around my neck, then took a big breath in and let it out. She let go of my neck, came down off her tiptoes, and wiped a tear out of her eye.

"Where should we start?" Kate said.

"NASAD's headquarters seems like as good a place as any," I said. "It appears to be the epicenter of all that has gone wrong and the most likely place to find Dr. Nemo."

"I agree," Kate said. "Manu and Mosi can take us in the Maybach. I have a home in Malibu that's not far from NASAD's offices in Westlake Village and you can stay in an extra room there."

That sounded fine to me except for the part about the Maybach. Despite having dispatched many a Maybach to an early grave, I had never ridden in one of the infernal machines. The thought of riding in one then made my stomach start to churn for the second time that morning. Still, it would be foolish to take more than one vehicle to Southern California, especially when the Maybach could easily accommodate all four of us - Manu, Mosi, Kate, and me.

"Sounds like that will work fine," I said. "How long do you think it will take us to get to your house?"

"Probably seven or eight hours," Kate said. "When do you want to leave?"

"Just as soon as I pack," I said.

"Should I track down Manu and Mosi while you pack and tell them that we'll be heading back down south soon?" Kate said.

"That's a good idea," I said. "Except please don't mention yet that I'm going with you. I want to break the news to Adelaide and Jeff myself."

"Got it," Kate said.

Kate turned to go.

"Kate, wait, I forgot something," I said.

She turned back around.

"It's probably best if you transfer all the relevant NASAD files you have on your iPhone to mine," I said. "That way I'll have easy access to them if I want to review them."

"Is it safe to transfer the files here?" Kate said. "You're sure your network is secure enough?"

"It's a little embarrassing," I said, "but the ranch's wireless network is even more secure than the one used in the White House. It was installed by, and at the insistence of, the U.S. military."

"Do you really need something that powerful?" Kate said.

"I did when I was on active duty," I said.

"Oh, right, of course," Kate said. "So you want Dr. Nemo's file, the pages I printed, and his voicemail?"

"Everything," I said. "Even the photos of the dead NASAD drone sub engineers and their families."

"Okay," Kate said. "Show me how to log on."

I showed her and we transferred all the files. Kate left then and I went to my bedroom to pack for the journey. I grabbed a few clean, light blue work shirts, jeans, underwear, and socks, and shoved everything in the tattered green canvas rucksack that had been in most parts of the world with me. I then tossed in a comb, some deodorant, a toothbrush, toothpaste, and was done.

I had considered packing a Glock as well, but, again, as a military man, I was already on shaky ground conducting an independent operation on domestic soil. I could take care of myself in most situations without a gun, and, given that I wasn't a NASAD engineer working on drone submarines, nor a NASAD employee of any type, I was unlikely to be a target. Last but not least, I didn't want to worry about some California cop giving me a hard time about carrying around an unlicensed firearm.

I threw my rucksack over my shoulder, exited the front door, bounded down the porch steps, and turned up the path that led to Grace's grave. I wanted to share some parting words with Grace before I left.

When I arrived at Grace's grave, I said, "Grace honey, I'm sorry, but a woman is here who has asked me to do an important job. I need to leave for a while, but I won't be gone long. I'm sure Adelaide and Jeff will be okay in my absence. I don't know what to make of it yet, but the woman has an uncanny resemblance to you. I know she's not you, but sometimes it feels like she is, and that you're with me again. Please don't be mad, but I like that feeling Grace. I really, really like it."

I neatened up the flowers I had left earlier that morning, and kissed Grace's headstone.

"I'll see you soon, my love," I said.

It took an effort of will, but I then tore myself away from Grace's grave and went looking for Adelaide and Jeff. Voices emanated from the direction of the jump tower and that is where I headed. The wind had picked up, bringing cold air from the northeast where tall, dark storm clouds continued to gather. The seagulls rode the wind westward towards a sky that was still blue and clear, and where the sun, slowly making its way toward Yosemite, was big and glowing. The cold air chilled my body, but the sun's rays felt warm on my face.

As I walked along the drying foot trail that wended its way through the pine forest to the jump tower, I tried to go over all that Kate had told me. I quickly realized, however, that then was not the time for such a review - I was still in a daze from the events of the morning and unable to think clearly. I also knew that I'd have plenty of time during the long drive ahead of me to think about the issues revolving around Milt Feynman and Paul Lennon, the dead NASAD drone submarine engineering project managers, Freddy, the FBI, Special Agent Burnette, disgruntled employees, and Dr. Nemo.

The voices from the jump tower grew louder as I continued on my way, but the pines were dense and I couldn't see anything other than the forest surrounding me. Despite my efforts to keep my questions regarding the situation at NASAD at bay, I suddenly found it impossible not to think about all the innocent people who had been murdered. The murders demanded justice. Some ideas about how that justice could be meted out bubbled up into my consciousness, but those ideas, or ones like them, were why there were hundred year old laws that prohibited men like me from operating on domestic soil.

CHAPTER 19

As I got closer to the jump tower, I found myself dreading breaking the news of my leaving to Adelaide and Jeff. I was sure they would consider me some kind of deserter. I tried to come up with what I would say to them, but nothing I thought of felt right. I decided I would just have to play it by ear and hope for the best.

When I finally exited the forest, I saw that Adelaide, Jeff, Kate, and the Samoans were at the jump tower. Their backs were to me, so they couldn't see me. Ashley had resumed chasing the mallards in her pond, but Eclipse was nowhere to be seen. I assumed Jeff must have put him back in his stall.

It appeared Jeff was instructing the giant Samoan twins in the art of parachute jumping. The twins were barefoot but had not bothered to remove their sopping wet black suits. Was it that they didn't mind sodden clothes, but didn't like the feel of soggy shoes? I didn't know.

Jeff, still wearing his blue and white striped jockey helmet and red riding jacket, barked orders as the twins hauled themselves up the ladder to the top of the thirty-four-foot tower. Adelaide had remained caked in mud.

The twins reached the top of the wooden jump platform. Both twins began to strap themselves into their jump harnesses. The harnesses were attached via small trolleys to a cable that ran all the way to the ground. The idea was to jump off the tower and ride the cable back to earth.

The purpose of the jump tower was, again, to train soldiers how to jump out of a plane and land after a parachute jump. Soldiers were trained in how to actually use a parachute and maneuver through the air only after they had learned how to land. The jump tower's construction was, in essence, very much like a zip line, except that the jump tower's trolleys did not have brakes, and the landings at the end of the cable were made at much higher speeds, and onto much harder ground.

After the twins were fully strapped into their harnesses, the first twin leapt into the air and started his descent. His brother quickly followed, too quickly in my opinion. I cringed as the first brother landed well -

touching down on the balls of his feet, then rolling onto the sides of his calf, hip, and torso - only to be slammed into by the second twin. Both twins lay on the ground, grunting and groaning in apparent agony.

Jeff yelled, "I told you you gotta wait for the first one to clear before the second one jump!"

The twins must have been hardy souls, as even in the midst of their suffering, they managed a sheepish nod in Jeff's direction. A few moments later they both got to their feet, dusted off their suits, and staggered back up the jump tower.

I quickly covered the ground between myself and the tower. Only Kate seemed to hear my approach. She turned around. Her eyes appeared to key instantly on my small rucksack.

"I hope you're planning on staying more than twenty-four hours," Kate said.

Jeff turned, stared right at me, and his face looking decidedly accusatory, said, "That'll last him six months at least. Question is, where he goin'?"

I felt myself withering under Jeff's glare. I knew right then and there that nothing I could say would ever convince him, or Adelaide, that I wasn't a turncoat or a dirty double-crossing deserter, and that I actually had a good reason to leave them behind at the ranch and go to Southern California to help Kate. I felt I had to try, however, and so, full of dread, I took a deep breath and...

Kate spoke before I had a chance to say anything.

"Adelaide and Jeff, I feel comfortable being open with both of you since General Wilder clearly holds each of you in such high regard," Kate said. "Where General Wilder is going, is with me. I work at the North American Space and Defense company - better known as NASAD - which, Adelaide, as you may or may not know, is a large defense contractor for the United States military. Top-level engineers are being murdered at NASAD, and I believe there may be a significant security breach that threatens the safety of the U.S. Armed Forces. The FBI is not only useless, but clueless. My father, Milton Feynman, who founded NASAD, and my husband, Captain Paul Lennon - who I believe you knew, General Bradshaw - told me that if things ever got really bad, the only person they would trust to help them was General Wilder. Well, right now things are really bad. We have very serious issues at NASAD."

Adelaide took an aggressive posture - thrusting her chest forward and putting her knuckles on her hips and her elbows out wide - and rolled her eyes.

"So you say, missy, so you say," Adelaide said. "More likely the only serious issue any of us got is that Uncle Jack's having a hard time keeping his dick in his pants after you waved your little ass at him."

Jeff nodded.

"She do have a nice ass," Jeff said.

I was mortified. How could Adelaide and Jeff treat Kate so horribly? But then, I looked at Kate's face, and she seemed unaffected by their outburst, as if, perhaps she had expected it might be coming and knew not to take it personally. I was both surprised and impressed by how Kate had reacted.

Jeff said to me, "Can't see how anything at NASAD more important than what you and I gotta do in Saudi Arabia."

I didn't say anything, as I didn't want to contradict or embarrass Jeff in front of Kate with another discussion of his 'twin', or the IED's under his bed. Adelaide, however, seemed to have no compunction about such matters. She spit onto the ground and shook her head.

"What exactly you planning on doing in Saudi Arabia, Jeff?" Adelaide said.

"None of your business, Adelaide," Jeff said.

"Wouldn't have something to do with the Chinese would it?" Adelaide said.

Jeff didn't say anything.

"Because no matter what that bowl of mush you call a brain is thinking, CENTCOM doesn't need your help," Adelaide said. "And if they did, we might as well surrender right now."

I said, "Be careful what you say, Adelaide. Jeff spoke with CENT-COM today."

"Bullshit," Adelaide said. "No goddamn way."

"Way," Jeff said. "Told them I'm ready."

"Jeff, please," Adelaide said. "The only thing you're ready for is another trip to the looney bin."

I could see where Jeff and Adelaide were headed and I was pretty sure it wouldn't end well. I also knew that if I said or did anything to Adelaide in an attempt to stop her behavior while Kate was present, things could easily spiral out of control, since Adelaide would like nothing better than to show an outsider how tough she was.

I said, "Kate, would you mind leaving us alone for a moment?"

"Why?" Kate said. "I'm enjoying this."

Adelaide glared at her.

"What the hell does that mean?" Adelaide said.

"You and Jeff remind me of how my brother and I treat each other," Kate said.

"Does Jeff look like my brother to you?" Adelaide said.

"Uh, well, no," Kate said.

"Good answer," Adelaide said.

Kate looked at me.

"It's okay, Kate," I said. "Adelaide, Jeff, and I will have a little private conversation and I'll come get you when we're done."

"Alright," Kate said. "I should probably check on Manu and Mosi anyway to make sure they don't have concussions after that last jump."

Adelaide said, "Yeah, you probably should."

Kate headed over towards Manu and Mosi at the jump tower. I waited until Kate was out of earshot before I spoke to Adelaide.

"Could you be any ruder?" I said.

"Yes," Adelaide said.

Jeff said, "I'll second that."

I sighed.

"Look you two," I said, "what Kate needs me to do is extremely important. NASAD's employees are being murdered, and whoever is doing it has shown no signs of stopping. There could easily be many more murders to come. There's also the chance that whatever is going on at NASAD could represent a potentially serious threat to national security. I owe it to Kate's father, Milt Feynman, her husband, Paul Lennon, and indeed to our country, to try to figure out what's going on. Now, I want both of you to promise me you'll treat each other well until I get back."

"I promise I'll treat her well," Jeff said, "but I'm not guaranteeing we'll both be here when you get back."

Adelaide said, "Yeah, Jeff will be in Saudi Arabia."

"Weren't talking about me," Jeff said.

Adelaide glared at Jeff. The two of them appeared to know something I didn't.

"You going somewhere Adelaide?" I said.

"Me?" Adelaide said.

"You're the only Adelaide here," I said.

Adelaide gave me her 'how could you possibly think that?' look. She lifted her left leg, pulled back the cuff of her pants to reveal her ankle monitor, and extended her leg toward me.

"In case you forgot, this stylish little bracelet I'm wearing is a court-ordered tracking device," Adelaide said.

I turned to Jeff.

"It appears Adelaide believes you're mistaken, Jeff," I said. "Would you care to explain your last comment?"

"No," Jeff said.

"Why not?" I said.

"Because I'm not getting in the middle," Jeff said.

"You already did get in the middle," I said.

Jeff shrugged.

I turned back to Adelaide. I knew something was up with her. I just didn't know what it was.

"You leave the ranch, they're going to put you in jail," I said. "Won't be a thing I can do about it."

"I'm not going anywhere," Adelaide said. "Besides, I wouldn't believe you even if you said you could do something about it. You're not a man of your word."

"What's that supposed to mean?" I said.

"You promised you'd help me complete my training," Adelaide said. "Now you're leaving, and there are a lot of things I still have to learn."

Jeff said, "You got that right."

"Screw you, Jeff," Adelaide said.

A sickening thump, followed by a loud scream, came from the jump tower behind us. Adelaide, Jeff, and I turned to look. One of the Samoan twins was writhing on the ground, holding his ankle. Kate and the other twin didn't look too concerned, however. Adelaide, Jeff, and I turned back around and picked up where we had left off.

I said, "I'm sorry if you think I lied to you, Adelaide, but I'm not abandoning you. In all honesty, I think things at NASAD may be actually worse than Kate described. I need to be there. I promise we'll finish your training when I get back."

"And if you don't come back?" Adelaide said.

"Why wouldn't I come back?" I said.

"Things really as bad as you say they are, you'll probably get killed," Adelaide said.

Jeff said, "Hate to agree with Adelaide, but everything you and Kate said is giving me a bad feeling."

I said, "I have to do this, Jeff."

"I better go with you then," Jeff said.

"You know there's plenty of reasons why that can't happen," I said.

Jeff said nothing.

"I'm glad you understand," I said. "I'll call you once I get to Southern California. I'm sure I'll need you to help me figure things out." I turned to Adelaide. "Adelaide, this is what we'll do when I get back…"

"Don't waste your breath," Adelaide interrupted. "I'm not listening to anything you say."

"Fine, I don't need you to listen," I said, "but I'm going to talk anyway. We'll keep it simple. Upon my return we'll resume battlefield communications, nighttime navigation without instruments, and medic training. Until then, Jeff will work with you on close quarter hand-to-hand combat."

"Jeff?" Adelaide said.

"I thought you weren't listening?" I said.

"Yeah, well when someone says something incredibly stupid sometimes it's hard not to hear it," Adelaide said.

"I assume that means you're questioning Jeff's hand-to-hand abilities?" I said.

"That's exactly what I'm doing," Adelaide said.

"Jeff happens to be the best close quarter fighter I've ever seen," I said. Jeff nodded, smiled.

"Lots of things you don't know about me, girl," Jeff said.

"Ha," Adelaide snorted. "I'll believe that when I see…"

Jeff, moving faster than a striking cobra, grabbed Adelaide's shoulder, twisted her hip over his hip, then flipped her over onto the ground so that her face and belly were in the dirt. He pinned Adelaide down by putting his knee on the small of her back.

Adelaide, stunned, spit dirt out of her mouth.

"That was a cheap shot Jeff," Adelaide said. "You think it takes talent to jump someone when they aren't expecting it?"

"Tell that to the hostile slitting your throat," Jeff said.

"How about I slit yours?" Adelaide said.

Adelaide reached for the SOG tactical knife in the scabbard on her belt, but Jeff grabbed her arm before she could unsheath the knife. Jeff bent Adelaide's arm against her back and shifted his knee so that it pinned her arm as well as her body. Adelaide struggled, lashing at Jeff with backward kicks and swings of her free arm. Jeff calmly avoided her attempts at mayhem.

"Let me go asshole!" Adelaide screamed.

I looked over at Kate and the Samoans. The twins were frozen in place atop the jump tower, and they, along with Kate, were staring at us. I gave all three of them a small wave.

"Everything's fine," I yelled. "Adelaide's just getting a lesson."

Jeff looked up at me.

"I'm happy to teach Adelaide some hand-to-hand," Jeff said. "But if it's all the same to you, I prefer we do knife throwing first."

Adelaide continued to flail her free fist and viciously kick her heels. Jeff, after appearing to wait for just the right moment, snared Adelaide's left leg, and while gripping her leg between his elbows, unlaced her Army Ranger boot, and ripped the boot off her foot. He kept Adelaide pinned with his knee as he studied the boot, turning it over in his hands and sniffing it.

"Ooh girl," Jeff said. "You got some powerful odor. I think we gonna have to kill this boot."

Adelaide, much to my surprise, suddenly stopped thrashing and craned her neck around to look at Jeff.

"What'd you just say, Jeff?" Adelaide said.

"I said I think we gonna have to kill this boot," Jeff said.

Adelaide nodded her head ever so slightly, an enigmatic smile crossing her face.

If I'd been Jeff, Adelaide's reaction might have made me stop and think for a moment before my next move. But I wasn't Jeff and he wasn't me...

Jeff, putting the boot in his right hand, wound up by his shoulders by pulling his left shoulder back, dropped his right arm across his chest, and flung the boot backhanded into the sky. The boot swiftly rose, rotating end over end, shoelaces flapping.

Jeff, keeping both eyes on the boot, pulled a Walther Tanto Tactical Folding Knife from his pants pocket. It should be noted that, not only was Jeff not supposed to be handling guns at that time, but any knife other than a butter knife as well. Things were happening too fast for me to say anything to him at that moment, however.

The boot was one hundred feet high and still rapidly ascending when Jeff flicked the Walther open.

Adelaide's enigmatic smile broadened.

Jeff flung the knife at the boot. The knife, with a loud whoosh, sky-rocketed blade over handle, handle over blade, retracing the boot's path.

Adelaide began to laugh, softly at first, then hysterically.

The boot, with the knife in hot pursuit, reached the apex of its flight and began to fall back to earth. Just as it fell, the knife slashed through the boot's rubber sole and leather tongue. The conjoined boot and knife tumbled out of the sky like a wounded bird, crashed into the ground, bounced three times, and came to a rest.

Adelaide was laughing so hard she seemed to be convulsing.

"You find that amusing, huh?" Jeff said to Adelaide.

Adelaide somehow managed to nod her head in between spasms.

"You ain't gonna be laughing after I slash your other one," Jeff said.

Adelaide bent back her right leg and waved the remaining boot in Jeff's face.

Jeff reached for the boot, but then stopped dead in his tracks. His eyes looked like they might pop out of his head, his nostrils flared, and his breath came in short quick bursts. Spittle formed at both sides of his mouth.

"Goddamnit!" Jeff yelled.

I had no idea what was going on, but I was afraid Jeff was going to give himself a stroke.

"Hey buddy, I don't know what's bothering you, but you better chill,"

I said. "Otherwise, you're gonna hurt yourself."

"Bitch wearing my boots!" Jeff screamed.

I suppose because what Jeff had just said was so unexpected, it took me a moment to fully absorb the significance of his words. When I did, I started laughing almost as hard as Adelaide.

Jeff dove down and clamped his hands around Adelaide's neck. Adelaide kept laughing and somehow managed to garble out something I couldn't quite hear, but sounded pretty close to "Can't believe you didn't even recognize your own boots."

Jeff shook Adelaide's neck back and forth, her head flopping like a rag doll's. Adelaide somehow kept laughing, but her face was turning red. I was fairly certain Jeff wouldn't kill her, but why take a chance? I stepped forward, used both of my hands to grab the back of Jeff's fox hunting jacket collar, and yanked him off Adelaide.

"Enough, please," I said.

Jeff, frothing at the mouth, struggled, but I pulled him further away from Adelaide and planted his ass firmly on the ground.

Adelaide slowly caught her breath between laughs.

"You owe Jeff a new pair of boots, Adelaide," I said.

"Why?!" Adelaide said. "What did I do?"

"You stole his boots," I said.

"I borrowed them," Adelaide said.

"Did you have Jeff's permission to borrow them?" I said.

Adelaide said nothing.

"Borrowing without permission is stealing," I said. "Order some new boots online for him, please."

Jeff, who was quickly calming down beneath my grip, said, "Better be brand new boots too. Don't want no used ones."

Adelaide said, "Fine. I'm sure there's a website having a sale somewhere."

I said to Jeff, "If I let you up, are you going to behave yourself?"

"'Course I will," Jeff said. "Just got myself a new pair of boots."

I let him up. I opened my arms wide and gestured with my hands to both Adelaide and Jeff.

"Okay, the two of you come in here," I said.

They looked at me like I was out of my mind.

"That wasn't a request," I said. "It was an order."

It took them another moment, but they begrudgingly stood up and came beside me, Adelaide to my right, Jeff to my left. I put my arms around them and hugged them.

Ashley, who seemed to have a sixth sense about any affection being doled out on the ranch, came running up to us. Still wet from her adventures in the pond, she got up on her back legs, put her front paws on my chest, and licked my face. Adelaide, Jeff, and I closed ranks and I extended the hug to include Ashley as well.

"Promise me you'll both behave," I said to Adelaide and Jeff.

They both nodded.

"I'll have my cell," I said. "I'll call every day to check in and you can call me anytime. If there's an emergency, I can get back here on a NASAD jet in under an hour."

Jeff said, "That go ditto for me."

"Ditto for you, what?" I said.

"I don't give a damn about your reasons for me not going with you," Jeff said. "You got an emergency of your own down there, you call me. I'll come."

"Jeff...," I said.

"Hush," Jeff said. "Not another word. Unless you want me to get angry."

"Well, I certainly don't want that," I said.

The four of us tightened the hug. We stayed that way for a moment until I pulled out of it, ready to get on my way.

*

PART II
THE JOURNEY SOUTH

CHAPTER 20

At a little before 9:30 a.m., about two and a half hours after I had first spotted the Maybach on my ranch road, I led Kate and the Samoan twins off the ranch's plateau and down to the stream. I lowered the drawbridge, then the four of us used the drawbridge to cross the stream and headed for the Maybach.

The dark storm clouds that had been closing in since dawn obliterated the sky, and with it, the sun. The temperature fell to the low fifties. Gusting winds made it feel colder than that. Normally, if either Adelaide, Jeff, or I were taking a short trip off the ranch, we would leave the drawbridge down until we returned. As I thought I would be gone at least a few days, I had asked Jeff to raise the drawbridge back up after Kate, the Samoans, and I left.

The Samoans, covered in dust, their long, stringy black hair and clothes still drying from their dunking in the stream earlier that morning, piled into the Maybach's front seats. Kate and I - my stomach churning and bile rising into my mouth - got into the rear ones. Most cars didn't have enough room to comfortably accommodate my six foot three frame, but the Maybach's reclining beige leather rear seats with extendable footrests suited me just fine.

The rear cabin had a soundproof glass partition between it and the front cabin. The glass could be raised and lowered, and at that moment it was down. The rear cabin also had real walnut trim, Bose speakers, its own refrigerator, fold-out stainless steel food tables, expensive, deep, plush carpet, and electric window curtains. I could see how assholes the world over could appreciate such luxury and felt bad when I found myself beginning to enjoy it. I did, however, resist the urge to play with the curtain buttons.

The twin behind the steering wheel started the engine while the twin in the front passenger seat craned around to look at me through the cabin partition.

"If you want a drink General, we have soft drinks, beer, and wine in the refrigerator," the twin in the passenger seat said. "We have snacks too."

"Thanks," I said. "I beg your pardon, but which twin are you?"

The twin smiled.

"I'm Mosi," Mosi said. "Manu is driving."

I turned to Kate.

"Did you know that?" I said.

"Yes, I did," Kate said. "But only because I know Mosi hates to drive."

Manu wheeled the Maybach around and headed us out on the ranch road. The wind and sun had dried out the road and the Maybach's going out would be easier than its coming in. After we had gone only a short distance, my thighs started getting hot. Rear seat warmers. Nice, I thought. My stomach started to calm down and the bile began to stop short of my mouth.

I looked out the back window. Adelaide, Jeff, and Ashley stood atop the bluff watching our departure. A pang of regret washed over me as I wondered again if I was doing the right thing leaving them alone. I waved, but then felt foolish when I remembered that the windows were heavily tinted and that I was completely invisible to them.

Manu, his massive hands on the steering wheel, craned his head around to look at me, not slowing the car one bit as his eyes came off the road.

"Coriolis effect means the world is rotating and snipers need to adjust for it, right General?" Manu said.

"Yes," I said.

"Do you have to account for the Coriolis while driving a car?" Manu said. "Like you go around a curve, and the curve moves, and then you go over the side?"

"Maybe," I said. "But probably the most important thing to do while driving a car, Manu, is to keep your eyes on the road. And right now might be a good time to start doing that."

Manu looked befuddled for a moment, but then, seeming to process my words, he quickly turned face forward where he couldn't help but notice that the Maybach was headed directly for a roadside boulder. Manu jerked the steering wheel left and barely missed the boulder.

"Whoa, that was close," Manu said.

Kate seemed unperturbed.

"That didn't bother you?" I said to Kate.

She smiled.

"Not my car," Kate said.

Mosi laid his ham-sized left forearm across the back of his seat, and using his arm as an anchor, pulled the massive bulk of his body around and looked at me.

"You much of a parachutist, General?" Mosi said.

"I've done some jumping in my time, Mosi," I said.

"You think I've got what it takes?" Mosi said.

"I think you did very well for a beginner," I said.

"See, what'd I tell you?" Mosi said to Manu.

Manu said, "General wouldn't be saying that if he knew how many times you landed on your head before he started watching us."

"Well, you're lucky the general didn't see how many times you landed on your ass," Mosi said.

"I resent your implication," Manu said.

"Implication a pretty big word for an ass-lander," Mosi said.

"I ain't no ass-lander," Manu said. "You better watch your mouth."

Kate reached down and pushed the button to raise the soundproof glass partition between the cabins. We were mercifully spared the remainder of the Samoans' somewhat mystifying argument.

Kate then turned on an iPod that was connected to the Maybach's rear sound system. Cat Stevens's 'Hard Headed Woman' began to play, the music softly filling the cabin.

I looked over at Kate. Why did she have to choose *that* song out of all the songs the iPod surely held?

"Cat Stevens is a little before your time, isn't he?" I said, my voice suddenly hoarse.

"I first heard 'Hard Headed Woman' on an oldies station when I was in high school," Kate said. "I loved it. I bought the whole album."

"Tea for the Tillerman," I said.

"You know it?" Kate said.

Did I know it? Of course I knew it. My wife Grace had been an avid rock historian and had filled my head with a massive amount of rock trivia. Tea for the Tillerman, though it was decades old, had been one of Grace's favorite albums, and 'Hard Headed Woman', one of her favorite songs. Grace said she was my hard headed woman and that I was lucky she had such a hard head, as no other woman would ever be able to put up with me. I was pretty sure Grace was right about that, so she never heard a peep of protest from me whenever she said it. But what were the chances that 'Hard Headed Woman' was one of Kate's favorite songs as well? I didn't understand what was going on. I felt like I was drifting off into an alternate universe for what seemed like the umpteenth time that morning.

"Yes, I know it," I croaked.

Kate, apparently responding to the odd sound of my voice, said, "You okay?"

I tried to speak, but couldn't.

I nodded instead.

Kate rolled her body toward me, drawing up her knees to her chest as she did. Her new position tightened the fabric of her jeans and more clearly outlined her slim hips and thighs. Kate's movements also gently stirred the cabin's air, heightening the jasmine scent of her perfume.

"We should get some things out in the open," Kate said.

"Okay," I squeaked.

"You're a very handsome man, movie-star handsome actually," Kate said. "I never thought I would ever be attracted to another man after Paul died, but I am to you."

I didn't say anything.

"Don't you feel it too?" Kate said.

My tongue felt heavy and my throat tight. I couldn't have spoken even if I knew what to say.

"I didn't take you for the shy type," Kate said.

"Normally I'm not," I somehow forced out.

"I'll take that to mean the feeling is mutual," Kate said. "But for the sake of the project, we need to shove these feelings aside."

What?

Kate didn't really just say that, did she?

"Umm," I said.

"For the sake of the project, and also because my feelings for you can't go anywhere since I swore I would never get involved with another soldier," Kate said.

Never get involved with another soldier?

What's wrong with soldiers?

And how could our feelings for each other possibly harm the project?

Well, maybe she was right about that.

But then again, she could be wrong too, couldn't she?

I felt like I was falling down a deep hole. I wanted to tell Kate how one should never say never, how, yes, perhaps our feelings could get in the way of our project, but surely it would be folly to try to stand in the way of such a strong mutual attraction.

But I couldn't even come close to mustering the courage to say either of those things, or even anything remotely similar to them.

Instead of sharing my true feelings, what I choked out was, "Probably a wise decision on your part."

"Good," Kate said. "I'm glad you understand."

My head nodded, but it felt like it was nodding on its own. The hole I had fallen into seemed to have become a deep cosmic wormhole, a wormhole that I was sure would turn out to be bottomless.

"I also believe," Kate continued, "that though we may have these mutual feelings, there is a high likelihood that your feelings may come more from the fact that I look like your wife, not from who I really am."

Now hold on there. My feelings weren't based just on how Kate *looked*. What about the way Kate's lips felt just like Grace's lips when she kissed me? Or that Kate smiled just like Grace? Or that Kate's skin, in its softness and warmth, felt just like Grace's skin? What about 'Hard Headed Woman'? Everything said Grace, Grace, Grace.

I somehow stopped my fall into the wormhole and climbed back to what I could best describe as the present reality of that moment.

"Your feelings are real but mine aren't?" I said.

"It sounds harsh the way you put it," Kate said.

"It sounds harsh the way *you* put it," I said.

"You're right," Kate said. "I'm sorry. However, such feelings still would not be the basis for a healthy relationship. It would be too emotionally risky for me."

I said nothing.

"You look like you're pouting," Kate said.

I was pouting.

"I'm not pouting," I said.

"You sure?" Kate said.

"I'm not sure about anything right now," I said.

"That makes two of us," Kate said. "But that's all the more reason, isn't it?"

"All the more reason for what?" I said.

"To shove our feelings aside," Kate said.

I didn't say anything.

"Come on now," Kate said. "You know I'm right."

I was pretty sure Kate wasn't right. In fact I was pretty sure she was dead wrong. However, I also didn't think I'd get anywhere at that moment by trying to fight her about what she believed.

"Fine," I said. "We'll shove our feelings aside."

Kate smiled.

"Thank you," Kate said.

She then reached out and gently touched my arm.

Wait.

Wait, just a goddamned minute.

She talks like that, but then she touches me like this? With a jolt of radiant heat that traveled straight from where her fingers had landed right to the center of my chest? A jolt that ignited my heart so that it felt like it was glowing?

I looked into Kate's eyes, and for an instant, she held my gaze. But the instant passed. Kate looked down at her hand and removed it from my arm almost as quickly as she had put it there.

"I'm sorry, I don't know why I did that," Kate said.

"I like it when you touch me," I said.

"I'll try not to do it anymore," Kate said. "The project comes first. It's too important. Failure is not an option."

I felt that I'd taken enough of a beating from Kate by then to argue anymore about feelings. If that was the way she wanted it, I could play it cool too. I shifted into my professional mode.

"Failure?" I said. "What's that?"

CHAPTER 21

Kate and I continued on in silence for a while, each staring out our respective windows as the Maybach made its way along the ranch road. Manu and Mosi were rhythmically swaying in the front cabin. I assumed they had turned on some music that I couldn't hear through the cabin partition.

I thought about NASAD and kept coming back to the idea that everything I had heard so far seemed to have started with Milton Feynman's death. There was at least one good motive for murdering Feynman, NASAD's founder and president. Control of the company. I was pondering that notion when the raindrops the dark clouds had been threatening to unleash at any moment finally began to fall. The raindrops splattered on the Maybach's windshield, then formed into little silvery liquid streams that flowed down the glass. Lightning flashed, briefly illuminating the distant granite peaks. Rolling thunder followed a few seconds later and shook the car. Kate shuddered slightly.

"Thunder bother you?" I said.

"A little," Kate said.

"I've got some questions," I said. "How about we take your mind off the weather with them?"

Kate nodded.

"Obviously things had to have changed at NASAD after your father Milt died," I said. "What was the biggest one?"

"That's easy," Kate said. "My brother Freddy took over."

"Milt was grooming him?" I said.

"No, my father was fighting him," Kate said.

I gave Kate a questioning look. Lightning flashed nearby and another thunderclap shook the car. Kate shuddered, but less than she had before.

"Freddy had a lot of ideas my father didn't like," Kate said. "Chief among them was opening up manufacturing plants in Malaysia to save money on labor."

"I remember Milt as being very loyal to his employees," I said. "I wouldn't think he'd ever consider giving their jobs away to workers in another country."

"You're right," Kate said, "My father would never consider that. But it wasn't just the employee issue. My dad hated the idea of allowing secret technology to get into the hands of foreigners. He thought it would come back to bite us. That, someday, one of the foreign managers of a foreign-based NASAD factory, or a foreign executive at that factory, would get a big payday selling NASAD technological information to the highest bidder. Our enemies would then have obtained knowledge they could use to defeat us."

A flash of lightning struck a boulder less than twenty feet away from us. Kate shuddered again. A half dozen rabbits, apparently spooked by the lightning, dashed out from under a manzanita bush and sprinted across the road.

"What did Freddy think?" I said.

"Freddy thought it was silly," Kate said. "He said there was no reason to think someone in Malaysia, Viet Nam, Cambodia, or wherever else he could find cheap labor, was any less trustworthy than an American."

"Did Freddy share these views with your father?" I said.

"Yes," Kate said.

"How did your father respond to him?" I said.

"My father," Kate said, "told Freddy he was shocked Freddy could not see that even the most dishonorable American alive would, in all likelihood, at least be motivated by self-interest in his or her own safety, and, if that was not enough, then the harsh penalties for treason would certainly be an effective deterrent. My father also pointed out we could monitor for leaks much better with the vast security expertise we had at home in America."

"Freddy didn't buy it?" I said.

"Freddy laughed," Kate said. "Freddy said my father was old-fashioned and naive. He told my father that my father just didn't understand the way modern capital markets worked. Freddy said, that since the Europeans had sold a chunk of EADS to the Russians, it showed they clearly didn't care about that kind of stuff and neither should we."

"I think the Europeans absolutely cared about the potential security threat of the EADS's deal, but I think the Europeans also cared about money more," I said. "After the deal, EADS changed its name to the Airbus Group. I always thought it was a public relations maneuver, a way to distract everyone from the fact the deal had ever even occurred, and thus making it unlikely that anyone might start questioning the wisdom of doing the deal in the first place."

"I agree," Kate said. "The Airbus Group. A very warm and cuddly name for one of the largest military and defense contractors in the world. A contractor that also just happens to have access to many of the West's military technological secrets."

Overhead a flock of seagulls was beating its way west, trying to stay ahead of the storm. Three lightning bolts flashed in quick succession near the base of the granite peaks that were miles away. The granite appeared for a moment like a shimmering silver mirror.

"So you don't believe the Chinese wall that was supposed to keep those secrets from the Russians is doing what it's supposed to?" I said.

"Do you?" Kate said.

"I don't think those kinds of arrangements have ever worked in all of human history, so no," I said.

"Exactly," Kate said. "I don't think they've ever worked either. Neither did my father, which is why when Freddy tried to justify what he wanted to do by using the EADS deal as an example, my father, who rarely lost his temper, went ballistic. My father told Freddy that he wished he had never sent him to Yale Business School, and that all the money he'd spent on the school was a complete waste if that was the kind of garbage Freddy was going to spew. He said that Freddy needed to take his head out of his ass and stop acting like the rest of those greedy, stateless money men who viewed the security of the U.S. as just one more tree from which to pluck bushels of dollars."

"Freddy had an answer for that too, I assume?" I said.

"Of course," Kate said. "Freddy said that we were businessmen, not philosophers. The business of business is to make money. Nations were a thing of the past, and the new world was only going to be divided along the lines of who had money and who did not. You were either going to be one of the elite or you were going to be one of the unwashed masses."

"Let me guess," I said. "Freddy doesn't see himself as one of the unwashed masses?"

Kate laughed.

"Hardly," Kate said. "Freddy is entirely guilt-free about it too. If you asked him, he'd happily tell you that the only way he'd join the masses was over his dead body."

Another lightning bolt hit into a brace of pines about fifty yards in front of the Maybach. Kate shuddered again. A deer with a six point rack ran out of the pines, onto the ranch road, and raced down the road. I lost track of the deer when it cut around a bend in the road that was guarded by big boulders and manzanitas.

"I assume Milt didn't buy Freddy's argument about nationless states?" I said.

"He didn't," Kate said. "What my father did do was to wish Freddy good luck, because he said that luck was the only thing that would keep him alive if Freddy put his fate in the loving hands of his elite friends in China and Russia. Freddy said he knew my father was being sarcastic, but that my father was only behaving that way since my father was ignorant. The world elite, Freddy said, is bound by common interest, and everyone would act to protect those interests, both their own and their like-minded brethren's."

"At which point your father gave up," I said.

"If not right then, then pretty soon thereafter," Kate said. "How did you know?"

"I didn't know," I said. "But since I don't believe there's much else you can say to the Freddies of this world, I assumed your father probably came to the same conclusion."

"He did," Kate said. "But my father held out hope Freddy would grow up and see things differently one day."

"But then your father died," I said.

"Then he died," Kate said.

Two lightning bolts landed in quick succession on either side of the car. The thunder followed almost immediately. Kate shuddered once more.

"We're safe in the car," I said.

"I know that," Kate said. "It doesn't help."

"I understand," I said. "Which side are you on, Freddy's or your father's?"

"I don't know," Kate said. "Let me think about it."

"Sorry, bad joke," I said. "Has Freddy gotten his wish? Are there overseas plants working on sensitive technology?"

"No," Kate said. "The majority of the NASAD board remains loyal to my father's philosophy."

"The board keeps Freddy on a short leash?" I said.

"Very," Kate said.

"Other than Freddy taking over, any other significant changes?" I said.

Kate closed her eyes and rolled her tongue over her upper teeth as she seemed to think about my question. Her teeth and lips glistened. I tried not to stare.

"There is one thing," Kate said, opening her eyes. "Pennsylvania Avenue Partners. Since the board wouldn't let Freddy build plants overseas, about two years ago they threw him PAP to shut up his constant whining about NASAD's lack of sophisticated modern financial engineering. My father wouldn't let Carter Bowdoin near NASAD while he was alive, but Pennsylvania Avenue Partners has had a stake in NASAD for two years now. Freddy and Carter spend a lot of time together."

Carter Bowdoin, son of Howard Bowdoin, the former president of the United States, ran Pennsylvania Avenue Partners, or PAP. PAP was one of the most successful private equity groups in the world. Their business model was based on the one perfected by the Carlyle Group wherein former generals and defense personnel are recruited after they retire from service so that their contacts and knowledge of the military procurement system can be used to secure contracts for PAP. PAP, however, had outdone Carlyle by light years, and counted not only Carter's father as a board member, but two former defense secretaries, the former head of the NSA, and numerous retired senators. PAP controlled large stakes in defense companies who seemed to magically obtain huge contracts with the U.S. military shortly after PAP bought out those companies for a fraction of what they were worth at the time of purchase. PAP had extremely wealthy investors from all over the world, but claimed to only take money from countries who didn't pose a threat to the U.S. A large portion of PAP's money came from the Saudi royal family, but at that time, at least, there was no evidence the Chinese or Russians had invested in PAP.

"Carter is a successful guy," I said. "He's revered by a lot of people in the military who dream of the vast sums of money he'll bestow on them upon their retirement."

"Are you one of them?" Kate said.

"If I get a lobotomy, yes," I said. "Are pediatric cardiac surgeons allowed to operate on adult brains?"

"For you, I can make an exception," Kate said.

Kate leaned forward and opened the refrigerator.

"Do you want anything?" Kate said.

"Coke please, if you have it," I said.

"Regular or diet?" Kate said.

"You have both, huh?" I said. "Very classy joint you're running here. Regular please."

Kate took out a can of Coke, opened the flip top, handed me the can, and took out a bottle of Pellegrino for herself. She closed the refrigerator, unscrewed the cap on her bottle of water, and took a sip.

"I don't think what Pennsylvania Avenue Partners does should be legal," Kate said. "Neither did my father."

"That train left the station a long time ago," I said. "So I take it Carter was wooing Freddy before your father died?"

"Yes, Freddy idolizes him," Kate said. "They first met briefly at Yale when Carter was a senior and Freddy a freshman."

"How charming," I said. "How much of a stake does PAP have in NASAD?"

"Ten percent," Kate said. "I don't like Carter, but at least he seems concerned about what's going on in the drone submarine division."

"Is Carter more concerned with the employees in the drone sub division who lost their lives, or the potential monetary effect on NASAD?" I said.

"Carter pays lip service to dead drone sub engineers," Kate said. "But, honestly, I think all he really cares about is the money."

"Shocking," I said.

"Isn't it?" Kate said.

CHAPTER 22

There's only one way in and out of my ranch, and that's through an opening in the wood post and barbed wire fence that encircles the entire property. The opening is guarded by a tubular steel gate and lies at the point where the ranch's dirt road meets an asphalt-paved county road. The county road extends east and west for mile after deserted mile as it makes its way through a pumice plain populated by manzanitas, pines trees, and scrub brush.

A little less than thirty minutes after we had left the drawbridge and the stream, Manu stopped the Maybach at the gate. Mosi got out of the passenger side door, and covering his head against the rain, dashed to the gate. Mosi unlatched the gate, and pushing against the gate's heavy steel spring, swung the gate open and held it there. Manu drove the Maybach out onto the asphalt, turned left, and stopped. Suddenly the rain turned to hail. Mosi looked up at the sky in wonderment and, seemingly not caring that his face was being pelted by small frozen pellets, stood like that for almost thirty seconds until Manu gave a short burst of the car's horn. Mosi let the gate clang shut, re-latched it, then ran across the asphalt and jumped back into the Maybach.

The soundproof glass partition was still up. I flipped on the Maybach's intercom so that I could talk to the two brothers. The sound of '6 Foot 7 Foot' by Lil Wayne came through the intercom.

"Never seen hail before, Mosi?" I said.

"What is hail?" Mosi said.

"It's what people call the flying ice that's bouncing off the windshield," I said.

"We don't have hail where I come from," Mosi said.

"Where's that?" I said.

"Carson," Mosi said.

"Is Carson somewhere south of Los Angeles and next to a freeway?" I said.

"Yes, sir," Mosi said. "We're right off the 405."

I was pretty sure that meant the twins were from the same Carson that Jeff had said they were from. I wasn't surprised, however, that Jeff had been correct. I had no idea how Jeff did it, but his guesses were more often right than wrong.

I switched the intercom off. Lil Wayne was no more.

Manu headed west through the curtain of hail. From where we were, it would take close to forty minutes to reach reached Highway 395, the north-south road that would take us all the way to Southern California.

As the Maybach rolled along the county road, I watched the hailstones bombard the asphalt, the pellets bouncing up and down in diminishing arcs until they rolled to a stop. I began to think about the EADS deal Kate and I had just discussed, along with other defense industry deals just like it. It seemed to me all those deals could never have been accomplished unless the politicians making them had possessed a very cavalier attitude toward national security. Why let your enemies know the ins and outs of your military secrets? How could anyone believe that if your enemies were privy to those secrets that they wouldn't use those secrets against you?

Luckily, worrying about politics wasn't my job. My job, nearly always with Jeff accompanying me, was to come in and clean up the politicians' nastier messes before they turned into irredeemable disasters. Before Jeff and I had taken our leaves of absence and decamped to my ranch, we had done our job well. But what, if anything, may have been brewing out there unbeknownst to us while we had been out of commission during those last two years was entirely beyond my ken.

Kate, who also had been watching the hail, turned away from the window and flashed a smile at me. Her blue eyes seemed to dance. She once again rolled over on her seat to face me, bringing her knees up and resting on her side. She gently pushed her silky flaxen hair away from her face. Her movement stirred the air and I caught a whiff of her jasmine perfume.

"Forgive me if this question is premature," Kate said, "but do you have any thoughts yet on who might be killing my people?"

"I have a lot of thoughts," I said. "I don't know if any of them are any good. Tell me something, though. I should have asked this before, but the drone submarine program - is it just in the planning stages, or are any of the subs currently active?"

"The subs are active," Kate said. "Six of them are being tested at sea right now."

"Ohios and Seawolves?" I said.

"Just Ohios," Kate said.

"Are they fully armed?" I said. "Do they have nuclear weapons on board?"

"Yes," Kate said. "They weren't designed to be complete drones, however. Once the test phase is done, they'll still need about seven crew members."

"How many crew members are being used during the test phase?" I said.

"Seventy," Kate said.

"About half the number for a normal Ohio, then?" I said.

Kate nodded.

"Are you worried about the same thing I'm worried about?" Kate said.

"What's that?" I said.

"Maybe someone is attacking our drone sub program because they're after our nukes?" Kate said.

"It'd certainly be bad if someone were," I said. "But my gut says no."

"Why no?" Kate said.

"I can't think of a reason for anyone to do it," I said. "One, our major enemies already have their own nukes. Two, those enemies probably aren't worried about NASAD's drone subs, since the drones, by not needing full crews, represent more of a cost saving to the U.S. Navy rather than a tactical advantage. Three, because the drones have crews on board, it's hard to imagine how a hostile entity could take over the drone without boarding it themselves. Undersea boardings are extremely difficult, so it seems highly unlikely such a boarding would be attempted. Four, even if a hostile entity, like Iran, for example, considered boarding a nuclear sub a possibility, I think they would decide buying a nuke from Pakistan, North Korea, or a rogue Russian general would be an easier way to go. Iran itself has already tried to buy nukes from all three countries, and each time Iran has been thwarted."

"How do you know that Iran already tried?" Kate said.

"If I told you I'd have to kill you," I said.

"Another one of those, huh?" Kate said.

The hail suddenly became much heavier. For a moment it sounded like the Maybach's exterior was being pounded on by hundreds of jackhammers. But then, just as quickly as the hail had increased, it died back down again.

"Yes," I said. "However, I will say that Jeff and I became very closely acquainted with the rogue Russian general shortly before the general's death."

"I believe I understand what you mean," Kate said, "But I won't commit to anything beyond that as I value my life. What about terrorists? Could they be behind everything?"

"My guess is that terrorists would behave similarly to Iran when it came to the procurement of nuclear weapons," I said. "But with the execution style killings in Vegas, terrorists can't be ruled out."

Kate nodded.

"Should we even consider one of our competitors might be trying to disrupt our drone sub program?" Kate said.

"A competitor would certainly be able to muster up the resources to do so," I said. "But I don't think they'd take the chance. They'd not only lose their business, but go to prison as well."

"I know we made fun of Agent Burnette's idea of a disgruntled employee being responsible for everything, but is there any way he could be right?" Kate said.

"I can't see how any one NASAD employee would have the resources to pull off everything that has happened to date," I said. "Could it be a group of employees? Possibly. But how often do you hear of a group of employees ganging up to commit a string of highly organized murders spanning years, and never once taking credit or making their disgruntled feelings known far and wide to whoever will listen?"

"How about never?" Kate said.

"Never sounds good to me," I said. "The only other place I can think of to look for suspects right now would be in any part of NASAD where there might have been a significant reorganization or change in leadership that took place after your father's death. Has there been anything like that you can think of?"

"Other than what I told you about Freddy's elevation to CEO, and Carter Bowdoin and Pennsylvania Avenue Partners buying a piece of

NASAD, no," Kate said.

"I don't see any way Freddy or Carter would benefit by hurting NASAD, do you?" I said.

Kate seemed surprised by my question.

"Freddy would never kill anyone," Kate said.

"Okay," I said.

"There's also no way he could benefit from the murders of the drone sub engineers," Kate said.

"What about Carter Bowdoin?" I said.

"Carter doesn't seem like the murderous type to me," Kate said. "It's hard to imagine how Carter could profit from the engineers' deaths either."

"I agree," I said. "I guess if Pennsylvania Avenue Partners was a public company, and Carter Bowdoin had somehow caused the problems at NASAD in order for PAP's investment in NASAD to drag down the value of PAP as a whole, Carter could sell his PAP stock short. But PAP, as I remember it, is privately held."

"It is," Kate said.

"Well, I guess we've covered everyone and everything," I said.

"But we've ruled everyone and everything out," Kate said.

"We have," I said.

"What are we going to do, then?" Kate said.

"Good question," I said.

Kate frowned.

"I thought you said you wouldn't do that anymore," Kate said.

"Do what?" I said.

"Not take things seriously," Kate said.

"I think I acknowledged it may sound like I don't take things seriously at times, but I don't remember agreeing to stop sounding like that," I said.

"So you are serious, but you can't resist making jokes?" Kate said.

The Maybach's rear end skidded sideways. Manu had apparently guided the car into a patch of road that was especially slippery. He quickly regained control and we continued on our way.

"Didn't you call it deflecting?" I said.

"Fine," Kate said. "So seriously, what are we going to do?"

"Our best bet is probably going to be to find Dr. Nemo, since his voicemail said he knows the entity who is behind the murders," I said.

"Dr. Nemo also said the same entity had put our country at grave risk in the event of a war," Kate said.

"He did," I said. "Which is why we need to find Dr. Nemo sooner rather than later."

"What if we don't find him?" Kate said.

"Then we'll poke around NASAD and see if we can come up with anything," I said. "It's possible we entirely missed a potential suspect, and that at some point we might be able to flush that suspect out into the open. It's also possible we didn't fully list all the motives of the entities we just discussed, and that we might discover a motive for one of those entities that would explain why NASAD is being attacked."

"But, as of now, we really have no solid suspects?" Kate said.

"Correct," I said. "However, that's pretty much how all missions like this start out."

Kate's and my discussion of potential suspects and their motives for the murders of the NASAD drone sub engineers made me begin to think about the deaths of Milt Feynman and Paul Lennon. If the two men had been murdered, those murders would have both caused harm to NASAD and affected the control of the company. Causing harm to NASAD and affecting control of the company seemed like reasonably sufficient motives to murder Milt and Paul - though, again, Kate and I had been unable to identify a suspect who would benefit from those motives. But I had a nagging feeling I was missing another motive. A simple and important motive, but one I could not grasp at that moment, no matter how hard I tried. I didn't share any of those thoughts regarding the murders of Milt and Paul with Kate, however. There was, of course, a chance my suspicion that Milt and Paul had been murdered would turn out to be completely unfounded, and there was no reason to unnecessarily upset her.

"You always figure it out in the end, though, right?" Kate said.

"Absolutely," I said.

"And you see no reason why this mission won't have a successful conclusion, just like all your others?" Kate said.

"Actually, I can see a million reasons," I said.

"You're joking, right?" Kate said.

"Sort of," I said.

"Come on!" Kate said.

"Sorry," I said. "I'm sure we'll figure it out. But it's not going to be easy."

CHAPTER 23

Another loud thunderclap shook the Maybach. The veil of hail was so dense and opaque there hadn't been even a hint of a lightning flash. We were getting closer to the Minarets in the Mammoth Lakes area. I thought the Minarets, with their massive peaks, might hold back the storm and give us a chance to make the downhill run to the town of Bishop under clear skies. But Mammoth was still over thirty minutes away. I checked on Manu. His eyes were locked on the road ahead.

"I have some questions for you," Kate said. "They're not necessarily about NASAD."

"Do I have to answer them then?" I said.

"You sound scared," Kate said.

"Don't know the meaning of the word," I said.

"Uh huh," Kate said. "Question number one. Jeff has PTSD, doesn't he?"

"I was right to be scared," I said.

"You don't have to answer if you don't want to," Kate said. "I am a doctor though. We're sworn to confidentiality. All secrets are safe with me."

I believed Kate wouldn't divulge any secrets I shared with her, but I wasn't sure if it would be appropriate for me to discuss Jeff's private issues with Kate.

"What made you ask that about Jeff?" I said.

"Did you hear Jeff talking with me about Herodotus?" Kate said.

"Yes," I said.

"Herodotus was one of the first historians to comment on the psychological effects of warfare," Kate said.

"From that you got Jeff has PTSD?" I said.

"That and two other things," Kate said. "One, I got a strange vibe when I talked to some of my husband Paul's friends about you and how to find you. A couple of them let something slip about you taking care of a sick fellow officer - they didn't say anything specific, and they were very respectful, but I got the impression the officer wasn't suffering from a physical illness. And, two, well...Adelaide did say Jeff was nuts."

"Way to go Adelaide," I said.

"So?" Kate said. "Yes or no?"

I sighed inwardly. If Jeff's condition had been a secret before, it really wasn't one then. I suppose I could have lied to Kate, or just refused to answer, but doing either just didn't feel right. And Kate *was* a doctor, and Jeff in his own way seemed to have told her what was going on.

"Yes," I said.

"It's good he has a friend like you to take care of him," Kate said.

"I really didn't have much choice," I said. "Jeff was in Walter Reed. He was in bad shape and getting worse, so I took him out. He would have done the same thing for me."

"Didn't the Army doctors put up a fight?" Kate said.

"Might have," I said, "if they knew what I was going to do."

Kate looked surprised.

"You took Jeff out of the hospital without telling anyone?" Kate said.

"More like here one day, gone the next," I said. "And good luck finding us."

Kate laughed her soft, throaty laugh. Her teeth had glistened when she laughed. I liked both the laugh and the glistening.

"One would think the Army would be good at treating PTSD," Kate said. "But everything I've heard is that they're terrible at it. It's shameful. Was Jeff on a lot of medications?"

A pickup truck traveling much too fast for the conditions zoomed by us on our left side. The hail was so thick, and the truck was moving so fast, that the vehicle had just looked like a white blur as it passed us. The truck's windows were fogged over as well and it was impossible to see inside its cabin. For some unknown reason, the idea popped into my head that the truck was piloting itself. The idea produced a chill down my spine.

"Gabitril, Prozac, Risperidone, and Valium, among others," I said. "Don't remember the rest."

"Jackasses probably more concerned about themselves than Jeff," Kate said.

It was my turn to raise my eyebrows.

"They'd be afraid Jeff might get violent," Kate said.

"If Jeff had, the entire hospital staff wouldn't have been able to stop him," I said.

"I believe that," Kate said. "What's he on now?"

"Water," I said. "Mountain air."

"You're kidding," Kate said.

I shook my head.

"No wonder you won all those medals, General," Kate said. "You really are brave."

"Not sure about that," I said. "Anyway, Jeff claims he's got it all figured out."

"Jeff's got PTSD figured out?" Kate said.

"Uh huh," I said.

"Care to share?" Kate said.

"Main problem's the flashbacks," I said. "If the flashback becomes your reality, you're in trouble."

Kate nodded.

"You start reacting to enemies, bombs, and gunfire that aren't really there," I said. "Jeff says he has found a way to tell if the flashback is a flashback or something actually happening in real life."

"I know there are methods that are supposed to help, but I've never heard of anything that really works," Kate said.

"Yeah, Jeff got an earful of those methods," I said. "Breathe deep, remind yourself it's just a flashback, wrap yourself like a baby in a blanket to feel more secure, return to the present. Lot of other horseshit that didn't work either."

"So what does Jeff do?" Kate said.

"Runs a test," I said.

"A test?" Kate said.

"He asks himself what the mission is and how he was inserted," I said. "Flashback doesn't know that and can't make it up."

"So if Jeff doesn't know the mission, he knows what he's seeing isn't real?" Kate said.

I nodded.

"Amazing," Kate said. "Is it working? Is Jeff improving?"

"I thought so until you made a diagnosis after having spent all of maybe half an hour with him," I said. "Guess we've wasted two years of our lives."

Kate didn't say anything.

I suddenly felt like I'd sounded like a whiner. I hate whiners. I decided to stop whining.

"So," I said, "what Jeff says he needs now is immersion therapy."

Kate grimaced.

"That's completely theoretical and totally unproven," Kate said. "How'd Jeff hear about it?"

"Internet," I said.

"I assume by immersion, he means combat?" Kate said.

I nodded.

"Not so sure that would be a good idea," she said.

"You and me both," I said.

CHAPTER 24

Kate opened the Maybach's refrigerator and took out another can of Coke for me and another bottle of Pellegrino for herself. We had about ten minutes before we would make the turn south on Highway 395. The hail still came down in torrents. Manu had the Maybach's defrosters on high and the windshield wipers on full speed. The wipers swept back and forth, almost dizzyingly so, the windshield clearing for a moment, then filming over in a cloud of rapid fire hailstones.

I popped the tab of my Coke and drank some. Kate took a few sips of her Pellegrino.

"I still have some more questions," Kate said. "You ready?"

"No," I said.

"Too bad for you, then," Kate said. "You've been out of commission a long time. What's your official status with the Army?"

"Jeff and I are on leave," I said.

"For how long?" Kate said.

"Indeterminate," I said.

"That's allowed?" Kate said.

"Since we're not really in the Army, yes," I said.

"What do you mean you're not really in the Army?" Kate said.

"If I told you I'd have to kill you," I said.

Kate smiled.

"You keep using that excuse for not answering some of my questions," Kate said. "Haven't you figured out by now I don't scare easily?"

"Unfortunately, I have," I said.

I took another swallow of Coke.

"It would almost be easier to tell you what I'm not," I said.

"And then you wouldn't have to kill me either," Kate said.

"There's that," I said. "The United States is overloaded with intelligence agencies and departments. We have the CIA, the NSA, Homeland Security, Defense Intelligence Agency, National Counterproliferation Center, National Counterterrorism Center, and the National Reconnaissance Office. And that's just for a start."

"Do we need all those?" Kate said.

I suddenly felt the Maybach begin to hydroplane. We were at a low point on the highway, and I assumed it had been flooded by the storm. The Maybach's tires violently threw the water underneath us into the car's wheel wells. It sounded like we were being sucked into some monstrous washing machine. The Maybach kept a straight path, however, and we quickly passed out of the flooded area.

"Most of the people employed by them think so," I said. "All those agencies are so weighted with bureaucracy and oversight that it's nearly impossible for them to get anything meaningful done. They need so many people in those bureaucratic positions, that there are not enough truly talented people in this country, let alone the world, to staff them."

"You're saying that, in effect, there are so many incompetent people trying to enforce so many rules and regulations, that they're getting in the way of the few competent people accomplishing anything of real value?" Kate said.

"You said that, not me," I said.

"But you clearly implied that," Kate said.

"So says you," I said. "If I agreed with you..."

Kate interrupted me.

"You'd have to kill me," Kate said.

"And it wouldn't be pretty," I said.

"Seems like a situation that might annoy a person like you," Kate said.

"And a person like Jeff too," I said.

"So the two of you did something?" Kate said.

"Hypothetically, we might have accepted an invitation," I said.

A loud thunderclap shook the Maybach again. Kate startled again, but she barely missed a beat in our conversation.

"An invitation extended by who?" Kate said. "Hypothetically, of course."

"Of course," I said. "Hypothetically, the people at the top of all those aforementioned agencies are not fools. They realized that ofttimes not much good was being accomplished. Hypothetically, they might have looked the other way when another solution was created."

"The solution you and Jeff accepted an invitation to," Kate said.

"If it existed, yes," I said. "Such a solution might hypothetically get some real work done while not even existing. The CIA, NSA, and organizations of their ilk could run around doing their own thing and occasionally succeeding, but also perhaps create distractions to divert attention from what the 'solution' was doing in regard to some really important things."

Kate thought this over.

"The leaders of the NSA, CIA, and organizations of their ilk, might even be happy there was a solution for things that needed to be done that they could not be caught doing," Kate said. "Hypothetically, of course."

"Nothing like a little ownership to make people feel invested," I said. "As you can imagine, something that doesn't exist might be able to be very flexible when it came to leaves of absence."

"Especially if they granted the leaves to people they believed were irreplaceable," Kate said.

"Not sure who you're referring to," I said.

"Well, if we may pretend for a moment that I don't exist, then I'd be referring to you and Jeff," Kate said.

"Why would we have to pretend you don't exist?" I said.

"If I don't exist, then I can safely say things like that without you feeling like you need to kill me," Kate said.

I nodded.

"Good thinking," I said.

Kate took another sip of Pellegrino.

"I suppose if I were after the truly perfect solution, I might attach this entity that does not exist to the Army," Kate said. "That way the people in the entity could have access to the best military resources this country has to offer."

"The majority of those resources - since they are the best after all - most likely having been built by NASAD," I said.

"How kind of you," Kate said. "By the way, what would I call this truly perfect 'solution'?"

"I don't know," I said. "Maybe the 'Military Interagency Department of Special Operations', or 'The Department' for short. Or 'MOM'. Or 'That Whose Name Cannot Be Said Aloud'. Or 'Ice Station Zebra'."

"Let me guess," Kate said. "'Ice Station Zebra' is one of Jeff's favorite books?"

"Uh huh," I said.

"I further suppose that if I were in charge of 'MOM', or 'Ice Station Zebra', or 'That Whose Name Cannot Be Said Aloud', I might promote some of my best operatives to the rank of general so that no one would think they could tell them what to do?" Kate said.

"Too bad it's all hypothetical," I said.

"Too bad, indeed," Kate said.

CHAPTER 25

It was midmorning, a little less than an hour since we had used the drawbridge to cross my ranch's moat, when we turned left onto Highway 395 from the county road and started heading south. The hail was coming down more heavily, pinging loudly against the hardened steel roof and sides of the Maybach. The sheer volume of the ice stones seemed to form a crystalline membrane around us and reduced visibility to twenty yards. The car's tires thrummed softly as they hydroplaned on pavement made wet by the melting hail.

Kate pushed a button and her seat reclined fully.

"Last night's lack of sleep is catching up with me," Kate said. "That plus the fact we got up at 4:00 a.m. to come see you."

"Hope it's been worth it so far," I said.

Kate smiled. Her eyes seemed to light up from within again. Just like Grace's eyes used to do.

"No question about that," Kate said. "Please forgive me, but I need to take a nap."

"Sweet dreams, Grace," I said.

"You just called me Grace," Kate said.

"Did I?" I said.

"You did," Kate said.

"Sorry," I said.

"No need to apologize," Kate said. "I took it as a compliment."

"That's very gracious of you," I said.

"That's not a pun is it?" Kate said.

"Pun?" I said. "No, but I could see how you might think that."

"I'm teasing you, Jack," Kate said.

I didn't say anything.

"I would like one more thing from you before I go to sleep, please," Kate said.

"What's that?" I said.

"A bedtime story," Kate said. "Well, a bedtime question actually."

"Another question," I said. "Why am I not surprised?"

"You never finished telling me why Adelaide is on probation," Kate said.

"That's hardly bedtime fare," I said.

"I'm sure it's not," Kate said. "But I'd like to know, please."

Outside, the hail seemed to suddenly harden and become even more rocklike in character. The frozen, jagged crystals smashed into the Maybach's front windshield. For a moment, I thought the windshield might shatter. The windshield's bullet-proof Lexan easily repelled the hail, however, and the icy pellets left not even the slightest mark.

"There's no easy way to put this," I said. "Adelaide's parents - her mother was Grace's sister - were killed by a drunk driver when she was fourteen."

"How awful," Kate said.

"Was and is," I said. "Adelaide's father was an Army Ranger. Except for the fact that Adelaide, ever since she was eight years old, had wanted to be an Army Ranger like her dad, she was like most kids her age until her parents died. But with her parents gone, she started having anger issues. About a year after her parents' death, three teenage boys jumped Adelaide after school and tried to rape her. Adelaide fought the boys off, but what she did during the fight got her arrested."

"Wouldn't fighting off three boys trying to rape her be self-defense?" Kate said.

"Initially it was," I said. "Only, after Adelaide got all three boys on the ground, she kept kicking their heads in, and continued to do so long after they had lost consciousness. At which point she started on their groins. Barring a medical miracle none of them will be fathers."

"Not a problem for me," Kate said.

"Me either," I said. "However, the district attorney wasn't happy. He wanted to charge Adelaide as an adult for aggravated assault and attempted murder. Said Adelaide should have stopped once she had adequately defended herself. I was able to get a lawyer to talk the DA out of it. The final deal included me taking Adelaide and keeping her on the ranch with me."

Kate appeared to think this over.

"Adelaide seems to be doing very well with you as her guardian," Kate said.

"Thank you," I said.

"Between her and Jeff, I guess you really were stuck on the ranch," Kate said.

"I don't look at it as being stuck," I said.

"Sorry, that came out wrong," Kate said.

"No need to apologize," I said.

"Thank you for telling me that story," Kate said.

"I only did as you asked," I said.

"Yes, you did," Kate said. "And luckily I'm so exhausted even that grim tale won't be able to keep me awake."

"As in the Brothers Grimm?" I said

"Something like that," Kate said.

She smiled at me, then turned her head, closed her eyes, gently snuggled her cheek against the seat back, and was asleep almost immediately. Kate's breath slowed, and her face relaxed, making her look almost childlike and even more beautiful.

Grace too was able to fall asleep immediately upon laying her head down, and Grace, when she slept, also looked just like Kate did now. As I watched the nearly imperceptible rise and fall of Kate's chest, Kate became Grace. I felt myself drifting into a dream world, one in which Grace was still alive. Grace and I were walking through a pine forest, the air cool, the light falling in shafts that illumined tiny floating flecks of dust, and the ground beneath our feet spongy with pine needles. I was fully into that world, luxuriating in Grace's presence, suffused with her love and warmth when a booming voice came seemingly from out of nowhere.

"What the hell you doin'?!" the voice said.

I was instantly awake and found myself looking at Jeff. He was sitting across from me in Kate's seat and was wearing his jockey helmet and red riding jacket. I checked on Manu and Mosi. They were both oblivious to Jeff's presence and still rocking to a beat I couldn't hear at that moment.

"What are you doing here?" I said to Jeff. "What did you do with Kate?"

"That's none of your business," Jeff said.

"It is too my business," I said. "How did you get here?"

"There are more things in Heaven and Earth, Horatio, than are dreamt of in your philosophy," Jeff said.

"Hamlet?" I said.

"The immortal bard himself," Jeff said. "Now, how come you screwing up so bad I'm forced to be saving your ass?"

"Why do you say I'm screwing up?" I said.

"Because you be having that pretty little chat with Kate about suspects and motive and all in regard to who is killing all those NASAD drone sub engineers, but you completely missing the point," Jeff said.

"I am?" I said.

"This whole mission with Kate isn't just about those murders," Jeff said. "It about CENTCOM's Chinese insurmountable edge too."

"What the hell are you talking about?" I said.

"Dr. Nemo told you plain as day in his voicemail that the same entity that is responsible for the NASAD engineers' murders also will be putting the country at grave risk in time of war," Jeff said.

"Dr. Nemo did say that, didn't he?" I said.

"He surely did," Jeff said. "What else gonna be putting us at grave risk other than an insurmountable edge?"

I suddenly remembered I hadn't told Jeff about Dr. Nemo. How did he know about him?

"Hold on a second," I said. "How'd you find out about Dr. Nemo?"

"That beside the point," Jeff said.

"What is the point?" I said.

"Point is you gotta figure out what that insurmountable edge is," Jeff said. "And the other point is that since those drone subs can't be the source of a grave risk, they also can't be the insurmountable edge either. You already proved that to yourself."

I thought about that for a moment.

"You're right," I said. "The sub drones can't be the source of the risk or the insurmountable edge."

"So if those subs aren't the edge, what is they?" Jeff said.

"What is they?" I said.

"Damnit, don't just be repeating what I say," Jeff said.

"I'm sorry," I said. "I'm completely lost."

"Jeez, you dense, boy," Jeff said. "But I'll take mercy on you. I give you a clue."

"Thanks," I said.

"William the Conqueror, Stonewall Jackson, and Pas-de-Calais," Jeff said.

Jeff's face began to flicker, appearing and reappearing as if his face was on a television screen that couldn't hold its signal. His face was strangely colored too. The colors were the bright psychedelic hues - red, green, yellow, orange, purple, and blue - of a Peter Max poster from the 1960's. I squeezed my eyes shut for a moment trying to wipe the image from my vision. I didn't expect that simple approach to work, but it did. When I opened my eyes Jeff was back to normal.

"What's wrong with you?" Jeff said.

"Nothing's wrong with me," I said.

"Why you squeezing your eyes shut like you've got a migraine or something?" Jeff said.

"My vision got blurry for a moment," I said. "I was just trying to refocus."

"How come I don't believe you?" Jeff said.

"I don't know," I said. "Maybe you're just being your normal suspicious self. Now, as to William the Conqueror, Stonewall Jackson, and Pas-de-Calais, that's three clues, not one."

"No, they one clue, fool," Jeff said.

"I understand those three clues might add up to the same one answer, but they're still three clues," I said.

"I'm not in the mood for one of your stupid-ass philosophical discussions," Jeff said.

"Don't be arguing with me then," I said.

"Just as long as you don't be taking the fact that I'm moving on as some kind of confirmation you're correct," Jeff said. "It's purely an acknowledgment that I'm the bigger man and am foregoing any stupid-ass philosophical discussion at the present time for the greater good of the mission."

"Duly acknowledged," I said. "Now would you like me to tell you how the clue or clues are all related?"

"I'm all ears," Jeff said.

"William the Conqueror, Stonewall Jackson, and Pas-de-Calais are related because they all have something to do with diversions," I said. "In fact, the diversions they're related to are some of the greatest diversions in the time-honored, historical pantheon of military deceptions and diversions. William the Conqueror made a feigned retreat at the Battle of Hastings. Stonewall Jackson got the enemy to believe he and his Army were heading in a different direction than they were actually heading by having his scouts map a false route along the Shenandoah Valley during the Civil War. The United States and its allies used fake warplanes and landing craft at Dover during World War II to fool the Nazis into believing their D-Day invasion would take place at Pas-de-Calais, rather than Normandy, their true landing zone."

"Maybe you aren't so dense after all," Jeff said.

"Thank you," I said. "I assume the reason you gave me that clue or clues in the first place is that you believe the murders of the NASAD drone sub engineers are a diversion? And that the murders of the engineers are meant to draw everyone's attention to the NASAD drone sub program while the real target is something else that NASAD produces?"

"The answer to both those questions be yes," Jeff said. "You told Kate the drone subs didn't have much value other than for saving on crew. Smaller crew might also make those drones able to stay at sea longer, but who cares? Neither of those potential advantages worth all the energy and planning that's gone into killing those engineers for the last two years." Jeff paused. "Of course all that energy and planning coulda been going on for longer than that if that plane crash in Alaska that killed Kate's father, Milt Feynman, and Kate's husband, Paul Lennon, turns out to be a murder."

"How'd you know about their plane crash?" I said. "I never told you about it."

"Same way I know about Dr. Nemo," Jeff said.

"You going to tell me what that same way is?" I said.

"Not right now," Jeff said. "However, while we on the subject of the diversion, I want to point out there's a whole lot of serious escalating going on."

"You're talking about those three over-the-top executions of the NASAD drone submarine engineers in Las Vegas last week?" I said.

"Uh huh," Jeff said.

"I'd have to say I agree with you," I said. "In the past, the engineers were murdered one at a time, and months could go by between the murders. But in Las Vegas, the bad guys killed all three NASAD engineers at once. The killings in Vegas were also extremely garish and clearly designed to call attention to themselves. The previous 'accidental' murders were designed to do anything but call attention to themselves."

"Disguising those previous murders as accidents was a pretty clever idea too," Jeff said.

Through the shroud of hail, I thought I could see the turnoff from Highway 395 that led to the road to Deadman's Summit. There was a fence in the field surrounding the road and the fence began to take on the same shimmering quality and psychedelic hues that Jeff's face had taken on a moment ago. A hangman's gallows suddenly materialized in the field. Three men with nooses around their necks and black hoods over their heads were dangling from the gallows. The gallows and the men began to shimmer in psychedelic hues as well.

The vision was disturbing, even more disturbing than most of the odd things I'd seen ever since Jeff had pointed the CheyTac at me earlier that morning. My best explanation for the odd things I'd seen was that they were due to stress, stress that was directly related to Jeff's pointing the rifle at me. Though I'd never experienced such visions before, I had often been highly stressed in my combat career. Since those previous episodes of stress had always passed fairly quickly, I assumed this current episode would also soon pass, and so was not too concerned about it.

What did concern me at that moment, however, was finding a way to get rid of the strange gallows vision as quickly as possible. I knew that if I squeezed my eyes shut to try to clear the vision, Jeff would again ask me what was wrong with me. To avoid such questioning, I simply turned my head away from the gallows. Luckily, after a few seconds, the vision cleared. Jeff appeared none the wiser.

"I assume you're referring to the fact that, by making the deaths appear accidental, our enemy may have used those deaths, in combination with the executions in Vegas, to control the timing of the diversion's maximum effect?" I said.

"That's what I'm referring to, yeah," Jeff said.

"Then, yes, I'd have to agree with you on that as well," I said. "It's a very clever idea, but in an evil, insidious way."

"Especially since that idea is working so well," Jeff said. "The three executions in Vegas forcing anyone investigating the 'accidental' deaths of all those NASAD drone sub engineers to conclude the 'accidents' were actually murders. Once an investigator figure out the accidents are really murders, they then gotta conclude the reason those previous murders were disguised as accidents was to cover up something. And that something that being covered up is that someone is attacking the NASAD drone sub program - even though you and I know that isn't what that someone really be doing."

"The murders in Vegas make it nearly impossible for any investigator to *not* come to those conclusions," I said.

"Diversion is in its full glory," Jeff said.

"It sure looks that way," I said. "Everyone seems to be running around in a panic about the NASAD drone subs. We have nothing to suggest that anyone is even considering that whoever committed the murders of the NASAD engineers may be targeting a completely different product at NASAD than the drone subs."

"That true target be what we after," Jeff said.

"Truth is like the sun," I said. "You can shut it out for a time, but it ain't goin' away."

"Elvis?" Jeff said.

"The king himself," I said. "Aren't you at all worried no one else seems to be thinking like us in regard to the diversion?"

"Most times no one else be thinking like us," Jeff said. "And most times when no one thinking like us, we right and they wrong."

"You're implying we go with our standard operating procedure in this mission?" I said.

"I'm doing that, yes," Jeff said. "Even if no one else believe what we believe, we still stick to our guns until such sticking is proved to be in error."

"Agreed," I said. "So, back to the true target. I assume we both believe that if the true target really is something NASAD produces other than the drone submarines, then Dr. Nemo knows what the true target is?"

"That be exactly what we believe," Jeff said. "However, that NASAD product which be the true target also got a third component intrinsic to its existence."

"It's the source of Dr. Nemo's grave risk and also the Chinese insurmountable edge?" I said.

"Odds say so," Jeff said.

"I can't believe I didn't put the whole thing together sooner," I said.

"That why you have me," Jeff said.

"That is why," I said. "Even my cannily brilliant linking of the name 'Dr. Nemo' to Jules Verne's 'Twenty Thousand Leagues Under the Sea' was probably an error, wasn't it?"

"Verne's Nemo be a captain, not a doctor," Jeff said.

"Yeah," I said. "And our Dr. Nemo, whether he's really a doctor or not, knows those drone subs have nothing to do with the insurmountable edge."

"That exactly what he knows," Jeff said.

I paused, rolling something over in my mind.

"We might have a problem, though," I said.

"What problem?" Jeff said.

"If Milt Feynman and Paul Lennon were murdered, their murders don't fit the same pattern as the murders of the NASAD drone sub engineering project managers," I said.

"If they are murders, then they were murders that were made to look like accidents, weren't they?" Jeff said.

"Yes, but Feynman's and Lennon's murders still don't fit our diversionary theory," I said.

"Why you say that?" Jeff said.

"Milt Feynman and Paul Lennon held fundamentally different positions at NASAD from the positions held by the NASAD drone sub engineering project managers," I said. "Milt Feynman was the founder and CEO of NASAD, and there was no one higher than Milt at the time of his death. Paul Lennon was also a high-level NASAD executive at the time of his death. The two men's executive positions would have given them broad oversight at NASAD, and, unlike the engineers, they wouldn't have been involved in the drone sub program any more than any other NASAD program. Feynman's and Lennon's positions of broad oversight meant that if any investigator ever started looking at their deaths as murders - and as far as I know you and I are the only ones that are even considering that the two men were murdered - that investigator would have no reason to directly link their murders to the

NASAD drone sub program. Because an investigator wouldn't directly link Feynman's and Lennon's murders to the drone sub program, their murders wouldn't have the same diversionary effect on an investigator as the drone sub engineers' murders. The investigator, if he or she looked for a motive behind Feynman's and Lennon's murderers, would have to consider thousands of NASAD products, and the drone sub program is just one of those thousands."

"I don't see how that contradict our drone sub diversionary theory," Jeff said.

"How can you not?" I said. "I just explained how their murders, unlike the drone sub engineers' murders, don't solely point at the drone subs. That's a clear contradiction."

"It's a clear contradiction if you thinking like a moron and not like your usual self," Jeff said.

As much as I would have liked to have continued arguing my position to Jeff, I did not. When Jeff was as adamant about a topic as he was about the current subject of our conversation, his position usually turned out to be correct. Besides that, I was well aware I wasn't anywhere close to my usual self.

"I admit I'm not feeling so hot," I said.

"You don't need to admit nothing I already know," Jeff said. "I seen how your face look when we passing that field near Deadman Summit. You weren't squeezing your eyes shut since your vision was blurry."

I didn't say anything.

"I'll take your silence to mean you don't want to talk about what really going on at Deadman Summit," Jeff said. "But at least try not to think like an idiot for a moment, and tell me why Milt Feynman's and Paul Lennon's murders don't contradict our diversionary theory."

The Maybach passed the sign to Devils Postpile that is just before the Mammoth turnoff. I swore I could see a psychedelic Mephistopheles atop the sign. The psychedelic Mephistopheles had clawed hands and feet, dragon wings, a long tail with a razor-sharp triangular tip, and was breathing fire. I quickly looked away.

"I'm sorry," I said. "I guess I must be an idiot or a moron or both. I still don't see how Feynman's and Lennon's murders can fit our diversionary theory, since their murders don't directly point at the NASAD drone subs."

"You going to make me tell you the answer, aren't you?" Jeff said.

"I think that would be the simplest thing, yes," I said. "Our only other option would be for you to berate me some more and keep telling me how stupid I am, but I don't believe that would get us anywhere."

"For both an idiot and a moron, what you just said actually makes a lot of sense," Jeff said.

"Thank you," I said.

"Okay, then," Jeff said. "We need be returning to our notion that the true target of our enemy is a product made by NASAD other than the drone subs."

"Alright," I said.

"That NASAD product, whatever it is, likely been corrupted in some way so that it can serve as the Chinese insurmountable edge," Jeff said.

"That's what probably occurred, yes," I said.

"The NASAD product that be corrupted could be any one of thousands of products, because that's how many products NASAD makes," Jeff said.

"Any one of thousands, other than the drone subs," I said.

"Yes," Jeff said. "Now, if you was going to target any one of thousands of NASAD products in order to subvert one of those products for your own nefarious purposes..."

"Nefarious is a good word," I said.

"Thank you," Jeff said.

"And an insurmountable edge would also be as nefarious as it gets," I said.

"Thank you again," Jeff said. "Continuing then, if you were targeting any one of a thousand products at NASAD, what person or persons would you most like to get out of your way?"

I thought for a moment.

"Well," I said. "The person or persons at NASAD I would most like to get out of my way would be a person or persons who were very smart, had been at NASAD a long time and during their tenure had a vast overview of all that NASAD was producing, and was a person or persons who could not only spot what I was doing, but had the power to put an end to my nefarious plans."

"Can you think of any people at NASAD who might fit that bill?" Jeff said.

"Can I think of any people at NASAD who..." I said. "Damn, you really gotta rub it in, don't you?"

"Just answer the question, please," Jeff said.

"Milt Feynman and Paul Lennon," I said.

"Maybe you ain't so dumb as you appear to be," Jeff said.

"I hope so," I said. "So if our overall, big picture working theory is that one of the thousands of products at NASAD is the Chinese insurmountable edge, then Feynman and Lennon were killed in order to clear a pathway to turn that one in a thousand product into the edge?"

"That's the way I see it," Jeff said. "It also appear that one of our enemy's strategies along the pathway to their insurmountable edge was to use the NASAD drone subs as a diversion."

"Which would mean that our drone submarine diversionary theory is a subtheory - 'subtheory' as in subordinate, not as in submarine - of our overall working theory?" I said.

"Uh huh," Jeff said. "And if that be the case, that get rid of your contradiction, don't it?"

"It does," I said. "The murders of Feynman and Lennon and our diversionary theory both fit nicely together under our big picture working theory of the insurmountable edge. The murders of Feynman and Lennon would not only make it easier for our enemy to put their drone sub diversion into play, but easier for our enemies to gain possession of their insurmountable edge as well."

"By George," Jeff said. "I think you've got it."

I realized then, of course, that clearing a pathway for our enemy to obtain their insurmountable edge was the simple and important motive I had missed earlier when I had been considering potential motives for the murders of Milt Feynman and Paul Lennon. I saw no need to tell Jeff anything about that realization, however.

"My Fair Lady?" I said.

"Close enough," Jeff said. "Now that we got all that out of the way, and now that we are in agreement Feynman and Lennon were murdered so that our enemy could target a NASAD product other than the drone subs, we still got a big problem, though."

"We do," I said. "Since NASAD produces thousands of vital defense-oriented products, and we have nothing yet that would point to any particular product, identifying which product is the true target seems at the moment to be a monumental task."

"Anyone gonna figure out which NASAD product it be, it us," Jeff said.

"Usually, I'd agree with you," I said. "But..."

"But what?" Jeff said.

"As you so politely pointed out earlier, I'm not really anywhere close to my normal self," I said. "And you haven't been your normal self for quite a while."

"We just going to have to adapt to a new normal," Jeff said.

"That's one way to look at it," I said.

"It's the only way to look at it," Jeff said.

"You're probably right," I said.

"I'd like to move on to another topic if I may?" Jeff said.

"You may," I said.

"Dr. Nemo says there's an 'entity' who is killing all the drone sub engineers," Jeff said. "Nemo also says that same entity will be putting us at grave risk if there's a war, and that NASAD will be blamed. Who you think that entity is?"

"If we stick with the idea that Dr. Nemo's grave risk and the insurmountable edge are the same thing," I said, "and that the insurmountable edge is something produced by NASAD, one could easily leap to the conclusion that China is Nemo's entity, since it's China that supposedly possesses the edge." I paused. "But my gut says the entity isn't China."

"Why do you say that?" Jeff said.

"I think that Nemo would have named China, or at least used the word 'country' instead of 'entity', if it was China he was referring to," I said. "There's also no reason I can come up with for Nemo *not* to name China, if China is indeed the entity."

"It certainly seems to me Nemo would have named China if that who he thinks the entity is," Jeff said.

"So, if the entity isn't China, who is the entity?" I said.

"I got no idea," Jeff said. "I haven't seen anything that points to anyone or anything in particular."

"Neither have I," I said.

"I do, however, have a suggestion on how we should proceed in determining the entity," Jeff said.

"Which is?" I said.

"It's too early rule out *any* entity," Jeff said.

"That's what I was afraid you were going to say," I said.

"Since that be the case, we essentially at square one in this investigation," Jeff said.

"We are," I said. "If it is any consolation, though, we have been in similar situations lots of times before."

"And it just mean we gotta follow any and all clues that present themselves to us," Jeff said. "No matter who they might implicate, or where they might lead."

I heard a loud thump on the Maybach's trunk behind me. I turned around. The psychedelic Mephistopheles from the Devils Postpile sign was sitting on his haunches on the trunk's lid and staring right at me. He laughed and spit fire in my face. I drew back in shock.

"Now what's wrong with you?" Jeff said. "You look like you seen the devil himself."

"I have no idea what you're talking about," I said.

"I think you do," Jeff said. "You're hiding something from me again. I know it."

"Like I told you before, it must be your normal overly suspicious self at work," I said.

"It isn't," Jeff said.

"Fine, whatever you say," I said. "Can we please get back to what we were talking about?"

"Just so long you admit you feel bad about lying to me," Jeff said.

"I'm not going to admit anything of the sort," I said. "As to what you said about clues, I agree we have to follow them no matter where they might lead. Deep down, however, I still think that finding Dr. Nemo is our best, if not only hope, for solving the NASAD murders and determining what the grave risk is that has him so worried. If the grave risk ultimately turns out to be the Chinese insurmountable edge, so much the better." I paused. "I just thought of something. If the diversion is, as you said earlier, in its full glory, it's in that glory for a reason. The true product being targeted at NASAD, whatever it is, may be about to come under serious assault."

"Or be put in play," Jeff said.

"Put in play?" I said.

"If the true target at NASAD is the insurmountable edge, Chinese might be getting ready to deploy it," Jeff said.

I considered what Jeff had said.

"That would make sense, wouldn't it?" I said. "The Chinese are going to start their war in a month, so whoever is behind the insurmountable edge is ramping up the diversion to the max. With the diversion working as well as it is, the bad guys have to feel safe no one is ever going to figure out what the insurmountable edge is. Everyone is looking at the NASAD sub drones, and not the product the bad guys have actually been targeting at NASAD all along."

"Which be why we can't let no diversion distract us and keep us from finding out what's really going on at NASAD," Jeff said. "'Course it could also turn out the murders of the NASAD drone sub engineers weren't a diversion. Subs could turn out to be the Chinese insurmountable edge after all. We gotta investigate that possibility too."

"We just said the drone subs couldn't possibly be the insurmountable edge," I said. "Are you trying to drive me nuts?"

"Some people might say you're already nuts," Jeff said.

"Thank you," I said.

"But I didn't say what I did to make you more nuts than you already are," Jeff said. "I said it to highlight how difficult our job gonna be."

"There's no question it's going to be difficult," I said. "But, when the going gets tough…"

"The tough get going," Jeff said.

I shook my head.

"Damn," I said. "We sound like a couple of idiots, don't we?" I paused. "You know what? I'll bet Sun Tzu originally came up with that saying."

"Wouldn't surprise me," Jeff said. "Now, you want to know how I know about Dr. Nemo and also Feynman and Lennon and their plane crash?"

"Yes," I said.

"Because I'm you, you moron!!" Jeff said. "Now get up and get to work!!"

Jeff slapped me sharply across my face. I woke up, this time for real, my interludes with Grace and Jeff apparently part of one continuous dream. I looked down and saw my own hand in front of my face. Clearly, I'd slapped myself.

Kate was in her seat, still asleep next to me. Manu was staring at me in the rearview mirror. I assumed he must have seen me slap myself. In any event, I'm sure I looked pretty silly staring at the hand in front of my face. When confronted with that type of potentially embarrassing situation, one can generally respond with either a sheepish grin or a hard stare.

I chose a hard stare.

Manu turned away.

I thought about what Jeff and I had talked about in my dream. I got a bit pissed off that Jeff had been saying 'we' gotta do this and 'we' gotta do that, when it was clearly me that was going to have to do everything. The pissed off feeling quickly passed, however, when I reminded myself it was me - me as myself, and me as Jeff - who had actually been the one saying everything.

The feeling that didn't quickly pass was the anxiousness that overcame me when I confronted the dream's underlying message. There was no way I could escape the fact that at that moment, the amount of genuine, verifiable knowledge I had concerning Dr. Nemo and his grave risk, the murders of the NASAD drone sub engineers, the NASAD drone sub program itself, the potential murders of Milt Feynman and Paul Lennon, the identity of the NASAD product that might represent the malevolent entity's true target, and the Chinese insurmountable edge, was agonizingly, horribly, and terrifyingly, insufficient, meager, and scant.

Almost anything was possible.

Nothing could be ruled out.

And, as if that wasn't enough, it also appeared my mind was playing tricks on me.

Aiyeee!

CHAPTER 26

Almost half an hour had gone by since we made the turn south onto Highway 395. It was by then about 10:45 a.m., nearly three hours and forty-five minutes since Kate and the Maybach had showed up on that Monday morning. The hail was coming rapid-fire, the ice stones sounding like a thousand steel heeled and toed dancers in the throes of a violent tarantella atop the Maybach's roof. Outside, the exit for Mammoth Lakes Airport whirred by in a shroud of misty fog so dense I could see less than fifty yards down the road that led to the airport itself.

A flash of lightning somehow penetrated the grey gloom. The lightning was followed closely by a clap of thunder. The still sleeping Kate appeared not to have been affected by the light or the sound. Up front, the Samoans continued to sway to a beat I could not hear. I watched the windshield wipers sweep back and forth. The wipers cleared the hail off the glass, but the ice stones reaccumulated almost as fast as they were swept away.

I took out my iPhone and looked at the photos Kate had transferred to it. The first photos I looked at were of Milton Feynman and Paul Lennon. I began to think about Feynman and Lennon's plane crash, and how, as the plane plummeted into the sea, they must have known they were going to die. Thinking about good people living out their final moments watching death come inexorably upon them always disturbed me. Maybe it shouldn't have disturbed me. Maybe I should just have accepted it as an occasional cost of the great gift of human consciousness. But I didn't accept it. In a just world, good people would die quietly in their sleep.

I looked at Kate. Her sleeping face was beautiful, untroubled, and at peace. I began to think about the loss of Feynman's and Lennon's lives from Kate's perspective. Earlier in the day I had gotten the sense that, other than for her children and her brother Freddy, the deaths of her father and her husband had left Kate pretty much alone in the world. There were no clear reasons I could enumerate to support that notion, and I knew it could turn out I was completely mistaken, but that was how I felt. I didn't like the thought of her being so alone.

I came up with an idea that might help me determine the true nature of the plane crash that had taken Feynman's and Lennon's lives. The idea entailed gaining access to certain resources. Accessing those resources would mean involving my team at MOM/That Whose Name Cannot Be Said Aloud/Ice Station Zebra. I hadn't had contact with anyone on my team during the entire two years I'd been on leave on the ranch with Jeff, and I wasn't absolutely sure if contacting them would be a good idea. There was always the risk my colleagues might want more from me for any favor I might ask of them than I was willing to give them in return. I would have to put some thought into handling what could be a tricky situation.

A strong gust of wind, whistling loud and shrill, suddenly shook the Maybach and rattled its doors. White hailstones flew into us like bullets, making a rat-tat-tat sound on the Maybach's windows. The only other sound was Kate's breath as it came in the shallow and slow rhythm of sleep.

Sleep.

Sleep...

When my wife Grace had died she had just closed her eyes and fallen asleep one last time. I had held her hand and watched as her breaths came less and less often. When it seemed her breaths were about to stop forever, I tried to will my heart to cease beating so that I might go with her. It hadn't worked. I hadn't died.

But that first failure to die didn't stop me from trying again. In the weeks that followed Grace's death, there were many times I again tried to stop my heart from beating, hoping to be taken to her. None of those times worked either.

Ultimately, I took a different tack. I stopped trying to die, and instead tried to bring Grace back to life in my mind as vividly as I could. I learned how to close my eyes and slow my breath and be with Grace as if she had never gone. I did that then in the back seat of the Maybach. I closed my eyes and slowed my breath and Grace and I were together again at her favorite spot on the ranch, the spot on which her grave then sat. But in my mind's eye, at that moment, there was no grave. I had gone back to an earlier time, when Grace was still alive, and there were only mountains, trees, sky, and fresh, pure air surrounding the two of us.

Suddenly, in the midst of that beautiful, sylvan interlude, I heard Jeff's voice again.

"You drifting off course again," Jeff's voice said.

Jeff sounded so close by I could have sworn he was in the Maybach's rear cabin with me. I spun my head looking for him. I couldn't find him anywhere. The only other person in the cabin with me was the still sleeping Kate.

"Jeff, where are you?" I said.

"Not important," Jeff's voice said. "What important is you wake up and get back to work."

"Wake up?" I said.

"Yeah," Jeff's voice said. "You fell asleep. Again."

"Did not," I said.

"If you can't tell if you asleep or awake there's something seriously wrong with you," Jeff's voice said.

"Look who's talking," I said.

Jeff's voice said nothing.

"Besides, if there's something wrong with me, it's your fault," I said.

"My fault?" Jeff's voice said.

"I think you gave me PTSD when you shoved the CheyTac in my face," I said. "I'm having all sorts of weird visions, I'm having trouble thinking straight, and I'm falling asleep for no reason."

"Show how little you know," Jeff's voice said. "Takes weeks for PTSD to show up. If this thing last, maybe you got it. But right now, all you got is a stress reaction."

"Stress reaction, huh?" I said. "Who says I didn't already have PTSD and you shoved me over the edge. Maybe I caught it from you months ago."

"PTSD ain't contagious, asshole," Jeff's voice said.

"Fine," I said. "It's probably Stockholm syndrome then."

"Stockholm syndrome when the prisoner start taking on the characteristics of their captors," Jeff's voice said.

"Exactly," I said.

"You ain't my prisoner," Jeff's voice said.

"Then it's reverse Stockholm syndrome," I said.

"You sound like an idiot," Jeff's voice said. "Which I suppose be why you so focused on Feynman and Lennon plane crash that you forget what else MOM could do for you."

I was in no mood to give Jeff an excuse to gloat over thinking of something I hadn't. I thought about what the 'what else' MOM could help me with could possibly be. I drew a blank.

"Seven seconds," Jeff's voice said.

"Seven seconds, what?" I said.

"You got seven more seconds to come up with what you aren't going to come up with before I tell you what it is," Jeff's voice said.

"Seven seconds is a pretty arbitrary length of time, don't you think?" I said.

"Three...two...one..." Jeff's voice said. "Time's up. You got to send MOM Dr. Nemo's code so they can decipher it."

"I'm absolutely sure there's no way you can know about Dr. Nemo," I said. "I never mentioned him to you."

"Like I said," Jeff's voice said. "You sound like an idiot."

"I don't understand," I said.

"That's why you're an idiot," Jeff's voice said. "While you at it, send MOM Nemo's voicemail too."

"The voicemail was sent using a voice altering device," I said.

"Just do it," Jeff's voice said.

CHAPTER 27

I awoke for the second time that day from a dream in which Jeff had appeared just as the Maybach broke free from the storm and its darkness and fog and hail and cold, and entered into bright sunlight. The car was passing over a ridge just past the Highway 395 turnoff for the Owens River. Up ahead was the Crowley Lake valley, shimmering with brilliant shades of gold, green, orange, and umber. The valley stretched before us for nearly ten miles and was surrounded by pine-covered, snow-capped volcanic peaks. Seagulls soared in the cloudless aquamarine sky above. Kate remained sound asleep, her breath slow and soft. The giant Samoans continued to dance in the front seats.

I struggled to recall what Jeff, or rather I as Jeff, had been talking about in the dream. After a moment, I remembered that I had exhorted myself to send Dr. Nemo's coded message and also his voicemail to MOM. Sending the message made obvious sense, and as I thought it over, so too did sending the voicemail.

MOM's voice identification technology could help identify who Nemo was despite the fact his voice had been altered. The technology, by looking at the speaker's choice of words, their sentence structure, and the time lag between the words, syllables, and even letters, could come up with a pretty good idea of the speaker's age, sex, level of intelligence, education, and native language. The voice identification software, by exploiting subtle patterns within the speaker's phrasing, could also determine the speaker's accent, which would in turn help pinpoint the geographical location where the speaker had most likely been raised.

As we passed Lake Crowley, the road ahead was dry and fast, and the two southbound lanes of Highway 395 were so empty we might as well have had them to ourselves. Manu opened up the Maybach's big engine, and we flew past Tom's Place and the cascading gorges of the Owens River. During the downhill run to Bishop, I began to think about what I, as Jeff, had said in my dream about stress reactions. A stress reaction seemed like a good explanation for the tiredness and strange mental issues I had been experiencing so far that day. I knew stress reactions were manageable. If I was careful, it might not get worse.

We pulled off Highway 395 in Bishop and stopped at the Shell gas station in the north end of town to refuel. The air was warmer at Bishop's lower altitude and the temperature was in the low eighties. Manu and Mosi, still barefoot as their socks and shoes had not yet dried from their morning's aquatic activities in my moat, got out of the Maybach. There was a lightness to their step as they moved between the car and the gas pump bay, the twins seeming to enjoy the heat that was radiating into their bare soles from the station's cement roadway. They put the fuel pump's nozzle into the Maybach's gas tank opening, started the gasoline flowing, and went into the station's mini-mart.

Kate awoke. She stretched her arms above her head.

"Where are we?" Kate said.

"Bishop," I said.

"How long was I asleep?" Kate said.

"Probably about an hour and a half," I said.

I felt my iPhone vibrate in my pocket.

"Excuse me a second, please," I said.

I took out the phone. I had a text from Jeff.

"Needs to talk about letter Adelaide received," the text said.

"What letter?" I texted back.

Kate said, "What's wrong?"

"Who said anything's wrong?" I said.

"I can see it on your face," Kate said. "You look worried."

"I'm that transparent, huh?" I said.

"You are," Kate said.

"It's Adelaide," I said.

"Is she in some kind of trouble?" Kate said.

"I don't know," I said. "If she's not yet, I think she might about to be. This morning, before we left, Adelaide and Jeff had a somewhat cryptic exchange. I got the distinct impression Adelaide was planning on running away."

"Does Jeff know about it?" Kate said.

"I think so," I said. "He didn't tell me probably because he didn't want to feel like he was being a tattletale."

"That's an interesting way for a grown man to act," Kate said.

"Jeff tends to fall to Adelaide's level when the two of them are together," I said.

"I guess I could see how that could happen," Kate said. "I thought Adelaide wore had an ankle monitor, though."

"She does," I said. "She made a big show of hiking up her pant leg and displaying the monitor to me when I warned her about not leaving the ranch. In retrospect, it was probably too big a show."

"The lady doth protest too much, methinks," Kate said.

"Yeah, something like that," I said.

"Wouldn't Adelaide have to take off or disable her monitor if she didn't want to be found?" Kate said.

"She would, and it would violate her parole if she did," I said.

"Which would mean she would go back to prison?" Kate said.

"Yes," I said. "I don't think she really comprehends how badly it would mess up her life if she did."

"You're right to be worried then," Kate said. "Where would Adelaide run away to?"

"I have no idea," I said. "But Jeff just texted me something about a letter Adelaide got and I'm guessing that has something to do with her plans."

"Because of him texting you about the letter so close in time to their cryptic discussion this morning?" Kate said.

"That, and because other than that discussion, I haven't even had a hint of anything that might be a serious cause of concern for me about her," I said. "Other than my normal serious causes of concern for her, of course. But I can't see any of those having anything to do with a letter."

"I assume you texted Jeff back asking him about the letter?" Kate said.

"I did," I said. "He hasn't responded yet."

"Why don't you call him?" Kate said.

"Good idea," I said.

I dialed Jeff's number. It rang and rang, finally went to voicemail.

"Jeff," I said into the phone, "please call me as soon as possible about the letter you mentioned in your text."

I hung up.

"Perhaps you should call Adelaide as well?" Kate said.

I nodded.

I dialed Adelaide's number. Her phone rang and rang until it too went to voicemail.

"Adelaide," I said, "it is very urgent you call me right away."

I hung up.

"Are you more worried than you were before, now that you couldn't reach either of them?" Kate said.

"Honestly, yes," I said.

"Should we go back to the ranch?" Kate said.

"It's very considerate of you to offer that," I said. "But that would probably be an overreaction. Let's wait to see what Jeff says."

The chattering voices of Manu and Mosi came from somewhere outside the Maybach. Both Kate and I turned to see the twins exiting the mini-mart. The men's arms were laden with two six-packs of root beer, a gallon of chocolate milk, and a jar that looked like it contained about a hundred strawberry Twizzlers.

"Manu and Mosi don't like the snacks in the car?" I said to Kate.

"Not sweet enough for them," Kate said.

The twins replaced the pump nozzle, closed the Maybach's fuel door, climbed back into the car, and excitedly divvied up their booty. Mosi rotated around in his seat toward Kate and me, and offered some Twizzlers to us by waving them at us from behind the glass partition. Kate and I both shook our heads, and I mouthed the words 'no thank you' to him.

We left the Shell station and the Maybach crawled through the stop-and-go traffic of Bishop's main street. I was still worrying about Adelaide and how I was sure she truly didn't understand the ramifications of what would happen to her if she was caught violating her parole.

I tried to distract myself by focusing on the small-town world we were passing through. Lining the street were family restaurants, a theatre, and fishing tackle and furniture stores. A variety of older-model, dust-covered pickup trucks were traveling in both the north and southbound sides of the street. The Maybach stopped for a red light behind a red Dodge Charger with the vanity license plate 'IXCLR8'.

"I accelerate," Kate said.

It took a moment for her words to wend their way through the

Adelaide-inspired anxious haze clouding my brain.

"What did you say?" I said.

"That car's vanity plate," Kate said, pointing at the Dodge. "It says, 'I accelerate.'"

"You got that pretty fast," I said.

"I like word games," Kate said.

I saw a northbound Chevy Silverado 1500 pickup with a heavily tinted windshield across the intersection in front of us. The Chevy was also stopped at the light and had a vanity plate on its front end bumper that said 'B8ME'.

"What about that one?" I said, pointing at the Chevy.

"Bait me," Kate said. "He must be a fisherman."

The light turned and the Chevy and the Maybach crossed by each other as we both drove through the intersection in opposite directions. The Chevy's driver side window was not as heavily tinted as the windshield. I could see that the driver was wearing a floppy canvas bucket hat with lures stuck on it, and that there were a half dozen fishing poles laid horizontally on a rack across the Chevy's back window.

"Looks like I was right," Kate said.

"You were," I said.

Something seemed to flit behind Kate's eyes then, as if she'd had some sudden thought or realization.

"What if Dr. Nemo is an anagram?" Kate said.

"An anagram?" I said. "How'd you come up with that?"

"We were just talking about word games, and since anagrams are a form of word game, I guess anagrams just popped into my head," Kate said.

"Okay," I said. "How'd you get to Dr. Nemo, though?"

"Anagrams are a form of code, aren't they?" Kate said.

"Yes," I said.

"Dr. Nemo sent me that entire file in code, so it appears he likes codes," Kate said. "Maybe he chose Dr. Nemo since it's a code as well."

Kate's line of thinking may not have been as logical or direct as she seemed to believe it was - in fact, her thinking felt pretty intuitive to me - but I liked it.

"Maybe Dr. Nemo lives on Omen Road then?" I said.

"Or his real name is Ned Mor," Kate said.

"Not too many people who spell their last name 'M-O-R,'" I said.

"It would make it easier to find him if he did, though," Kate said.

"True," I said. "Are there any 'M' drones being made at NASAD?"

"Not that I'm aware of," Kate said. "But I know why you asked." She paused. "You know what? I'm starting to think Dr. Nemo may be one of NASAD's younger employees."

I actually had just had the same thought. But I was curious as to how Kate had been led to that idea as well.

"What makes you say that?" I said.

"If Dr. Nemo really is an anagram, then it seems like kind of a playful thing to do," Kate said. "I've also always thought the voicemail Dr. Nemo left me was overly formal, as if a young person was trying to phrase things in a way he thought a lawyer, for example, might phrase them."

"Great minds think alike," I said.

"You had the same hunch?" Kate said.

The Maybach left the south end of Bishop and picked up speed again.

"I did," I said. "All these thoughts you're having are good, as they might help us narrow our search for Nemo, at least in the initial stage. We can start with wherever the anagrams might lead, and we can also focus on younger suspects first."

"So I'm actually adding some value to the investigation?" Kate said.

"Yes," I said.

"The FBI never thought so," Kate said.

"Shows how little they know," I said. "Now, you've got about seventy-five thousand employees, right?"

"Yes," Kate said.

"Do you have any idea how many of those employees would be capable of using the type of sophisticated cryptography that was used in the file you received from Nemo?" I said.

"My guess is it would be less than one thousand," Kate said. "I know who I can ask to find out for sure. Should I send them a message now?"

"Let's wait to send the message until we get to your house," I said. "I like that you've been keeping your phone off so that you couldn't be tracked since you left yesterday, and I'd feel safer if we don't change that just yet."

"Okay," Kate said.

The Maybach continued to roll south through the high desert of the Owens Valley. Lush grasses and leafy trees dotted the landscape, the valley much greener than I had ever seen it. The valley's residents had recently won their long fight over water rights with the Los Angeles Department of Water and Power, and it appeared their victory was already bearing fruit.

I thought about Dr. Nemo as we drove. The more I thought about the syntax of his voicemail, and his use of a code name, the more I became convinced that the likelihood of him being young was extremely high, indeed almost a certainty. That certainty made my respect for him grow. The risks to Nemo were huge, and I felt it must have taken an enormous amount of guts for a person so young to do what he had done. Nemo had all the markings of a true hero.

I began to worry about Nemo too. Because I wasn't sure if Nemo fully understood the risks he had taken. He mentioned his fear of the penalties he might face for violating his security oath, but the risk to him went far beyond that. There was no question in my mind, that if the entity that was behind the murders at NASAD found out what Nemo was up to, that entity would then quickly determine Nemo represented an unacceptable threat to them, and would hunt Nemo down and kill him. For all I knew, they might already be hunting Nemo at that moment. If they were, that meant I not only needed to find Nemo, but find him fast.

About five miles north of Lone Pine, I heard the whine of an aircraft overhead. I craned my neck back to look up through the Maybach's rear window. A single-engine plane was flying low behind us and seemed to be following the highway south, just as we were. I couldn't make out any markings on the plane, but there were plenty of signs along the highway that said "patrolled by aircraft". I thought perhaps the plane was piloted by a California Highway Patrol officer looking to spot drivers exceeding the speed limit from the air. I leaned forward and looked over Manu's shoulder at the speedometer. We were only doing seventy, so I sat back and said nothing. A few minutes later, the plane peeled off and headed west, and I didn't give it another thought.

My iPhone vibrated in my pocket. I took it out and saw there was a text from Jeff. Kate watched me as I read the text.

"All is fine re letter," the text said. "I fixed the problem. Everything is under control. Can't talk now. Will call this afternoon."

"Phew," I said under my breath.

"Good news?" Kate said.

I showed her the screen.

"So maybe Adelaide isn't going to run away?" Kate said.

"I certainly hope that's the case," I said.

"But you're still going to worry about her anyway until Jeff calls you?" Kate said.

"For only just having met me, you know me pretty well," I said.

CHAPTER 28

Shortly after 1:00 p.m., Manu pulled off the highway and into the Coso Junction rest area that lies seventy-five miles north of Mojave. The rest area, consisting of a few shade trees and wooden structures housing its restrooms, was deserted when we entered its large blacktop parking lot.

I wasn't surprised by the fact the rest area was deserted. After all, it was midday on a Monday, and we were pretty much in the middle of nowhere on a very lonely stretch of road. Indeed, the only other vehicle visible at that moment was one out on the highway approaching the rest area from the south. The vehicle was traveling well above the speed limit, a dangerous maneuver to my mind as that stretch of 395 was fairly well patrolled by the California Highway Patrol.

Manu parked the Maybach between the white lines of one of the rest area's parking spaces. Kate sat up in her seat, grabbed her door handle, and opened the door. A blast of desert heat rushed in through the opening. It must have been well over a hundred degrees outside.

"You coming?" Kate said.

"I'm good," I said.

"Suit yourself," Kate said.

She exited the car, as did Manu and Mosi. The three of them, mindful of the heat, quickly shut their doors behind them. They walked along the hot asphalt path to the restrooms, the Samoans quite gingerly in their still bare feet. Above them, chirping came from a bird hidden in the leaves of one of the rest area's trees.

The vehicle I had seen rapidly approaching from the south suddenly slowed and made the right turn into the rest area's entrance off of 395. I watched as it moved down the winding main road to the rest area and continued into the parking lot. The vehicle was a white Ford Econoline van, maybe seven to eight years old, with a slightly battered body, and no windows other than in the forward cab. The van silently slid into a space about seven spaces to the right of the Maybach and came to a stop.

Two men hopped out of the van's front passenger door. The driver stayed put. Neither of the three men appeared to pay any attention to me, most likely because it was next to impossible to see me behind the Maybach's tinted windows.

Both of the men who had exited were agile and sinewy, and appeared to be in their early twenties. They also both wore identical lightweight, dark green windbreakers and had bowl-cut haircuts that reminded me of special forces commandos from Kazakhstan, Uzbekistan, or some other similar such dump of the former Soviet Empire. It was true I hadn't been out much lately, but I didn't think their haircuts were some new 'do' adopted by young American males.

It wasn't just their do's that made me think they were Kazakhs or Uzbeks, though. Their features had that distinct look of mixed Caucasian and Mongoloid blood unique to the Kazakh and Uzbek homeland, and they both wore heavy black leather Russian Army boots as well. Certainly there were Americans that had those same features, but I was pretty sure Americans would have had a hard time finding those boots, not to mention a barber with just the right kind of bowl, anywhere close to home.

The men moved quickly and headed toward the restrooms. When they got close to the restrooms' entrances, they veered away from the men's room, and took up positions a few yards away from and on opposite sides of the women's restroom door.

I made the brilliant deduction the men weren't there to piss.

The man on the right side of the women's restroom crouched behind a pillar that would block him from the view of anyone who might exit the restroom door. The man on the left took up a similar position on the other side of the door. Both men removed Sig Sauer P226 9 mm pistols from their jacket pockets and pulled back and released their pistols' slides to load a bullet from the magazine into the firing chamber. Their positioning suggested they knew what they were doing - the barrier-like nature of the pillars, combined with the angle between their positions, would make it impossible for a single hostile shooter to get a sight line on both of them at the same time from any one location. Their positioning also meant that if a hostile shooter took out one or the other of them, the remaining man would have time to react and take out the hostile shooter in return.

If there had been any doubt in my mind before, there was none then.

The two men were commandos until proven otherwise.

The men/commandos held the guns at the ready, fingers across the trigger guards, barrels pointing down. Their gun work, coupled with how they had stationed themselves, suggested they were not just commandos, but very professional, and well-trained, commandos.

Only not well-trained enough.

Somewhere along the line their teachers had left out a crucial lesson.

Either that or the gunmen had been asleep during that class.

Because they had not done one important thing.

The idiots hadn't checked the Maybach to see if there was anybody in it. Yes, the Maybach's windows were tinted, but all they would have had to have done is put their faces right up to the glass. Their failure to perform wasn't just a military issue, but also a common sense one. Maybe common sense wasn't taught in the elementary schools of satellite countries of the crumbling Soviet empire. Perhaps it was a funding problem. Maybe the school district sent all the money to Moscow. Maybe all that extra money ensured the little tykes of Moscow's ruling elite got better educations than the peasants.

Then again, maybe common sense could not be taught.

At that moment I didn't have time to wonder how Russian-style commandos had made it into the Mojave Desert, an area that was deep inside United States territory, or who might have financed the long journey from Kazakhstan or Uzbekistan. I figured that could wait for later. Right then what I had to attend to was what looked like a potential kidnapping at best, and an assassination at worst. Since the men were outside the women's room, I didn't think the target was Manu and Mosi.

Which meant the target was Kate.

If the gunmen thought I was going to give up Grace now that she had finally come back to me, well, that wasn't going to happen was it?

Except...

Maybe it was going to happen.

I sat there feeling as close to paralyzed as I ever had. Could I really do this, I wondered? Could I really do what needed to be done after spending the previous two years pretty much wasting away as a babysitter for Adelaide and Jeff?

Would my mind know what to do?

Would my body be able to follow?

And then there was my budding stress reaction...

What if its symptoms surfaced in the middle of whatever I attempted to do?

Damnit Jeff.

I opened and closed the fingers on both my hands a few times, looking down at them as I did. My fingers seemed to be moving too slowly, like there was some kind of delay between my brain's orders and their reaction. My knuckle joints felt like they were rusty, like they needed some oil, maybe even a complete lube job.

How was I ever going to pull this off?

The sniper shot I had made earlier that morning played back in my mind. All well and good. But that was on a range. No one was shooting back. And no one was going to die if I failed.

Grace was going to die if I failed.

Screw this, I thought to myself.

It was now or never.

Like it always was.

And maybe always would be.

I carefully opened my door on the left side of the Maybach, and exited the car. When my left foot hit the ground, my knee, having been immobile for over an hour, felt like someone had lit a magnesium flare in it. Despite the pain, I felt familiar juices start to flow with my body's movement.

I began to feel...

Improbably...

Impossibly...

Like my old self again.

Certainly not all the way back, but hell, I was getting close. Maybe even ninety percent of the way there. Well, maybe not ninety. But at least fifty.

Fifty was good, wasn't it?

I made my way in a crouch toward the back of the Maybach, using the car's body to shield me from view of the gunmen and the van's driver. I stopped behind the Maybach's trunk and took a close look at all three men. From the gap between the top of the restroom's outer wall and roof came the sound of Manu and Mosi laughing, as if they didn't have a worry in the world.

The driver of the van had rolled down his window and was staring straight ahead, watching what his companions were up to. He had the same haircut and wore the same green windbreaker as the two gunmen.

Stylish.

Maybe I was making a mistake. Maybe they were just part of a visiting Kazakh or Uzbek dance troupe. If they were, I might set back American-Kazakhstan or American-Uzbekistan cultural relations for centuries. So what if I did? There wasn't anyone who could care, was there?

Had I really just had those thoughts?

Yes, I had.

Which was good.

Because only a guy who was loose could think like that on the precipice of mortal combat.

And loose was good.

Loose meant I really was back.

Maybe more than fifty percent back, maybe even eighty.

One last thing, though.

Shouldn't I at least say something to the gunmen before I killed them? Give them a chance to give up? That would be the fair, gentlemanly thing to do, wouldn't it? Sure, I was unarmed, and there were three of them and one of me, and they were ruthless professional killers in the middle of executing an ambush, but still, wasn't there a chance they would lay down their arms without bloodshed?

Uh...

No.

If I said anything, anything at all, everyone on my side was going to wind up dead.

I crabbed low towards the van until I was next to the driver's door, just below his window. The flaming magnesium in my knee felt like it was melting my leg bones. I can be very quiet when I want to, and I wanted to be very quiet then as I stayed below the driver's door for a moment, feeling my body gathering up. Some guys pontificate on being able to apply just the right amount of pressure or force to knock a guy out for a minute, or an hour, or a day. I didn't buy it.

Instantaneous death was always better.

Instantaneous death solved things cleanly and quickly, leaving no room for potential loose ends.

I reached up, grabbed the driver's head, my left hand on the top, my right hand under his chin, and twisted, hard and fast. I felt and heard his neck bones snap. Crunchy feeling, crunchy sound. The driver's head was all the way around then, so that he looked like he was getting ready to back the Ford out. His body went limp.

I looked up. The gunmen at the restroom appeared not to have heard a thing. They still seemed to be focused on the women's restroom door, waiting for Kate to emerge.

I figured I had maybe fifteen more seconds before Manu and Mosi came out of the men's room and did something stupid and got themselves killed, or Kate came out, and, at best, became a hostage.

There were ways to handle what I would have to do next without a gun, but a gun would make it so much easier. I had hoped that since the driver was dressed just like the gunmen, he would be similarly armed as well. I reached into the dead driver's windbreaker pocket, and, voilá, came out with a Sig P226 identical to the ones the other two gunmen had. With my head inside the cab, I noticed a few things I would have to take a closer look at later, but right then had no time for.

The same guys who pontificate about the fine points of breaking, or not breaking, someone's neck also pontificate about not ever using a gun in combat situations unless you're sure the gun works and have practiced with it.

Fine in theory, but again, pretty useless in the current situation.

I pulled the Sig's slide back and forth to load a round in the firing chamber, and scuttled around for cover behind one of the rest area's shade trees. From there, I had a clear shot at the commando stationed to the left of the women's restroom. Again, because of the two men's positioning, it was impossible to get a sight line on both of them at once. Which also meant, even though I had a gun, I still couldn't call for their surrender or give them a chance to lay down their weapons. Any such delay would allow one or the other of the men to go in after Kate, something I was sure they would do.

I was going to have to kill them both.

Since the Sig I held in my hand was not silenced, I was going to have to kill them fast too. If I wasn't fast enough, when I shot the gunman on the left, the one on the right would hear it and have a chance to grab Kate, kill me, or both.

I cradled the Sig in my right hand and raised my right arm at the same time I brought my left arm up to use as a brace. Then, slowly and steadily, I extended my right arm toward the commando stationed on the left side of the women's room, carefully sighted in on his head, and took a deep breath.

Just then one of the Samoan twins, I could not tell which, came out of the restroom.

Early.

The twin saw me and the gun. Got scared fast.

"General Wilder," the twin said, "is something wrong?"

Maybe the American school system wasn't any better than the Soviet's.

Both the commandos turned to look at the Samoan and took a bead on his head with their Sigs.

It was like I wasn't there.

Like they couldn't see what they didn't expect to see. I pulled the Sig's trigger and put a bullet behind the ear of the one on the left, sprinted out from behind my shade tree cover, and dove in a somersault across the restroom path.

The gunman on the right had heard my shot and sighted in on me. He was good and quick. He fired off three rounds that blew up the ground in front of my head, the dust exploding around my eyes.

The only reason he didn't hit me was because I kept rolling. It's hard to hit a guy doing somersaults. I landed on my side, raised my arm, and put two rounds between his eyes.

CHAPTER 29

The sound of my last shot reverberated through the rest area. When the reverberations finally stopped, there was nothing but dead silence and absolute stillness. The bird no longer chirped. No fly buzzed. No leaves rustled.

I continued to lie on my side and did a quick sight check of my body. There were no new holes. I pushed myself up and looked over at the first gunman I had shot. He lay unmoving on the ground outside the restrooms. I walked up to him, kneeled down, and looked for signs of life. There weren't any.

I walked over to where the second gunman also lay unmoving. As I walked, I thought about how strange it was, yet how comforting it was, that I was able to react as quickly as I had to the commando's attack, despite my two years of hibernation-like exile. I suppose the shot I had made on the sniper range really should have tipped me off that I would be able to react to a mortal threat as capably as I just had done. But, again, the context of what had happened on the range was so different than what I had just experienced, I didn't feel I could be blamed for having had my doubts, for not realizing what my shot with the CheyTac seemingly foretold.

I reached the second gunman, bent down, and checked his carotid artery for a pulse. There was none. He was dead as well.

My initial cursory inspection of the two bodies thus complete, I turned my attention to the Samoan twin, who, moments ago, had exited the men's room with such unfortunate timing. The twin appeared to be frozen in some kind of shock. His face was pale, a slight sheen of sweat had broken out on his upper lip, and his eyes were glassy.

"It's okay," I said to the Samoan in as soothing a tone as I could muster. "They can't hurt you now."

He gave me the barest perceptible nod, but no other part of his body moved.

"By the way, which twin are you?" I said.

"Mosi," he said.

"Okay, Mosi," I said. "Be a good idea if you sat down for a moment. You don't look so good."

Mosi sat down. I turned to face the women's room.

"Grace, you done in there," I yelled.

"It's Kate, Jack," Kate said, her frightened voice carrying from behind the restroom wall.

Damn. I was going to have to find a way to stop doing that.

"Right," I said. "Sorry."

"What just happened?" Kate said, her voice still tremulous.

"We had a little incident," I said. "But it's all over now. You can come out."

"What about me?" Manu called from the men's room.

"You too," I said.

Kate and Manu exited their respective rooms and looked at the two dead men. They then looked at me, back at the men again, then back at me. Kate went pale and drew her hand up to her mouth, but for the moment seemed like she would remain upright.

Manu had a little different take. His knees buckled, he went down on all fours, and vomited. Mosi, watching him, rolled forward from his sitting position onto all fours as well, and also vomited.

Must be some kind of twin thing, I thought.

Like telepathy or something.

I went to Kate's side, gently took her right arm in my hands, and felt her wrist. Her skin was cold and her pulse was thready. She had done well to that point, but I didn't want to push my luck.

"I'm going to help you to the car," I said.

Kate nodded.

I supported her weight, and together we walked slowly to the May-bach. I opened the Maybach's rear door. Before I could put Kate in, she turned her head to look at the van, saw the unmoving driver with his neck at an unnatural angle.

"Is he dead too?" Kate said.

"Yes," I said.

"Okay," she said.

I laid Kate down on her seat on the left side of the Maybach's passenger compartment. I walked around the Maybach's hood, opened the driver side front door, reached inside, and popped the trunk. I took my rucksack out of the trunk, returned to Kate, and placed the rucksack under her calves. I wanted to get her legs as high as possible to help raise her blood pressure. Kate smiled weakly.

"Standard special forces cross-training, right?" She said.

"Yes," I said. "I'm a general and a medic."

"You learned well," she said.

"Coming from you, Dr. Lennon, I will take that as a great compliment," I said. "I'm going to send Manu and Mosi back here. Once they're inside the car, I want the doors locked and no one is to open them for anyone but me."

I jogged back to where Manu and Mosi were still on the ground. They were moaning a bit, but looked much better.

"Some paratroopers you guys are," I said.

They didn't seem to appreciate my comment.

"Think you can stand up?" I said.

They groaned, then stumbled to their feet.

"Go to the car," I said. "Get in your seats. Put them all the way back and put your feet up on the dash. Then lock the doors and don't open them for anyone but me. And don't forget to turn on the engine and get the air conditioning going."

They shuffled back to the car. As Manu and Mosi opened the Maybach's doors, they appeared to notice the dead man at the wheel of the Ford van. I thought the twins both might be sick again, but they quickly turned their heads away, got in the Maybach, and shut the doors behind them.

I assumed whoever planned the just aborted Soviet-style commando operation probably figured the three man team would have no problem taking down Kate and her not too well-trained bodyguards. So, I doubted there was a second fire team anywhere close by. One can never be too careful though, which is why I had put Kate and the twins in the Maybach. They would be safe inside the car.

Hmm.

Did I really just have a nice thought about Maybachs for the second time that day?

I wanted to see if I could find out anything more about who the three dead men were and where they came from. I went to the gunman farthest from the car, the one who had been on my left and I had killed first, and bent over him. I was careful not to step in the spreading pool of blood that lay around his corpse. I didn't want to leave any bloody footprints next to the bodies, lest someone question why I had needed to come in so close to them, maybe even start to wonder if I had tampered with the crime scene.

Tampering, of course, was exactly what I was going to do. I was going to search the three men, and if I found anything interesting, I was going to keep it for myself.

I uncurled the first gunman's fingers from where they still clutched his Sig and shoved the gun under the waistband on the left side of my pants. Since I had already stashed the Sig I had taken from the van driver in the waistband on the right side of my pants, I now had two guns I could draw upon. Just like Wyatt Earp.

I searched the dead guy's pockets.

No identification, no money, no keys.

But I did find one thing.

A Koran.

It looked new.

Like it had never been read or even opened.

The Koran was interesting, but I didn't need to take it with me, so I put it back in his pocket.

I found a stick and used the tip of it to push back the hair behind the gunman's ears. The skin there was tattooed with the cobra and crucifix insignia favored by certain elite sections of the Kazakhstan special forces. The Uzbekistan half of my hunch regarding the man's origin was out, and the Kazakhstan half was in.

Kazakhstan being in begged two obvious questions.

One, since it couldn't have been an easy task to bring Kazakh special forces into the U.S., somebody had gone to a lot of trouble to do it, and that somebody had to have some pretty sophisticated resources. Who was that somebody?

Two, what was this Christian fellow with a crucifix tattoo doing carrying around a Koran?

There wasn't much I could accomplish pondering those questions at that moment, so I added them to my mental list of things that needed answering.

I should also note that the cobra and crucifix insignia was of personal interest to me. Because the insignia was the same one tattooed on the Kazakh mercenaries who had been part of the ambush that had been the direct cause of Jeff developing PTSD, and thus, secondarily, the life Jeff and I were then living.

Was it possible that particular Kazakh and/or his two dead comrades knew the members - or perhaps themselves had even been members - of the mercenary group that had ambushed Jeff?

I supposed it was.

But I didn't see any way I could possibly determine the answer to that question, and I gave it no further thought. It did appear, however, that mercenaries who had received their training in the Kazakh special forces certainly had no reservations about plying their trade in any far-flung corner of the globe.

I took a photo with my cell phone of the dead man's face and tattoo, then went to the second dead man. Same result. His pockets were empty except for a brand-spanking-new Koran, and his skull was tattooed with a cobra and crucifix. I took photos of his face and tattoo as well. I also took his Sig and slid it under the waistband at the small of my back. Now my pants felt tight and I didn't feel like Wyatt Earp anymore. I don't know what I felt like. A man with too many guns?

I walked over to the van. The driver's head didn't look any less crooked. I shot a photo of the van's license plates, then took a closer look at the two items I had previously noticed inside the van, but at that earlier moment had been unable to take the time to examine closely.

Item number one. A very sophisticated, military-grade computer was lashed onto the floor next to the driver's feet. It was connected to a screen on the dash next to the steering wheel. The screen showed the path of the Maybach since it had left Bishop and also high-definition photos of Kate, Manu, and Mosi.

Item number two. In the back of the van, a chair had been bolted to the center of the van's metal floor. The chair looked like an old barber's chair. It had stuffed, red leather upholstery and its arms and center mounted swivel support post were made of stainless steel. Ugly heavy-duty leather straps with big, bronze buckles encircled the chair's back and bottom seat cushions and dangled from both armrests. There was a box of syringes filled with a yellow-colored fluid next to the chair.

I decided my initial instinct had been confirmed. The three men had planned to kidnap Kate. The chair and syringes were to be used for her. Since there were no provisions for Manu and Mosi, I assumed the rest area had been meant to be their eternal one.

I refocused on the dead van driver and searched him. Behind his ear, he had the same crucifix and cobra tattoo as the two gunmen had. In his right front pocket he also had a brand-spanking-new, unopened Koran. But he also had something else. A crinkled up foil bag. I uncrinkled it. It was an empty bag of pork rinds made by a Kazakhstan food company. Pork rinds, crucifix tattoos, and Korans? If things weren't adding up before, they were adding up even less now. I thought the foil bag might also ultimately reveal other secrets about the Kazakhs. I kept the bag and put the Koran back. I took a photo of the van driver's face and his tattoo.

The high-pitched whine of straining engines suddenly caught my attention. Five identical black Crown Victorias, the kind favored by government agencies, were barreling north up 395. They were doing at least a hundred and ten miles per hour and their headlights were flashing and their red rooftop strobes whirling. I hoped they would pass right by, but the vehicles made screeching right turns off the highway and headed in my direction.

I guess that was my day for unexpected visitors.

I assumed the government agents in those cars had probably just traveled close to a hundred miles, as that was how far the rest stop was from the nearest reasonably large metropolitan area. Agents dashing that far across the desert would probably be hot, thirsty, and cranky. I didn't think they'd want to be greeted by a guy with three guns in his pants.

But then again, if I wasn't armed I might not get any respect.

I left the guns where they were.

I stuffed the crinkled foil bag in my right sock. If they decided to search me, I figured they probably wouldn't look inside my sock.

I wanted to confirm one thing before the Crown Vics arrived. It looked like I had about twenty more seconds before they did.

I walked over to the Maybach, rapped on the driver's side window.

The window rolled down. I leaned my head in.

"One of you used your cell when we stopped at the Shell station in Bishop, didn't you?" I said.

Mosi nodded sheepishly.

"Who'd you call?" I said.

"My mom," he said.

"Is the phone still on?" I said.

Mosi took his cell phone out of his pants pocket and looked down at it.

"Guess I forgot to turn it off," Mosi said even more sheepishly than he had nodded.

"Okay," I said. "Manu put the window back up. Everyone stay in the car."

Before the window had rolled up completely and the tinting had blocked my view, I saw Manu give Mosi a dirty look. Mosi seemed to try to give him one back in return, but appeared to be overtaken by another wave of nausea before he could muster up anything significant.

I took a seat on the front of the Maybach's hood and waited for the Crown Victorias to arrive. I felt I was more in my element now. Until the events of the last few minutes, the NASAD issue had had an amorphous feel to it, the enemy unseen. Now I had some dead Kazakhs. The Kazakhs were most likely hired guns, but if I was able to discover the path they had taken to get to the rest area, and then backtracked along that path, who knew, maybe their bosses would be at the other end.

And, as the Kazakhs' bosses had sent the Kazakhs to kidnap NASAD's very own Kate Lennon, weren't the Kazakhs' bosses likely to also be the malevolent entity behind the killings of the NASAD drone submarine engineers? And if the Kazakhs' bosses had killed the drone sub engineers, then consistent with my new way of thinking, wasn't it likely those bosses could also be the malevolent entity behind the Chinese insurmountable edge?

All in all, finding the Kazakhs' bosses could turn out to be a very good thing.

I hoped the empty foil bag that had once contained pork rinds, and was now lodged in my sock, would turn out to be a signpost along the path that led back to the Kazakhs' bosses, a sort of distant cousin to

Hansel and Gretel's trail of bread crumbs in the forest. I also hoped that the birds in the story, the ones that gobbled up the children's crumbs before they could be put to their intended use, didn't have any distant metaphorical cousins running around in the present day who might believe it was their duty to get in my way.

I felt it was possible, perhaps even probable, however, that some of those metaphorical cousins were in the approaching Crown Vics. But it was also possible, and perhaps even probable, that the arrival of those cousins, rather than being a bothersome intrusion by individuals intent on getting in my way, could actually turn out to be a fortuitous event. Because the Crown Vics' occupants might be able to provide me with some additional useful information about the dead Kazakh commandos. Not willingly, of course. Government agents usually don't like to share information. In fact, they can be disgustingly stingy when it comes to sharing information. But, maybe with a little luck, I could find a way to get the agents in the Crown Vics to say some things they normally wouldn't say.

CHAPTER 30

I maintained my perch atop the Maybach as the five black Crown Victorias barreled toward me down the rest area's winding entrance road. Each Crown Vic followed the exact path of the Crown Vic in front of it, seemingly duplicating every twist and turn to the minutest detail, as if they were not individual cars at all, but one long undulating black python. It was a strange display that would have reminded me of a Busby Berkeley musical - if Busby had made horror films.

Cars being driven in such an anally compulsive manner were sure to be toting around assholes of the highest order. To achieve my goal of getting those assholes to cough up information I could use about the Kazakhs, or anything else for that matter, I felt my best plan was going to be to annoy the hell out of them. I hadn't yet decided on the details of such a plan, but whatever the plan was going to be, I had about thirty seconds to finalize it, as that was how much time I figured I had before the Crown Vics were fully upon me.

I knew one single, solitary, isolated act on my part probably wouldn't cut it.

But a few things in combination might have a chance.

I was thinking maybe something analogous to a professional prize-fighter's repertoire.

A few feints.

A couple of jabs.

A hook followed by a haymaker.

Since the Crown Victorias' occupants were likely U.S. federales, and thus, at least in theory, on the same side I was, I didn't want to hurt them too badly. Which meant I'd have to stay away from physical abuse and stick to the verbal variety.

Trash talking would be a good start.

Ignoring any and all orders directed my way would be effective.

I could also make fun of their guns.

First impressions were important too, however. So, I thought it would be best if I were to begin with a good visual presentation before nary a word passed between us.

But what would that visual presentation be? How should I appear when first they laid eyes on me?

Hmm.

How about super casual?

With just the right touch of insouciance.

As if I was a guy without a care in the world.

Guys with big guns who prided themselves in the pretentious way they drove around in their big pretentious cars wouldn't like that. No way. They'd be annoyed as hell.

And when it came to super casual, I knew just the right cat to imitate.

The King of Cool.

The Mac.

Mr. McQ.

The one.

The only.

Steve McQueen.

Steve McQueen in 'The Great Escape', to be exact.

With Steve's visage in mind, I leaned back, rested my hands on the Maybach's hood, dangled my legs over the side of the car, and assumed my best super casual Steve McQueen King of Cool pose. I pushed my hair off my forehead, smiled in a close-lipped, almost elfin way, and squinted slightly while trying to make my eyes sparkle. As I was doing all those things, it came to me that if Steve had three new Sig P226's, he would take full advantage of the opportunity they provided. He wouldn't leave one of the Sigs hidden behind his back. No way. He'd make sure all three were clearly visible and displayed for maximum effect. Which meant that's what I had to do too. So, I moved the Sig I had shoved in the back of my waistband to the front of my waistband. As soon as the Sig had settled in there, and I had adjusted it just right, I knew I'd done good and Steve would have been proud. If Steve were still alive, he maybe even would have wanted to star in the movie of my life. We would call it 'The Man With Three Guns'.

Just then my thirty seconds were up and all five Crown Victorias, engines screaming, headlights still flashing, and rooftop beacons still whirling, were no more than a hundred yards away, hurtling closer and closer with each passing moment. When the Vics were fifty yards out, their line split up in a very coordinated, elegant move that had each car peeling off at precisely equal intervals so that they could better surround me. At ten yards, all the Vics simultaneously skidded to a halt amid squealing springs and screeching tires, the tires leaving wicked fantails of flying gravel in their wake.

One would have expected after all that frenzied activity that more frenzied activity was sure to quickly follow.

But nothing followed.

Everything just came to a complete standstill.

I waited.

Nothing.

The Vics just sat there, four of them in a tight semicircle in front of me and one behind me. All the Vics' windshields, front, back, and sides, were heavily tinted so that I couldn't see what was going on inside any of them.

I craned my neck around to look at the Vic behind me. From a tactical perspective, its positioning was highly questionable, even stupid. Well, that wasn't my problem. Might be something to make fun of later, though.

I turned back around to look at the four Vics in front of me. They remained eerily quiet. No movement at all. I thought maybe the Vics' occupants were hatching a plan to use against me. They were probably very afraid of my three guns and felt they needed extra time to come up with their best plan possible.

Then suddenly, just when I was starting to believe they'd never have the guts to confront me, there was a flurry of activity.

All ten of the Vics' front doors whipped open.

Ten men leapt out, each of them taking cover behind an open door.

Each man trained a weapon on yours truly.

Three Heckler and Koch MP5 submachine guns.

Four Ithaca 37 shotguns.

Three Glock 23 automatic handguns.

Red laser dots danced across my head and heart.

Game on.

The ten men were clearly part of a team. Each one wore neatly pressed blue pants with a crease down the front and cuffs at the bottom, a crisp, starched collared white dress shirt, a carefully knotted red and blue striped tie, highly polished black leather shoes with rubber soles, white socks, and a shiny blue nylon windbreaker.

Nine of the men wore blue cotton baseball-style caps.

The tenth man wore a porkpie hat.

The porkpie hat was made of brown felt and had a black velvet band circling the crown. The brim was wider in front than in back and a little red feather was stuck in the band. It looked like it was suitable for summer wear as long as it was the summer of 1942.

The porkpie hat had nothing written on it, but the blue windbreakers and the blue baseball caps were imprinted with big blocky yellow letters across their fronts.

The big block yellow letters spelled out 'FBI'.

Which led me to my second brilliant deduction of the day.

"I bet these guys are FBI agents," I said to myself.

"FREEZE!" the FBI agent wearing the porkpie hat said through a yellow bullhorn.

I didn't freeze, but neither did I make a move for any of my three guns.

The FBI agent who had said 'freeze' seemed to be in charge. Why did I think that? Mainly because it seemed like only someone in charge would dare wear a porkpie hat - and a way out of date one at that - and also because besides being the only agent with a giant yellow bullhorn, he was also the only one with a gold-plated Glock with a pearl handle.

Gold-plated Glock with a pearl handle?

Wasn't that a little girl's gun?

The FBI agent with the gold-plated Glock and the porkpie hat didn't resemble a little girl in any other way, however. He was big and burly, around six feet tall, and two hundred and fifty pounds. Maybe burly was too kind. His gut hung out in a roll over his belt. Fat would thus be more accurate than burly. I guessed he was in his mid-fifties. His small, dark, piggy eyes, floppy jowls, blubbery lips, and chubby, pink, sweaty cheeks were screwed up in an expression he was probably hoping conveyed 'hard-ass'. All I was thinking was 'lard-ass'. His porkpie hat was just rakishly askew enough so I could see that his hair was fashioned in a blondish crewcut. It looked like it was a crewcut whose style he hadn't changed since high school - the dead Kazakhs' bowl cuts looked positively chic by comparison.

Then I remembered.

I knew who the fat man in the porkpie hat with the gold-plated, pearl handled Glock was.

He was Special Agent Burnette, the agent who had been assigned to the NASAD case, and he looked exactly as Kate had described him to me.

I maintained my super casual Steve McQueen King of Cool pose as the red laser dots continued to flicker across my body. I smiled my close-lipped, elfin smile at the FBI agents. They did not smile back. I was making some progress though, because most of them were starting to look pretty annoyed.

Probably because I had not yet frozen.

In addition to their annoyance, I found something else about the FBI agents' behavior interesting. Not one of them had noticed the bodies of the three dead Kazakhs, even though the bodies were barely fifty feet from us. I took that to mean that the agents probably hadn't come across the desert looking for three Kazakhs. Because if they had been looking for the Kazakhs, surely the first thing they would have done is look for them right? And then finding them, they would have further searched and secured the area. But they had not done that. They only had eyes for me.

Knowing the FBI agents were not looking for the Kazakhs was thus a fairly good start for my free intel gathering program.

Unfortunately, the free intel wasn't really free.

It came with a cost.

A mental cost.

Because it raised a new question that I had to consider.

If the FBI wasn't looking for the Kazakhs, why the hell had they just raced across the desert in a five car Crown Vic battalion? Something had to be going on, but what was that something? The agents had made their Busby Berkeley beeline for the Maybach. Sure, most people would find the Maybach was a nice car and all, but, on its own, was it really enough to warrant the attention of ten heavily armed FBI agents? Which had to mean the FBI was interested in the Maybach's occupants. Hard to imagine the agents would go through so much trouble for the Samoans, even as sweet and wonderful as the twins might be. So that left Kate. But why had they come for her? And, again, what was the big emergency that made them use five cars to do that?

That was another question that was going to have to wait, because just then the agent in charge, AKA Special Agent Burnette, again shouted, "FREEZE!" through the yellow bullhorn.

"Dude," I said, still smiling. "It's gotta be a hundred and five out here. So, unless you're secretly Bobby Drake, AKA the X-man the 'Iceman', that ain't gonna happen."

"Hands over your head!" Burnette screamed.

"Be honest," I said. "The hat and the bullhorn - you got them as part of the special G-man package last month at Walmart, right?"

"Hands up or we're gonna blow your goddamned head off!" Burnette yelled.

I didn't raise my hands, just continued smiling my elfin smile and trying to make my eyes sparkle. I realized then that Steve McQueen most likely wouldn't have dignified Burnette by entertaining thoughts about Burnette while using solely Burnette's real name. I needed a better moniker for him. Goldi-Glocks? No reason to denigrate a fine old fairy tale by associating it with this clown. Bullhorn Boy? Nice ring to it, but...no. How about Porkpie? I felt a little tingle in my spine that I took to mean Steve would have liked that. Okay, Porkpie it was.

Burnette, newly christened as Porkpie, seemed pretty annoyed, maybe even about to reach his boiling point. Boiling would probably be a bit too high. Simmering was ideal. I decided it would be best to say nothing in the hopes that would turn down the heat and I could let him stew for a moment. Saying nothing seemed to work.

While he was stewing, I took a moment for myself. I breathed in the pungent smell of overheated engines and burning rubber. I listened to the pleasant pinging sound the Crown Vics' engines made as they cooled. I felt the gentle rumble of the Maybach's own engine beneath me as it powered the air conditioning for Kate and the Samoans. I watched the dust the Crown Victorias had kicked up float gently back to earth.

And then, as often happens when we allow ourselves to truly pay attention to the world around us and momentarily lose ourselves in all it has to offer, I had an insight. I realized that as annoyed with me as

Porkpie might be, I was at least as equally annoyed with him and his men. I didn't like that Porkpie and his FBI cohorts, no matter how well they drove, or how snazzily they dressed, had been late to the party. I didn't like that their lateness could have resulted in Kate's death. I also didn't like that I had already deduced it wasn't the Kazakhs that had been worrying them. Because shouldn't that have been what was worrying them? Wasn't it their job to know that the Kazakhs had been after Kate? They were the goddamn FBI weren't they? Why didn't they know about the Kazakhs? They had no excuse. Kate shouldn't have been put in any danger at all. They should have been here for Kate. And I shouldn't have had to do their job for them, either.

But again, the question still remained as to why the FBI was on the scene at all. Apparently *something* had set their minds atwitter and racing off to find Kate. What was it?

Annoyed as I was, I probably shouldn't have done what I did next.

I'm fairly certain other mortals probably wouldn't have done what I did either.

They would have responded differently.

They would have stopped, or at least slowed down, before they acted.

But I didn't stop, and I didn't slow down.

I forged full speed ahead.

My forging was driven not just by my aforementioned annoyance, but by a powerful stew of other reasons.

One, I was experiencing a huge adrenaline rush from my just concluded gun battle with the Kazakh commandos.

Two, I was under the spell of a sudden, unexpected euphoria fueled by the realization that my former warrior self, which though it had been buried for well nigh two years, was not only not dead, but alive and well and ready for action.

And three - this third reason the one that actually sent me completely over the edge - being my anger with Burnette for not just failing to protect Kate from the Kazakhs, but also for his total botching of the NASAD investigation. Because Burnette's botching of the NASAD investigation was a major botching, indeed, a world class botching. His botching was, in my opinion, the direct cause of most, if not all, of the murders of the twelve NASAD drone sub engineers. I couldn't honestly have expected Burnette to uncover the plot against the engineers after only the first few deaths, but to let the murders go on as long as they had been was unforgivable. I believed that the engineers, in the absence of such botching, would have still been alive that day.

And so, all those reasons, mixed in with my abiding inability to suffer fools gladly - yes, it's a fault - made my behavior, and all that happened next, a fait accompli.

"Hey asshole," I said. "Your name wouldn't happen to be Burnette would it?"

Porkpie's piggy eyes narrowed slightly and his lower lip quivered. It was a reaction that provided absolute confirmation for me - not that I needed it - that Porkpie was, in fact, Burnette.

"We're the ones asking the questions here," Burnette said.

I understood what Burnette meant about the questions, even though, technically, I didn't believe he had asked any questions yet.

"Indeed you are the one asking the questions, Agent Burnette," I said, "indeed you are. And please note that I'm ready, willing, and able to answer any and all questions, especially ones you might have about the dead guys arrayed in various locations around this fine rest area. Truth be told, I'm actually somewhat disappointed you haven't asked already."

Both of Porkpie's eyes narrowed again, and the left eye also twitched. His lips didn't just quiver, but spasmed into a corkscrew-like shape he seemed to have trouble releasing. I took pleasure in the fact I had made his face do that. It felt like sport. I began to hope Porkpie/Burnette might fall apart and dissolve into a mass of quivering jelly.

Unfortunately, he didn't, however.

What Porkpie/Burnette appeared to do instead was to keep trying to do his job, despite whatever feelings of embarrassment, inadequacy, or self-doubt I felt certain I'd caused to arise in him. A kinder judge might have awarded Porkpie points for that. I did not. Mainly because I'd gotten the distinct impression Burnette had had plenty of past practice dealing with such issues, and, truth be told, the degree of difficulty of just doing his job also wasn't all that high. After all, all Burnette had to do was...

Look right.

Look left.

See the Kazakhs lying next to the restroom entrances.

Shout out an order.

And after a moment, all those things are exactly what he did do.

"Conklin, Finlayson, check it out," Burnette said into his giant yellow bullhorn.

Conklin and Finlayson must have been the two FBI agents shielding themselves behind the doors of the Vic closest to the dead men. Because they were the agents who broke cover from that Vic's front doors and ran toward the bodies, one going to the dead Kazakh on the right, and the other to the one on the left. Each agent knelt down, did a quick investigation, and nodded at Porkpie.

I said, "Well done, Conklin and Finlayson. Well done. Feel free to scamper back from whence you came. I'm a dangerous man with three guns after all."

Conklin and Finlayson didn't say anything. They hustled back to their Vic, took cover, and, once again, pointed their weapons at me.

I turned to Porkpie.

"Agent Burnette," I said, "aren't you going to ask me about the other one?"

"Other one what?" Burnette said.

"Dead body," I said. "What else would I be talkin' about, fool?"

Porkpie took some deep breaths, slowly taking air in and slowly letting it out. The other nine agents and I were forced to participate in his little ritual, as the sucking in of his breath came loud and clear through the giant yellow bullhorn's speaker. The breaths seemed to forestall Porkpie's usual quivering and twitching.

"Where is it?" Burnette said.

"Where's what, Agent Burnette?" I said.

"I know you think you're funny, wiseass," Burnette said, "but you're not."

"Oh, you meant the dead body?" I said. "You took so long with all that breathing, I forgot what we were talking about. It's in the vehicle."

That time Porkpie's face metamorphosed in a completely new way. His eyes didn't narrow or twitch, but widened into two big saucers. His lips didn't quiver or twirl - his whole jaw dropped. I assumed he thought I was referring to the Maybach, which to him probably would have raised the disastrous notion that Kate Lennon was the 'other' dead body. Which was what I wanted him to think. Because I wanted him to suffer. For the twelve dead NASAD engineers. For being late for Kate. And for his presumed overall history of being an arrogant, incompetent jackass.

"You look worried, Agent Burnette," I said. "Is it something I can help you with?"

"Screw you," Burnette said.

"I thought FBI agents weren't allowed to swear," I said. "Good for you."

Burnette said nothing.

"Actually Agent Burnette, I know what you're thinking," I said.

"You have no idea what I'm thinking," Burnette said.

"Ah, but I do," I said. "You're worried Dr. Lennon is dead."

He did not respond.

"But I wasn't talking about the Maybach," I said. "I was talking about the Ford Econoline van."

Porkpie's eyes immediately tracked to the van.

"Sterling, the van," he said into the bullhorn.

Sterling must have been the agent crouching behind the passenger door of the Vic farthest to my left. Because it was that agent who dashed over to the van, peered into the van's driver side window, stuck his hand in, checked for a pulse, then pulled his hand out, turned, and nodded to Porkpie.

"Got another dead guy here," Sterling said.

Porkpie turned to face me. He stared at me, not saying anything.

I smiled helpfully at him.

Finally, Burnette said to me, "Any others?"

"Nope," I said. "That's it."

"You do this?" Burnette said.

"I could have let them kill Dr. Lennon," I said. "Would you have preferred that?"

Burnette said nothing.

"Oh dear," I said. "Did I make a mistake telling you that? Do I need a lawyer now?"

"You're a real piece of work, aren't you?" Burnette said. "Where's Dr. Lennon?"

"What?" I said. "No 'thank you'? Isn't that the least I deserve for doing your job for you, Agent Burnette?"

"Screw you, asshole," he said.

"There's that swearing again," I said.

"If you want to leave here in something other than a body bag," Burnette said, "you need to tell me where Dr. Lennon is, and you better do it right now."

"I need some ID first," I said.

Porkpie did his deep breathing thing again, each sucking breath broadcast far and wide by the yellow bullhorn.

"Look man," I said. "Don't take it personal. I'm just following orders. There are some pretty pissed off Samoans inside this little ol' Maybach and they have some pretty big guns pointed at your heads right now."

Hearing this, the other nine FBI agents simultaneously moved their eyes off of me and focused on the Maybach's windows. They seemed to try to peer in through the heavily tinted glass.

Which of course didn't get them anywhere.

Burnette said, "Is Dr. Lennon in the car?"

"ID first, then we talk," I said.

Sweat had begun to pour down Porkpie's face. He stared at me as he took a handkerchief out of his back left hip pocket, flipped his porkpie hat higher up his forehead, wiped his entire face, then shoved the handkerchief back in the pocket. He then reached into his back right hip pocket, fumbled around for a moment, and pulled something out that looked like a small wallet. He tossed the wallet to me. I caught it. It turned out to be his identification case. I opened it, held it out in front of me, and read the card inside.

"John Burnette, FBI, Special Agent in Charge," I said. "Would have been so much easier Johnny if you'd just said, 'Yes', when I asked you a minute ago. Anyway, this makes me feel a whole lot better. If you were FBI SWAT, I would've been deeply concerned by how far their physical conditioning standards had fallen."

"Your turn, asshole," Burnette said.

I tossed his case back to him.

"Relax those trigger fingers boys," I said to the assembled multitudes. "Wallet's in my back pocket."

I gently removed my wallet and side-armed it to Burnette. He opened it and studied my Armed Forces identity card.

"Jack Wilder," Burnette said. "Uniformed Services. U.S. Army. Says here you're a general, Jack. You expect me to believe this bullshit?"

"Believe what you want," I said.

"You're a long way from base, Mr. Wilder," Burnette said.

"On leave," I said.

"Assuming you are who you say you are, I don't know how many laws you've broken regarding military personnel involvement in domestic affairs," Burnette said. "Not to mention obstruction of justice, resisting arrest, and interfering with a federal agent in the discharge of his duties."

"Please don't talk like that," I said. "I scare very easily."

Burnette tossed my wallet back to me.

"Where's Dr. Lennon?" He said.

"We're almost there," I said. "First, however, we - the Samoans and I - would like to know why you assigned so little importance to this mission that you brought along inexperienced personnel? Dr. Lennon's life deserves more respect than a training exercise."

"All our men are highly qualified," Burnette said.

"Liar, liar, pants on fire," I said.

Burnette did not say anything.

"What about those two?" I said.

I jerked my thumb back a couple of times, indicating the two agents behind me, the ones who had parked their Vic - the fifth Vic - in the aforementioned tactically questionable position. It was tactically questionable because it put them and the other eight agents directly in each others' line of fire.

"Those men are top-notch agents," Burnette said.

"Really?" I said. "Are all your top-notch agents as stupid as they are? Where I come from, even the lowliest recruit knows not to place himself and his comrades in the line of fire. Somebody starts shooting, I'm just going to duck under this Maybach and watch you guys blow each other away."

I expected Burnette's face to do that eye narrowing and lip quivering thing again. But it didn't. Which probably should have tipped me off he wasn't as weak as I had taken him to be, had heretofore unseen hidden abilities, or that all that deep breathing had worked some powerful magic on him. Any or all of which would have made me be a little more careful going forward with him, and maybe even intuited Burnette had developed some kind of plan for dealing with me in that chubby head of his. But since I had already messed up that day by not paying enough attention to the airplane I had seen following us on the highway - an airplane I was by then reasonably certain had been given our location and sent to track us after Mosi had made the unfortunate error of calling his mother on his cell phone, the airplane's tracking made easy in the extreme since Mosi had also failed to turn his cell phone off after the call - it shouldn't have come as a surprise that any such potential tip off went completely unnoticed by me.

"Lunn, Jeske," Burnette said to the agents behind me. "Bring that vehicle over here."

Lunn and Jeske got in their Vic and pulled it next to Burnette's own vehicle. They then exited their car, crouched behind the front doors, and once again, aimed their weapons at my head.

Burnette said to me, "Feel better now?"

I did feel better. Not having weapons aimed at your back is always a good thing.

"Much," I said. "One more item and then I'm pretty sure the Samoans will be okay with letting you talk to the good doctor. Actually two more items. That is, if you don't mind..."

"I do mind," Burnette said. "But that's not gonna stop you from going on your merry asshole way, is it?"

"Good point," I said. "First, lose the bullhorn. I can hear you just fine."

Burnette shrugged like it was no big deal. He leaned into his car, put the bullhorn down on the front seat, came back out, and faced me.

"I appreciate that," I said. "I know we just had Agent Sterling checking out the van, but I want to see what you think as well. Please go over there and take a look behind the dead guy's left ear."

"Your wish is my command, shithead," Burnette said.

Burnette walked over to the Econoline, bent his head under the driver's side windowsill, and pulled back the dead driver's ear.

"What do you see?" I said.

"A tattoo," Burnette said.

"What's it look like?" I said.

"A crucifix and a cobra," Burnette said.

"Give the man a prize," I said. "Know what it signifies?"

Burnette pulled his head out of the window and turned to me.

"No," Burnette said. "But I'll bet doughnuts to dollars you do."

"The other two dead guys also have the same tattoo," I said. "The driver and his buddies are, or were, members of an elite branch of the Kazakh special forces. Have you come across any other men like this?"

"I'm not discussing that with you," Burnette said.

"Dr. Lennon is going to feel a lot more comfortable if you do," I said. "If you don't discuss it with me, then I'm going to tell the Samoans to fire up the Maybach, start driving, and not stop until they get home."

"We're not going to let that car go anywhere," Burnette said.

"That's a high security Maybach, Johnny," I said. "You'd need a tank to stop it. Now, please be sure you answer my question with the whole truth and nothing but the truth. Samoans have a sixth sense when it comes to lies."

Burnette wiped the sweat off his face with his handkerchief again, then took a closer look at the Maybach. He seemed to realize the windows weren't just tinted, but were also thick bulletproof resin. And that the Maybach's body was armored and the tires solid rubber.

"No," Burnette finally said. "The FBI is not aware of any Kazakhstani special forces in the U.S."

Chalk up another victory for me and my little quest for free knowledge.

"No special work permits for mercenaries?" I said. "No government sponsored programs for cross cultural exchange of killers?"

"No," Burnette said.

"How'd you find us?" I said.

"That's classified," Burnette said.

"I'm sure my clearance is higher than yours," I said. "Go ahead, you can tell me."

Burnette just stared at me.

"Haven't you learned by now resistance is futile?" I said.

Burnette took a deep breath, then turned his head to the side and spit on the ground.

"We tracked the driver's cell phone," Burnette said.

"You can't tell them apart either, can you?" I said.

"What the hell does that mean?" Burnette said.

"It's an easy mistake to make," I said. "But for the record, it wasn't the driver's phone, it was his twin brother's."

"Do you think I give a rat's ass?" Burnette said.

"Did you send a plane up to get visual confirmation?" I said.

Burnette spit again.

"No, we did not send a plane up to get visual confirmation," Burnette said.

Which meant, that even though I had been nearly certain it was the Kazakhs' bosses who had sent aloft the plane that had tracked us earlier, I was then absolutely certain it was them. I wasn't sure what I could do with that knowledge, but at least it was consistent with everything I had learned so far, namely that NASAD's enemy appeared to have seemingly endless resources.

"In regard to the Kazakhs," I said. "You clearly didn't expect to find them here. So, I'm wondering, Johnny, what the hell *are* you doing here?"

"That's between Dr. Lennon and me," Burnette said.

"What did I just say about resistance?" I said.

"I don't care what you said, shit for brains," Burnette said. "I'm not discussing that subject with you. "

"Really?" I said.

"It's non-negotiable," Burnette said.

I didn't see any reason to push Burnette at that moment on the subject of what had brought him to the rest area, as I felt quite sure I would come by that information soon enough, with or without his help. Burnette would certainly explain to Kate at some point what he had been doing here, and Kate would tell me. I tried to think of some more questions for Burnette, but couldn't. I thought I had done reasonably well for a guy with ten guns pointed at his head.

"I'll let you have that one, Johnny," I said. "Thank you. You've been very helpful."

"Are we done here?" Burnette said.

I nodded. I pushed myself off the Maybach's hood, turned, and rapped on the Maybach's driver window. It slid down. Burnette approached carefully, poked his head in. In front of him were just three weak and woozy people. No angry men with guns. Burnette made some kind of barely perceptible movement that I wasn't quick enough to read. An agent Tasered me from behind. From what I'd heard, I thought Tasers were supposed to be a less harsh option for law enforcement. I didn't think a person was supposed to lose consciousness.

But I did.

The last things I remember thinking were, one, I wasn't as quite up to speed as I had thought I had been - fifty percent, not ninety percent, had probably been the right number after all - and two, maybe, just maybe, I shouldn't have pushed those guys so hard.

*

PART III
THE MOJAVE

CHAPTER 31

I woke up in a jail cell. Eight foot high steel bars, no window, cement floor, barren walls painted a hideous green color, harsh fluorescent lighting. The astringent smell of ammonia disinfectant filled my nostrils and the low hum of big institutional air conditioners throbbed in my ears. There was not a clock in sight. I had no idea what time it was, how long I'd been in the cell, or even if it was night or day.

There were four other cells next to me and they were all empty. I had just a stainless steel toilet to keep me company. I was sitting, my back against the wall farthest from the bars, my feet splayed in front of me, and my wrists cuffed behind me. My wrists hurt, my back hurt, my left knee burned, and my mouth was very dry. I felt groggy. Like I'd been tranquilized. There was a pinch in my right biceps where I assumed the needle had gone in. Drugging me seemed like something a guy like Burnette would order up. Maybe he even pushed the plunger himself. At least I could still feel the foil wrapper I had taken from the dead Kazakh driver wedged under my sock.

A voice said, "Are you really a general?"

I looked up. The speaker was a beautiful Latina in a Los Angeles County Sheriff's Department uniform. She appeared to have just stepped out from behind a nearby post in the hallway. She was about five feet, five inches tall with an hourglass figure, laughing brown eyes, and a pretty mouth full of white teeth. Her dark hair fell down around her shoulders. The way her breasts pushed against her shirt, and her pants outlined her ass, made it hard for me to believe her tailoring was regulation. There were sergeant's stripes on her arm and a nameplate that said 'Aguilera' on her chest.

"Yes," I said. "But I know at least one guy who doesn't believe it."

"You wouldn't be talking about Special Agent Burnette, would you?" Aguilera said.

"One and the same," I said.

"He's the asshole who brought you in here," Aguilera said.

"I can see you're a good judge of character, Sergeant Aguilera," I said.

"Please call me Laura," said Aguilera. "Agent Burnette's driving everyone here nuts. My momma always taught me guests should mind their manners."

"I think I'd like your momma, Laura," I said. "By the way, where's here?"

"Los Angeles County Sheriff's Substation, Lancaster, California," Aguilera said.

"That puts us about seventy miles north of Los Angeles, doesn't it?" I said

"Yes it does," Aguilera said.

"You like it in Lancaster, Laura?" I said.

"Been out here a couple of years," Aguilera said. "I'm still undecided."

"Me too," I said. "People seem friendly. Accommodations are a bit iffy though."

Aguilera smiled.

"Laura, do you know what time it is?" I said.

She looked down at her watch.

"3:23," Aguilera said.

"A.m. or p.m.?" I said.

"P.m.," Aguilera said

"Still Monday, June fifth?" I said.

"Uh huh," Aguilera said.

Which meant, since I had been Tasered at about 1:15 p.m., I had only been unconscious for over two hours. It felt like it had been a lot longer.

"Thank you, Laura," I said.

"You're welcome," Aguilera said. "Tracey and I think you're too cute to be a general. We think you're a movie star playing a general."

"Who's Tracey?" I said.

"Me," said Tracey.

A light-skinned woman with blonde hair and blue eyes and a nameplate that said 'Apple' who otherwise could have been Laura's twin - same figure, same tailoring - stepped out from behind another post.

Aguilera said, "Sergeant Apple and I were hoping you might have to pee."

I said, "Actually I could use some help with these cuffs."

"Oh, no, the cuffs have to stay on," Aguilera said.

Tracey said, "But we can still provide assistance."

I guess it was a side effect of the tranquilizer, but it took me a moment to understand what they were offering. I never got the chance to take them up on their offer, however, as we were interrupted by the sound of footsteps pounding down the hall. I figured the footsteps were probably Burnette's because the jail floor shook with each and every one. A moment later I was proved correct.

Burnette, still wearing his porkpie hat and his pearl handled, gold-plated Glock at his side, rounded a corner in the hallway and came into view. I thought Burnette had probably just eaten, since his belly looked bigger than when I had last seen it. Next to Burnette was the substation's captain. The captain's nameplate said 'Halford'. Other than the name-plate, he didn't look anything like Tracey and Laura. He was about five foot five, thin as a snake, bald, had yellow teeth, and was wearing glasses with a shiny black plastic frame and thick, Coke bottle lenses. The lenses made his eyes appear three times larger than a normal human's.

Burnette and Captain Halford stopped outside my cell.

Tracey and Laura scattered.

"I wouldn't want to be you right now, Wilder," Burnette said.

"Funny," I said. "I was just thinking the same thing about you."

"Laugh while you can," Burnette said. "The United States Attorney for the California Central District just choppered in here to personally interrogate you."

"Interrogate me?" I said. "I would have thought you already did that while I was under the influence of whatever drugs you pumped into me."

"A cowboy like you couldn't possibly understand this," Burnette said, "but at the FBI we take pride in following the rules."

"You're sure it's not because you're just so stupid you didn't think of it?" I said.

Burnette turned to Halford.

"Get him out of the cell, Halford," Burnette said.

Halford opened the cell door, stepped through it, grabbed my handcuffed wrists from behind, yanked me to my feet, and shoved me out the cell door. Even with the cuffs on, it was unlikely the two of them could have stopped me if I had tried to escape then and there. I didn't think trying to escape would be a good idea, though. To escape, I would have had to attack Burnette and Halford, and attacking the two of them was probably just what Burnette would have loved to see me do. Because, even if he wouldn't admit it to anyone, I was pretty sure somewhere deep down Burnette knew he couldn't make any charges stick based on what I'd done so far. Assaulting him and Halford would be a different matter, however. Besides, I didn't see any harm in talking to the U.S. Attorney. It was hard to believe he could be as big a knucklehead as Burnette, and if it turned out he was, well, I'd cross that bridge when I came to it. Right then, however, there was nothing to prevent me from doing a little interrogating of my own. I didn't expect to get much, but even if I didn't, there was a pretty good chance I'd at least annoy Burnette. And annoying Burnette could never be a bad thing.

"I hope by now you've handed over Dr. Lennon to someone who can actually keep her safe," I said to Burnette.

Burnette ignored me, just nodded at Halford. Halford gave me another shove, and, still holding my cuffed wrists, pushed me along so that he and I moved down the hallway and away from the cell. Burnette followed close behind.

"Okay, I understand you don't want to talk about how badly you messed up with Dr. Lennon, Johnny," I said, craning my head around to look at him. "It's gotta be a real sore point for you."

Burnette still ignored me.

"Since I'm in such a good mood, I'll do you a favor and change the subject," I said. "What we doin' in Lancaster? You guys run out of gas on the way to L.A.? I know those Crown Vics are real guzzlers."

"You're one of those jackasses who speaks just to hear the sound of their own voice, aren't you?" Burnette said.

"You wouldn't be talkin' to me like that if I still had those three Sigs," I said.

"You want your guns back, do ya?" Burnette said.

"Yes," I said. "Can you arrange that?"

"Sure can," Burnette said. "Your sentence should be up in about sixty years. I'll be there with the Sigs waiting for you right outside the prison gate."

Burnette laughed at his own joke.

"Oh damn, I forgot," Burnette said. "Convicted felons can't own guns can they? Guess I'll just have to keep them for myself."

"That's actually a good idea," I said. "You're gonna need something to use when you have to give back that gold-plated, pearl handled piece of shit you been packin' to the ten year old girl you stole it from."

"Nobody here thinks you're funny but you," Burnette said. "But I guess you get told that a lot, don't you?"

We kept walking. My interrogation of Burnette wasn't going so well. But I don't give up easily.

"What about the Kazakhs?" I said. "You find out how they got in the country yet?"

"You just won't quit, will you?" Burnette said.

"Not unless I have a good reason to," I said. "How about we discuss your namby pamby rules for a moment?"

"Happy to," Burnette said.

"I've got cuffs on and I was just in a jail cell," I said.

"Huh," Burnette said. "I hadn't noticed. Thanks for pointing that out."

"You're welcome," I said. "However, I don't remember being formally charged."

"You want me to read you your rights?" Burnette said.

"I think it'd be the classy thing to do, don't you?" I said.

"Okay," Burnette said, "you have the right to remain silent. And, considering how goddamn sick I am of your voice, I pray to the Lord you immediately exercise that right."

Burnette chuckled, apparently having amused himself again.

We had progressed to a part of the hallway where the linoleum floor had a nice sheen to it, like it had been freshly waxed. The fluorescent lighting seemed less harsh than it had been in my cell and the hallway's walls were painted beige instead of puke green. I figured we were getting closer to where the jailers hung out as opposed to the jailees.

And we were.

Because a moment later, we arrived at an interrogation room and stopped. Standing outside the room was a handsome black man dressed in a well-tailored dark grey pin-striped suit, white dress shirt, and a crisp yellow tie with white polka dots. His skull was clean-shaven and glistened under the fluorescent lights. He was about six two, very fit, with strong arms and chest. He looked like he was both a runner and a lifter. He had eyes that were very clear and very sharp.

"U.S. Attorney Vandross, this is Mr. Jack Wilder," Burnette said. "Please advise us when you are done with Mr. Wilder so that we can transport him to the MDC."

The MDC is the Metropolitan Detention Center and is the federal holding facility in Los Angeles. I knew the name, because about seven years before, Jeff and I had been tasked with tracking down and bringing back to the United States a very bad man who had escaped from the MDC and made his way to a Bolivian rainforest. The United States considered the man to be very bad because he was an Islamic terrorist, originally from Jordan, who had set up a drug operation in Bolivia and was using the proceeds from that operation to fund Al-Qaeda cells. One of the things those cells liked to do was behead American tourists in various countries around the globe. By the time Jeff and I got to the rainforest, the very bad Jordanian had enlisted about fifty equally bad friends to help prevent his capture and return. Unfortunately, that didn't work out too well for him or his friends, and technically at least, not for Jeff and me either. I say 'technically' because Jeff and I failed in our original mission in that we were unable to return the Jordanian to the MDC. We instead had to settle for turning the Jordanian and his bad friends into a nutritional compost pile on the rainforest floor. One might still be able to find the site of our skirmish today, recognizing it by how much more lush it is - trees taller, canopies fuller, and richer, more tasty fruits for the squirrel monkeys and toucans - than the surrounding area.

I said, "I hear the MDC is very comfy."

Burnette ignored me.

"Nice to meet you U.S. Attorney Vandross," I said as I rotated a bit to show my cuffed wrists. "I'm sorry, I'd shake your hand, but mine are indisposed at the moment."

Vandross also ignored me.

"Thank you, Special Agent Brunette," Vandross said. "I will take it from here."

"It's Burnette, sir," Burnette said.

Vandross seemed not to understand.

"My name, Attorney Vandross, is *Burnette*, not *Brunette*," Burnette said.

"Oh, of course, Agent Burnette," Vandross said, dragging out the 'r'. "So sorry."

"If you'll forgive me, sir, I do not think being alone with Mr. Wilder is a wise idea," Burnette said. "Mr. Wilder is a dangerous, unstable man."

"I'll be fine," Vandross said. "Thank you Special Agent, and thank you Captain Halford. I'll call for you when I'm done."

CHAPTER 32

Vandross led me into the interrogation room. In the center of the room, two steel chairs faced each other on either side of a metal table that had been bolted to the cement floor. A thick metal ring, which could be used to chain and secure a prisoner's ankle shackles, had been bolted to the floor beneath the table. A brown leather briefcase and a microphone were on top of the table. There was a two-way mirror with curtains on one wall. The curtains were open. On the wall above the curtains was a clock that said it was 3:32. The other walls were barren. The room reminded me a lot of the cell I had just called home. I guessed the same architect had designed both rooms and found it hard to let go of his minimalist motif.

"There was a special forces major at Fort Bragg named Vandross," I said. "When he left the service he went to Harvard Law School."

Vandross smiled.

"Thank you for remembering," Vandross said.

Vandross closed the curtains over the two-way mirror, then reached into his right front hip pocket where his hand appeared to fumble around in search of something. For a moment I had the disconcerting notion he was looking for a pair of brass knuckles. Instead, he brought out a key, stepped around behind me, and unlocked my handcuffs.

"Sorry about the cuffs, General," Vandross said. "I hope your wrists are not too sore?"

I shook my head.

"No, no, they're okay," I said.

"Good," Vandross said. "Please have a seat."

"Thank you," I said.

I sat down in one of the steel chairs. I rubbed my wrists. The blood started to flow. I rubbed my throbbing left knee. It didn't help.

Vandross disconnected the tabletop microphone from its jack and sat down opposite me. He opened the briefcase and removed a thermos, two bottles of water, two styrofoam cups, and a bag of beef jerky.

"I assumed you would be hungry and thirsty, General," Vandross said. "What can I do you for?"

Hmm. First he takes off the cuffs, now he's offering me food and drink? What's going on here? I wasn't ready to let my guard down, but I also didn't see any harm in playing along.

"That thermos have any coffee in it?" I said.

"Indeed it does," Vandross said.

He opened the thermos and poured me a cup of coffee.

"Sorry I don't have sugar and cream," Vandross said.

"No problem at all," I said. "Don't use it."

"Jerky?" Vandross said.

"If you insist," I said.

He opened the bag of beef jerky and slid it over to me.

"You have an interesting interrogation style," I said.

"I'm honored to be in your presence, General," Vandross said. "Please call me Carl."

Wow. This guy might actually be on the level...

"Okay, Carl," I said. "Please call me Jack."

"Thank you, sir," Vandross said. "I performed a security check on the room while I was alone. It is fully soundproof. With the curtains closed and the microphone turned off, no one can hear or see us."

I considered this for a moment and took a sip of coffee. It was very hot and a good quality Sumatran blend. I took out a piece of jerky and offered it to Vandross.

"Would you care to join me, Carl?" I said.

"No thank you, General," Vandross said.

"Jack," I said.

"Sorry, sir," Vandross said. "The service misses you, Jack. How is General Jeffrey Bradshaw, sir?"

"Getting better," I said. "Thank you for asking."

Now I really was feeling pretty good about things. This might turn out in my favor after all...

Vandross took a cell phone out of his pocket and handed it to me.

"The phone is encrypted with the highest level AES using a Rijndael variant," Vandross said. "Please turn it on."

AES stands for Advanced Encryption Standard and is used by the United States military. I had a very small hand in its initial implementation when I worked with Kate's father, Milton Feynman, at NASAD. As far as I knew, NASAD still maintained all the military's communications systems. The Rijndael variant Vandross had referred to was a cipher. It was developed by two Belgian cryptographers and is a play on their names, Joan Daemen and Vincent Rijmen.

And Vandross was correct.

There was no higher standard.

"Phone's up and running," I said.

"Please go to FaceTime and push connect," Vandross said.

I did. After a moment a face came up on the cell phone screen. The face was the face of someone I knew. Maybe I was getting soft, or it was just the stress of the last few hours, but I found my eyes tearing up for the second time that day.

But that time they were tears of joy.

CHAPTER 33

The face on the iPhone's screen belonged to Jim Hart, the four star general who was my boss, and headed the Military Interagency Department of Special Operations/The Department/MOM/Ice Station Zebra/ That Whose Name Cannot Be Said Aloud. I had not seen nor spoken to General Hart in nearly two years, ever since I had gone on leave and brought Jeff home to my ranch.

Hart was sixty-five years old, but he didn't look it and never had - he always looked younger than his years. He had a handsome face, his cheekbones and jaw were sharply chiseled, and his steel grey eyes were fierce and intensely intelligent. His hair was close-cropped and sandy brown. His mouth, which always seemed to convey a look of deep concern, did so then. Hart was as tall as I was, but the iPhone screen only showed him from his strong shoulders and above. He was hatless and wearing a tan shirt with no visible insignia to mark his rank.

As usual, Hart also appeared to be on the move. To the left of his onscreen visage was what looked like the open window of an armored Humvee. Outside, a barren, dusty countryside rolled quickly by.

General Hart and my father were special ops soldiers together. They were best friends. They fought together in Africa, South America, and Viet Nam. In 'Nam, Jim Hart, barely conscious and bleeding to death after having taken three rounds to the chest in a firefight, had been carried by my father through five miles of dense jungle to a clearing where they were met by a Medevac chopper. The chopper airlifted Hart to a field hospital where he was treated and survived. Unbeknownst to Hart, my father had made that five mile carry while mortally wounded himself. My father made it into the chopper along with Hart, but didn't survive the flight.

Jim Hart says one of the few things he knows for sure in this life is that he would be dead if it hadn't been for my father's actions. I was as yet unborn on the day of Jim Hart's rescue and my father's death. But, since my birth, Jim Hart had always been there for me. He would call my mother once a month to check on me until I was old enough to talk myself, and then he would talk directly to me. At least once a year, Hart, despite his busy schedule, would take me on fishing or hunting trips, always telling me stories about my dad. My mother died when I was ten, and after that, my maternal grandparents raised me. While nothing could make up for never knowing my father, between my grandfather, Jim Hart, Kate's father Milt Feynman, and my two hundred year old journal of my paternal ancestors' writings, I believe I grew up with as much good fathering as anyone in my situation could have had a right to expect.

Jim Hart never pushed me into a career as a soldier, but knowing I was my father's son, he nurtured what he saw in me. Jim had been very close with Milt Feynman and it was Jim who had helped set up that relationship for me. It was also Jim who snatched Jeff and me from special forces fifteen years ago. Jeff and I had been working for Jim Hart and MOM ever since.

"Good to see you, General," I said.

"Good to see you, General," Hart said on screen.

"I'm not used to you calling me that yet," I said.

"You earned it son," Hart said, "you earned it."

"Where are you, sir?" I said.

"Congo," Hart said. "Trying to free a couple of dozen UNICEF workers taken hostage by Boko Haram. In other words, doing your job for you."

I didn't say anything. On the iPhone screen, three giraffes ran behind Hart's head.

"How's Jeff?" Hart said.

"Not so good," I said. "His twin was running around the ranch last night dodging an ambush."

"Jeff doesn't have a twin," Hart said.

"That's the problem," I said.

"Post-traumatic stress disorder's a bad disease," Hart said. "Damn Army is clueless when it comes to treating it. You did the right thing taking him home. Still, we've missed both of you. Glad to at least have one of you back on board."

I didn't like the sound of that.

"Back on board, sir?" I said.

"Don't be coy Jack," Hart said. "You know this is a serious situation."

"This meaning...?" I said.

"NASAD," Hart said. "What else would I mean?"

I didn't respond. I felt the back of my neck getting hot. I took a deep breath. I had assumed that Hart, who always knew everything there was to know about the men under his command, had somehow heard of my arrest and kindly decided to give me a hand. But this was beginning to look like something completely different. Hart was not above manipulating me, or anyone else who worked for him, for that matter. Of course, if you asked Hart, he would say he never manipulated anybody. He would tell you that if you thought that way, you were mistaking manipulation for motivation and that whatever he did was always for a soldier's own good and the good of the unit. As far as my individual case went, I always considered Hart's manipulations/motivations pretty harmless as I had my own way of dealing with my boss/dad on this issue. If Hart wasn't above manipulating me, well, then I wasn't above disobeying his orders from time to time, was I?

But the current situation was looking not only different from I what I had expected, but different from all my previous situations with Hart. Along with looking different, it didn't feel right and it didn't feel good either. Had Hart manipulated/motivated me, or at least played some role, in getting me involved with NASAD's problems?

Hart said, "You look like you're getting a little hot under the collar, son."

I was getting more than hot. I was building up a rage. But I didn't know why. It was as if my emotions were being driven by some unseen force. Was the idea that Hart was manipulating me that unseen force? It shouldn't have been. I mean, I was used to his antics, wasn't I? Maybe what was different that time was that I felt Hart's manipulations had caused me to leave Adelaide and Jeff at the ranch alone, thus putting not just me at risk, but potentially Adelaide and Jeff as well? I didn't really believe that was it, though. After all, wouldn't I have done what I did no matter what Hart may have concocted behind the scenes? Duty had called. Feynman and Lennon were dead. The engineers had been murdered. Wives and husbands and partners had buried their loved ones. Children had buried their parents. Our troops could be at risk.

Why was I getting so angry, then?

"If you say so, sir," I said.

Yikes. I had been trying to make light of his comment. But my words came out sounding like some obnoxious, whiny little brat. I couldn't remember talking like that. Ever.

Hart didn't flinch, however.

"Yes, I do believe I say so," Hart said. "Lord knows if anyone can tell when you're getting angry, it's me. Why, I think I probably witnessed one of the first tantrums of your terrible twos. And then there was that time..."

"If you're trying to ingratiate yourself with me, it's not working," I said.

That time my words sounded even more full of childish petulance and spite. It felt like some other being was taking over my body.

"My, aren't we touchy today?" Hart said. "What's the problem, son?"

His words sent me over the top. I knew it was nuts, but I wanted to reach through the screen and strangle him. I tried to calm myself. But it was a no go. Maybe it was the drugs Burnette had given me, or Jeff and the CheyTac, or the Kazakhs, or the fourth anniversary of Grace's death, or something else entirely. Whatever it was, it was bad.

"Problem?" I screamed. "Who said there was a problem?"

Screamed? Me? Oh man, that was not just bad. It was terrible. I was out of control. I was certifiable.

"Settle down, son," Hart said. "You're out of control."

What? Was Hart reading my mind now? I'm not proud of what transpired over the next few moments. But there had been nothing I could do to stop myself.

"I'm out of control?" I screamed. "No! You're out of control!"

Vandross seemed not to know what to make of my behavior. He looked very uneasy, maybe even worried. It takes a lot to worry a special ops major, even a retired one. Vandross got closer to me, made a move that was probably meant to calm me. Hart must have been watching what was going on through the iPhone camera, because before Vandross could actually touch me, Hart interrupted.

"Vandross. Leave him alone," Hart said. "I'll handle this."

I screamed, "You? You can't handle anything!"

"Take some deep breaths, son," Hart said. "You're having a stress reaction."

Stress reaction? Wasn't that exactly what Jeff had called my then current state? Hart's words, which were clearly intended to soothe me, had the exact opposite effect and only added more paranoia to the equation.

"What!?" I shouted. "You and Jeff have been talking behind my back, haven't you?! Admit it!"

"I haven't been talking to Jeff, Jack," Hart said. "Please, just breathe."

"I'll breathe just as soon as you tell me you had nothing to do with getting me involved in the NASAD situation," I shrieked.

Again, a part of me, most of me in fact, didn't care if he had gotten me involved or not. But something else was in control then. All I could do was go along for the ride.

"I'm not going to lie to you," Hart said.

"So, I'm right!" I howled. "You tricked me into all of this!"

"Well, I don't think 'tricked' is quite the right word," Hart said.

"You like 'dupe' better?" I roared. "How about 'con'? Does that work for you? Wait, I've got it. You 'hornswoggled' me. That's it."

Hornswoggled? I didn't even know I knew that word.

"Jack, listen to yourself," Hart said. "Hornswoggled? Who talks like that?"

"Me! That's who!" I wailed.

"Okay," Hart said. "I hornswoggled you. Just try to breathe okay?"

Then all of the sudden, I didn't know why, things changed almost as quickly as they had started. I felt myself calming a bit. Maybe it was because I had been able to get in a few deep breaths. Or maybe it was because I had just kept repeating the word 'hornswoggled' in my mind, trying to figure out where it came from. I remembered thinking that was what crazy people probably did, repeat nonsense words over and over in their heads, until, until...well I didn't want to think about what happened after until. I took a few more deep breaths. The anger lessened a bit more.

Hart said, "There you go. Just keep breathing."

I suddenly felt very, very weak. I slumped in my chair. I put my elbows on the table and cradled my head in my hands.

Vandross, apparently thinking quickly, took the iPhone from my hands and propped it against his briefcase so that its camera pointed at me.

Hart said, "Good, Jack. Just keep doing that. I'll tell you a little story."

I felt myself nod. I say 'felt myself' because it seemed like my body was still acting on its own. Like I was far, far away, and just an observer.

Hart said, "As you know, I've known Kate Lennon since she was born..."

Which was clearly another manipulation on Hart's part. I had absolutely no idea that Kate and Hart had known each other 'since she was born'. I also knew that Hart - because he was so sneaky, and again, made it his business to know everything there was to know - knew that I didn't have any idea either. Despite the calming I had felt just seconds before, I normally would have expected Hart's further manipulation to have re-enraged me. But, surprisingly, the manipulation had the opposite effect - I only felt even more drained, like some floppy, worn out rag doll, devoid of all energy and emotion. As drained and raggedy as I was, however, it wasn't in my nature to let such a comment go unchallenged.

"Stop right there," I said - it had been an effort just to make my mouth move, "how could I possibly have known that? I didn't even know Milt had a daughter."

Hart smiled the smallest of smiles on the iPhone's screen. I knew the little bastard wouldn't have smiled like that unless he had seen something in my face, or heard something in my voice, that led him to believe the worst was over, that I had escaped from whatever evil jinni had had me in its clutches. And then Hart, being Hart, apparently couldn't resist instantly shifting into his normal mode with me when I was feeling my absolute worst, but he knew, for all intents and purposes, I was safe. That normal mode was to give me an even harder time. He showed me no mercy.

"Wow," Hart said in his most disingenuous tone possible, "that surprises the heck out of me."

My head had started to throb. I squeezed it between my hands. It didn't help.

"Jesus Christ," I muttered softly. "You are such an asshole."

Hart laughed. Vandross looked at us like we were both crazy.

Hart said, "I have no idea why you would say such a thing."

"Screw you," I said. "Just go on, will you? I want to hear your little story."

Hart said, "Yes. Where was I?"

"You were saying you knew Kate since she was born," I said.

"Right," Hart said. "As you said, there was no way you could know that, since you didn't even know Milt had a daughter. Be that as it may, ever since Milt died, Kate has occasionally contacted me for advice. A year ago she asked me to look into some deaths at NASAD. Kate told me the FBI said the deaths were accidents, but she was convinced they were not. I spoke with the FBI, did a little nosing around on my own, and in what could turn out to be the biggest mistake of my career, also came to the conclusion the NASAD deaths were accidents. I advised Kate of what I had found. She begged me to reconsider. I did. But in the end, I found nothing to change my original belief. I told Kate I had done all I could, and what with it being a domestic issue, I really couldn't involve myself any further. Kate and I talked plenty over the last year, but it was always about other things, and the deaths never came up again. Then last week the three NASAD drone engineers were executed in Vegas, and all hell broke loose."

"Go on," I said.

"The executions, combined with the previous deaths, and some new information that came across my desk, made me concerned we had a significant problem, not just in regard to NASAD itself, but on the military side as well," Hart said. "So, my hand was forced. I had no choice but to get MOM involved. But I still didn't know how to get around the domestic issue. Then, out of the blue, I was handed a gift. Kate called and said she thought the situation at NASAD was much worse than before, and could in fact threaten the future of the company. Kate said she understood I couldn't get involved, but that she wanted to know if I could help her contact you. She said Paul and Milt worshipped you and had told her if they ever needed anybody in a dire situation, you were the one they'd turn to. I didn't tell her about my keen new interest in NASAD's problems or how I would love to have you back at work, but I did tell her how to find you."

My head was really throbbing by then. Every heartbeat seemed like an earthquake in my skull. I was so tired I had trouble sitting up. But I still wasn't going to let Hart keep trying to get away with saying whatever he wanted.

"That's not what Kate said," I mumbled. "She said she found me by contacting some of Paul Lennon's old friends."

"I think we can both agree that Paul was a friend of mine, can't we?" Hart said.

"Friends with an 's,'" I said. "How much you want to bet if I ask Kate she'll tell me she didn't talk to anyone but you?"

Vandross, who appeared to have been listening and watching carefully, seemed to have decided that things between Hart and I had stabilized enough so that he might hazard joining the conversation.

Vandross said, "I'll take part of General Wilder's bet."

Hart said, "Thanks. I appreciate your support, Vandross."

"I know a good bet when I see one, sir," Vandross said.

"Anyone who went to Harvard wouldn't know a good bet if it punched them in the mouth," Hart said. He paused for a moment, then addressed me. "Jack, you're right. Kate didn't talk to anyone else. But don't blame her. I told her not to tell you it was only me she talked with. I was afraid you wouldn't come if I was involved, which, is also of course why I didn't call you myself."

My energy level was falling lower and lower. It took everything I had in me just to continue the conversation.

"I'm not so sure you should have dragged me into this, sir," I said. "Adelaide needs me. Jeff needs me. You've got a good stable of talented people. You don't need me. And look at me. I'm a mess. It would probably be best if I turned around and went right back home to the ranch."

"I don't agree," Hart said. "What you call home is not a good place for you right now. You were rotting away up there. You need to do this. Believe me, it's for your own good."

There it was. Classic Hart/boss/dad. For my own good. Sometimes he was right, though. In all honesty, while I was fully committed to tending to Adelaide and Jeff, I had at times wondered whether devoting myself full time to them truly was the right thing for them, or me for that matter. Before I could think much more about that, I was distracted by the sight of a large baobab tree whizzing by in the Hummer's window.

There were about two dozen baboons sitting on the tree's limbs. The baboons were grooming themselves en masse. Even the babies were hard at work on whatever monkey was closest to them. I had never seen anything quite like it. Then the Humvee moved on, and the baboons were gone from view. I was left staring at a dry, parched landscape and an empty sky. As I watched the barren land roll by, I realized I had forgotten what I had been thinking about before I had seen the baboons and been so taken with what they were doing.

Oh, yeah.

For my own good.

Was it or wasn't it?

Whether it was or not, I knew I just didn't have the brain power to think about it just then. Besides, a new question had popped into my mind, one I really wanted answered. Hart had said something that just didn't seem to fit with everything else he was telling me.

I said to Hart, "You claimed to have told Kate you couldn't get involved in domestic affairs. It's not just you, is it though? It's all of us at Ice Station Zebra. Mind telling me why that excludes me?"

"You're on leave, Jack," Hart said. "Different animal."

"Different animal, huh?" I said. "So you're saying a guy on leave *can* get involved in domestic affairs? That idea been tested, or you just hoping it's so?"

"I find hope in the darkest of days, and focus in the brightest," Hart said. "I do not judge the universe."

"Leave the Dalai Lama out of this," I said.

"It's never been tested," Hart said. "But I promise I will take care of it if it becomes an issue."

I felt so weak just then that my arms collapsed under me and I hit my chin on the table. It was all I could do just to turn my head and lay it on its side.

"Yeah, yeah, yeah," I said groggily. "This can't be a good idea."

I rolled my eyes toward Vandross.

"How do you feel about this, Carl?" I said.

"Don't look at me," Vandross said. "I'm just a little ol' U.S. Attorney. Seems to me you need someone more along the lines of a Supreme Court justice on this one."

Hart said, "Shut up, Carl."

I said, "Don't you have any other guys on leave that can do this?"

"We need the best, Jack," Hart said. "We need you. I know what happened at the rest area. Kate would be kidnapped or dead if not for you."

"That was luck," I said. "Pure luck."

"No, it wasn't," Hart said. "Besides, there's something else. Something I didn't tell you yet. Something's happened that is going to make things very bad for Kate. She's going to need you."

By then I was almost asleep. My emotions, which had been so high a moment before, were almost numb, and my body was like a lump of lead. I had no idea why I just didn't slide off the table and chair and onto the floor.

"Something's happened, huh?" I said. "What?"

I heard Hart take a deep breath in and slowly let it out.

"Tell him, Vandross," Hart said.

Vandross appeared a bit reluctant, but I knew very few special ops majors who got where they were by disobeying direct orders from men like Hart. In fact, I didn't know of any except me. Vandross took a moment to steady himself, then spoke.

"We believe Dr. Lennon's children might have been murdered this morning," Vandross said. "The victims were stoned to death in an abandoned housing development near here."

A jolt of electricity went through my body. I tried to use it to power my muscles but could not. My muscles were flaccid, as if they had been turned into jelly. My mind was even more useless. Like all the circuits had been cooled into a nonconductive state. That was awful, horrible news and yet my feelings remained numb. In retrospect, I could see how it might have been a good thing. Who knew if I could have survived another shock that day? The logical part of my brain, however, continued to function on some minimal level. It told me I had to get to Kate. I tried to move again, but again nothing happened. All I was able to do was eke out one word.

"Stoned?" I said.

"It appears to have been done in accordance with Islamic ritual," Vandross said. "We're still waiting for more details, but reports from the crime scene place the children's time of death around 9:00 a.m."

"Where is Dr. Lennon?" I said, my words slurred.

"Waiting outside the substation," Vandross said. "The bodies of Dr. Lennon's children are currently at the morgue operated by the Los Angeles County Coroner's Office in Lancaster. The coroner still needs Dr. Lennon to make a final identification. Dr. Lennon refuses to go to the morgue without you."

Using every last bit of energy I could find - I still don't know where that energy came from - I slid myself out of the chair, crashed to the floor, and started crawling to the door.

Vandross, apparently thinking quickly again, picked the iPhone off the table and pointed its camera at me so Hart could follow the action.

Hart said, "Where are you going?"

I kept crawling. I wasn't getting very far, but that didn't stop me from trying.

"To help Grace," I mumbled. "You guys are barbaric. How can you make her wait? You should have told me before."

"You said Grace," Hart said. "I know Grace and Kate look alike, but you meant Kate right?"

"Grace, Kate, Kate, Grace," I said. "What does it matter? You're still barbarians."

"In case you don't remember," Hart said, "it was only a few minutes ago that you regained consciousness in that cell the FBI threw you into. We're moving as fast as we can."

"Not fast enough," I said.

Then I collapsed face first on the floor. I couldn't move my arms, but I did my best to keep moving forward by pushing off on my toes.

"Jack, you can't help anyone in your present state," Hart said. "Your body is in some kind of shock. Just let it rest for a minute."

"Uh uh," I said, a bit of drool escaping out of the corner of my mouth. "Rest later."

Then I passed out completely.

CHAPTER 34

When I woke up I was still in the Sheriff's Substation interrogation room, only then I was lying on my back on the metal table, my left leg dangling over the table's side. Vandross was standing over me, talking on the Rijndael AES variant encrypted iPhone. I realized I had been unconscious, but at that point, I didn't remember anything that had happened in the room prior to that moment, other than Vandross leading me inside the room after we had said goodbye to both Burnette and the substation's captain, and then taking off my handcuffs. I looked up at the clock on the wall above the curtains covering the room's window. It said it was 3:47. I didn't think Hart and Vandross would have left me lying on the table for twelve hours, so that meant it was 3:47 p.m., not a.m. Which also meant, even if I had been unconscious since I had entered the room, it couldn't have been for more than a few minutes.

"Looks like he's coming to," Vandross said into the iPhone.

"Let me talk to him," Hart's voice growled through the phone.

Vandross turned the iPhone around and pointed its camera at me. Hart came into view on the screen.

"Don't say a goddamned word," Hart said. "I've got things to say and you're going to stay put until I'm done."

What the hell is he so mad about, I wondered. Then everything that had happened earlier in the interrogation room all came flooding back to me. The strange interlude where I had felt possessed. The extreme weakness that had followed. And then Kate. Hart and Vandross had said Kate's children had been stoned to death. Hart could say whatever he wanted, but I wasn't going to hang around to listen.

"It'll have to wait," I said. "Right now I'm going to Kate."

I slid my body across the table to my left, pushed myself up, and dropped both feet to the ground. When my left foot hit the floor it felt like a jackhammer had smashed my reconstructed left knee. I took a step to the door, but when I did, my left leg yanked against something and I was unable to move it any farther. The yank also made my knee hurt much worse, like someone had tried to tear my lower leg off at the joint. I turned around to see what the problem was. My left ankle had been shackled with the handcuffs to the metal floor ring that was bolted to the floor under the table.

"This confirms it," I said. "You're both nuts."

"What did I just say, Jack?" Hart said. "Just shut up and listen for a minute."

"Vandross, gimme the key," I said.

Vandross didn't say anything, just backed away from me.

Hart said, "I'm sure if there's anyone who can take down Vandross while their leg is shackled it's you. But that's only if he lets you near him. Which he won't."

"We'll see about that," I said to myself.

I lunged at Vandross.

The cuffs held me back and I missed him by a good two feet. My lunge had been so forceful that my left leg pulled violently against the cuffs when I reached the end of their tether. My knee pain instantly became infinitely worse.

Hart said, "Listen to me, Jack. I don't know what you think I'm capable of, but one of those things is not hurting Kate. I promise you she's in good hands right now. It sounds cruel, but Kate's children are dead. There's nothing you can do for Kate right now that can't wait a few more minutes."

His words went in one ear and out the other. Because I wasn't paying attention to him. What I was doing was trying to figure out how to free my leg. I didn't think I could tear the bolt out of the floor. It looked like it was in there pretty good. The cuffs looked very strong too. I wasn't going to be able to break their chain. The only thing I could do was saw off my leg. I started looking for something to do that with.

Hart said, "Jack, do you really think you can handle this project alone? You're going to need help if you're going to assist Kate in fixing the problems at NASAD. The best thing you can do for Kate right now is to hear me out."

I knew Hart was saying something, but I still wasn't listening. I hadn't been able to find anything to saw with. I realized the only thing I had that I could use were my teeth. I sat down on the floor, pulled up my left pant leg, bent the leg as close to my mouth as I could, and tried to get my teeth in a position from which they could do some damage.

Hart said, "I admire your commitment, son, but that's not going to work."

Hart's words filtered through that time. He was right. No matter how I tried to twist all the parts of my body, I couldn't get in a position that would allow me to sink my teeth into anything meaningful. I didn't think it would work, but I felt it would at least be worth a try to see if I could slip my left ankle and foot through the cuffs. I took off my left shoe and sock, grabbed the steel cuff ring encircling my left ankle, and pulled it down toward my toes with all my might.

Hart said, "Jack, ask yourself. Would a sane person do what you're doing now?"

I kept tugging to no avail.

"Jack, look at me for Godsakes!" Hart yelled, his voice so loud it rang in my ears.

I looked up at the iPhone screen.

"What the hell do you want?" I said. "Can't you see I'm busy?"

Behind Hart's face I could see a brilliant blue African sky beginning to fill with dark storm clouds. Vultures were circling overhead. Hart's Humvee kept moving and the vultures disappeared from view.

Hart said, "You were in a gun battle, Jack. You were Tasered. Then you were drugged. Isn't it just a teensy weensy bit possible your thinking is off?"

"So now you're saying I'm weak, is that it?" I said.

I tugged some more on the cuffs. I started to think there was no way I was going to get the cuffs off with that technique. I looked around the room to see if there was anything else I could use.

"I'm not saying you're weak," Hart said. "You're the strongest man I know."

I didn't say anything, just kept looking around the room. I decided my best bet would be to try to break off one of the legs of the table, then wedge the leg into the metal ring that the cuffs were chained to, and then try to snap the cuffs' chain by forcing the chain against the ring.

"And I'm sorry about the cuffs," Hart said. "I saw no other way."

What did Hart just say? Did he actually apologize? General James Hart never says he's sorry.

"What did you just say?" I said.

"I said I was sorry about the cuffs," Hart said.

"What kind of shit are you trying to pull?" I said.

"What are you talking about?" Hart said.

"You just said you were sorry," I said. "Twice."

"You got a problem with that?" Hart said.

"It's not like you," I said.

"I'm sorry you feel that way," Hart said.

"There you go again," I said. "How am I supposed to concentrate on what I'm trying to do if you're going to force me to think about why you're behaving so inconsistently?"

"I'm behaving inconsistently?" Hart said. "What about you?"

"Don't change the subject," I said.

Hart sighed.

"You want us to take the cuffs off?" Hart said.

"What the hell do you think!" I said.

"You going to stay put if we do?" Hart said.

"Depends," I said.

"Depends on what?" Hart said.

"I'll decide after you take the cuffs off," I said.

"How about this," Hart said. "You promise me you'll give me two minutes, and we'll take the cuffs off."

"Two minutes?" I said.

"Two minutes," Hart said.

I looked at the table legs, the metal floor ring, and the cuffs. I figured it would take at least two minutes to rip the table leg off and try to break the chain. There was always the possibility it wouldn't work either.

"Two minutes," I said. "That's it."

"Vandross, take the cuffs off," Hart said.

Most other men might have been a little leery of approaching me at that moment, but Vandross didn't flinch. Keeping the iPhone camera aimed at me, he walked over to me, bent down, took the cuffs' key out of his pocket, and unlocked the cuffs.

I said, "Thanks, Vandross."

"You're welcome, sir," Vandross said.

I reached for my sock and shoe to put them back on, then looked up at the iPhone screen.

"Clock's ticking," I said.

"You're such an asshole," Hart said.

"I had a good teacher," I said.

"Touché," Hart said. "Alright then, please listen carefully. We have it from very reliable sources within the Chinese military and Chinese politburo that the Chinese invasion of Saudi Arabia will commence near dawn on the morning of June 16th. That is less than eleven days from now. CENTCOM and the joint service chiefs are convinced the Chinese would not make this move unless the Chinese thought they had an insurmountable edge."

"Eleven days?" I said. "Boy, the Chinese must really want that Saudi oil bad."

"It appears that way," Hart said.

"From what I heard, however, a Chinese offensive won't start for at least four weeks," I said.

"Who told you that?" Hart said.

"John Martinez," I said. "He called me this morning. You're not the only one who wants my help."

"Well Martinez was right about the four weeks when he talked to you this morning," Hart said. "But things have changed since then. The Chinese are moving faster than anybody anticipated. Eleven days is how much time we have left before the invasion commences."

"I guess I'll have to take your word on that," I said. "And by the way, Martinez told me about the Chinese insurmountable edge too. Jeff also knows about it."

Hart said, "Jeff?"

"Steve Kent called Jeff this morning," I said.

"He did?" Hart said.

"Would I say it if it wasn't true?" I said.

Hart seemed to think over what I had just said. He didn't look happy. I said, "Time's a wastin'. I suggest you do your thinking later."

"What do you mean?" Hart said.

"Your two minutes are almost up," I said.

Hart sighed.

"Our same sources in the Chinese military and Chinese politburo have also informed us that 'edge' is due to a weakness in something produced by NASAD," Hart said. "If we go to war without finding out what the edge is, we're looking at a potential catastrophe. We could lose the war and a lot of good men and women will die in the process. A *lot* of good men and women. Problem is, NASAD, as you know, is a key military contractor and they've got their hands in nearly every part of the Armed Forces. Aircraft, guided weapons, nukes, submarines, computer security, communications, drones, you name it. Not only do we have no idea what system has been compromised, but we have no idea how it may have been compromised. The edge might allow the Chinese to disable one of the systems, take control of a system, or maybe just eavesdrop on whatever we are doing. I'm sure you'll agree any of those options are completely unacceptable."

What had Hart just said? He believed the insurmountable edge emanated from something within NASAD? Hadn't I also considered earlier that day the possibility Dr. Nemo's grave risk, the Chinese insurmountable edge, and NASAD were all connected? Hart could have been wrong, but he'd made his guess after having access to a hell of a lot more information than I'd had.

I said, "Yadda, yadda, yadda. You don't think I already thought of that?"

"You did?" Hart said.

"Of course I did," I said. "I also already know what you're going to say next."

"You do?" Hart said.

"You're going to remind me again that MOM can't take the kind of direct action you would prefer in regard to NASAD since most of NASAD's operations take place on domestic soil," I said. "And then you're going to say you also won't call in the FBI, Homeland, or the NSA to help you with the edge - even though the FBI is already on the case - since you'd rather die than let the fate of the U.S. military be put in anyone's hands but yours."

I finished tying my shoe, then slowly stood up, carefully straightening my left leg as I did. Carefully straightening the leg didn't help and I hadn't really expected it to - searing pain enveloped my knee.

"Okay, close enough," Hart said. "I'm sure you'll understand then if I also remind you it is imperative that you take every precaution to keep the FBI and Homeland, or anyone else outside the military, from even getting wind the Chinese insurmountable edge might exist. I can't afford for anyone outside of MOM to come charging into this like a bull in a china shop and mess up any chance we have to fix this thing before it's too late. "

"Don't shoot the messenger," I said. "But that train already left the station."

"What does that mean?" Hart said.

Behind Hart's head I could see a herd of wildebeest. The wildebeest spooked as the Humvee raced past them. The wildebeest stampeded, kicking up a dust storm with their hooves.

"People outside the military already know," I said. "Those people may not be calling it the insurmountable edge, but they know that there's an enemy out there that might be able to turn something NASAD produces against us in a very destructive and lethal way."

"You're sure about that?" Hart said.

"As I just said, would I say it if I wasn't?" I said.

Hart nodded.

"Understood," Hart said. "Can you tell me who those people are?"

"I'm thinkin' about it," I said. "Not sure if you deserve to know or not."

"Jesus, Jack," Hart said.

"Alright, calm down, no reason to get your undies all in a knot," I said. "Kate knows. Dr. Nemo knows."

"Dr. Nemo as in 'Twenty Thousand Leagues Under the Sea' Nemo?" Hart said.

"That was Captain Nemo, sir," I said.

"Whatever," Hart said. "Who the hell is Nemo and how the hell does Kate know about the edge?"

For the first time in my life I sensed a significant amount of desperation coming from Hart. I could have teased things out a little longer, which would have been torture for him. But, since for all intents and purposes he was the only dad I had left, and I loved him, I just couldn't bring myself to do it.

"Dr. Nemo is a code name for someone who appears to be a NASAD employee," I said. "He, or she, left a voicemail for Kate. Let's call him a he for now since that's what my gut says he is. Nemo says something about a 'grave risk' in his voicemail. Nemo's grave risk pretty much matches what you've been saying about the insurmountable edge and the threat it represents. Dr. Nemo also sent Kate an encrypted file. I think we can infer from other statements Dr. Nemo made in his voicemail that that encrypted file will most likely tell us what Dr. Nemo believes his grave risk is. If we're lucky, the grave risk and the insurmountable edge will turn out to be one and the same. But the only way we'll know for sure is if we find Nemo or decrypt his file."

"Code name? Encrypted file?" Hart said. "What the hell is wrong with this guy? Why didn't he just come forward like a normal person would?"

"Dr. Nemo's afraid if he reveals anything he knows, he could run afoul of national secrets laws," I said.

Hart's face reddened and his nostrils flared. He looked like he wanted to kill something with his bare hands.

"Goddamned Homeland," Hart said. "Goddamned FBI. Bloody, goddamned NSA. If they weren't all so goddamned heavy handed and pigheaded in everything they do, I guarantee you this Nemo guy would have told us what he knows and we'd already have this thing licked."

"That's your department, sir," I said. "But it does kinda have a ring of truth about it."

"How we gonna find Nemo?" Hart said.

"I've already made finding Nemo my top priority, sir," I said. "If you can get my iPhone back to me, I'll send you Dr. Nemo's voicemail. Hopefully you can work up a profile based on it that will help us identify him. I'll also send you the encrypted file, but my hunch is we're not going to be able to crack it until Dr. Nemo gives us the key."

"Vandross will get your phone to you before you leave the Sheriff's Department," Hart said.

"Good," I said. "Are we done now, sir?"

"One more thing," Hart said. "While I said the insurmountable edge could reside in any of the weapons or systems NASAD provides to us, the majority of MOM's analysts believe we should be pursuing NASAD's drone subs as the edge's most likely source. I agree with the analysts. The drone subs are our best bet."

I didn't say anything.

"Cat got your tongue?" Hart said. "Not like you to not weigh in with your opinion."

At that point, I could have told Hart about my hunch the real issue was not the drone subs and that I thought the subs were just a diversion. But I didn't. Why didn't I? One, even though I had little doubt my hunch was correct, I wasn't sure I could adequately defend my position to Hart at that moment. Two, we had already gone beyond the two minutes I had promised Hart, and if I took a stab at defending my position, it would probably lead to an argument that would only further delay my rejoining Kate. And three, there was always the possibility Hart might believe I was so completely off base about my diversion theory, he would think about ordering me to pursue the drone subs, or at the very least attempt to interfere with the path I wanted to follow. Experience told me if I wanted to do things the way I wanted to do them, it was best to keep Hart in the dark.

I said, "I can see how the analysts would feel that way. The Ohios carry nukes, which make them a real threat, and all the dead engineers are from the NASAD drone sub division."

"Glad you agree," Hart said. "This Humvee's taking me to an airbase near Kisangani. From there I'll fly to the Persian Gulf to meet with Admiral Bagley on the Washington."

Admiral Bagley was chief of U.S. Naval Operations. The George Washington was a supercarrier.

"You hate carrier landings though, sir," I said. "Carrier landings are the only thing in the world that makes your nuts draw up into their sack."

"Thanks for broadcasting that, Jack," Hart said.

I looked over at Vandross.

"You didn't know?" I said.

Vandross shook his head.

I turned back to look at Hart.

"Sorry, sir," I said. "What's so important it's worth getting your testicles tied in a knot?"

"You done?" Hart said.

"Yeah," I said.

"I'm visiting Bagley because I need to convince him to take the drone subs offline," Hart said.

Since I'd already thought that the Navy would take the drone subs offline in response to the potential threat they represented in light of the problems at NASAD, I felt it was likely Bagley would do as Hart wanted. But, since I also didn't believe the subs were the edge, I didn't believe taking the subs offline would actually do much good.

I said, "Hopefully, Bagley listens to you, sir. I assume CENTCOM has been checking that all the drone subs' equipment and systems are in working order and there are no signs of sabotage?"

"Triple checking," Hart said. "Everything is clean so far."

"Great," I said. "I'll be going then.

"Going?" Hart said.

"Didn't you say a moment ago you had just one more thing and then told me that one more thing?" I said.

"Yes, I did," Hart said.

"Didn't you also just tell me we were working under a deadline?" I said. "Eleven days is what you said, sir. It's best if I get started right away, don't you think?"

"I was hoping you might tell me what you were you going to do," Hart said.

"You mean my plan?" I said.

"Yes, your plan," Hart said.

"Sorry, I thought that was kind of obvious," I said.

"Humor me," Hart said.

I sighed. I very badly wanted to get to Kate. I had also already given Hart much more than the two minutes he had agreed to. And, there really wasn't much point in telling what I planned to do next, because no matter what I had told him right then and there, I was still going to handle the investigation of NASAD in any way I wanted, and the way I wanted could change at a moment's notice. But Hart was being so nice, which was so unlike him, and he was, again, the only dad I had left, a dad I hadn't seen in so very long, and the poor guy was clearly under a lot of stress and seemed to very much want to know what I was going to do. So, really, what choice did I have?

I said, "Well, sir, as we discussed, my top priority is to find Dr.

Nemo, as, if he is real, we have a chance to quickly learn from him who is behind the problems at NASAD and possibly determine what the Chinese insurmountable edge is as well. But I will also be looking for who is behind the killings of the drone sub engineers, as it seems likely those killings and the insurmountable edge are related."

"Do you really need to find Nemo to determine that the drone subs are the insurmountable edge?" Hart said. "As I said, all of MOM's analysts are solidly behind the idea that the Chinese consider something about the drone subs to be their edge."

There he went again, spewing that nonsense about the drone subs. Again, to my mind, the drone subs were a diversion, which meant the insurmountable edge had to lay elsewhere within NASAD, though exactly where, I hadn't a clue. I definitely intended to investigate the drone subs, however. An investigation into NASAD's drone sub program might help lead me to the NASAD murderers, and the murderers themselves, in turn, might, if I applied the proper techniques, reveal to me the true nature of the insurmountable edge.

"Sorry, sir, I misspoke," I said, lying through my teeth. "I meant to say that Nemo might be able to tell us how the drone subs function as the insurmountable edge."

"Understood," Hart said. "Besides the murders of the drone sub engineers, won't you also be looking into the murders of Kate's children and the failed attempt to kidnap her?"

"I'll definitely look into those issues too," I said. "I believe we have to assume the attempt to kidnap Kate, and all of the murders of anyone associated with NASAD, including the murders of Kate's children, are related until proven otherwise. Solving any one of those crimes may do us just as much good in terms of confirming the details of the edge as finding Nemo. And, as long as when I find whoever is behind the murders I'm allowed to question them in any manner I deem fit, then I'm sure we'll get the answers we seek."

"You damn well better question them in any manner you deem fit," Hart said.

I looked over at Vandross.

Vandross said, "What are you looking at me for?"

"You also on board with 'in any manner in which I deem fit'?" I said.

"You're on leave," Vandross said. "You can do whatever you want."

"You speaking for the Justice Department or just yourself?" I said.

"For the department," Vandross said. "And I suggest you don't ask any more questions."

"Why can't I ask any more questions?" I said.

Hart said, "Shut up, Jack. It's been taken care of, okay? Just run with it."

"Okay," I said.

"Vandross, is there anything else we need to add before we send him into the fray?" Hart said.

Vandross said, "No, sir. We're good to go."

"Good luck, Jack," Hart said.

I was about to say goodbye to Hart then and there, but I stopped myself. I realized that as much as I truly wanted - needed - to go to Kate's side, it would be better for both Kate and me if I took an extra moment to run by Hart some of the more important questions that had been running through my head since the morning. Hart, even if he couldn't immediately provide an answer to me, had access to all of MOM's resources, and there was no one better at finding the answer to even the most difficult and vexatious of questions than MOM. I'm certain that if the team at MOM had been around in the fourth century B.C., they could have untied the Gordian Knot.

"Not so fast, sir," I said. "Before I go, I'd like to ask you, in regard to the NASAD murders disguised as accidents, did you ever think the deaths of Milt Feynman and Paul Lennon were part of the same chain?"

I saw Hart suck in his breath as he appeared to consider this.

"No," Hart finally said. "But I see your point. I can't believe I missed the connection."

"It happens, sir," I said.

"Not to me," Hart said.

"You were close to Milt Feynman, sir," I said. "Maybe that clouded your thinking. Milt's and Paul Lennon's deaths also occurred almost a year before the NASAD engineers began to die, so there was a separation in time as well."

"All true," Hart said. "But still no excuse."

"How about this then, sir?" I said. "You're old and getting older."

"Okay, Jack," Hart said. "I think we can stop there."

Behind Hart, I saw a lone zebra standing by the road. There was a small bird sitting on the zebra's head.

"In any event, I've been thinking about their deaths, sir," I said. "When my thoughts are a little clearer, I may need to ask MOM for help on that as well."

"Of course," Hart said. "Anything else?"

"Yes," I said.

I bent over, took off my right shoe, and rolled down my sock. I removed the empty foil bag that I had found on the dead Kazakh driver. I held the bag out where Hart could see it.

Hart said, "What's that?"

"Empty bag of pork rinds I took from one of the dead Kazakhs," I said. "It was right next to his Koran."

Hart shook his head.

"That idiot Special Agent Burnette is running around screaming we're up against Islamic terrorists," Hart said.

"Let him," I said. "I think the bag looks just like the kind of bag an airline flight attendant would hand out as a snack. Maybe the Kazakh ate the pork rinds on the plane and shoved the empty bag in his pocket or maybe he saved the rinds for later. Doesn't matter, though, because either way, I don't think he'd carry around an empty bag for long."

"So you think the Kazakhs had only been in the country a short time when you met up with them?" Hart said.

"Uh huh," I said. "I'd appreciate it if you could get someone looking for the plane they came in on."

"Consider it done," Hart said.

"Thanks," I said. "Kazakhs also had the same crucifix and cobra tattoo behind their ears as the mercenaries on the fire team that took down Jeff's crew in the Sudan."

"What do you make of that?" Hart said.

"Nothing yet," I said. "I'm still thinking about it. But I thought you should be aware."

Hart nodded.

"Anything else?" Hart said.

"Not right now," I said.

"Vandross will clear you with the FBI," Hart said. "Oh and Jack, make sure Kate doesn't discuss Dr. Nemo or his 'grave risk' with anyone, okay?"

"I think Kate is smart enough not to do that," I said. "But I'll remind her."

"I'll feel better if you do," Hart said. "Good luck, Jack."

Hart's image disappeared from the screen.

I turned to Vandross.

I said, "You're a busy man, aren't you Carl?"

"How so?" Vandross said.

"U.S. Attorney *and* working on the sly for MOM," I said.

Vandross smiled.

"It's a living," Vandross said.

"Until it gets you killed," I said.

Vandross smiled again.

"There's always that," Vandross said.

I shoved the foil bag back in where it had been inside my right sock and pulled my shoe on.

Vandross, watching me tie my laces, said, "You and General Hart appear to have a very complicated relationship."

"That's one way to describe it," I said.

"You're not related are you?" Vandross said.

"Related?" I said.

"Hart seems to talk to you like a father would talk to his son," Vandross said.

"You're a very astute observer, Carl," I said. "What else did you see?"

Vandross seemed not to want to answer.

"Go on," I said. "Don't be shy."

"Well," Vandross said, "you kinda did the same."

"I talked to him like he was my son?" I said.

"Very funny," Vandross said. "No. Like he was your father. You took liberties with the general most people wouldn't have dared hazard."

"Also very astute," I said. "It's a long story, Carl. One day maybe we can find the time to sit down over a cup of coffee and I'll tell it to you."

Vandross and I walked to the door together. Vandross took hold of the doorknob. I grabbed his arm and held it before he could turn it. He looked surprised.

I said, "One more thing."

"Yes, sir?" Vandross said.

"Think that stress reaction is going to do me in?" I said.

"No, sir," Vandross said quickly.

"You sound pretty sure of that," I said.

"I've had one," Vandross said. "I think all of us have had one at one time or another. Comes with the territory. With what we do and see, I don't think it can be any other way."

"No one talks about it, though," I said.

"No," Vandross said. "We don't."

I nodded and let go of his arm.

"Please take me to Dr. Lennon now," I said.

CHAPTER 35

Vandross led me through the double glass doors that served as the Sheriff's Substation's rear entrance. We stopped on an elevated concrete landing outside the building. The sun was at its apex and the sky was cloudless. The air was dry, hot, and still. I saw the Maybach parked in a corner of the station's asphalt parking lot. The asphalt looked like it was melting and waves of oily, vision distorting vapor rose from its scorching surface. I could hear the Maybach's engine idling.

The landing's stairs emptied onto the parking lot. Burnette and three of his agents were standing in the lot about thirty yards away from the stairs and in the shade of the substation's building. Burnette, who was smoking a cigarette, threw the cigarette on the ground and stubbed it out with his foot when he saw Vandross and me. Burnette then signaled to his three agents, and all four of them started walking towards us.

I said, "Carl, when Burnette and his dance team arrived at the rest area, I was pretty sure they hadn't come looking for the Kazakhs."

"They hadn't," Vandross said.

I raised my eyebrows.

"What were they doing then?" I said.

"Burnette wanted to be sure he was the first one who told Dr. Lennon her kids had been murdered," Vandross said. "Hart and I figured that since Burnette was at least partially responsible for the kids' safety, he wanted to try to soften any blows that might be coming his way due to his gross incompetence."

"Why did Burnette need five Crown Vics to deliver the message to Dr. Lennon?" I said.

"Who knows?" Vandross said. "To show he cared?"

"And Burnette never thought Dr. Lennon herself could be in danger?" I said.

"Burnette said he profiled the crime scene where the kids had been murdered and was certain whoever stoned the kids was not a threat to Dr. Lennon," Vandross said.

"Wow," I said. "Burnette is stupider than he looks. Which begs another question."

"And that is?" Vandross said.

"How do we know Burnette didn't foul up the identification of the kids' bodies?" I said, "Maybe the dead kids aren't Dr. Lennon's."

"I thought of that," Vandross said. "I checked with the FBI techs who had been at the crime scene. The bodies were badly mutilated, but they were the right size and age. One boy and one girl, the boy older than the girl. Hair and eyes matched Dr. Lennon's kids. The girl had a locket with her name on it, and the boy was carrying a cell phone that belonged to Dr. Lennon's son. FBI showed pictures of the kids' clothes to Dr. Lennon's brother, Freddy Feynman, and he said he recognized them. The boy also had a note pinned to his shirt. The note said, 'Dear Dr. Lennon, please accept this gift with our compliments.' It was signed by the 'Free Arab Islamic Jihad Militia.'"

"More grist for Burnette's bullshit terrorist theory," I said. "Only problem for him is those Kazakhs this morning at the rest area weren't terrorists."

"You can fool some of the people all of the time," Vandross said. "And all of the people some of the time...,"

"But, you can always fool Burnette all of the time," I said.

"Exactly," Vandross said.

"So if the bodies have been so clearly identified, why do we have to put Dr. Lennon through the torture of going to the morgue?" I said.

"Protocol," Vandross said. "Not official until there's a visual by a relative."

"Her brother Freddy refused to do it?" I said.

"Freddy said Dr. Lennon was already out here and there was no reason for him to travel such a long way when she could do it herself," Vandross said.

"Doesn't Freddy live near NASAD?" I said.

"He does," Vandross said. "In Malibu."

"That's like what, ninety minutes from here?" I said.

"Yep," Vandross said.

"That's screwed up," I said. "The body identification protocol itself is screwed up too."

"It is," Vandross said.

Vandross took my iPhone out of his suit jacket pocket and handed it to me.

"Sorry," Vandross said. "Almost forgot about this. I put my number in your phone in case you need to reach me."

I put the iPhone in my pants pocket.

"Thanks," I said. "What about my guns?"

"The three Sigs you took off the Kazakhs?" Vandross said.

"Finder's keepers, loser's weepers," I said.

"Hart and I think it's better legal-wise if you don't have a gun on you," Vandross said.

"Legal-wise?" I said.

"You prefer law-wise?" Vandross said.

"Nah," I said. "Legal-wise is good."

"It's not personal, General," Vandross said. "The State of California just isn't too receptive to military men packing heat off base. Wouldn't want some highway patrolman to give you a hard time."

I cupped my hand and spoke into it as if it was a cop's radio microphone.

"21-50 to headquarters," I said, using as deep a snarl as I could muster.

"Headquarters by," Vandross said.

I was surprised.

"You recognized that?" I said.

"Damn straight," Vandross said. "Broderick Crawford in 'Highway Patrol'. Series debuted in 1955. Clint Eastwood guest starred in one of the episodes."

"I'm impressed," I said. "General Bradshaw would be impressed too. He loves that show. You and Jeff would get along real well."

I felt the concrete landing tremble beneath my feet as Burnette and his three agents climbed the stairs below Vandross and me. Burnette's cheeks looked more red and puffy than they had before, his belly had swelled even larger, and there was a dark sweat stain circling the crown of his porkpie hat.

Burnette and the three agents surrounded us when they reached the top of the stairs. The other agents hung back a reasonable distance away from us, but Burnette moved in close enough to breach every boundary any normal person with a working sense of society's minimal requirements for proximity to other humans would have respected. Vandross and I backed away from him. I don't know about Vandross, but I moved too late to avoid a whiff of Burnette's scent. He smelled like he hadn't bathed in a week.

Burnette said, "You removed his cuffs Mr. Vandross. That's not a good idea."

Burnette snapped his fingers at the agent closest to him. The agent removed a set of handcuffs from where they were hooked on his belt and handed them to Burnette.

"Face the wall and put your hands behind your back, Wilder," Burnette said.

Vandross said, "That won't be necessary."

"With all due respect, it's protocol, sir," Burnette said. "We have a long ride to L.A."

Burnette turned around, pointed at a black, windowless van parked about ten yards away.

"Gonna be hot too," Burnette said. "Air conditioner in the prisoner area in the back of the van seems to be on the fritz."

"General Wilder is not going with you, Agent Burnette," Vandross said. "The Department of Justice has determined that the general was acting in the best interests of the United States when he valiantly saved the life of some of its citizens today. No charges are being considered now, nor will any be considered in the future."

"Excuse me, sir, but that's a very bad decision," Burnette said. "The Director of the FBI is personally following this case, and I have been ordered to take Mr. Wilder into custody. Maybe you'd like to talk to him."

Burnette took out his cell phone and thrust it at Vandross.

"Put that away please, Agent Burnette," Vandross said. "I'm afraid you're a little behind the eight ball on this one. I've already spoken to the Director. The two of us agree it is in everyone's best interests for General Wilder to continue in his role as security consultant to Dr. Lennon and NASAD. The Director also asked me to advise you that you're to give the general every accommodation and assistance he may request of you. Oh, and please stop referring to the general as Mr. Wilder. From now on, it's General Wilder to you. The general's record of service to this country demands nothing less."

I said, "Geez, Burnette, I wonder why the Director didn't tell you all that himself. Did you check your cell phone battery? Must be out of juice."

Burnette opened his mouth seemingly to speak, but closed it before saying anything. Unfortunately for me, however, Burnette had opened his mouth wide enough so that I couldn't help but notice that he had all sorts of food particles - they appeared to be mainly bits of beef and lettuce - stuck between his top teeth. Burnette, even after closing his mouth, kept looking like he was going say something, and we - Vandross, I, and the other agents - all waited expectantly for the momentous event. Ultimately though, nothing came out of Burnette's blubbery lips, and he just grimaced instead.

Burnette remaining silent was so out of character for him that I thought I might be dreaming for a moment. I pinched myself. It hurt. I was awake, or, as Jeff would have said if he had been with me, "Yet mad I am not...and very surely I do not dream."

I shook Vandross's hand.

"Thank you for your assistance, U.S. Attorney Vandross," I said.

"It was an honor to meet you, General," Vandross said.

I turned to Burnette.

"I forgive you for Tasering me in the back, Agent Burnette," I said. "I understand it's much easier not to fight like a man. I also forgive you for pumping me full of tranquilizer. You were right to be worried about what I might do to you and your team if I regained consciousness before you had me safely ensconced in one of the sheriff's cells."

I walked past Burnette and the other agents and continued down the steps. When I reached the bottom of the steps, I quickly texted Hart the files on my iPhone that contained Dr. Nemo's voicemail and coded message, then put the phone away, and set off across the parking lot towards the Maybach. The parking lot's asphalt was so hot it felt like it might scald my feet through the bottoms of my shoes. The Maybach's front passenger door opened and Mosi stepped out. I was happy to see Mosi was wearing his shoes again, as I shuddered to think what would have happened to the soles of his feet if he hadn't been.

Mosi opened the Maybach's right rear door for me.

"Thank you, Mosi," I said.

"You are welcome, General, sir," Mosi said.

A black Suburban of the type favored by SWAT teams suddenly pulled up next to the Maybach. The SUV's windows were heavily tinted and I couldn't see inside. There was a federal license plate under the SUV's back bumper, but, besides the plate, there were no other features to identify any organization that might claim ownership of the vehicle.

Mosi nodded at the SUV.

"That's our new escort," Mosi said.

"Different squad than Burnette's?" I said.

"Very different, sir," Mosi said.

I stepped into the Maybach, sat down on my seat, and closed the door. Kate was in the seat next to me and looked much worse than when I had left her hours before. Her beautiful face was pale, her features devoid of any expression, and her blue eyes rimmed with red and nearly glazed over. Tears stained both cheeks. She barely breathed.

It seemed to take a moment for Kate to realize I was sitting next to her, but when she did, she leaned across her seat towards me, put her head on my shoulder and her arms around me. She held on tightly. I put my arms around her and held her as well. Her cheek was both hot and wet against my neck. Her chest was warm against my side.

"Kate, I'm sorry I didn't get here sooner," I said. "I can't imagine what you're going through."

"They wanted me to identify my children's bodies," Kate said. "I told them I wouldn't go to the morgue without you."

"I understand," I said.

"I really don't think I can do it though," Kate said.

"We'll get you through it," I said.

"What kind of animal stones children to death?" Kate said.

I didn't say anything, just held her tighter.

I knew the answer to her question, however.

What kind of animal stones children to death?

An animal that would soon wish it had never been born.

CHAPTER 36

The Maybach pulled out of the Lancaster sheriff's substation, made its way to Avenue I, then headed west. Our new SUV escort followed right behind. Kate had withdrawn into herself again and was sitting in a fetal position up against the Maybach's door. I felt it best to leave her alone. I took out my iPhone and punched up a map of our route to the coroner's office. According to the map, the drive would take about fifteen minutes. I then used the phone to find out as much as I could about the Lancaster morgue in the hope I would be able to make the process as easy as possible for Kate when we got there.

When I was done with my research, I looked out the Maybach's window at the surrounding scenery. We passed through residential areas, then a commercial section with a nail spa, pawn shop, Power of Praise Ministry, AutoZone, IHOP, McDonald's, Jack in the Box, and a Subway sandwich shop. As we got closer to the morgue, my side of the street took on a different kind of desolation. It was lined by dead weeds and barren trees. There were crows in the trees' branches. The only structures were abandoned wood buildings. The buildings were as dry as kindling and sat on vast sand covered, otherwise empty lots. A jackrabbit scampered across the dunes.

Kate very softly said, "Elizabeth still hasn't answered any of my texts."

I turned to look at Kate. She was staring numbly down at her iPhone. She seemed to be in a trance, her face drained of all emotion.

"Kate, who's Elizabeth?" I said.

Kate didn't react. It was as if she couldn't hear me.

"Kate, who's Elizabeth?" I repeated.

That time Kate startled. She turned and looked up at me.

"You know Elizabeth?" Kate said.

"No," I said. "Who is she?"

"Elizabeth Wells," Kate said, "She's the children's nanny."

"Elizabeth was taking care of your children today?" I said.

"Yes," Kate said. "I left them with her yesterday and she wasn't supposed to go off duty until I got home today."

"I'm sorry Kate," I said. "I didn't know about Elizabeth. No one mentioned her to me."

"I told the FBI," Kate said. "They're supposed to be looking for her."

"Then she wasn't...," I said.

"No," Kate said. "Elizabeth wasn't with my children when the sheriff found them. I've left her voicemails and text messages. She hasn't responded to any of them."

"Does the FBI know when the last time was that anyone saw Elizabeth?" I said.

"The FBI said my housekeeper told them Elizabeth left at around 7:30 this morning with the kids in one of my cars," Kate said.

"That sounds kind of early," I said. "Does she often take the kids out that early?"

"Sometimes, yes, especially since school is out for the summer," Kate said. "I give Elizabeth a lot of latitude in deciding what she thinks the children will like to do. She recently took them fishing and they left at 5:00 a.m. It was still dark outside when they drove away."

"Does the housekeeper know where Elizabeth was taking the kids today?" I said.

Kate shook her head.

"The only thing Elizabeth told my housekeeper was that she'd be back by 6:00 p.m.," Kate said.

"What about the car?" I said. "Did the FBI find it?"

"If they did, they haven't said anything to me about it yet," Kate said. "I told the FBI what kind of car it was and I gave them the license plate number. They said they would look for it."

"That's good," I said. "Did you give the FBI Elizabeth's cell phone number too?"

"Yes," Kate said. "The last thing the FBI said was they were trying to locate her phone, but that it wasn't showing up anywhere on the system."

"Not sure we can make much of that," I said. "It could just mean her battery is dead."

Kate's eyes narrowed slightly.

"Do you really believe that?" Kate said.

"It's better than the alternative," I said.

"I think you're trying to spare my feelings," Kate said. "What you really believe is that Elizabeth was also killed."

"I didn't say that," I said.

"But what if she was, Jack?" Kate said.

"It'd be horrible," I said.

Kate nodded.

"Why would anyone kill my children and their nanny?" Kate said.

I sighed.

"I wish I knew, Kate," I said. "I wish I knew."

"Yes," Kate said. "I wish I knew too."

Kate leaned her head back in the seat and closed her eyes. Her face, which had become slightly animated during our conversation, suddenly looked depleted once again, her beautiful features drawn and slack.

The Maybach rolled on past more vacant lots, the U-shaped shoulders between the lots and the highway littered with broken glass, empty beer cans, and dried out tumbleweeds. I thought about Kate's nanny. Was the nanny missing or was she dead? Was the nanny in on the killings? Whether she was or wasn't, I struggled to make sense out of the killings of Kate's children.

Vandross had said the killings had most likely taken place early that morning. 9:00 a.m. was the current best guess, he had said, and that was well before the Kazakhs had tried to kidnap Kate. It was nearly impossible to believe that whoever had hired the Kazakhs to kidnap Kate wasn't also behind the killings of her children. But if the Kazakhs' bosses had had the children killed, why hadn't they simply killed Kate as well? Had I been wrong about what the Kazakhs had intended to do at the rest stop? I didn't think so. The van at the rest stop had been outfitted for a kidnapping, not a murder. Also, if the Kazakhs had wanted to kill Kate, their best course of action would have been to shoot her with a rifle from the van and be done with it. They wouldn't have bothered to take up the positioning they had, a positioning that was clearly meant to facilitate a capture, not an execution. And since the Kazakhs hadn't killed Kate, didn't that mean the Kazakhs' bosses must have wanted something out of her?

What could that something be?

Something Kate knew?

Something Kate had?

Both?

But...

If the Kazakhs' bosses wanted something out of Kate, wouldn't they hold the children as hostages? What more effective way was there to get a mother to talk than to threaten to harm her children?

They had had Kate's children killed, though.

It didn't add up.

My head felt like it was spinning.

I took a few deep breaths and tried to relax for a moment. But as soon as I started to relax, I remembered Jeff still owed me a call to explain his strange, disconcerting text message about Adelaide. I re-checked my iPhone for any emails, messages, or voicemails from him. There was nothing. I began to worry.

The worry quickly turned to guilt, however.

Who was I to be so concerned with my own relatively petty issues when the children of the woman sitting next to me had just been murdered?

Manu suddenly slammed on the brakes, launching both Kate and me forward, our bodies straining against our seat belts. I looked up to see a coyote walking across the street in front of us. I quickly craned my head around, worried that our Suburban escort, following as closely as it was behind the Maybach, might hit us. But the Suburban was slowing down smoothly, seemingly effortlessly, and was never in danger of making contact with us. Manu, it appeared, had been right. Whatever team was behind the SUV's tinted windows probably really was much different than Burnette's squad, and different in a good way.

I turned to Kate.

"You okay?" I said.

She nodded.

The Maybach hadn't moved yet. The coyote was still blocking us as he continued his journey across the asphalt toward the desert on the other side of the road. The coyote was mangy, underfed, and his jaw seemed much too big for his skull. When he reached the other side of the road, he stopped for a moment and looked at us with his small yellow eyes. He howled, yipped, and yelped in his strange, indecipherable coyote language, then scampered off and almost instantly disappeared into the sagebrush.

Manu got the Maybach moving again, but suddenly stopped when another coyote, this one with two pups in tow, exited from the desert. The three animals followed in the footsteps of the first coyote, making their way across the road and then disappearing into the brush. Manu waited a moment, and when no more coyotes made themselves visible, started the Maybach rolling.

The mother coyote and the pups made my thoughts turn back again to Kate's nanny. It was an ugly notion to consider, but when all was said and done, wasn't the nanny the most likely candidate to have taken Kate's children? It would've been easy for her. The nanny had access to the children, the children trusted her, and no one would suspect anything was amiss until long after her crime had been committed. The nanny would have had to have been a real monster to stone the children to death, but there were monsters in the world.

If the nanny had truly killed the children, I doubted we would ever find her. Everything about the murders of NASAD's engineers, the probable murders of Feynman and Lennon, and the attack by the Kazakhs earlier that morning suggested a well organized, well financed enemy. An enemy like that would have whisked the nanny out of the country hours ago, and she would have had by then a new, untraceable identity - or have been re-united with her old identity if the one she had been using while employed by Kate was fake - but either way, she was most likely lost for good among the vast human seas of the planet Earth.

The more I thought about the nanny, however, the more I began to have my doubts about her complicity. I had a hard time imagining that Kate, with all the resources she had at her disposal, wouldn't have had the nanny carefully and completely vetted before she hired her. Then was not the time to ask Kate about the nanny's vetting, however, and I made a mental note to ask her about it later.

I began to focus on the insurmountable edge and what it could be. It had to be something all encompassing didn't it? Something that could bring the entire U.S. military to its knees? Something that could disrupt our weapons' guidance systems perhaps? Or interfere with command and control of our troops? Or maybe allow the Chinese to intercept our communications and thus anticipate our every move?

That last thought was as far as I got at that moment, because just then I was stirred from my reverie by gentle contractions of the muscles on the right side of my body, contractions I realized were due to the action of centrifugal force. I looked up.

The Maybach was turning left on 60th Street.

The coroner's office was very close.

Up to that moment I had been so concerned about what I would do to help Kate when we got to the coroner's office, that I must have been suppressing my own unconscious emotions about what was going to happen once we arrived there. But right then, I saw myself standing next to Kate as she identified the bodies of her dead children, and a feeling of dread began to rise within me. It rose slowly, but inexorably, and quickly became excruciating.

CHAPTER 37

Manu parked the Maybach in a space in front of the coroner's office and our SUV escort slid in next to us. By then it was about 4:30 p.m. - nine and a half hours since I had first spotted the Maybach on my ranch - and the sun a yellow blaze suspended in the cyan skies above Lancaster.

The coroner's office itself was part of the L.A. County coroner system and occupied a box-like trailer. The trailer was just where my iPhone had said it would be - plunked down in a corner of the large asphalt parking lot that lay behind a tall multi-storied building. The tall multi-storied building had once been the home of Lancaster's High Desert Hospital. The hospital had long since moved out, and the building then housed the offices of various business enterprises, including a facility for day surgery and urgent care, a flower shop, and, most importantly for us, the morgue.

I got out of the Maybach, circled the rear of the car to Kate's door, opened it, and helped her out. I gave our SUV escort a quick check. I still couldn't see inside the vehicle, and no one got out. Shouldn't they be coming with us, I thought? Wasn't it possible whoever had sent the Kazakhs after Kate that morning was still hunting her? Then, out of the corner of my eye, I caught movement on top of the multi-storied building. I turned to look. There were two FBI snipers on the building's roof keeping a careful watch on Kate and me. More proof, as far as I was concerned, that our new FBI escort was a much better organized and run unit than Burnette's Busby Berkeley squad.

I gently put my arm around Kate's shoulder and led her through the scorching heat and dry desert air into the coroner's trailer. The interior of the trailer was typical of county offices throughout America. It had a steel desk, some worn couches, dirty windows covered by warped Venetian blinds, multiple cork bulletin boards on every wall - sun bleached notices to the public regarding the coroner's rules and regulations were tacked to the boards - and a little white plastic disc with red clock hands sitting on top of an ancient computer monitor. The little white disk also had the words 'Back at' stenciled on it, and the red clock hands were set to 4:55 p.m. At least the air conditioner was on.

"You would have thought the FBI would have told the coroner's staff we were coming," I said.

"Maybe they did," Kate said. "Maybe the staff just didn't care."

Kate closed her eyes, put her face in her hands, drew in a long breath. She looked like she was trying to do all she could to hold back a flood of tears from bursting forth.

"Four fifty-five is almost half an hour from now," Kate said. "I can't wait that long."

"We're not going to wait, then," I said. "The morgue is in the old hospital building. We should be able to go directly there. Come on."

We left the trailer, walked across the parking lot - the heat again burning the soles of my feet through my shoes - and entered a lobby in the back of the multi-storied building through the lobby's wide double glass doors. The lobby was two stories high, its walls covered with faded yellow wallpaper, and its floor a checkerboard of interlocking squares of deeply scratched black and white vinyl tile. The air was hot and stale and had a vague medicinal smell that seemed to be a mixture of alcohol, formaldehyde, and iodine. The light, which was dim, came from plastic globes mounted on the ceiling. The globes appeared to have once been white, but were then covered in a brown sooty film.

The flower shop my iPhone had told me about was on the right side of the lobby, about thirty feet away from where Kate and I stood. There were red roses, white carnations, and yellow tulips on shelves lining the shop's walls. The flowers were dry and wilted and looked as if they had been there for months. There were no customers, but there was a girl in a stained blue smock behind the sales counter. The girl, who looked to be about sixteen years old, had pallid white skin, spiky black hair with pink tips at the end of the spikes, a silver nose ring, and black lipstick. Her ears were covered by big chartreuse headphones that were connected to an MP3 player. The girl was moving spasmodically, and her eyes, wreathed in black eye shadow applied in a raccoon-like style, were closed. I assumed her spasmodic movements were somehow being provoked by the sounds inside the headphones.

"Kate," I said, "I assume the morgue is in the basement, but I'm not sure how to get there. Do you want to wait here while I look around, or do you want to come with me?"

"Why don't we just ask the girl in the flower shop for directions?" Kate said.

"Not sure that would be a good idea," I said.

"Come on," Kate said. "She's the only one here."

Kate and I walked up to the girl.

"Excuse me, miss," Kate said. "I'm wondering if you might be able to help us with some directions."

The girl spasmed a few times, but otherwise there was no response.

I said, "Miss, would you mind turning down the music for a moment so you can hear us?"

Still nothing.

I reached forward, grabbed the cord that connected the girl's headphones to her MP3 player, and pulled out the plug. The girl's eyes, which were a dull grey with specks of red and green - a coloration I had mercifully never encountered before - shot open.

"What the hell is wrong with you?" the girl said.

"Where's the morgue?" I said.

"What's a morgue?" the girl said.

I hesitated for a moment, uncomfortable answering that question with Kate by my side. Kate, however, perhaps sensing my discomfort, or maybe driven by her own frustration with the girl's seeming thick headedness, said sharply, "A place where they keep dead people."

The girl did something with her mouth that I assumed was her attempt at a sly smile, but to me only made her appear to be even more moronic. Her smile also revealed a set of crooked black teeth. I couldn't tell whether her teeth looked like they did because they had been smeared by her lipstick, or because they were rotting away.

"Somebody you know died, huh?" the girl said. "You wanna buy them some flowers?"

Kate and I exchanged a look.

"No, we don't want to buy any flowers," Kate said. "Just directions, please."

"Why would I know where they keep dead people?" the girl said.

I said, "The morgue is someplace in this building. Do you know where it is, or not?"

"There's dead people in this building?" the girl said. "Like right now?"

"Let's try someone else, shall we?" I said to Kate.

Kate nodded. We returned to the lobby. There were three corridors that extended off the lobby, one center, one right, and one left.

"Your choice," I said.

"How about the center one?" Kate said.

I took Kate's hand and we walked down the center corridor until we came to a point where the corridor jogged left, then dumped us into a different lobby. The new lobby had thick glass double doors that opened onto the front of the building. The lobby didn't have a flower shop, but it did have a desk with a plaque on top of it that said 'Information'.

A woman sat on a swivel office chair behind the Information Desk. The woman appeared to be in her mid-fifties, had bleached blond hair piled in a stiff beehive, heavily pancaked makeup over what appeared to be pale blotchy skin, very long fingernails on which someone had painted little red ladybugs with black polka dots, and an overly plump body that she had shoved into a shapeless purple dress. She appeared to be engrossed by something on her cell phone screen.

"We better not get too close to her hair," Kate said. "We might get stung."

Kate smiled weakly as she said that. Very weakly. My heart sagged at the thought of how hard it must have been for her, and how much effort she must have expended, in trying to add some lightness to the nearly unbearable situation she was being forced to live through at that moment.

"Don't look at me like that," Kate said.

"Like what?" I said.

"Like you're taking pity on me," Kate said. "If I think you're pitying me, it will make it even more impossible for me to get through this."

"Sorry," I said. "I won't do that anymore. It's just that..."

"Yes, I know," Kate said. "I was looking pitiable. But I'm going to stop looking that way since I'm going to stop pitying myself, at least for the moment. I owe my children this last duty and I'm going to get it done."

"Got it," I said.

We walked over to the Beehive Lady. I leaned in close to her and smiled.

"Ma'am?" I said.

The woman remained fixated by her cell phone and didn't look up.

"Seems like it's going to be a toss up," Kate said.

"As to who is going to be more unhelpful?" I said. "Flower Shop Girl or Beehive Lady?"

"Um-hmm," Kate said.

Kate snatched the cell phone out of the Beehive Lady's hands.

"You're a quick learner," I said to Kate.

"Thanks," Kate said.

Beehive Lady looked at Kate, her eyes wide, her mouth curled in a snarl.

Beehive Lady said, "Are you out of your mind?"

Kate showed me what was on Beehive Lady's cell phone screen. Two cats were having some kind of swimming race in a pool.

"I didn't know cats could swim," I said.

"Neither did I," Kate said, then added to Beehive Lady, "The morgue. Where is it?"

"Give me my phone back," Beehive Lady said.

"Directions first," Kate said. "Then phone."

Beehive Lady sneered.

"Won't do you any good," the lady said.

I said, "Why not?"

"It's closed," the lady said and gave a self-satisfied chuckle.

"When did it close?" I said,

"About an hour ago," the lady said.

"When does it reopen?" I said.

"Six a.m.," the lady said.

"What happens if somebody dies in the meantime?" I said.

"What?" the lady said.

"What happens if somebody dies in the meantime?" I said. "Do they wait in the lobby with you?"

"You're a couple of goddamned smart asses aren't you?" Beehive Lady said.

Kate said, "No, we're not a couple of goddamned smart asses. He's a general in the United States Army and I'm a physician. And as a physician, I know how morgues work. Somebody must be attending it, whether it's closed to visitors or not."

"What's the big rush?" Beehive Lady said.

"The big rush is my children have been murdered and their bodies are now in your morgue," Kate said. "I'm not waiting until morning to identify them."

"Somebody's there," the lady said, "but they won't help you." She sneered again.

Kate had just told Beehive Lady her kids were dead and this was how she the lady was treating her? Had the world gone completely insane while I had been cooped up on my ranch?

"Ma'am," Kate said to the lady, "whether whoever is attending the morgue helps us or not is none of your business. Your business is to provide information, just like it says right there on your plaque. So, unless you want me to shove this cell phone up your goddamned fat ass, you'll tell me how to get to the morgue and do it now."

"You wouldn't dare," the lady said.

Kate positioned the cell phone in her right hand so that one end of it was protruding between her thumb and forefinger, and then seemingly gripping the phone as tightly as she could, she circled around the desk to get at Beehive Lady. The lady's eyes went wide again, only this time I assumed from fear rather than indignation. She grabbed the bottom of her chair with both hands and seemed to try to shove her ass down onto it, as if somehow that would protect her ass from Kate's onslaught.

"You're crazy!" the lady said. "Chill, okay?"

"Chill?" Kate said. "Aren't you a little old for that kind of language?"

"What are you implying?" the lady said.

"I'm not implying anything," Kate said. "I'm just suggesting you use more age appropriate language."

"How old do you think I am?" the lady said.

"Eighty? Eighty-five?" Kate said.

"Screw you," the lady said.

Kate moved closer to her and menacingly pointed the cell phone at her.

"Okay, okay," the lady said. "You want to waste your time, it's not my problem. Take that corridor on the right until you get to an elevator bank. Take the elevator to the basement. Turn right again. The morgue will be in front of you."

The corridor she spoke of was on the opposite side of the lobby from the corridor from which Kate and I had entered.

"Thank you," Kate said.

"Can I have my cell phone back?" the lady said.

"Sure," Kate said.

With a backward flick of her wrist that sent the cell phone spinning, Kate tossed the phone high above Beehive Lady's head. The lady caught it with both hands, rather artfully I thought, as it fell back to earth. Needs must when the devil drives.

"Just remember I told you so when you don't get anywhere," the lady said.

"We'll do that," Kate said.

Kate and I strode off towards the corridor that would take us to the elevators to the morgue.

"What kind of selection criteria do they use to hire people around here?" Kate said. "Laziness? Meanness? Disagreeability?"

"I'd say it's all of those," I said. "Plus a proclivity for poor grooming choices?"

"I bet Cruella de Vil wrote the HR manual," Kate said.

"I wouldn't doubt it," I said.

"You know what?" Kate said. "We should invent a new app."

"What would it do?" I said.

"Tells you not only how to find a place, but also warns you about all the foul creatures you'll encounter within it," Kate said.

"We'd probably sell a million of 'em," I said.

We reached the elevators and I pushed the down call button. The middle elevator doors shot open and an unseen bell made a high-pitched clang. We entered the elevator, the doors closed, and we began our descent.

CHAPTER 38

The elevator reached the basement and the doors slid open. Kate and I found ourselves staring out at an empty hallway and were immediately met by a blast of very cold air and painfully bright fluorescent light. The odor of formaldehyde was much stronger than when I had first detected it in the upstairs lobby. The hallway was utterly silent, and the silence, coupled with the fact there were no shadows due to the intense lighting, made everything seem timeless and unreal.

We stepped out of the elevator. The basement floor beneath our feet was brown linoleum and bore the scuff marks from what seemed like a millennium of passing shoes. The walls were lime green and the paint was peeling. The low hum of ventilating machinery appeared to emanate from all directions.

To our right was a set of swinging double doors. The doors were made of scratched and dented pale oak. Small windows were set in the center of each door at about head height. The windows were so grimy it was impossible to see through them. The word 'MORGUE' was written in big, black, blocky letters on the wall next to the left door.

I made a move to enter the doors, but Kate reached out, grabbed my arm, and stopped me.

"I'm sorry, Jack," Kate said. "I thought I could be strong, but I just don't see how this can be happening. It was only yesterday when my kids were running around the house playing hide and seek. When I told them I had to go on a trip, they hugged me and kissed me and said they'd make a welcome home banner for me even though they knew I'd only be gone a day and a half."

"Look," I said. "Maybe we shouldn't do this right now. Maybe we can wait until tomorrow, or maybe even find another way to handle it."

Kate seemed to consider what I had said for a moment, then shook her head.

"No, I have to do it, and I have to do it now," Kate said. "My children need me."

We walked through the swinging doors and entered a room that served as the morgue's antechamber. There were three empty white plastic chairs lined up against the right wall of the antechamber and there was no sign of human life. The room was about ten by twelve feet in size, its walls a deeper shade of green than the walls in the hallway, and its floor a black linoleum even more scuffed than the hallway's floor. Across from us was another set of swinging double doors. The doors were made of ancient and damaged oak and looked exactly like the doors we had just walked through, except that they didn't have any windows. 'No' was written on the left door, and 'Admittance' on the right.

"Last chance to turn back," I said.

"No," Kate said. "We're going in."

I took Kate's hand, and with the elbow of my free arm, shoved open the new set of doors. We found ourselves in the morgue itself, a vast windowless room with a high ceiling. The light was dim and had a grayish cast to it that was almost mist-like. It was much colder inside than it had been in the hallway, and the smell of formaldehyde was stronger still. Three stainless steel autopsy tables were lined up in the center of the room. At the head of each table was a weighing scale. An organ bucket was attached by a bracket to the bottom of each scale. Above each table hung a ceiling mounted halogen bulb lighting system. The lighting systems had control arms that both rotated and moved up and down so that any procedures being performed by the forensic pathologist would be adequately illuminated. Hand washing stations lined one wall and banks of storage drawers used for the corpses lined the opposite wall. The floor was damp and made of cement, and there were drains set in it at regular intervals. I didn't want to think about what kinds of things had been washed down those drains.

Only one of the halogen lighting systems was currently in operation. It was suspended above the dissecting table farthest from the doors through which Kate and I had just entered. A dead body lay on the table and a small man in a white lab coat was hunched over the body. The small man's coat was stained with blood along with other unidentifiable yellow and green fluids and he was standing on a stainless steel footstool with thick black rubber caps on each of its four legs. The man was washing the body and appeared to be absorbed in his work. The water the man was washing with came from a hose that had been clamped to a fitting extending out of the ceiling. The spray from the hose was so loud I could hear it from across the room.

"Kate, would it be okay if I go over first and take a look at what the man is working on?" I said.

Kate nodded.

I walked over to the table and circled around it so that I might engage the man face to face. Perhaps the sound of the water spray had muffled my approach, or perhaps the man was so engrossed in his work that he'd had no room to pay attention to anything else, but whatever the reason was, the man seemed not to be aware of my presence and just continued washing the dead body on the table. Up close, I could see the body being washed was not one of Kate's children, but rather that of a white-haired and very old man.

The man in the white lab coat, however, appeared to be middle-aged. The name tag on his coat said 'Dr. Dimguiba', with no first name or anything that would identify his job title. The man had a round face, deep set eyes, and dark brown skin. His hair was as black as obsidian and cut short. He wore tortoiseshell framed glasses that were much too large for his face, and the pupils of his eyes behind the lenses looked like pieces of compressed charcoal. His hands were encased in clear plastic gloves and his exposed skin above the wrist end of the gloves looked nut hard, I assumed from years of exposure to harsh chemicals.

I suddenly heard a loud gasp. I looked up to see Kate staring at something across the room from her. Kate's hand was over her mouth and her face was frozen in a look of sheer horror. The gasp had been loud enough to be heard over the hose's spray and had attracted Dr. Dimguiba's attention as well. The doctor still didn't seem to be aware of me, but he did turn to look at Kate just as Kate's face unfroze long enough to allow her to wail.

"Oh my God!" Kate said.

Dimguiba instantly twisted a valve on the hose's nozzle that shut off the water.

"What are you doing in here?" Dimguiba shouted at Kate. He had a heavy Filipino accent and his small shoulders hunched up in an aggressive posture.

Kate ignored Dimguiba and ran across the room. I already knew where she was headed as I had tracked her eyes and had seen what she had seen. Piled on two stainless steel tables tucked well back in the morgue were what looked like some children's clothes. As best I could make out, there was a small pair of blue jeans, a yellow Lakers jersey, and a little pink dress.

I ran after Kate.

She reached the tables with the clothes on them just before I did. Kate lifted the clothes in her arms and hugged them close to her chest. She swayed from side to side, sobbing.

Dimguiba jumped off his footstool and came toward us. "How dare you!" Dimguiba screamed. "This is an outrage. Put those clothes down right now!"

Kate and I ignored him. I put my arm around her.

"I'm so sorry, Kate," I said.

Kate just kept sobbing and hugging the clothes. Up close, I could see that the little pink dress had tiny blue elephants on it. The Lakers jersey had 'O'Neal' and the number '34' written on the back of it.

I felt a tiny hand grab the back of my shoulder. I turned around. Dimguiba was glaring up at me, his thin mouth contorted in a snarl, spittle gathering at the corners of his lips.

"Are both of you deaf?" Dimguiba said.

"No, we're not deaf," I said.

"Well, then, didn't you hear what I said?" Dimguiba said. "You can't be in here. We're closed."

"We heard you loud and clear," I said. "We came to identify the bodies of the two children who were brought in here today. That woman is the children's mother."

"I don't care who you are, or why you're here, you have to leave," he said.

"Will you witness the identification?" I said.

"I'm not witnessing anything," Dimguiba said. "The children's bodies are being transported to the coroner's office in downtown Los Angeles tomorrow. You can view them there."

"Which drawers contain their bodies?" I said.

"That's none of your business," Dimguiba said.

I looked at Kate. She was still hugging her children's clothes and appeared lost in her grief. Her pain was almost palpable, and I couldn't bear the thought of Kate going through the agony of actually having to look at her children up close. Instantly, I made a decision. I would examine the children's bodies just long enough to gather enough details to share with Kate so that she could make the identifications from my descriptions alone, and then both of us would get out of this hellish place.

I walked to the bank of drawers and reached to open the first one. Dimguiba, who had followed me, grabbed my arm. I gave him a backhand swat that knocked him down and sent him skidding across the floor. For a moment, Dimguiba lay stunned, his eyes glazed, his body unmoving. I walked up to him and stood over him.

"If you touch me again," I said, "the next thing you'll see is the inside of one of these drawers. Only you won't actually be seeing anything, since you'll be dead."

Dimguiba's eyes rapidly cleared and he once again glared at me.

"I'm getting a security guard," Dimguiba screamed. He pushed himself to his feet and ran off toward the autopsy room's entrance.

"You do that," I yelled after him. "Make sure you bring more than one. Hell, bring an Army of 'em. I could use the exercise."

I watched him disappear between the double doors.

What was it about this place? I couldn't remember ever having encountered so many unhelpful assholes under one roof. Kate was probably right about Cruella de Vil having written the HR manual.

I checked on Kate. She still appeared to be in a daze. I went back to the bank of body storage drawers. I opened and closed them, one after the other. The first nine drawers contained adults' bodies, but the tenth drawer contained the corpse of a small girl. I opened the eleventh drawer. There was a dead boy inside of it. Both of the young corpses looked just like other bodies I had seen where the victims had been stoned to death. The bodies were crushed and mutilated. It appeared as if nearly every bone had been fractured at least once.

I took a close look a the girl. Her skull bore a deep indentation above her brow, her teeth had all been shattered, her lips were torn to shreds, and her head was at such an odd angle it could only have meant her neck was fractured. The girl's eyes were open and stared blankly up at the ceiling, and her hair was matted with blood and dirt and glued down on her head. The girl's hair looked brown, but there was so much blood it was hard to tell what color it really was.

I took a few strands of the girl's hair in my left hand and stripped off some of the blackened blood and dirt with my right. With the blood and dirt removed, it was clear her hair was red. I checked the roots too. The roots were red and there was no hint her hair could have been dyed.

I then leaned my face in close to the girl corpse's face and examined her eyes. The eyes looked brown, but I knew eyes can turn color after death, usually to black or brown. There had also been some bleeding into the irises, bleeding probably induced by the trauma of the stoning, bleeding that could also make the eyes look brown. I looked closer. Just around the edges of the irises there was still some color. The color looked like it was fading, but it was blue, not brown. In life then, the little girl's eyes had been blue.

I checked on Kate. She clutched her children's clothes tight to her chest and seemed to have sunk even deeper inside of herself. She still appeared to be completely oblivious of her surroundings. I was tempted to go to her and comfort her, but knew the best thing I could do was finish my task as quickly as possible.

I turned my attention to the boy. His skull was worse than the girl's. It had been caved in on all sides so that his head was narrow and flattened top to bottom. His right eye socket was empty as if his eyeball had been plucked out and the left orbital bones looked like they had been smashed to bits. The left eyelids were swollen up like a baseball and sealed shut. The boy's right ear was missing - all that remained was some ragged flesh where it had once been. His face and hair were caked in dried, almost black blood. His hair looked brown, but there was so much caked blood and dirt in it, it was impossible to be sure. As I had done with the girl, I took a few strands of the boy's hair in my left hand and with my right hand cleaned off as much grime and blood as I could. When I was done, it was clear the boy's hair was not brown, but blond. I looked at the roots too. The roots were blond. And again, as with the girl, I could not see any evidence of any dye being used. I didn't really want to do what I did next, but I didn't think my investigation would be complete unless I did. I pried open the boy's left eyelids. There was an eyeball there but it had been so lacerated, and so much of its interior fluids were gone, that it was beyond recognition.

I felt Kate's eyes boring down upon me. I turned around. My body had been obstructing Kate's ability to see what I had been doing, but since I had last checked on her she had moved sideways so that she had at least a partial view of what was inside the open drawers. Kate, looking like she was in a trance, and clutching the children's clothes, moved toward me.

I took a step closer to her and blocked her path.

"Kate, please stay back," I said. "I don't think you should see this."

"Please get out of the way, Jack," Kate said.

For a moment I was seriously tempted to scoop Kate into my arms and carry her out of the morgue. From what Vandross had told me there was no reason to question the identifications. But then I remembered the 'protocol' Vandross had also mentioned. I realized that that protocol - even though I had only moments earlier suggested to Kate that perhaps we could find another way to complete the identifications of the bodies - would probably make it impossible for Kate to avoid doing the identifications herself. If we left and didn't complete the identifications right then and there, I thought there was a high likelihood we would have to come back again. For Kate's sake, I felt that was the last thing we should do.

"Listen," I said. "I think it's much better if we do this without you looking. I'm going to describe them to you."

"I want to see my children, Jack," Kate said.

"They need to be cleaned up," I said. "They're in no state for viewing. Just don't move, okay. Your son has blond hair, yes?"

"Blond hair?" Kate said.

"Yes," I said.

"What are you talking about?" Kate said.

This was going to be harder than I had expected. Kate was clearly in denial, her grief overwhelming her ability to rationally process her thoughts.

"I'm sorry, Kate," I said. "I don't want to do this any more than you do. I'm not going to ask you any more questions than I have to."

Kate did not say anything.

"Okay, let's try again," I said. "Your son has blond hair, correct?"

"My son does not have blond hair," Kate said. "He has brown hair."

I studied Kate's face for a moment. Grief does strange things to people. Maybe she wasn't in denial, but just confused. I didn't want to keep pushing Kate, but if I wanted to get the process over with, I had no other choice.

"I know this is very tough and that you're feeling as bad as a person can feel, but please try to focus and think about the color of your son's hair," I said.

"I don't need to focus," Kate said. "My son's hair is brown. Why are you giving me such a hard time?"

"I'm not trying to give you a hard time," I said. "In fact, I'm trying to make this as easy as possible on you."

"It sure doesn't seem that way," Kate said.

"I'm sorry," I said. "But please, I need to know. You're absolutely positive your son's hair is brown?"

"I know the color of my own son's hair, Jack!" Kate said.

I studied Kate's face again. She was clearly grieving, but had I been too quick to assume she was either confused or in denial? What if Kate was right? What if the person who had told Vandross that the boy corpse's hair color had matched that of Kate's son had been mistaken? Maybe that person had thought the boy corpse's hair was brown when it was really blond? But then again, maybe it was me who had made the mistake? Maybe I had seen the boy's hair as blond when it really was brown?

There was only one thing to do.

"Don't move, okay?" I said.

"What's going on?" Kate said.

"Just give me a second," I said.

It seemed to me that Kate was reluctant to accommodate my request, but after a moment, she nodded.

I turned back to the bodies and quickly repeated my examination. My findings were the same. The boy's hair was blond. The girl's hair was red and her eyes were blue.

I turned back to face Kate.

"What color is your daughter's hair?" I said.

"My daughter's hair is brown," Kate said. "Do you want to argue about that too?"

"No," I said. "What color are your daughter's eyes?"

"My daughter's eyes are brown," Kate said.

"Kate," I said, "these bodies don't belong to your children."

"What?" Kate said.

"They aren't your children," I said. "The dead boy in the drawer has blond hair, and the girl has blue eyes and red hair."

Kate looked confused, as if she couldn't comprehend what I had just said. Her confusion seemed to give way to the smallest possible hint of hopefulness, but a hopefulness tinged with anxiety, as if she couldn't bring herself to dare to accept that my assessment had been correct. Kate didn't say anything further, just walked over to me, pushed me aside, and peered into one drawer, then the other. She put her hand to her mouth.

"Oh no!" Kate moaned.

"What?" I said.

Kate kept staring at the bodies.

"It's Sam and Lizzy," Kate said.

"Sam and Lizzy?" I said.

"Yes," Kate said.

Kate slowly craned her head around to look at me.

"This is so terrible, Jack," Kate said. "So unbelievably terrible."

Kate still appeared to be in a trance, but the quality of the trance appeared to have changed. She seemed somehow less devastated and her eyes seemed to be focusing on a new target, as if they were readjusting ever so slightly to a new future, one that had not been there for her moments ago. She turned her head back to the body drawers, leaned over the one containing the dead girl, and gently stroked the girl's hair.

"Poor, poor Lizzy," Kate said to the girl. "I'm so sorry, Lizzy."

I stepped in close beside Kate and watched her tenderly minister to the girl.

After a few moments, I very softly said, "Kate, who are Sam and Lizzy?"

Without looking up, Kate said, "Paul's children. My husband Paul's children."

"Paul had children with his first wife before he married you?" I said.

"Yes," Kate said.

CHAPTER 39

I felt it inevitable that the disagreeable little physician Dr. Dimguiba would return. I therefore wanted to leave the morgue as soon as possible so as to avoid the unnecessary unpleasantries that would surely result from such return. But Kate seemed to want to spend more time with Sam and Lizzy, and I couldn't bring myself to tear her away from them. She was leaning over Lizzy's body stroking the little girl's hair with one hand, while her other hand still clutched her own children's clothes to her chest. The smell of formaldehyde grew even more pronounced, the hum of the ventilating machinery was the only sound I could hear, and the air in the room had grown so cold it chilled my bones. Light from the pathologist's autopsy lamps had caused the two children's body drawers to cast shadows on the morgue's cold, cement floor, shadows which seemed to me to have almost taken on a life of their own.

Kate moved away from Lizzy and turned her attention to Sam. Kate didn't stroke Sam's hair as she had done with Lizzy, but instead just looked at the dead boy. I couldn't read Kate's mind, but by the sad, reflective expression on her face, I believed she was most likely mourning the life Sam would never have. Kate remained lost in her inner reverie for nearly a full minute before she came out of it with a sigh. She bent over Sam's lifeless body, kissed his forehead, then straightened, and turned to face me.

"I hate to admit this, Jack," Kate said, "but, even though I feel awful about Sam and Lizzy, a part me feels better now that it's not my own children lying here."

"No one could fault you for that," I said.

"No, probably not," Kate said. "But it really doesn't change anything either, does it?"

"Change anything?" I said.

"Come on, Jack," Kate said. "You and I both know my children, Carolyn and Dylan, are dead too."

What Kate had said was certainly justified in light of all that happened that day, but I had also been giving the fate of Kate's children some thought during those last few moments. My response to her, then, was not just some well-intentioned fabrication meant to spare Kate's feelings or give her false hope, but what I honestly believed.

"Let's not go there yet, Kate," I said. "I could be wrong, but I truly believe there's a good chance your children are still alive."

Kate shook her head.

"That doesn't make sense, Jack," Kate said. "These people are monsters. They have to have killed my children too."

"There's no question they're monsters," I said. "But I think there's at least two reasons they may not have done that."

"Let me hear them," Kate said.

"I'm afraid you might not find much comfort in the first reason," I said. "It's pretty disturbing on its own."

"Nothing could be as disturbing as my children being dead, Jack," Kate said.

"I understand," I said. "There's no easy way to put this, but if I were one of one of the bad guys, your children's value as hostages would keep me from killing them."

"Hostages?" Kate said. "Hostages for what? Money?"

The ventilating machinery suddenly kicked into a higher gear and the morgue was flooded with cold air. At the same time, a noise came from the direction of the morgue's entrance doors. Kate and I tensed, Kate probably thinking exactly what I was - the loathsome Dr. Dimguiba had returned. We both quickly turned to look at the swinging doors. The doors quivered back and forth a few times, but there was no sign of any human presence. I assumed the doors must have been moved by a blast of air from the ventilation shafts.

We both turned back to look at each other.

Kate said, "I thought that awful little man had come back."

"Me too," I said. "We should probably go before he does."

"You afraid of his reinforcements?" Kate said.

"Afraid *for* his reinforcements," I said.

Kate smiled.

"Yes, I could see that," Kate said. "I can also see how it might be fun to watch if they try to move you out of here before you're ready."

"That's nice of you to say," I said. "I'm ready to go now, though."

"I'm not," Kate said.

"You're not?" I said.

"Not until you finish what you were saying about hostages," Kate said.

Since our discussion seemed, if only for the moment, to have distracted Kate away from the horrible pain she had been suffering through those last few hours, I decided it was worth the risk to stay a little longer. A very little longer.

"I don't think it's money they want," I said. "Sam and Lizzy's killers, or at least whoever is behind them, seem to have all the money they could possibly need. So it must be something else they want from you."

"What?" Kate said.

"I can't say for sure," I said. "Maybe something they think you know, maybe some kind of information they think you can provide them with."

"Like something about NASAD?" Kate said.

"That would be the most likely scenario," I said

"I know a lot about NASAD's business, but I don't know anything that's worth kidnapping and killing for," Kate said.

"That doesn't matter," I said. "What matters is the killers probably think you do."

"But I don't," Kate said.

"Actually you might, but just not realize it," I said.

"You're saying I might know something, but not know I know it," Kate said.

I nodded. Kate frowned.

"I'm sensing some frustration coming from you," I said.

"How astute of you," Kate said.

"Would you mind if I share a little lesson with you?" I said.

"What lesson would that be?" Kate said.

"One I learned at West Point," I said. "As you know, West Point teaches the cadets a lot of important lessons meant to help us become good officers. The most important of those important lessons is taught in the first hour of the first class on the first day of the first year."

"What was it?" Kate said. "To confuse the hell out of whoever you are talking to so that they feel really stupid and do whatever you say?"

"That was the second day," I said. "The one I am referring to is 'Don't shoot the messenger.'"

"Sorry, but that doesn't work for me," Kate said. "Because I'd sure as hell shoot you right now if I could."

"Funny," I said. "Look, what if the killers think you know something that has to do with Dr. Nemo? What if the killers are on to him? Maybe they suspect Nemo contacted you and they want to know what he told you."

Kate appeared to consider this.

"I guess if what Nemo told me was true, I could see the killers being worried about what I know," Kate said. "I probably should have thought of that myself."

"Given some time, I'm sure you would have," I said.

"Not so sure about that," Kate said. "What's your second reason?"

"Second reason?" I said.

"You said there were two reasons the killers may not have killed my children," Kate said.

"The second reason is there's a real chance Sam and Lizzy's killers don't even have your children," I said.

Kate looked at me in disbelief.

"Actually, the more I think about it," I said, "the more I believe that's the most likely scenario."

Kate shook her head.

"Stop, Jack," Kate said. "Please, stop."

"Stop?" I said.

"Yes," Kate said. "I can see what you're trying to do."

"What do you mean?" I said.

"Don't tell me things you know aren't true just to try to make me feel better," Kate said. "Because it'll just make me feel worse in the end."

"That's not what I'm doing," I said.

Kate took the children's clothes out from under her arm and thrust them towards me.

"No?" Kate said. "These are Carolyn's and Dylan's clothes. Their names are sewn into the collars. They were both supposed to go to summer camp next month, and I sewed the names there myself so the clothes wouldn't get lost while they were there. The FBI also found

Carolyn's locket around Lizzy's neck and Dylan's cell phone next to Sam."

The ventilating machinery kicked on again and the same flapping sound came from the direction of the room's double doors. Kate and I both turned to look. The doors were swinging, but there was no one there. We turned back to face each other.

"There are other explanations for all of that other than the killers having your children," I said. "The locket, the cell phone, the clothes, everything could have been stolen from your home."

"And all of those things could have just as easily been taken off my kids too," Kate said.

"True, but people, especially bad people, usually take the path of least resistance," I said. "And I'm sure you'll agree it's a hell of a lot harder to kidnap your children than steal some of their things."

"They killed Sam and Lizzy, Jack," Kate said. "Was that a path of least resistance?"

"To the killers it might have been," I said.

"Killing Sam and Lizzy is the path of least resistance?" Kate said. "Do you have any idea what that sounds like?"

"What does it sound like?" I said.

"It sounds like you're insane," Kate said.

"Well, I've had a rough day, but I don't think I've completely lost it," I said. "Not yet anyway."

Kate sighed.

"Your rough day is all my fault too, isn't it?" Kate said.

"I didn't have to accept your assignment, Kate," I said. "I could have stayed back at the ranch."

Kate said nothing.

"The theory of the path of least resistance isn't insane," I said. "In this instance, the theory says that if the killers could have achieved their goals by killing Sam and Lizzy without having to kidnap or kill your children too, that's what they would have done."

"That just makes me feel worse," Kate said. "I'm responsible for Sam's and Lizzy's deaths aren't I?"

"No, the killers are responsible for their deaths," I said.

The air conditioning stopped suddenly and a flapping sound came from the direction of the entrance doors again. Both Kate and I tensed and turned to look at the doors. The doors were swinging back and forth, but no one was there.

"It doesn't feel that way," Kate said. "And it sounds like you're relying on a pretty big 'if' to get to my children aren't kidnapped or dead."

"It's not a big 'if' in context of everything that has gone on today," I said. "Ever since I was told your children were murdered, I've thought that killing them just before attempting to kidnap you didn't make any sense."

"Why not?" Kate said.

"Whoever is behind all of this must have had a reason for wanting to kidnap you," I said. "The most likely reason is they want something from you. If they want something from you, what better way is there to get it than to threaten to harm your children? If your children are dead, that doesn't work."

"Your hostage theory, again," Kate said. "Why you believe they won't kill my children even if they have them?"

"Yes," I said.

"But why kill Sam and Lizzy?" Kate said.

"As a demonstration," I said. "To give you a taste of what would happen if you didn't cooperate with the killers."

Kate thought this over for a moment.

"And they don't need my children to send that message?" Kate said.

"Right," I said. "It sounds terrible as far as Sam and Lizzy are concerned, but the killers might think killing them was enough."

"But that doesn't mean that they don't have my children, Jack," Kate said.

"No, it doesn't," I said. "The theory of least resistance and my gut tell me they don't though."

"We're going to rely on some dubious theory and your gut to dictate our actions?" Kate said.

"Of course not," I said. "We'll proceed as if they do have your children. And we'll go to the ends of the earth to bring them back if they do."

A loud bang - a sound much different than the flapping we had heard when the ventilation machinery turned on - came from the direction of the morgue's doors. Kate and I both tensed again and turned to look. It wasn't, however, the dreaded Dr. Dimguiba and his promised team of security guards. A large yellow plastic mop bucket was coming through the door on four rubber wheels. The bucket had a six foot long wooden-handled mop sticking out of a wringer attached to the rim of the bucket. The movement of the bucket was causing the bucket's water to make loud sloshing sounds. Following the bucket into the room was a pleasant looking, mildly plump, middle-aged Hispanic woman wearing a white hairnet, white shirt and pants, and black comfort mocs. The woman had been humming when she entered, but stopped suddenly when she saw us.

The woman said, "Oh, I am so sorry. I did not think anyone was in here."

That was the first 'sorry' I'd heard from anyone who worked in the building. It warmed my heart. I hoped it wasn't because she was new and simply hadn't read Cruella de Vil's HR manual yet.

"That's alright," I said. "You're not disturbing us."

"I will come back later," the woman said.

"You can stay if you wish," I said.

I saw the woman's eyes quickly take in the open body drawers, then Kate's face. She lingered on Kate's face for the barest of moments, during which time the woman's face seemed to take on a hint of infinite sadness.

"No, no, I go," the woman said. And with that she turned the bucket around and left as quickly as she had come.

Kate said, "She seemed nice."

"Yes," I said. "She did. Quite an anomaly for this place."

"So you were saying we would go to the ends of the earth to find my kids, correct?" Kate said.

"The ends of the earth," I said. "If we have to, yes."

"But you don't think it will come to that?" Kate said.

"Since I don't think the killers have them, no," I said.

"Okay," Kate said, "but if the killers don't have my kids, where are they?"

"My hunch is it might turn out to be something simple," I said.

"Do we give as much weight to your hunches as we do 'your gut' and the theory of the path of least resistance?" Kate said.

I smiled.

"I won't dignify that with a response," I said.

"You probably shouldn't," Kate said. "Give me an example of simple."

"My best something simple is that Elizabeth Wells is going to show up," I said. "They haven't found her yet, but the fact she's missing doesn't necessarily mean something bad has happened to your nanny. There could easily be an innocent explanation for her failure to contact you."

"An innocent explanation, huh?" Kate said. "Alright. And when Elizabeth shows up, she's going to show up with my kids?"

"You said she was good at her job, didn't you?" I said.

The barest hint of a smile appeared on Kate's face.

"Yes, I did," Kate said. "Elizabeth Wells is definitely good at her job."

"I think she's going to do it then," I said. "Now, I'm not sure what's taking Dr. Dimguiba and his enforcement squad so long to come back, but we've definitely overstayed our welcome. Before we hustle on out of here, however, it occurs to me there is something I haven't yet done, but need to do, in order to be sure we're not proceeding under any false assumptions."

"Sounds wise," Kate said. "What do you need to do?"

"Ask you some questions," I said.

"Ask away," Kate said.

"Paul was married before he married you, yes?" I said.

"I was his second wife," Kate said.

"And Sam and Lizzy are his children from his first wife?" I said.

"Yes," Kate said.

"I hate to push you on this, but are you absolutely sure the children here are Sam and Lizzy?" I said.

Kate turned and pointed at the dead boy's arm.

"You see that scar?" Kate said.

There was a scar on Sam's forearm. It was crescent shaped and about three inches long.

"Yes," I said.

"Paul stayed as close to his kids as he could under the custody agreement that followed his divorce," Kate said. "I was only too happy to support Paul in whatever he wanted, and I loved Sam and Lizzy, so it certainly wasn't hard to support him in regard to his relationship with them as well. When Paul and I went on vacation with our kids, we would often take Sam and Lizzy along too. One of those vacations was to Cancún, Mexico. My son, Dylan, was chasing Sam around the hotel room, and Sam ran right into the room's sliding glass door. The glass wasn't marked with any safety stickers and it wasn't tempered either - I guess they've got different rules in Mexico. Sam got a nasty laceration from the glass. There was blood everywhere. I stitched Sam up myself. That scar on Sam's arm is what remains of the laceration."

"What about Lizzy?" I said.

Kate moved toward the girl's body and gently folded Lizzy's right ear forward. The skin behind the ear had a birthmark that looked like an angel with spread wings.

"That's Lizzy's angel," Kate said. "I always told her she had nothing to fear since her angel would always protect her."

I got a lump in my throat. I couldn't have spoken even if I knew what to say.

Kate said, "I guess I lied to her, didn't I, Jack?"

I waited a few seconds. The lump went away.

"I'm not sure I'd call that a lie," I said. "Either way, you and I are going to make it up to Lizzy."

"We're her angels now, is that it?" Kate said.

"Yes," I said. "Her avenging angels."

CHAPTER 40

It was almost 5:00 p.m., nearly thirty minutes since Kate and I had disembarked from the Maybach and headed for the morgue to identify the bodies, when I gently pushed the drawers that held Sam and Lizzy's corpses back into their slots in the wall. The clicks the drawers made when they had returned to their closed position were some of the saddest sounds I had ever heard. I scanned the room one last time to be sure I hadn't missed anything that could have been of value to me in my search for the children's murderers. I found no such thing. There was then nothing more for Kate and me to do in that chamber of death. If we were to avenge Sam and Lizzy's souls, we had to keep moving into whatever uncertain future lay ahead of us.

Kate and I headed out of the morgue. We retraced our steps through the autopsy room's double doors, across the antechamber, out the antechamber's double doors, and into the hallway. Kate carried her children's clothes under her arm. I didn't have the heart to tell her the clothes would be considered evidence and that removing the clothes from the morgue may not be such a good idea. But I didn't see much risk in her actions either. Kate and I could always plead ignorance in regard to what she had done - I'm a soldier, not a lawyer after all - and we certainly weren't going to harm the clothes in any way.

As Kate and I journeyed through the basement's frozen, formaldehyde-tinged air, I contemplated what my best next steps would be. Earlier that day, I had come to the conclusion that finding Dr. Nemo was probably going to give me the best shot at solving the NASAD mystery and maybe stopping a war as well. Nothing had changed that notion, but my conversation with Kate regarding her kidnapping attempt had forced me to re-acknowledge that it was probably not just me that was looking for Nemo, but the bad guys as well. Which meant Nemo was very likely in danger even at that moment, and I had to concern myself not just with finding him for my own reasons, but for his sake as well.

NASAD was the obvious place to take up the hunt for Nemo. Since it was already so late in the day, and we were still a hundred miles from NASAD headquarters, I felt I had no other choice but to wait until tomorrow to begin my Nemo hunt in earnest. The site of Sam and Lizzy's stoning, on the other hand, was only a few miles away from the morgue. I decided that the best use of my time would be to visit the stoning site with the hope that something would reveal itself there that would bring me closer to the identities of the killers and their employers.

Knowing how I would proceed with the rest of my day, my thoughts turned to what, if anything, I could do to assist in the search for Elizabeth Wells. I still believed that when we found the nanny, she would also have Kate's children, Carolyn and Dylan, in tow. My contemplations on that matter, however, were interrupted by Kate just as we reached the basement elevator doors. Kate had apparently had been thinking along similar lines.

"Jack," Kate said, "if the killers have my children won't they try to contact me?"

"If they have them, yes," I said.

"Maybe the FBI should put a trace on my cell phone," Kate said.

"I'd be surprised if they haven't done that already," I said.

"Everything Burnette has touched has turned to shit," Kate said. "What makes you think he's done something as intelligent and logical as I just suggested?"

"When I said 'they', I wasn't thinking of Burnette," I said. "I'd be shocked if Burnette was completely off the case, but I'm pretty sure there's another, better FBI team also looking for your kids now."

Kate raised her eyebrows.

"I think our escorts in the Suburban are the real thing," I said.

"God, I hope so," Kate said.

I reached my hand out towards the elevator call button, but before I could push the button, I heard Kate suddenly breathe in sharply. She grabbed my arm and pulled it down.

"What's wrong?" I said.

"We have to go back, Jack," Kate said, her voice almost frenzied. "We need to clean up Sam and Lizzy. I can't bear the thought of leaving them lying there in such a terrible state."

"Your heart's in the right place, Kate," I said. "But if we did, it would interfere with the autopsy. If the murderers left any evidence behind that could help us find them, we can't risk contaminating or destroying that evidence."

Kate thought about this. She seemed to relax a bit.

"Yes," Kate said. "You're right."

Almost as soon she said this, however, Kate's gaze shifted down to the clothes she was carrying under her arm. A new look of worry crossed her face.

"Am I going to be in trouble since I took the clothes?" Kate said. "Maybe I should put them back."

"It wasn't like good ol' Dr. Dimguiba was taking extra special care of them," I said. "I say you keep the clothes for now, and if, when we get back up top, our escorts in the Suburban want the clothes, we'll give them to them."

"Okay," Kate said.

I pushed the elevator call button.

"The annoying thing," I said, "is that we probably could have cleaned up Sam and Lizzy, for all the good I think their autopsies are going to do."

"But I thought you just said the autopsies would help us catch the murderers," Kate said.

"They might, but it's doubtful," I said. "The FBI has access to huge databases of DNA and fingerprint records for both arrestees and convicted criminals. They'll try to identify the killers by comparing whatever they find at the autopsies to the databases, but I don't think it will do them any good."

"Why not?" Kate said.

"Whoever is behind NASAD's problems seems to favor out-of-country talent, at least for the killings of Sam and Lizzy," I said. "The out-of-country part is what makes it tough."

The elevator arrived and its doors opened. We stepped inside, I pushed the button for the lobby, the doors closed, and we started our ascent.

"'Out-of-country talent'?" Kate said. "Why do you think that?"

"The men who tried to kidnap you this morning were Kazakh mercenaries," I said.

"Burnette said they were Islamic terrorists," Kate said. "He said the stoning was done by Islamic terrorists too."

"The would-be kidnappers were Christians," I said. "They were carrying Korans, but they were crucifix tattooed, pork eating Christians nonetheless."

"You saw them eating pork?" Kate said.

"Found an empty pork rind wrapper in one of their pockets," I said.

Kate seemed to think this over.

"So, if the Kazakhs were being made to appear to be Islamic terrorists," Kate said, "then the stonings could also have been staged to appear to be the work of Islamic terrorists as well."

"Great minds think alike," I said.

"But that doesn't mean the ones who did the stonings were from outside our country too," Kate said.

"Wanna' bet?" I said.

Kate gave me a little smile. Somehow, despite how badly her physical being had been ravaged that day by exhaustion, grief, and worry, her face momentarily radiated its startling beauty.

"Don't let this go to your head, Jack," Kate said, "but betting against you seems like a bad idea."

"People do it all the time," I said.

"And the ones who did are probably all pushing up daisies, aren't they?" Kate said.

"No comment," I said.

Kate shook her head. I can't say for sure, but she may have even laughed slightly too.

"Clearly, it's too late," Kate said.

"Too late for what?" I said.

"To keep anything from going to your big, fat head," Kate said.

"Hmm," I said. "I think I stepped right into that one, didn't I?"

"You most certainly did," Kate said.

And that time she really did laugh.

The elevator jolted to a stop. The doors opened and we stepped out of the elevator.

Standing directly opposite us was Dr. Dimguiba, his diminutive form positioned against the wall of the elevator lobby. The good doctor was gesticulating wildly, his eyes were ablaze, and the spittle I had come to so adore was spraying from the edges of his vicious little mouth. It was clear why he hadn't made a triumphant return to the morgue. Dimguiba was surrounded by two heavily armored men who were keeping him pinned close to the wall. Neither Dimguiba nor the men had yet noticed Kate and me, but the men certainly looked like they knew what they were doing. The men were dressed in all black - black Kevlar helmets, black combat boots, and thick black bulletproof vests outside their black uniforms. They had goggles strapped atop their helmets, Glocks in hip holsters, body-mounted radios, and M4 carbines slung over their shoulders. Patches on their arms and chest read 'FBI'.

Which all added up, of course, to the two men holding Dimguiba being members of an FBI SWAT team, most likely the same FBI SWAT team that had been hidden behind the darkened windows of the mysterious black Suburban that had escorted our Maybach to the morgue. The question was, how had the SWAT team members known that Dimguiba represented a potential threat to Kate and me? Were there security cameras in the building, cameras I had somehow missed seeing earlier? I looked up at the ceiling of the elevator lobby. I saw no cameras there. But that didn't mean there weren't any cameras elsewhere and I planned to keep looking for them as Kate and I made our way to the exit.

Dimguiba screamed at the agents, "This is an outrage!"

Hadn't I just heard that somewhere before?

"Do you know who I am?" the Lilliputian continued. "Let me go, or as God is my witness, I will make sure you never work again!"

One of the SWAT members softly said something to Dimguiba that I couldn't hear. The teeny medico's outrage soared to new heights.

"Don't tell me to calm down!" Dimguiba said. "You calm down! Don't you realize you're aiding and abetting a criminal act!"

The FBI men said nothing. Dimguiba suddenly noticed Kate and me standing outside the elevator. He violently jabbed a finger in our direction.

"There they are!" He shouted. "Get them! Get them now!"

The FBI agents turned their heads towards the elevator and saw Kate and me. The agents gave us a little smile and friendly nod. The agent on the left said, "Dr. Lennon. General Wilder. Sorry about this.

Please pay Dr. Dimguiba no heed."

Kate and I smiled and nodded back.

Dimguiba screamed, "Pay me no heed!? No heed!? How dare you!?"

I said to the agents, "We'll catch you outside."

"Yes sir," the agent on the left said.

I took Kate's hand and we turned to go. Dimguiba, apparently hell-bent on preventing our escape, tried to make a run at us. The agent on the right grabbed the pint-sized demon by the throat, lifted him off the ground, shoved him against the wall, and held him there. Dimguiba's feet scissored back and forth, touching only air, as he futilely attempted to escape.

I enjoyed the sight of Dimguiba struggling so mightily, perhaps more than I should have. I had to hand it to him, though, there was no quit in the little nutjob.

Kate and I continued to the building's rear lobby. When we reached the double door exit, I noticed a tiny security camera mounted high above the door in the junction between the wall and the ceiling. I don't know why I had missed the camera earlier - and most likely also missed dozens of others planted in the building as well - but at least the camera's presence seemed to confirm my theory about how Dimguiba had come to be buttonholed by the two SWAT agents.

Kate and I exited the building and were met by dry, furnace-like air, and bright, almost blinding light from a sun still high overhead in the afternoon sky. I checked the building's roof. The two FBI snipers were still up there and keeping a watch on Kate and me. The Maybach and our black Suburban escort were also still parked outside the county coroner's office. We headed toward the vehicles.

"Jack, I've been thinking," Kate said. "Even if the killers are from 'out-of-country' as you say, couldn't the FBI find records of them in international databases?"

"Sorry, I should have been more clear earlier," I said. "When I told you I thought the FBI probably wouldn't be able to identify the murderers from any criminal databases, I was thinking of Interpol's records too. I don't think Interpol's records will be of any more help than the FBI's own records."

"Why not?" Kate said.

"Because while it's true that the men who tried to kidnap you were Kazakhs, and Kazakhstan is a signatory to Interpol, there are still at least two problems with expecting the Interpol records to be of help," I said. "One, the Kazakhs aren't the most reliable of international partners, and two, if records of the mercenaries who attacked us today currently existed in Interpol's database, I'm sure their employers wouldn't have used those particular mercenaries. That last point is probably moot, however, as if the mercenaries' employers are as well connected as I think they are, I'm pretty certain that even if the mercenaries' records had at one time been discoverable in the Interpol databases, their employers most likely could have had those records expunged any time they wanted to."

Kate nodded.

"It appears that General Jack Wilder doesn't allow himself to ever be guilty of underestimating the opposition," Kate said.

"Well, as Sun Tzu said, 'Move swift as the Wind and closely-formed as the Wood. Attack like the Fire and be still as the Mountain,'" I said.

Kate gave me a funny look.

"What does that have to do with what I just said?" Kate said.

"Nothing," I said. "I have no idea what it means either."

"Really?" Kate said. "It kinda makes sense to me."

"Good," I said. "Try it out and tell me how it works for you. Now, getting back to underestimating the opposition, let me ask you this - would *you* underestimate an enemy that has, in a seemingly meticulously planned operation spanning many years, killed twelve NASAD engineers, brutally murdered Paul's children, attempted to kidnap you, and, in all likelihood, possesses some kind of military edge that represents a serious threat to our national security, a threat, I might add, that Dr. Nemo, a presumed NASAD employee, apparently believes is so grave, he has not only gone through the trouble of creating some diabolically complicated coded message to try to warn you about it, but also in all probability risked his life in trying to deliver the message to you?"

Of course, I believed that Kate's father, Milt Feynman, and her husband, Paul Lennon, also belonged on the list of victims brought down by the enemy's meticulously planned operation. I felt it was still best, however, not to mention anything about that suspicion to Kate until I had proof the two men's Alaskan plane crash had indeed not been an accident.

"No, no, of course not," Kate said.

We were at that time not more than fifty yards from the Maybach. Kate suddenly stopped dead in her tracks and put her hand to her mouth.

"Jack, I can't believe I didn't think of this before," Kate said.

I turned to face her.

"Think of what, Kate?" I said.

"Sarah," Kate said.

Tears started to form in Kate's eyes.

"Who's Sarah, Kate?" I said.

"Someone's got to tell her, Jack," Kate said.

"Tell her what, Kate?"

Kate did not answer. She began to sob uncontrollably.

CHAPTER 41

Who was Sarah? What did Kate and I have to tell her? Why did just the thought of Sarah provoke such a painful reaction in Kate?

I didn't know.

What I did know was that Kate's condition was scaring me. Because she was crying so hard and her breaths were coming so fast and shallow, it seemed like she might have trouble breathing soon. Which, on its own, was something I believed her body could cope with. But it was 105 degrees as we stood there alone in the middle of that vast empty sea of a parking lot in Lancaster. The sun's rays felt like they were burning holes in our skin, the blisteringly hot air was searing our lungs, and the steaming asphalt was scorching the bottoms of our feet. I was worried Kate's hyperventilation, combined with her weakened state and the blazing heat, might cause her to get heatstroke. The building was fifty yards behind us and the Maybach was fifty yards in front of us. I was going to feel a lot better if I could quickly get her inside one or the other.

"Kate, let's go see how Manu and Mosi are doing," I said. "It's way too hot out here."

Kate didn't say anything, just kept crying, and shook her head.

"I'm worried you're going to get heatstroke," I said.

Kate, between breaths that I thought were becoming dangerously more rapid, managed to say, "I don't want anyone to see me like this."

"No one is going to care," I said. "They know what you've been going through."

Kate wobbled slightly.

"My head hurts, Jack," Kate said.

"Come on," I said. "I'll help you walk."

I took a step closer and reached for her hand. She pulled it away.

"No," Kate said. "Just give me a minute. I'll be okay."

But as she said this, the wobble I had just seen looked like it was going to turn into a full fledged topple. I grabbed both her shoulders and held her upright.

"Let go of me, Jack," Kate said. "There's people watching."

I didn't doubt she was right about that. There were probably at least a dozen eyes bearing down on us from the building's roof and from behind the tinted windows of the Maybach and the Suburban.

"And you're probably scaring them as much as you're scaring me," I said.

Kate wobbled again despite my grip on her shoulders.

"What's wrong with me?" Kate said.

"Heatstroke," I said.

Kate's eyes seemed to lose their focus for a second.

"Hold me tighter, Jack," Kate said. "I don't feel well."

The right thing to do at that moment probably would have been to just pick up Kate, carry her to the Maybach, and use the car's air conditioning to cool her down. But it's been my experience that when a beautiful woman says 'Hold me tighter' it can sometimes be pretty hard to do the right thing. Which is why, instead of doing the right thing, I quickly slipped my hands off of Kate's shoulders and hugged her close to me so that her face was pressed against mine. Her hot tears flowed down my cheek and neck.

"Thanks, Jack," Kate said. "Just keep doing that. I'll be okay in a minute."

"I'd rather take you to the car," I said.

"No," Kate said. "I'm already feeling better."

I felt her breathing getting slower and less shallow.

"Maybe you are," I said. "But maybe you aren't. If you start feeling worse..."

Kate interrupted, "I won't."

I chose to believe her and kept holding her. Her tears stopped and she seemed to slowly improve. I began to develop a problem of my own, however. The longer I stood there with Kate in my arms, the harder it became for me to suppress a thought that was forming deep within my mind. The more I tried to suppress the thought, the stronger it grew, until, finally, I wasn't able to hold it back any longer and it took full control of my consciousness. Kate felt just like my wife Grace. The warmth of her skin, the heat of her breath, the softness of her hair. I found myself stroking Kate's hair, but it was Grace's hair too.

I said, "I don't like it when you're sick, Grace."

Kate, her voice muffled since her face was so close to my chest, said, "You know you just called me Grace."

"Sorry," I said.

"It's okay," Kate said. "I'm glad you don't like it when I'm sick. What was it you said I had?"

"Heatstroke," I said.

"You still think so?" Kate said.

"You seem to be improving," I said.

"Is my skin red?" Kate said.

I pulled the hair back from her face to look.

"No, not really," I said.

"Is that perspiration on the back of my neck?" Kate said.

I stroked the damp skin on the nape of her neck.

"Feels like it," I said.

"Am I breathing better?" Kate said.

I put my ear closer to her mouth and nose.

"Yes," I said

"Who's the doctor here?" Kate said.

"You," I said.

"Who of us is more qualified to make a diagnosis, then?" Kate said.

"We're assuming the heatstroke hasn't made you delirious?" I said.

"Yes," Kate said.

"In that case, you," I said.

"And, that being the case," Kate said, "I'd like to state for the record I don't have heatstroke."

"Good to know," I said.

"I kinda like you holding me though," Kate said.

"I thought you said that was a bad idea," I said.

"I did," Kate said.

We kept holding each other.

Kate said, "I think I'm ready to call Sarah now."

"I'd still prefer you called her from inside the car," I said.

"I want some privacy," Kate said.

"You can put that window up between the front and rear seats," I said.

"No," Kate said. "I might break down even worse when I talk to her.

I don't want Manu and Mosi seeing me like that."

"Understandable," I said. "By the way, who is Sarah?"

"Sarah Lennon," Kate said. "Paul's first wife. Sam and Lizzy's mother."

Paul's first wife? Sam and Lizzy's mother?

Before I could process that information any further, I suddenly felt like I'd been smacked in the face. Hard. I instinctively whirled around, freeing myself from Kate as I did so. I turned my head from side to side, looking for whoever had hit me.

Absolutely no one and nothing was there.

I realized the palm of my right hand was hurting. I looked down at it. It was red, as if it had just hit something.

Had I hit myself?

Just like I'd done earlier in the Maybach shortly before we'd passed Lake Crowley?

What other explanation was there?

From behind me, I heard Kate say, "Jack, what's going on?"

Going on?

I'd just hit myself is what was going on.

But I wasn't going to tell Kate that.

I thought fast and used the first plausible excuse I could come up with.

"There was a bee on my cheek," I said.

"A bee?" Kate said.

I turned back around to find Kate looking at the air around my head, apparently searching for the bee.

"It already flew away," I said. "Don't worry."

She stopped searching.

"Are you allergic?" Kate said.

"Uh, no," I said. "Just didn't wanna get stung."

Kate studied me. She appeared to have her doubts about what I had told her about the bee.

"Pretty violent reaction for not wanting to get stung, don't you think?" Kate said.

"It's been a real rough day," I said. "I think my reflexes must be a bit on edge."

"Yes, it has been, but...," Kate said.

"But what?" I said.

"You sure you weren't hallucinating?" Kate said. "I got the impression you might have been hallucinating on the sniper range."

"Me? Hallucinating? Please," I said.

"You'd tell me if you were, wouldn't you?" Kate said.

"Of course," I said.

"Okay," Kate said.

She reached into her pocket, took out her iPhone, did some scrolling, then pushed a spot on iPhone's screen, and put the phone to her ear.

"You're calling Sarah?" I said.

Kate nodded.

"Wouldn't it be easier just to tell the FBI agents in the Suburban what's going on, and have them call Sarah?" I said.

"I want to do it myself," Kate said.

While Kate appeared to wait for Sarah to answer the phone, I thought about that vicious smack I'd given myself in the face. With all the other weird things that had been going on that day, I wasn't too surprised I had been capable of doing such a thing. I figured it was probably part of what Hart and Vandross had called my 'stress reaction'. And I also realized why I'd done it.

The smack was punishment.

For being so stupid.

It should have been obvious who Sarah was. Obvious to anyone with half a brain, that is.

But it wasn't just in regard to Sarah where I'd missed the obvious, was it?

The airplane that had tracked the Maybach in the desert, Burnette's team's Taser in my back, security cameras in the multi-story building that housed the morgue - all things, along with Sarah being Sam and Lizzy's mother, that I should have either anticipated, appreciated the significance of, known intuitively, or just plain observed, but did not.

It seemed like those failures of anticipation, appreciation, intuition, and observation were coming faster and faster. I didn't know what had caused those failures - rust due to inactivity, the effect on my mental state that my stress reaction was having, or something else - but the failures made me think I was a lot further off my game than I'd realized. And made me worry about how much further off my game I still might fall.

As I watched Kate wait for her call to be answered, I felt myself growing angry. I didn't like feeling incompetent. There were a lot of people relying on me to do my job. I had to do a whole hell of a lot better than I was doing. I had to get this sappy, slumbering brain of mine into a higher gear. The question was, how was I going to do that?

I took a few deep breaths trying to calm myself so that I could think about the answer to that question. Kate didn't seem to be paying any attention to what I was doing. She still had the phone next to her ear, waiting for a response.

I suppose if there had been a psychologist standing next to me, they might have said that my anger seemed a bit out of proportion to any real or imagined deficiencies in my performance, and that a lot of it was probably 'displaced' anger. That I was probably more angry at the slimebags that had murdered Sam and Lizzy than I was upset about my own failures. Luckily for that psychologist, however, he or she was not standing next to me and sharing his or her theories with me. Because if they were, and they had, I would have kicked their head in.

Kate, after a few more seconds of waiting for her call to be picked up on the other end, finally said, "Sarah, it's Kate. Please call me as soon as possible. It's important."

Kate took the iPhone away from her ear, touched the screen again, and put the phone back in her pocket.

"It went to voicemail," Kate said.

I nodded and took some more deep breaths as I continued to try to soothe my seething self. The breaths were working, but not fast enough. And, though I had hoped Kate wouldn't notice how agitated I was, she apparently had.

"That bee got to you that much?" Kate asked.

"It was a really big bee," I said between breaths.

"Uh huh," Kate said.

It appeared Kate still doubted my story about the bee. I could have tried to convince her that the bee had actually existed - even though it most assuredly had not - by making up some telling details about the bee. Things like the murderous look in the bee's eye, the razor-like sharpness of its stinger, and the scariness of its claws. But I had enough of my wits about me to recall the immortal bard's words that Kate, speaking in reference to Adelaide, had said about me thinking a person 'doth protest too much'. Rather than risk being accused of dothing that, I changed the subject.

"Hopefully, Sarah'll call back soon," I said.

"Hopefully," Kate said.

"In the meantime, we'll tell the FBI to get someone out to her house as fast as possible," I said.

"You think Sarah's in danger?" Kate said.

"No," I said. "Just an abundance of caution."

"An abundance of caution?" Kate said. "Is that another quote from Sun Tzu?"

"Uh uh," I said. "Lawyer in ancient Rome. 'Ex abundati cautela'. It makes too much sense for Sun Tzu to have said it."

"You know a lot of weird stuff, Jack," Kate said.

"You can blame General Bradshaw for that," I said. "Jeff knows more worthless shit than anyone on earth. Getting back to Sarah, however, shouldn't the FBI have had a harder time mistaking your kids for Sarah's? Are they that close in age?"

"My son, Dylan, is only two years younger than Lizzy," Kate said. "My daughter Carolyn is only a year and a half younger than my son. All four of them aren't that much different in size from each other, so the ages alone wouldn't have been a big enough tip off for the FBI to avoid the mistaken identification. That's still no excuse for how badly the FBI got it wrong, though."

"No, it's not," I said. "So you and Paul got married pretty quickly after he got divorced from Sarah?"

"Sarah and Paul got divorced when Sarah was in the early stages of her pregnancy with Lizzy," Kate said. "She didn't even know she was pregnant. Paul didn't want the divorce, but at that time Sarah was hooked on drugs and alcohol and she was borderline crazy. She dried out a few years ago and has been absolutely fine since then and a wonderful mother. Paul and I got married two years after the divorce and I got pregnant very quickly."

Just then, I got a pain in my gut that was so sharp it caused me to double over. I had to grip my hands to my knees to keep from collapsing to the asphalt. As I was struggling to stay upright, I heard a voice inside my head say, "You the one full of worthless shit, Jack."

Somehow, despite the pain, I was able to think clearly enough to realize it wouldn't be a good idea to let Kate hear me talking to myself, especially with the bee incident, and her doubts about me, so fresh in her mind. Silently, inside my head, I said, "Jeff?"

"You expecting someone else?" Jeff's voice said.

"What are you doing inside my head, Jeff?" I said.

"Not the first time I've been in here today is it?" Jeff's voice said.

"No, it's not," I said.

"And you think it's all because I shoved that CheyTac in your face, don't you?" Jeff's voice said.

I didn't say anything.

"Anyways, I'm not inside your head you idiot," Jeff's voice said. "I'm a simulation."

"A simulation?" I said.

"Yes," Jeff's voice said. "You simulating me. Just like you simulating yourself for that matter."

"I actually kind of think I know what you're talking about," I said. "But, you know, with the state I'm in, it might not be such a good idea for me to go there right now."

"Yeah, you so full of stupid, you don't know your ass from a hole in the ground, do you?" Jeff's voice said.

I felt another sharp wave of pain course through my stomach. I tightened my grip on my knees and tried to breathe as deeply as I could.

"I don't know if I'd go that far," I said.

"Oh no?" Jeff's voice said. His voice then continued in a high-pitched, whiny imitation of my own. "Get the FBI out to Sarah's house...Sarah'll call back soon...Just an abundance of caution...What the hell, dude!"

"You don't have to be so mean," I said.

"You prefer I kick your ass?" Jeff's voice said.

"I don't think what I said was so bad," I said.

"Uh huh," Jeff's voice said. "What's the FBI gonna find when they get to Sarah's house?"

"Sarah, of course," I said.

"Stop just flapping your mouth and think!" Jeff's voice said.

"My mouth isn't moving, Jeff," I said. "I don't want Kate to see me talking to you."

"You know what I mean," Jeff's voice said. "Use whatever pea-sized part of your brain that still works and scrutinize your candy-ass surmising."

Hoping it might shut Jeff up, I thought about what I'd said. A moment later I realized what he was talking about.

"Aw shit," I said.

"Aw shit is right," Jeff's voice said. "I'm going now. Try to stop being so damn dumb."

If one can feel a voice inside one's head disappear into thin air, then that's what I felt Jeff's voice do.

Which left me alone with the knowledge that Jeff had been right.

I was being incredibly stupid.

The FBI wasn't going to do Sarah Lennon any good. An abundance of caution wasn't going to help Sarah, nor was Sarah going to be calling back anytime soon. Not soon. Not ever. Almost a whole day had passed since Sarah Lennon's kids had been slaughtered and none of us had heard anything from, or about, Sarah. An optimistic type might have believed Sarah was out there frantically dealing with her local police, trying to get them to find her missing children. But if Sarah was indeed doing that, wouldn't one have to believe - considering all the information about the Mojave Desert murders of two kids named Lennon that was surely being broadcast that day on the California law enforcement airwaves - that some cop would have put two and two together by then? That maybe, just maybe, the murdered kids belonged to Sarah Lennon and not Kate Lennon? But no cop had put it together yet because they couldn't put it together. They couldn't put it together because no cop had even known Sarah Lennon's kids were missing in the first place. They didn't know, because Sarah hadn't told them. And Sarah hadn't told them because Sarah was dead.

CHAPTER 42

The pain in my gut continued to feel like someone had detonated a pound of C4 under my spleen. I remained bent over in the parking lot, breathing hard, and stuck in the limbo land between the hospital that was not a hospital and the Maybach. A strong breeze came up, but it did nothing to knock the edge off the sweltering heat.

The sound of jet engines momentarily distracted me from my pain. I carefully turned my head and watched as a jet thundered across the brilliant aqua sky. The plane was leaving stark white contrails that quickly elongated in its wake. Contrails that high and elongating that quickly meant they were probably being made by a military jet, maybe one that had taken off at nearby Edwards Air Force base. The jet might even be the kind of jet Jeff was thinking about when, earlier that day, he had dreamed of us catching a flight to Saudi Arabia.

I had by then realized, of course, that my stomach pain was most likely due not to any anatomical defect in my abdomen, but rather the handiwork of some ancient, primordial, reptilian messaging system deep within my brain. The messaging system had used the pain, along with a 'simulation' of Jeff's voice, to warn me off the foolish path I had been following regarding the fate of Sarah Lennon. The realization that the pain was some kind of phony mockup, however, had not made it hurt any less than the real thing.

Kate moved close up against my still bent over body. She put her arm around my shoulder and her mouth close to my ear.

"I don't want to make a big deal about this, especially since I don't want to embarrass you in front of those rooftop snipers who are watching our every move, but you don't look so good," Kate said. "What's wrong?"

The trill of Kate's breath in my ear, the warmth of her nearby mouth, and the touch of her arm worked wonders. My pain began to subside.

"My stomach hurts," I said. "Must have been something I ate."

"A bee, something you ate," Kate said. "If I hadn't seen what you did out at the rest stop today, I'd think you were one big pussy."

"I am a pussy," I said. "By the way, is my face red?"

Kate gently pushed my hair off my forehead and looked.

"No," Kate said.

"Is there sweat on the back of my neck?" I said.

She stroked the back of my neck.

"Yes," Kate said.

"Is my breathing irregular and shallow?" I said.

Kate pushed her ear close to my mouth.

"No," Kate said.

"Phew," I said. "I was worried I might have heatstroke."

She moved her mouth close to my ear again.

"You're a fast learner," Kate whispered.

"That's what they say," I said. "My stomach is feeling better now. If I stand up will you still keep your mouth next to my ear?"

"I'd like to," Kate said. "But I think we've already put on a good enough show for the snipers."

The sound of a car door being closed came from the direction of where the Maybach and the Suburban were parked. Kate and I swiveled our heads to look. A man appeared to have just exited the Suburban and was approaching us. He was dressed all in black - helmet, uniform, bulletproof vest, and boots - and looked just like the FBI SWAT agents who had corralled Dimguiba up against the elevator lobby's wall. The man also had a Heckler and Koch MP5 submachine gun slung over his shoulder and a Glock in his hip holster. His gait was steady despite the fact the breeze had stiffened and was at his back. The breeze both pushed him along and caused the sleeves of his uniform to flap.

Kate gestured with her chin at the approaching man in black and said, "And now we have a new guy to worry about as well."

"Him?" I said. "No way. Nothing fazes guys like that. They got nerves of steel."

"Perhaps," Kate said. "But isn't discretion the better part of valor?"

"You been speaking with General Jeffrey Bradshaw?" I said.

"No," Kate said. "Sir John Falstaff."

"Well," I said, "I guess he would know better than anyone."

Kate leaned her face in close to mine again, lightly kissed my ear, gently withdrew her arm, and stood up. I let out a deep sigh, pushed up off my knees, and stood up as well. The straightening of my left knee caused a shock of pain to sear up my left thigh and hip. With a sheer effort of will, I was somehow able to hide that new infirmity from Kate, however.

"I liked it better when we were bent over," I said.

"Me too," Kate said.

The man in black was rapidly closing the gap between him and us.

"Do you think he's going to arrest us?" I said.

"Fine with me," Kate said, "as long as we get to share the same cell."

Just then the breeze jumped up to a full-fledged gust. It blew Kate's gorgeous blond locks well off her face. The way the sunlight then fell on her cheeks and brightened the cornflower blue of her eyes made Kate look astonishingly beautiful. Grace was the only woman I had ever seen who could radiate such beauty, and once again, Grace started to become Kate, and Kate, Grace. I was able, however, through another force of will - or was it fear of additional embarrassment? - to keep from saying Grace's name aloud.

The man in black, propelled by the gust, rapidly completed the last few yards of his traverse across the parking lot and stopped next to Kate and me. Up close, I could see the man was about six feet, two inches tall, very fit, and had a strong jaw and clear blue eyes. He greeted us with a slight nod of his head and a two fingered tap to his helmet.

"Dr. Lennon, General Wilder," he said. "My name is Ray Carpenter. I'm the leader of the FBI SWAT team that has been assigned to provide security for Dr. Lennon."

My immediate sense about Agent Carpenter was that if there was such a thing as an anti-Burnette on the FBI payroll, Carpenter was surely it.

"Nice to have you aboard, Agent Carpenter," I said.

Kate said, "Good to meet you, Agent Carpenter."

"Thank you, ma'am," Carpenter said. "Uh, ma'am, I don't wish to appear rude, but I have an extremely urgent matter to discuss with the general."

I said, "What's on your mind, Agent Carpenter?"

"Forgive me, sir," Carpenter said, "but this is for your ears only."

"At this stage of the game, I'm not sure there's much Dr. Lennon can't be privy to," I said.

Carpenter did not reply. An awkward moment passed in which he seemed to become increasingly uncomfortable. Kate appeared to notice his discomfort as well. I was about to say something, but Kate interrupted.

"I'm afraid if I stay out here much longer I'll be guilty of renewing your fears about heatstroke, General," Kate said. "If you'll both excuse me, I'm going to go jump in the car with Manu and Mosi."

Kate headed off for the Maybach, her body leaning forward to counterbalance the force of the gusting desert wind. When she was out of earshot, Carpenter said, "It's an honor to meet you, sir. General Hart sends his greetings."

"You're with MOM?" I said.

"Yes, sir," Carpenter said.

"You look like a Seal," I said. "Were you a Seal, Agent Carpenter?"

"Yes, sir," Carpenter said. "I'm a former Seal, sir."

"But you're full time with the FBI now?" I said.

"Yes, sir," Carpenter said. "With MOM on the side."

"I assume Hart brought you up to speed on our fears about a Chinese insurmountable edge?" I said.

"He did, sir," Carpenter said.

"Did Hart also tell you about Dr. Nemo?" I said.

"That as well, sir," Carpenter said.

Out of the corner of my eye, I saw that Kate still had a ways to go to get to the Maybach. Mosi, however, had already gotten out of the car and opened the rear passenger door for her arrival. The wind made it a struggle for him to keep the door open.

"Before you discuss with me whatever it was you didn't want Dr. Lennon to hear," I said, "there's something I need to tell you."

"Yes, sir?" Carpenter said.

"The original identifications of the bodies in the morgue were incorrect," I said. "They're not Dr. Lennon's children."

"Yes, sir. I know, sir," Carpenter said. "That's why I wanted to talk with you alone."

I was momentarily taken aback. How could Carpenter have known the bodies didn't belong to Kate's children?

"Would you mind telling me how you knew that?" I said.

"We just found the nanny," Carpenter said.

"Elizabeth Wells?" I said.

"Yes, sir," Carpenter said.

"Alive?" I said.

"Yes, sir," Carpenter said.

"And the children?" I said.

"Safe and unharmed," Carpenter said.

"Well, obviously that's great news, Agent Carpenter," I said. "But why is it for my ears only?"

"I'm sorry, sir," Carpenter said. "My orders were not to tell you or Dr. Lennon about her children."

I felt anger rise in my throat. I kept it in check.

"You were ordered not to?" I said.

"Yes," Carpenter said.

"That seems a rather cruel order, Agent Carpenter," I said, "considering that not only has Dr. Lennon spent much of her day believing her children were dead, but continues to be worried sick about them."

"I agree, sir," Carpenter said.

The wind suddenly picked up even more strongly and it was all Carpenter and I could do to stay upright. It was impossible to speak and be heard, so our conversation was put on hold while we waited for the wind to die down. On the other side of the parking lot, Kate stepped into the Maybach's rear passenger compartment, as Mosi, his long hair blown over the front of his face so that it looked like he had some kind of dark, triangular pennant attached to his forehead, continued to struggle to hold her door open against the howling wind. An even bigger gust came up that ripped the door out of the giant twin's hands and slammed the door shut just as Kate disappeared from view. Then, almost as suddenly as it had come up, the gust was gone, leaving only a gentle breeze in its wake.

Carpenter and I were able to resume our conversation.

I said, "I would also find it impossible to believe that order came from General Hart."

"It didn't come from General Hart, sir," Carpenter said.

"Then who...?" I said. "No wait. Let me guess. Burnette."

"Yes, sir, Burnette gave the order," Carpenter said. "Obviously I knew I could tell you about the children, but, given the risks, I felt it best to leave it up to you about what to tell Dr. Lennon."

"Risks?" I said.

"I don't know Dr. Lennon, sir," Carpenter said. "If it gets back to Burnette I'd violated his order, I am sure he would get me removed from my posting."

"I understand," I said. "You did the right thing under the circumstances."

"Thank you, sir," Carpenter said.

"But there's no question we're going to tell Dr. Lennon," I said. "To do otherwise would be incomprehensible to me. She'll appreciate your situation, so I'm sure there'll be no blowback on you."

"Yes, sir," Carpenter said.

"I am very disappointed though," I said. "I had hoped you weren't under Burnette's command."

"Technically I'm not, sir," Carpenter said. "As of 14:00 today, Dr. Lennon's security is being handled separately from Agent Burnette's investigation of the problems at NASAD. The security detail assigned to her is under my direct control and outside Burnette's purview."

"What the hell is Burnette doing giving you orders, then?" I said.

"Clearly Burnette is not supposed to be giving me orders, sir," Carpenter said. "But, since Burnette outranks me in the overall FBI chain of command, I don't really have any choice other than to obey him."

"Fair is foul and foul is fair," I said. "Hover through the fog and filthy air."

"'Macbeth', sir?" Carpenter said.

I nodded.

"The witches, Act I, Scene I," I said. "And I bet, if we could ask those little harpies, they'd be in complete concurrence with my own views, namely, that Burnette's a goddamned asshole."

"May I speak off the record, sir?" Carpenter said.

"Always," I said.

"No question the harpies would, sir," Carpenter said. "Which means there's a lot of us thinking alike. You, me, the harpies, and everyone I brought with me."

I smiled.

Just then, a second black Suburban, identical to the one Carpenter had been in, circled around the medical building and stopped by its rear entrance. Two FBI SWAT agents - the same ones I had seen with Dimguiba in the lobby - exited the building and climbed into the waiting Suburban. They must have dumped the little doctor somewhere, as he was nowhere to be seen.

I nodded my head toward the Suburban.

"You have two full teams?" I said.

"Yes, sir," Carpenter said.

"Two teams is good," I said. "Tell me about the kids."

"Elizabeth Wells took the Lennon children to Disneyland this morning," Carpenter said. "Wells's cell phone died and she had no idea anyone was looking for her. One of the children wasn't feeling well, so Wells and the children left Disneyland earlier than they had planned. On the way home, Wells noticed a white Ford Econoline van that she thought was acting suspiciously and she believed might be following her. Wells was heading northbound on Interstate Highway 5 at the time and decided her best course of action was to go directly to the Buena Park police station. The station is right off one of the highway exits."

"Kate said Elizabeth was good at her job," I said under my breath.

"Sorry, sir, I didn't quite catch that," Carpenter said.

"It's not important," I said. "How long have you known about the children?"

"I was informed of the situation only five minutes ago," Carpenter said. "If I hadn't seen that you and Dr. Lennon were already headed my way, I would have gone to find you."

"The building's security cameras feed directly into your vehicle?" I said.

"Yes, sir," Carpenter said.

"Where are the Lennon children now?" I said.

"At the police station," Carpenter said. "Under heavy guard."

"Did Burnette deign to explain to you why he ordered you not to tell Dr. Lennon or me that the children had been found?" I said.

"He said it was because he was heading over there himself and wanted to assess everything before he discussed it with anyone else," Carpenter said.

"Burnette's actually on his way to the Buena Park police station?" I said.

"Yes, sir," Carpenter said. "He's requisitioned an FBI chopper. It should be picking him up within the next twenty minutes at the Lancaster Sheriff's Substation."

I shook my head.

"Pretty unbelievable, wouldn't you say?" I said.

"Sir?" Carpenter said.

"Burnette's stated reasons for his behavior," I said. "It's clear that jackass doesn't mind torturing Dr. Lennon so he can play the hero. I'm sure Burnette wants to personally deliver the children to her so he can cover up his role in the original mis-identifications."

"Yes, sir," Carpenter said. "Now that you put it that way, I certainly see how that's the most likely scenario."

Another jet from Edwards roared overhead. The firing of its afterburners caused the earth to vibrate beneath my feet.

"I don't want Burnette anywhere near those kids," I said. "Everything Burnette touches gets FUBAR faster than a spotted ass ape. I'll be damned if I'm gonna let that halfwit beefhead put those kids' lives at further risk."

"Halfwit beefhead," Carpenter said. "I like that, sir. You remind me of my commander at NAB."

"Thanks," I said. "I'll take that as a compliment."

"It was," Carpenter said. "What do you suggest we do, sir?"

"Make fun of Burnette some more," I said. "Or not. Before we make a decision about the kids, I'll need to know a few things."

"Yes, sir," Carpenter said

"First," I said, "where were you planning on taking Dr. Lennon when you leave here with her today?"

"To her home in Malibu, sir," Carpenter said.

"Had you considered a safe house?" I said.

"Yes, sir," Carpenter said. "However, the FBI Executive Assistant Director for National Security told me that when the NASAD engineers in Las Vegas were killed four days ago, he advised Dr. Lennon she should go to a safe house. The Assistant Director says Dr. Lennon told him to go to hell. He felt that trying again now, even though Dr. Lennon is clearly in even more danger, would just be a waste of time."

"I guess Dr. Lennon doesn't like safe houses," I said.

"Yes, sir," Carpenter said.

"Maybe I'll try to talk her into going to one myself at some point," I said. "What kind of security arrangements have you made for Dr. Lennon's home?"

"We're on a war footing, sir," Carpenter said. "Dr. Lennon and her brother Freddy Feynman's houses are located on a walled estate in Malibu. I have multiple teams in place and the Coast Guard is patrolling the shore below the seaside cliff on which the compound sits. Freddy Feynman had hired his own private security teams, but they've all been replaced with our teams."

"You comfortable with what you've done?" I said.

"Again, a safe house would be better, sir," Carpenter said, "but I think we've done the best we can under the circumstances. Hopefully, we'll be able to overcome our inability to enact ideal protocols."

I smiled.

"Your Commander at NAB teach you to be so reassuring?" I said.

"I believe I was born like that, sir," Carpenter said.

"Better to tell the truth than paint a falsely cheerful picture of a situation?" I said.

"Something like that, sir," Carpenter said.

"Couldn't agree more," I said. "Now, as to Dr. Lennon's children, I think it best if we involve U.S. Attorney Vandross. Do you know him?"

"Yes, sir," Carpenter said. "Hart told me Vandross is working with MOM on this matter."

"You know how to reach Vandross?" I said.

"I have his cell number, sir," Carpenter said.

"I want you to call Vandross and tell him to do whatever he has to do to get the Lennon kids securely on their way home before Burnette arrives in Buena Park," I said. "I want them there waiting for Dr. Lennon when you and she arrive."

"Yes, sir," Carpenter said.

"And tell Vandross that he has to make it look like the order to take the kids from the station came from him and him alone," I said. "That should take any heat off of you."

"Consider it done, sir," Carpenter said. "I take it you will not be accompanying us to Malibu?"

I noticed two more FBI agents exiting the rear of the medical building. I assumed they were the agents that had been on the roof, since they were both carrying sniper rifles. Both agents climbed into the second Suburban.

"I'm sure you can handle everything just fine without me," I said. "I'm going over to the stoning site to take a look for myself. I'll need transport there and a way to get to Malibu when I'm done."

"I'll arrange that, sir," Carpenter said.

"Will you please walk with me to the Maybach now, so I can give Dr. Lennon the good news?" I said.

"May I ask a question first, sir?" Carpenter said.

"Please do," I said.

"The children in the morgue, sir," Carpenter said. "Do you know who they are?"

"Sorry, I should have told you that before," I said. "Dr. Lennon was married to Paul Lennon, who is now deceased. The children are Paul Lennon's from a previous marriage."

"Paul Lennon was a special forces captain wasn't he, sir?" Carpenter said.

"Yes he was," I said. "And a fine one at that."

"Killing a fellow soldier's children doesn't sit well with me, sir," Carpenter said.

"Nor I, Agent Carpenter," I said. "Nor I."

"Whoever did this needs to pay, sir," Carpenter said.

"That's the plan," I said.

The breeze remained relatively calm as Carpenter and I walked together to the Maybach. As we walked, I knew there was something important I'd forgotten to tell Carpenter, but could not remember what it was. Manu, apparently having seen our approach, got out of the driver's door and opened the passenger door for me. When Carpenter and I reached the car we gave each other a small salute, then Carpenter headed over to his Suburban. As Carpenter was walking away, I'd realized what it was I'd forgotten.

I said to Manu, "Sorry Manu, one moment, please." I called after

Carpenter. "Agent Carpenter, one last thing."

Carpenter stopped. I walked to his side.

"Yes, sir?" Carpenter said.

"Sarah Lennon, Paul Lennon's ex-wife, is the mother of Sam and Lizzy, the children in the morgue," I said. "I think it best if you get someone out to Sarah Lennon's house as soon as possible. Dr. Lennon has been trying to reach her, but there has been no response. I'll get her phone number and address for you from Dr. Lennon."

I, of course, could have told Carpenter what I expected his cohorts to find at Sarah Lennon's house. But I did not. A small part of me, a very small part, was still holding out hope I had been wrong about Sarah's fate.

"Yes, sir," Carpenter said. "Hart gave me your cell number and I'll text you mine so you can send me Sarah's info. We'll check on Sarah once we get it from you."

"Excellent," I said. "Please keep me informed of your progress. Oh, and Carpenter?"

"Yes, sir?" Carpenter said.

"Do you need the clothes Sam and Lizzy were wearing when they were killed?" I said. "The clothes actually belong to Dr. Lennon's own children."

"Those are the clothes Dr. Lennon was carrying?" Carpenter said.

"Yes," I said.

"We can let her keep them for now," Carpenter said. "I'll get them from Dr. Lennon when we return to her estate."

"Very good," I said.

I had then considered my discussion with Carpenter to be at an end. However, as I was about to say my goodbye to him and return to Kate, I noticed he seemed to want to say something, but was perhaps afraid to get it out.

"Out with it, Agent Carpenter," I said.

"Sir?" Carpenter said.

"You've obviously got something on your mind," I said.

"Uh, yes, sir, I do," Carpenter said. "Sir, General Hart has explained to all of us at MOM the issues MOM faces operating on domestic soil. He made it very clear we can only have one of us directly involved in the investigation into the insurmountable edge, and that the rest of us are to avoid any direct involvement in the investigation."

"General Hart might just be being his normal paranoid self, but he's probably right," I said. "If any of our people who are on active duty with the Armed Forces or who are working at another agency - someone like you, for example - were revealed to be working with MOM right now, the mess might be a very hard one to clean up."

"That is how I understand it, sir," Carpenter said. "I just want you to know, that if it can only be one of us working on the edge, all of us at MOM are in full agreement that we're glad you're that one. We have no question that Hart chose the right man for the job. We're rooting for you, sir."

"That's very kind of you, Agent Carpenter," I said.

"I guess I better get going then, sir," Carpenter said.

We saluted each other. Carpenter headed for his Suburban. At the same time, on the other side of the parking lot, the second FBI SWAT Suburban pulled away from the rear of the medical building and headed toward us.

I walked back over to Manu. I noticed Manu's suit was even more snug around his massive body, its sleeves and pant legs even shorter than when I had first seen him back at the ranch. I assumed Manu's suit must have shrunk due to his little dip/near drowning in my ranch's moat.

"Miss me?" I said.

"Yes, General," Manu said. "Dr. Lennon told us about Sam and Lizzy. Terrible, isn't it, sir?"

"It is," I said.

"They were great kids," Manu said. "Mosi and I liked them very much. At least there's hope for Carolyn and Dylan."

"There's more than hope," I said.

Manu gave me a quizzical look.

"Give me a moment alone with Dr. Lennon," I said. "Then I'll fill you in."

I ducked my head, and carefully lowered my body onto the plush leather rear seat of the Maybach's passenger compartment. Manu closed the door behind me and climbed into the driver's seat.

I turned to Kate. She was looking at me, her face a mixture of both fear and hope.

"I heard what you said to Manu," Kate said. "Did you mean, please God, what I think you meant?"

"Yes, Kate," I said. "Elizabeth Wells did her job. Your children are safe and sound."

The hope and fear vanished from Kate's face and were replaced with a look of joy such as I had never seen. She sprang from her seat, veritably leapt across the divide between us, grabbed my shoulders with both her arms, and hugged me as tightly as I had ever been hugged. Kate's tears - this time of happiness - once again rolled down my neck.

CHAPTER 43

Before departing for her home in Malibu, Kate had given me Sarah Lennon's phone number and address and I'd texted the information to Carpenter. Carpenter had in turn arranged for a sheriff's deputy named Harold Blevins to drive me to the site where Sam and Lizzy had been stoned to death. The site was an abandoned housing development at the intersection of 85th Street and Avenue D in Lancaster. I would have preferred either Deputy Laura or Deputy Tracey, my jailhouse guards, to have been behind the wheel of the patrol car, but Deputy Blevins was not a bad substitute.

During the thirty minutes it had taken to travel east across Lancaster to get to the site, Blevins had regaled me with stories of the history of that great city. From what Blevins said, it appeared that other than the test flights of the Blackbird, U2, and stealth bombers, and the presence of Pancho Barnes, Chuck Yeager, and the Happy Bottom Club, not much had gone on in Lancaster since it was founded in 1884. Which might not have been so terrible, except for the fact that it had been decades since the stealth was first tested, which meant nothing of any worthwhile significance had occurred in Lancaster since the onset of the 21st century.

It was about 5:30 p.m. when Blevins dropped me off at the site. To the northwest lay the Tehachapi and Sierra Pelonas mountain ranges. The falling afternoon sun was still hours from disappearing beneath their rugged peaks, the bone dry air was absolutely still, and I could hear the hum of cars and trucks on the distant Highway 395. The temperature had dropped to a hundred degrees, but seemed to have stalled there and gave no hint of going lower. The only smell was the smell of heat.

The homes in the abandoned development were in various stages of completion - some nearly finished, others only framed - but all were rotting from years of exposure to the raging winds and alternating burning heat and freezing cold of the high desert. The houses bordered a stillborn golf course that consisted only of tufts of dead brown grass, sagebrush, tumbleweeds, and windblown sand. Each house was at least five thousand square feet in size and had a large backyard with a huge swimming pool. The backyards were barren and caked with dry dirt, and the walls of the pools were cracked and unpainted.

There was a massive FBI crime scene investigation in progress when I arrived and it was focused on the center of one of the extinct golf course fairways. The fairway itself was about five hundred yards long and seventy yards wide, but most of the FBI forensic techs were congregated within a single rectangle that had been created using yellow police tape and wooden stakes. The rectangle extended from a spot in the center of the fairway to the backyard of one of the decomposing homes on the fairway's northern edge. Three black FBI forensic vans and four black Crown Vics were parked next to the backyard.

I had harbored some illusions that my mission at the site, and perhaps even my broader mission at NASAD, would proceed without much intrusion by society at large. But what I saw before me shattered every last one of those illusions.

Because the FBI's forensic investigation had become a very public event.

Hundreds of gawkers ringed the golf course fairway. News teams had arrived as well, which meant untold millions were probably watching the goings on. Five television news satellite broadcast vans, one each from ABC, CBS, CNN, FOX, and NBC, were parked in the backyards of the two houses that were across the field from, and directly opposite, the houses where the FBI forensic vans were stationed. Each network had a two person team of reporters consisting of one man and one woman. The news reporters looked identical and interchangeable - they were all dressed in colorful, stylish clothes, wore too much makeup, spoke into microphones held closely to their mouths, and were bathed in bright, harsh light as cameramen filmed their every word.

A sheriff's helicopter circled overhead. Sheriff's and highway patrol cars had been placed at regular intervals around the fairway to keep the gawkers at bay. A separate deployment of a half dozen sheriff's deputies mounted on motorcycles had been tasked to keep the reporters from advancing any closer to the taped-off investigation area. The whirring blue, red, and yellow rooftop lights of the sheriff's and highway patrol cars, combined with the gawkers and news reporters, made me feel like

I had stumbled into a circus scene from a Fellini film.

I surveyed the spectacle for a few more moments, half expecting that lions, tigers, dancing bears, acrobats, clowns, or even Gelsomina and Zampano were going to appear. When they didn't, I started walking across the sand toward the rectangle of yellow police tape and wooden stakes. As I walked, I checked my phone for the umpteenth time in the last thirty minutes, hoping to have received a text or voicemail from Adelaide or Jeff. There weren't any. During my ride with Blevins, I had also repeatedly called Adelaide and Jeff, but they hadn't answered. I was still worried about Jeff's mysterious communication regarding Adelaide, but there was little I could do about it just then if neither of them were going to respond to me.

As I got closer to the rectangle, I was able to discern what the forensic technicians were doing. They were taking pictures, loading samples into plastic bags, making molds of footprints, and spraying chemicals that would help find even the smallest traces of blood.

The techs' work was all very exacting, but there was almost no chance it would do me any good. Why? Because in order to identify the killers, the evidence the techs were collecting would have to be compared against the killers' DNA and fingerprint data in an FBI accessible database. As I'd told Kate, I was sure nothing belonging to the killers would ever be found in such a database.

I did believe, however, that the investigation site might hold something of value. I wouldn't have come to the site if I thought that wasn't the case. I just knew I was going to have to find that value on my own.

I ducked under the police tape. A man in a blue windbreaker with 'FBI' stenciled in yellow on its front approached me. He appeared to be in his early sixties, was about five foot ten, stick thin, and very bow-legged. His face was darkly tanned and had the deep craggy lines of someone who spent most of his time outdoors under the burning sun. His windbreaker was open, revealing a black and red plaid flannel shirt, and he also had on blue jeans, a bolo tie with a turquoise enamel clasp, and a thick brown leather belt with a big silver buckle engraved with a longhorn on it. He walked with a slight limp.

"General Wilder?" the man said in a West Texas drawl. "Ray Carpenter said you would be coming. I'm Jerry MacKay, the agent runnin' this rodeo."

He extended his hand and I shook it. I noticed he was chewing tobacco.

"Pleasure to meet you, Agent MacKay," I said.

I meant it. It's not every day you get to meet a West Texas Irish cowboy.

"Heard you spent some quality time with Special Agent Burnette," MacKay said.

"Fine man, Burnette," I said. "Paragon of law enforcement leadership."

MacKay spit out some tobacco juice. He said nothing, just gave me a funny look.

"On the Bizzaro Planet," I said.

"Bizzaro Planet?" MacKay said. "Don't believe I know it."

"It's from Superman comics," I said. "Every inhabitant of the Bizarro World has taken an oath to do the opposite of whatever an earthling would consider good."

MacKay spit again.

"You sure you're a general?" MacKay said. "I'm a Marine and we didn't have no generals that talked like you in the Corps."

I didn't say anything.

MacKay punched my upper arm.

"Just ribbin' you General," MacKay said. "Know exactly what you're talking about. That shit for brains Burnette surely swore an oath against common sense."

"Against good taste too," I said.

"You referring to that sack of shit synchronized driving team of his?" MacKay said.

"Indeed I am," I said.

"Goddamned Burnette," MacKay said. He spit out some more to-bacco juice. "So, the way Carpenter tells it, Burnette screwed up the identifications of the kids' bodies something fierce."

"He did," I said.

"You pretty sure you got it right now?" MacKay said.

"Yes, I'm sure we've got it right now," I said. "Bodies definitely be-long to Sam and Lizzy Lennon, who were Paul Lennon's children by his first wife. Dr. Kate Lennon was Paul's second wife, and their children,

Dylan and Carolyn, are alive and well. Dr. Lennon did the identifications herself."

"The wheel was a' turnin' but the hamster was dead," MacKay said. "Burnette must've put poor Dr. Lennon through hell."

"More than hell," I said.

"Yeah, I bet," MacKay said. "I suppose you wanna hear what we found so far?"

"Please," I said.

"Well, little Sam and Lizzy were alive when they got here," MacKay said. He gestured with his head to the north side of the fairway. "Their footprints started out near the backyard of one of them houses. From there they headed to the center of the fairway."

Two food trucks joined the throng of onlookers standing outside the crime scene tape. There was a bit of a commotion as dozens of the onlookers rushed to get in line at the trucks.

"I assume they weren't unaccompanied?" I said.

"Hell no," MacKay said. "By the size and number a' the prints alongside the kids' prints, looks like three large males and one smaller male were with the kids." MacKay pointed to an area in the center of the staked rectangle. "Assholes brought Sam and Lizzy over to that spot right there and forced 'em to dig a grave."

"The children dug their own grave?" I said.

"Uh huh," MacKay said.

"How could you tell?" I said.

"Found two shovels next to the grave," MacKay said. "Shovels were small, kid size."

"I was already pretty pissed off, Agent MacKay," I said. "But I think I just got pissed off a whole lot more."

"You and me both, brother," MacKay said. "Anyway, best we can figure, Sam and Lizzy were stoned to death after they dug the grave. Small to medium-sized stones taken outta' the field first, then cinder blocks to finish 'em off. There's a pile of cinder blocks next to a half-built wall in the backyard of one of them houses. We're pretty sure that's where the blocks uh' come from."

"I was told the FBI thinks it was a ritual stoning," I said.

MacKay spit another big load of tobacco juice on the ground.

"Uh huh," MacKay said. "Sent pictures of the bodies and area surrounding the grave to Quantico. Quantico says everything's consistent with an Islamic stoning."

I knew that if things had happened the way MacKay just described them - and that was a big 'if' as far as I was concerned, given the pork eating, crucifix wearing nature of the supposed Islamic Kazakhstani terrorists I'd met up with earlier in the day - then the guys at Quantico would most likely turn out to have been right in their analysis. The reason I knew was because I had seen a similar stoning - actually as it turned out, a similar *attempted* stoning - when, many years ago, Jeff and I had come across one in progress in a remote Iranian village. A twelve year old girl named Fardokht didn't want to marry her uncle, so the villagers were going to stone her to death. Fardokht's two little brothers were part of the stoning crew and had already loaded up on some good-sized rocks. Jeff and I had just completed a mission that involved interrupting a supply of uranium to an Iranian nuclear reactor and were under strict orders to get out of Iran and stop for nothing until we were across the border. We both decided that stoning to death a twelve year old girl was not nothing. We snatched Fardokht, brought her back to the states, and found an extremely civilized Muslim family in Dearborn, Michigan, to take care of her. Last I heard, Fardokht was in dental school at the University of Michigan.

"No witnesses?" I said.

"None so far," MacKay said. "Don't expect any. I'm sure yuh' noticed as yuh' came in, this place is far from any currently inhabited area."

"I did," I said. "It made me wonder how it was that the bodies were discovered so quickly?"

"Deputy sheriff saw vultures circlin' the field and went to investigate," MacKay said.

"Didn't you say the kids were buried?" I said. "You got vultures out here with X-ray vision?"

"I said the kids dug their own grave," MacKay said. "I didn't say they were buried."

"What the hell was the grave for then?" I said.

"I don't know," MacKay said. "Maybe the kids' killers got interrupted. Maybe meant to bury 'em, but they thought they'd been seen and got outta here in a hurry."

"You said there weren't any witnesses, though?" I said.

"Might have been some who're 'fraid to come forward," MacKay said.

It was certainly possible MacKay was right about the killers being scared off, but it didn't feel that way. My instincts told me there was something else going on in regard to the grave, but just then I had no idea what that something else was.

"Alright, I guess I can see how it might have happened that way," I said. "So what got the FBI involved?"

"After a jihadist group claimed credit for the executions of those three NASAD employees in Vegas last week, anything to do with NASAD was upped to the FBI national terrorist watch list," MacKay said. "'Anything' included the name 'Lennon', and 'Lennon' was the name the deputy who found the bodies found written on the inside collars of the children's clothes. Soon as the deputy punched Lennon into the computer in his patrol car, all the bells and whistles went off."

"Bells and whistles, huh?" I said. "Just the kind of thing what would make a dog like Burnette come a runnin.'"

"I got here first," MacKay said. "It's my job to supervise any terrorist crime scenes in California, but yeah, Burnette was a close second."

"What'd Burnette do when he got here?" I said.

"Pulled rank on me and took over," MacKay said.

Two more food trucks arrived outside the yellow crime scene tape delineated perimeter. There was another scramble as dozens of onlookers rushed to be first in line at the trucks' service windows.

"Sounds familiar," I said. "Carpenter told me he did the same thing to him."

"That don't surprise me in the least," MacKay said. "Anyway, after he gets here, Burnette basically runs a fire drill, tramples over every FBI procedure and protocol known to man."

"He explain what the rush was?" I said.

"Didn't have to," MacKay said. "Obvious something scaring him big time."

"Obvious how?" I said.

"Soon as Burnette seen the children's bodies he just about shit his pants," MacKay said. "Burnette's face goes red, he starts sweating like a pig, and his lips got all blubbery."

"I've seen that look," I said. "Did he spit when he spoke?"

MacKay lobbed a big loogie of tobacco spit. If MacKay appreciated the irony of the moment, he didn't show it.

"Like a monsoon," MacKay said. "Burnette tries to reach Dr. Lennon and can't. Tries to reach the nanny. Can't do that neither. Burnette and his second moron in command huddle together. They're convinced the bodies they're looking at are Carolyn and Dylan Lennon."

"What did the convincing?" I said.

"Clothes labels, mainly," MacKay said. "Girl's locket and boy's cell phone too."

"They never stopped to think any of those items could have been stolen?" I said.

"You're kidding, right?" MacKay said. "Thought you were supposed to be a smart guy."

"You sure it wasn't a smart *ass*?" I said.

"That too," MacKay said. "And no, they didn't stop to think about nothin' bein' stolen."

"But it couldn't have just been the clothes, the locket, and the cell phone?" I said.

"No, Burnette and his sidekick were very scientific," MacKay said. "They moved on to the fact that the dead boy appeared to be older than the dead girl. And after that, they focused on the bodies also being the right size and age."

"Which sealed the deal," I said.

"Tighter'n a frog's ass," MacKay said.

"No one tried to get Burnette to slow down, maybe dig a little deeper?" I said.

"That would've been me," MacKay said. "But Burnette jus' screams, 'Who else could it be?!'. Told me to do my job and shut up."

"And knowing arguing with someone that stupid was a no win situation, that's exactly what you did," I said.

"Damn straight," MacKay said.

"What'd Burnette do next?" I said.

"Quantico picks up a trace on Dr. Lennon's driver's cell phone," MacKay said. "Burnette gets the news and he and his team take off on a road rally across the Mojave. You pretty much know the rest."

A scuffle broke out in one of the food truck lines. Two deputies hustled away from their positions manning the crime scene tape perimeter and made a beeline for the food truck.

"Sadly, I do," I said. "You have a time of death for Sam and Lizzy?"

"Best guess be 9:00 a.m.," MacKay said.

Which meant Sam and Lizzy had been killed while Kate and I were still at my ranch. It also meant that the Kazakhs would have had plenty of time to kill Sam and Lizzy and also meet up with us at the Coso Junction rest stop. But MacKay had said that three large males and one medium-sized male had been at the gravesite. There had been only three Kazakhs at the rest stop and I would not have described them as 'large' - the Kazakhs were strong and wiry, but they were more on the medium side size-wise. I suppose the medium-sized man at the stoning site could have been one of the rest stop Kazakhs, but I thought there was no way the three large men at the site could have been any of the Kazakhs I had seen at the rest stop. The rest stop crew also seemed like a pretty close knit team, so I doubted any of them would have split off to go to the stoning site alone. Which would mean that the medium-sized male at the stoning site was probably someone other than a member of the rest stop threesome.

Four men at the stoning site, plus the three dead Kazakhs at the rest stop, meant that whatever team the Kazakhs had belonged to had started out with at least seven players. My gut told me the team had not started with seven, though. Seven seemed too low. But no matter how many team members there were - seven, ten, fifteen, more - or whoever those team members ultimately turned out to be, or wherever they had originated from, or whatever method they had used to come to our shores, I knew one thing for certain. It wasn't just the three Kazakhs at the rest stop that were going home in body bags, but every single god-damned member of their godforsaken team.

"Thanks," I said. "Could I impose on you to show me around?"

"I better stay put," MacKay said. "I'm afraid the looky-loos and reporters might stampede and mess up mah' crime scene."

His comment seemed prescient, as, just at that moment, two of the reporters and their cameraman broke out of the news teams' containment area and made a dash for the center of the yellow rectangle. The sheriff's motorcycle deputies quickly corralled them and brought them back to where they belonged.

MacKay said, "See what I mean?"

"Yippee yi yo kayah," I said.

"Oh shoot," MacKay said. "Almost forgot. Carpenter sent a car for you. Said it was from a guy name uh' Mijtra."

"How do you spell that?" I said.

"Mijtra?" MacKay said.

"Uh huh," I said.

"I don't know," MacKay said. "M-I-J-T-R-A?"

"Could there have been an 'H' on the end?" I said.

MacKay gave me a funny look.

"Maybe," MacKay said. "Carpenter didn't spell it. Way Carpenter was talkin', I thought you knew the guy."

I did know the guy. The name was an anagram for 'Jim Hart'. Carpenter, or Hart, or both, were messing with me. In all honesty, I didn't know why I had asked MacKay to spell it. The question just kind of slipped out I guess, not unlike every other numbskull move I'd made that day. I'd at least had the presence of mind, however, to realize that if I told MacKay I actually did the know guy, there would then be two guys, MacKay and me, who thought I was a knucklehead. It was better to keep it at one.

I said, "Never heard of him. Wonder how Carpenter got that idea?"

MacKay shrugged.

"So, where's this car?" I said.

"Over yonder," MacKay said.

MacKay pointed at a banged up Toyota Corolla parked near the news vans. He fished the car's keys out of his pocket and handed them to me.

"Bit of uh' comedown from the Maybach," MacKay said.

"To tell you the truth, I'm not really much of a Maybach man," I said.

"That 'cause they so tough to blow up?" MacKay said.

"You've given it a try, huh?" I said.

MacKay laughed.

"No," MacKay said. "Special forces demolitions expert gave us a lecture at Quantico. Told us high security Maybachs a bitch ta' take down."

"That matches my experience," I said.

"You done it?" MacKay said.

"Too many times to count, unfortunately," I said. "Well, guess I better get started with my little tour."

"Already told the techs to give you anythin' you need," MacKay said, "but feel free to gimme a shout if there's something you ain't gettin'."

We shook hands. I turned and walked toward the yellow rectangle's center, which was then about fifty yards away from me, and also where most of the forensic investigative activity was taking place. I only had to cover about half of those fifty yards, however, to be able to see what was driving all that activity. Hollowed out in the desert sand near the center of the fairway was a child-sized grave.

i

CHAPTER 44

I stood near the grave Sam and Lizzy had dug in the abandoned field and watched the FBI forensic techs work. A slight breeze came up. The breeze didn't do much to knock the edge off the heat - it remained a hundred or so degrees - but even a little breeze was better than no breeze.

The FBI techs all wore blue windbreakers with the words 'FBI Laboratory' stenciled on the back in yellow block letters. The techs were either gathering evidence, putting evidence samples into plastic bags, or carefully labeling the bags. I didn't actually see what was written on those labels, but I knew the information would at least include the date, time, location, and description of the collection, along with something to identify the tech who had done the collecting.

All very well and good, but again, since the evidence the techs were gathering was mainly of the microscopic or trace chemical variety, I didn't believe any of it would help me. The lab results from that evidence would have to be compared against any databases that contained information about the world's criminals' DNA and fingerprints. Since there was almost no chance Sam's and Lizzy's killers were in any of those databases, even the most powerful DNA sequencers, electron microscopes, and mass spectrometers on earth wouldn't be able to identify the killers. If there was anything of use to me in that abandoned field, it was going to have to be something I could see with my own eyes right then and there.

The techs had laid out long, wide, white ribbons of some kind of plastic tape that seemed to be able to stick to the desert sand. The ribbons of tape outlined the areas within which the techs were focusing their investigation.

Two of those long, white ribbons had been laid out so that they ran parallel to each other. The pair of parallel ribbons demarcated a walking path. The path was about eight feet wide and fifty yards long, and extended from the north edge of the grave to the north side of the fairway. The path ended in the backyard of one of the homes on that side of the fairway. I could make out some faint footprints coming and going in both directions along the path.

Another similar pair of white ribbons marked a path that began at the southern edge of Sam and Lizzy's grave. That path headed out in a southeasterly direction at a forty-five degree angle to the grave. The path also had footprints along it. This second path was much shorter than the first path, however, and it extended only about twenty yards from the grave before it came to an abrupt stop in the middle of the abandoned fairway.

The spot at which the shorter path stopped was as nondescript as the rest of the vacant field. It was so nondescript, in fact, that I could see no reason for anyone to head for that spot over any other spot on the field. The spot didn't offer any spectacular scenic views, house any object of intense interest, nor did any rare animal or plant species seem to reside there.

At that moment, however, I believed I had a pretty good idea what that short ribbon-lined path meant.

It was an idea that made both my blood pressure skyrocket and the base of my neck flush hot with anger.

I knew anger wasn't going to do me much good right then, so I tried to calm myself. I told myself there was a chance my idea was wrong, and that it was silly to get all worked up before I had taken a closer look at the path in order to prove or disprove my theory.

Telling myself those things didn't help me, however, and my anger quickly escalated into fury.

I tried taking some deep breaths and focusing on my surroundings instead of my inflamed emotions. I saw that the sun, an orange eminence encased in an azure dome of sky, had continued to fall closer to the mountain ridges in the northwest. I became aware that the slight breeze that had come up carried the scent of sagebrush along with it. I listened hard and could almost hear the breeze rustling the dried weeds beneath my feet.

It was all almost idyllic.

Quite idyllic, in fact.

But, it did me no good.

My blood continued to boil.

Which I probably could have dealt with just fine if my vision hadn't also begun to blur, a blurring that was followed by a wave of dizziness that made me feel so unsteady I thought I might fall down.

Some warrior you are, Jack Wilder, I thought to myself.

I did the only thing I could do.

Which was to sit down on the desert floor.

Sitting down helped me to start feeling a tiny bit better.

But then a new problem rapidly developed.

The FBI forensic techs, who, other than for a few stolen glances, had pretty much ignored me up until then, were now all openly staring at me. I could also see MacKay looking directly at me from where he stood fifty yards away. I didn't think the techs or MacKay were in any way out of line, of course. After all, how often does one see a guy plop himself down on his ass in the middle of a crime scene?

I also quickly realized it wouldn't be long before the assembled gawking multitudes and the news crews would start to take an interest in me. The gawking multitudes had been growing too. They had grown so large in fact they had attracted yet another food truck, so that there were then five food trucks in total, all of which were supplying the crowd with cotton candy, popcorn, and soft drinks.

I didn't want to be the center of all that attention. But what could I do about it? I was still dizzy even though I was sitting down, and I knew if I stood up I'd probably at least keel over, or, at worst, lose consciousness.

I took some deep breaths and tried to gather my thoughts. The phrase 'Turn weakness into strength' flitted into my head, but I quickly discarded it. It sounded too much like something Sun Tzu might have said and it also nearly made me throw up.

I peeked out of the corner of my eye. The techs were still staring at me and the gawkers then seemed to be fixated on me. The sheriff's helicopter had made a beeline for me and was then hovering directly over my head. MacKay was also on his way over to me.

I decided my only way out of the mess was to pretend I had *chosen* to be on the ground. That I had taken to the desert floor because I had lost something and needed to look for it.

I took some more deep breaths to fend off my dizziness, and rolled onto my hands and knees. I crawled around and turned my head to and fro. I lifted handfuls of sand and filtered the sand through my fingertips.

I intermittently put my face close to the ground and pretended to be examining every detail of the sand below me.

I snuck another peek out of the corner of my eye. The gawkers were still gawking but MacKay was in retreat, apparently having fallen for my little show. I felt the wash of the helicopter's rotors as it moved on to greener pastures.

My vision began to clear and my wooziness lessened. I felt I could probably stand up and continue my investigation of the site. But I wasn't ready to do that just yet. Why wasn't I ready?

Pride.

Foolish pride.

Even though I was pretending to be looking for what was in actuality an imaginary object, I didn't want to stand up empty-handed. I thought the gawkers might think me a loser or a quitter. What could I give them though?

I scrabbled around in the sand some more while I thought about it. It was pretty much a choice between my iPhone and my wallet since those were the only things of value I had in my pockets. I decided the iPhone was best since it seemed like something that I either could have had out or could have slipped from my pocket. The problem was that I needed to get my phone out of my pocket without the audience seeing me doing that. I felt that could best be accomplished by using the magician's trick of misdirection.

I exaggeratedly studied the ground to my left. When I felt I'd done that long enough so that anyone observing me would be looking to my left, I slipped my right hand into my right front hip pocket as surreptitiously as I could, pulled my iPhone out, and dumped it on the ground just in front of my right knee. I kept looking left for a few more seconds, then looked right, bent down, and snatched my phone off the ground. Holding the phone aloft, I stood up and pantomimed a big sigh of relief.

Standing up as quickly as I had made my left knee scream in agony, but I did my best to shake off the pain and made a big show of wiping my iPhone off and checking its screen. I pretended to be satisfied with the phone, smiled, and put it back into my pocket. The techs and MacKay had already returned to what they were doing, but the multitudes clapped and whistled. I took a bow.

Having no desire at that moment to once again set my blood aboil, I assiduously avoided looking at the short ribbon-lined path to nowhere that extended from the southern edge of the grave, and instead focused my attention on the grave and the area immediately surrounding it. The area was enclosed by a white tape ribbon in the form of a square whose sides were about fifteen feet in length.

The grave itself was about three feet deep, four feet wide, and five feet long. Kid size. The grave's walls also suggested the grave could have been dug by children. The walls were not nice and neat like the ones made by backhoes in modern cemeteries, but rather were irregularly shaped and also inward sloping so that the base of the grave was narrower than its top. A big pile of dark sand was next to the grave, sand which I assumed had been dug out to create the grave.

Two shovels lay against the sand pile. The shovels were, as MacKay had said, also kid size. Their handles were only about thirty-six inches long and their blades only about eight inches wide.

Now that I had moved closer to the grave, I also saw that my initial count of only a half dozen FBI techs working the site had been wrong. There was a seventh tech lying face down on the floor of the grave.

The tech in the grave was not wearing a windbreaker like the others, but was instead garbed in a white jumpsuit, blue paper booties, light blue latex gloves, a disposable paper hat with an elastic bottom edge to ensure the hat didn't come off the wearer's head, and a surgical mask. Because of the tech's outfit, I wasn't able to tell if the tech was a man or a woman. The tech was propped up on his or her elbows meticulously photographing one of the stones that was on the grave's floor.

As I watched, he or she must have taken pictures of that stone from as many as twenty different angles. The stone being photographed was one of about three dozen blood-stained stones of various sizes that lay next to two large, bloody cinder blocks. I couldn't say for sure, but it looked like a few of the stones, and both cinder blocks, had bits of dried flesh stuck to them.

The blood and the flesh on the stones and cinder blocks made my own blood begin to boil again. I realized then that trying to keep my blood from boiling was a hopeless enterprise. There were just too many awful reminders out in that field of what had happened to Sam and

Lizzy. I resolved to carry on as best I could and not to let my anger interfere with my investigation.

I more closely studied the stones. Something about the stones' positioning seemed odd to me. At first, I couldn't quite put my finger on what I found odd about them, but after a minute, it came to me.

Most of the stones were piled against the east wall of the grave, but there were hardly any stones piled against the other walls. The grave's east wall was also the only wall that showed any pockmarks of the kind that would have been made by a stone hitting the wall with any significant force. Most of the pockmarks were very close to the top rim of the grave and there were no pockmarks near, or on, the grave floor.

One would have thought that if Sam and Lizzy were in the grave when they were stoned, then the killers would have had to have been standing outside the grave - and above the children - when they threw the stones down on them. That would mean that any stones that missed the children would most likely have made pockmarks on the grave floor and on the lower sections of the grave's walls as well.

One would also have expected that the stones, if violently thrown at a downward angle, would have scattered throughout the floor of the grave. But all the stones were piled almost directly on top of one another. It appeared as if the stones had not been thrown, but had fallen straight down and landed on each other.

I had an idea that could explain both the positioning of the pockmarks and the location of the stones. Before I pursued that idea further, however, I needed to confirm something with the tech photographing the interior of the grave.

"How's it going down there?" I said to the tech.

No response. Not even a twitch of recognition. The tech just kept lining up and focusing the camera and clicking away. Each click was accompanied by a flash from the camera's lighting system.

I tried another tack.

"Hi, my name's Jack," I said. "What's yours?"

The camera flashed, but nothing came out of the tech's mouth.

"I know you're really busy," I said. "I just have one quick question." Flash flash.

"That's a really cool flash on your camera," I said. "Are the batteries rechargeable?"

Flash flash flash.

"Actually, that wasn't my one question," I said.

Flash.

"Here's the question," I said. "You ready?"

Flash flash.

"Sorry. Strike that," I said. "'You ready?' could be taken as a question, but that's not what I wanted to ask."

I couldn't swear to it, but I was pretty sure I saw the tech take a deep breath in and out under the jumpsuit. Like they were trying to calm themselves. Either that or they were getting ready to punch me.

"Here's the real question," I said. "Did you, or anybody else, move any of the stones or blocks in the grave, or is what I see now exactly as you found it? A simple yes or no will be fine."

Flash flash flash flash.

It was time to take the gloves off.

"Your boss, Agent MacKay, told me I could expect full cooperation from all the techs in regard to my investigation," I said. "Do I need to ask him to come over here, or are you going to help me?"

The tech took the camera away from his or her face. He or she did not look up at me, but I did get an answer. It came in the form of a grunted low hiss that made it impossible to tell if the tech was even human, let alone male or female.

"Rephrase the question," hissed the tech.

Rephrase the question? It took me a moment, but I understood. My question had actually been a variation of a compound question that was impossible to answer with a simple yes or no. A yes or no answer to either of my question's compound sections would produce a response that was contradictory and opposite to the other section, even though both sections of my question had really asked the same thing.

"Yes, yes, of course," I said. "As far as you know, are these all the stones in exactly the position you found them in when you and your team arrived?"

"Yes," hissed the tech.

"Thanks," I said.

Flash flash flash.

I was then pretty sure my theory of the pockmarks' location and the positioning of the stones was correct. I was also just about as angry as I'd been in a very long time. Since I figured it was unlikely anything I saw next could make me any angrier than I already was, I decided it was time to revisit the short path to nowhere and give it the close examination it deserved.

I walked along the short path, studying the footprints on it as I did. I stopped when I reached the path's end, which was about twenty yards away from the grave.

There were two sets of smaller footprints that came out to where I stood but did *not* go back to the grave. There were also three sets of larger footprints that came out to where I stood, but did go back to the grave. The three sets of larger footprints, by their depth and stride length, made me believe that MacKay had been right - the three sets had probably been made by three tall men.

I also recognized the sole pattern of the shoes that had made the large prints. They were U.S. Army combat boots and they were a specific issue I had seen many times, but in only one place. That place was Afghanistan. The boots were the exact type that had been given to the Afghan soldiers who had been trained by U.S. Army advisors.

All the prints of the boots I was looking at belonged not to just some run of the mill Afghan troops, but to an elite subset of those troops, troops that had been trained by U.S. special forces units. I knew to whom the boots belonged, because all the bootprints showed that there had been a notch in all the boots' soles. That notch had been carved in the boots' soles by the special forces trainers to be able to track their elite Afghan students.

The notch was a subtle notch and the trainers of course didn't tell the Afghans about it. The trainers had put the notches on the soles because they faced a serious and chronic problem with some of the elite Afghan troops they were training. The problem was that once the troops had finished their training, the troops would sometimes turn that training back on the trainers and attack them. If a special forces advisor saw that notch on one of their attacker's bootprints, they knew one of their elite Afghan students had become an enemy.

There were only about two hundred elite Afghan commandos who had been given such notched boots. I considered the possibility that Sam and Lizzy's killers were not elite Afghan commandos themselves, but had gotten the boots from some of those elite troops. But the number of elite Afghan commandos in the world was so small, that I thought it unlikely three of them would just happen to have given their boots to non-commando compatriots who wound up killing little children on United States soil.

I thought it far more likely that whoever was behind the NASAD murders simply favored hiring elite mercenaries from Afghanistan's corner of the world. Afghanistan, after all, is just a hop, skip, and a jump from Kazakhstan, and Kazakhstan was the country from which the elite commandos at the Coso Junction rest stop earlier that morning had come.

As to why NASAD's enemy favored killers from that region, I had no clue.

But I meant to find out.

I was satisfied, at least for the moment, with my explanation for the probable origin of the three largest sets of footprints on that short path to nowhere. My thoughts turned next to the two smaller sets. The two smaller pairs of prints were tiny in comparison to the three larger pairs, and the smaller ones were also un-notched. I wished then I had taken a close look at Sam's and Lizzy's shoes in the morgue when I'd had the chance, but for whatever reason - the overwhelming emotions I had felt upon seeing the mutilated bodies of the dead children, lingering amounts of Burnette's tranquilizer drugs in my system, the stressful effects of the CheyTac being pointed at my chest, or overall rustiness from my two years of leave from active duty - I had not. The patterns of the soles of both smaller prints, however, were consistent with the rubber bottomed athletic shoes little kids would wear.

The smallest pair of the small prints looked to be just the right size to fit Lizzy, and the bigger pair of the small prints were the right size for Sam. Was there a chance the smaller prints didn't belong to Sam and Lizzy? I supposed it was possible, but it certainly wasn't something I was going to worry about.

There were other important things I noticed about the prints other than that Sam and Lizzy had made them, however. One, Lizzy's foot seemed to skirt along the line of Sam's right foot. Two, Lizzy seemed to have taken a lot more steps than Sam, and at times, I could see where the toes of Lizzy's shoes had not stepped at all, but rather been dragged away from the grave. Three, Sam's and Lizzy's prints both stopped at the path's end, and, unlike the three larger prints, the children's smaller prints did not return to the grave.

All of which said to me that the kids had made a run for it. Sam had probably figured out what fate awaited him and tried to drag his little sister Lizzy to safety.

I felt a tear come to my eye. That Sam had been one brave little boy. He and Lizzy deserved a lot better than they had gotten.

I took a moment to compose myself. I then refocused on what the prints were telling me. The pattern of all five sets of footprints also meant that the killers had caught Sam and Lizzy at the end of Sam and Lizzy's twenty yard run on the short path. The killers must have then carried the children back to the grave to be stoned.

I wasn't sure, however, what to make of the fact that there were only three sets of the larger footprints. Hadn't MacKay said there were four sets of larger prints? Had whoever had made the fourth set of larger prints just not given chase? Or maybe the owner of the fourth set of larger prints hadn't been graveside when the kids had made a run for it?

I walked back toward the grave and circled around it. I studied the tech's ribbon-lined path that marked the footprints that traveled back and forth between the grave and the house at the edge of the abandoned golf fairway. There were six sets of footprints on the path - four larger sets and two smaller sets.

The two smallest set of prints came out from the house, but did not return to the house. Not much mystery there. The smallest prints belonged to Sam and Lizzy. The children walked from the house out to the gravesite, but since they'd been murdered at the gravesite, they weren't going to be walking back the way they came.

The four larger sets of footprints on the path that came out from the house *did* return to the house, however. Three of those large footprint sets looked exactly like the large notched bootprints I had seen on the short path on which Sammy and Lizzy had made their ill-fated attempt to escape. The fourth set of the larger footprints on the path that led to and from the house, however, looked quite different from the other three pairs of large notched bootprints. That fourth set also had been the one that was not on Sam and Lizzy's escape path. That fourth set must have been the one that MacKay had been referring to.

The shoe that made the fourth set of the larger prints was smaller than the other three larger print sets, but still much bigger than Sam and Lizzy's footprints. The fourth set also didn't have the notched boot pattern of the three other larger prints, but rather had left a pattern that was consistent with the flat, treadless sole of a dress shoe.

The stride length of the person wearing the dress shoes was much shorter than the stride length of the men wearing the boots. The depth of the indentations made by the dress shoe in the sand was also much more shallow than the indentations made by the notched boots. That said to me the person wearing the dress shoes was lighter than my three presumed elite Afghan commandos who were wearing the notched boots.

MacKay had said he thought the small size of the fourth set of prints meant the person making them could have been a small male. But the apparent weight and stride length of the person who had made the prints suggested to me that that person could easily be a woman as well. Perhaps MacKay had been premature when he said a man had made the fourth set of prints?

Keeping in mind everything I had learned about that fourth set of footprints, I came up with six possible options for who might have made them. The options included a lightweight male or female with short legs and a short stride length, a lightweight male or female with long legs but limited stride length, or, lastly, a lightweight male or female with long legs who normally had a long stride length, but who had used a shorter stride length while at the site in order to disguise their identity. I had had no way to choose between those options at that moment, however. Perhaps a clue would arise later that would help me narrow the options down, and perhaps even zero in on an actual suspect.

It was time to further explore my theory about what had caused the locations of the pockmarks on the grave's east wall and the odd positioning of the stones on the grave's floor. I stood near the grave and scanned the area to the east and west of me for additional clues to support my hypothesis.

I scanned for the next ten minutes. The sun sank closer to the western mountain ranges and the sky around it turned a darker shade of orange. Another jet from Edwards roared overhead, its contrails flowing behind it. People walked away from the snack trucks drinking sodas and eating cotton candy and popcorn, but the lines of waiting customers at the trucks had grown longer and longer. A different pair of news reporters made a run with their cameramen for the grave and were quickly corralled by the motorcycle deputies. MacKay, watching the corralling, shook his head and spit.

My long range scanning exercise revealed nothing useful. All I got was hotter and more drenched in sweat. I realized that in order to find the clues I was looking for, I'd have to take a close look at a larger portion of the acreage surrounding the grave. My hunch was that the clues I was seeking would be found well outside the fifteen foot by fifteen foot ribbon square the techs had laid out around the grave.

There was only one way I knew of for one man to search an area as large as the area I needed to search and be sure he didn't miss anything of consequence. And that was to start at the center of the area to be searched and then walk outward from the search center in ever expanding concentric circles. The only drawback to conducting a search in that manner was that any forensic tech who chanced to observe my circular walk - and I had to assume it would be most, if not all of them - would probably think I was out of my mind. But, did I care what the techs thought?

No, I didn't.

I walked.

And walked.

And walked.

It wasn't until my fourth circle, a circle that had put me out about ten yards from the edge of the techs' perimeter - and fifteen yards from the grave - that all my circling had allowed me to see enough to confirm I'd found what I was looking for.

CHAPTER 45

I wiped the sweat from my brow and thought about what to do next. I wanted to bend down low to the ground in order to more closely study what I'd found. But if I did that, I risked tipping off the techs I'd found something of interest. Which might cause the techs to come over and take a look for themselves.

If the techs found what I had found, it was possible the techs would start questioning their theory of the murders of Sam and Lizzy - a theory that was then solidly focused on Islamic terrorists being the perpetrators. Such questioning might even get the techs to start thinking the way I was thinking, which was, of course, that Islamic terrorists had nothing to do with either Sam and Lizzy's deaths, or, for that matter, the deaths of the twelve NASAD drone submarine engineers, or the attempted kidnapping of Kate.

And the last thing I wanted was the techs thinking like I was thinking.

Because if the techs started thinking like I was thinking, they might share their thoughts with their FBI bosses. If their FBI bosses started doubting their Islamic terrorist theory, they could start pursuing a different theory. The FBI's pursuit of an alternate theory, no matter what that theory was, could tip off the bad guys that their terrorist diversionary gambit - a gambit the bad guys had clearly gone through a lot of trouble to both create and maintain - had been blown.

I didn't want the bad guys thinking their NASAD drone sub diversion was blown. I wanted them thinking their diversion was working just fine. Because if the bad guys thought their diversion was working, they probably wouldn't feel the need to create a new one. If they created a new diversion, I'd have to spend at least some time investigating their new diversionary actions to confirm the actions were actually diversionary, and not genuinely dangerous. With war possibly about to break out soon, I felt I needed all the time I had left to look for the enemy's true target, not a new, diversionary, false target. My hope continued to be that that true target would not only turn out to be what Dr. Nemo was referring to when he spoke of his 'grave risk', but also the insurmountable edge as well.

There were two additional reasons I didn't want the enemy to know I, or anyone else for that matter, was on to them. One, if the enemy believed no one was close to apprehending them, they might begin to let their guard down, which would make it easier for me to find them and dispose of them. And two, there was also the possibility, that if the bad guys thought anyone was on to them, they would get spooked and go so deeply underground I might never be able to find them. I wanted them out in the open where I had a chance to pick them off.

All of which is why, instead of taking a closer look at the ground beneath my feet just then, I once again circled the FBI techs' white ribbon perimeter surrounding the grave. I stopped circling when I was east of the grave and looking back at it. At that spot I could observe the odd collection of small stones that was lying on the desert earth between me and the grave. The stones were, for the most part, partially covered up by sagebrush.

Some of the stones were inside the techs' perimeter, but the majority of them were outside the perimeter. I had assumed the techs had either not seen the stones, or believed the stones had no significance. Otherwise, the techs would have cordoned off all the stones, not just the ones that were currently in their perimeter.

The odd stones, however, held great significance to me. That was because the stones lay among the sagebrush plants in a pattern that was clearly not of nature's making. That pattern consisted of nearly straight lines of stones that spread out like the spokes of a fan, or rays of the sun. The lines of stones ran in an east west direction, a direction that was almost perpendicular to the east wall of the grave. The stones were also in a fairly tight dispersion pattern.

There was only one way that pattern could have been created.

And that was by a human being or beings.

What it appeared that being or beings had done, was not only throw the stones at Sam and Lizzy, but that they had done so while standing a considerable distance away from the two children.

Throwing the stones in that manner was not consistent with an Islamic stoning. In an Islamic stoning, the stone throwers stand very close to their intended victim and throw the stones straight down onto the victim's body.

Which meant that what had happened to Sam and Lizzy was not an Islamic stoning but something else entirely.

I looked back at the grave. I observed that there were more stones in the ray-like lines closest to the center point of the grave than the northern and southern sides of the grave. I thought this would be consistent with someone aiming at something near the center of the grave. The heaviest concentrations of the fan-like, ray-like, pattern also seemed to form about five lines of stones, each with about eight to ten stones.

Extending from each of the stones was a short depression etched into the ground. The depression made it appear as if the stones all had a tail leading up to them. The stones' tails looked like they had been created when the stones had hit the ground at a high velocity and then skidded to a halt in the sand. The tails also pointed *away* from the stones and *at* the grave. The fact the tails pointed in that direction meant that if a person had thrown the stones at the same spot upon which I was then standing on the east side of the grave, that person would have had to have been standing either inside the grave or at a point somewhere west of the grave.

Throwing the stones from inside the grave itself made little sense to me. I assumed, therefore, that one or more people had thrown the stones from a spot somewhere west of the grave, a spot that would also be on the opposite side of the grave from where I was standing. The target of the person or persons throwing the stones was most likely Sam and Lizzy. Sam and Lizzy had also probably been standing in or near the grave when the stones had been thrown. The stones at my feet would have been the stones that had missed Sam and Lizzy.

Why had the techs missed the significance of the stones, indeed seemed not to even know of the stones' existence? The vast majority of the stones were almost fifteen yards away from the grave, so that was one possible explanation. Another explanation would be that the stones were too hard to see under the sagebrush.

I felt the best explanation, however, was that the techs were victims of the rule that people usually saw what they expected to see, and missed everything else. The techs had probably decided early in their investigation they were looking at a ritual Islamic stoning. From that point forward, anything the techs came across that didn't conform to their expectations of what an Islamic stoning should look like, simply remained unseen.

I moved to a spot that was five yards farther away from the grave. I was then parallel to the lines of stones and twenty yards away from the grave. I used that spot as the radius for a new circle. I started walking along that new circle towards a point on the circle's circumference halfway around the circle. When I got to that point I would be both twenty yards from the grave, and also directly opposite from where I had started. Since the circumference of a circle is $2\pi r$, my circle had a radius of twenty yards, and I was traveling halfway around the circle, that meant I only had to cover sixty yards in total.

I could cover sixty yards pretty quickly if I ran, but I couldn't run. If I ran, I might attract the techs' attention. So I walked and tried to appear as nonchalant as possible as I did so. My heart, however, was anything but nonchalant. It was pounding.

But my heart wasn't pounding from the walking I was doing. My heart was pounding because the anticipation of what I would find when I reached the point on the circle that was opposite and equidistant from my starting point was making me angrier than I already was.

Because I knew what I would find there would confirm the heartlessness and unspeakable evil of Sam and Lizzy's killers.

A few moments later I reached the equidistant point. I took a glance down at the ground, then quickly looked away. The glance had shown me the thing I had expected to see. Someone had kicked the thing in, probably trying to make it look like the thing had never existed. But there wasn't any question in my mind what the thing was.

It was a baseball pitcher's mound.

And if my twenty yard estimate was right, the mound was exactly where a pitcher's mound should have been if the grave was home plate - sixty feet away.

MacKay noticed me standing where I was and gave me a nod. I returned his gesture with a small wave. When MacKay turned back away, I raised my right arm to my face and pretended to wipe away the sweat on my forehead with the sleeve of my shirt. I peered down under the cover of my arm at the area around the mound. I saw that a very narrow footpath extending from the mound to the grave had been smoothed in an attempt to make it look like the path also had never existed.

Who had made the mound, and who had walked along the footpath?

Could it have been anyone other than the Afghans who had worn the notched boots?

Highly doubtful.

The members of the U.S. special forces units that had trained the elite Afghan fighters - the Afghan fighters who wore the same type notched boots that the Afghans who had stoned Sam and Lizzy had worn - had also taught those elite Afghan fighters the finer points of American style baseball during the downtime between combat missions. Assuming as I did, that the Afghans who had done the stoning were those selfsame elite Afghan fighters, then the Afghans who had done the stoning would have known how far a pitcher's mound was supposed to be from home plate. If Sam and Lizzy's grave was home plate, then the Afghans had put the mound just where it belonged.

Elite Afghan fighters were also expert in covering their tracks. Most people would have been misled by the Afghans' efforts to hide the footpath they had traveled between the pitcher's mound and the grave. But I had known what I was looking for. The unnatural smoothness of the footpath's sand had given away the Afghans' attempt to hide their tracks.

I took my arm away from my face and turned towards the western horizon. I stared at the ridges of the distant mountains where those ridges intersected with the desert's blue sky and recreated in my mind what had actually happened in this abandoned field earlier that morning.

What had happened wasn't a ritual stoning.

That was for sure.

No, the Afghans had played baseball.

Not a full game.

Just the pitching part.

The fan-like, ray-like, distribution pattern on the other side of the grave was consistent with pitches that had missed their mark. As one would expect, there were also a lot more stones outside the grave than in. More misses than hits.

The mound also explained the pockmarks on the wall of the grave and the fact that the stones were not scattered around the grave, but were mostly piled at the base of the east wall. Stones thrown from the mound would hit the upper part of the wall, but not the lower. Stones that hit Sam and Lizzy would have had their momentum absorbed by the children's bodies and pretty much just fallen to the grave floor near their feet.

The dispersal pattern of the stones on the other side of the grave - the side of the grave farthest away from me - also suggested Sam and Lizzy had not been a moving target. The Afghans had been aiming at something that had been fixed in space. Did one of the Afghans hold the kids still for the pitchers? Not unless the one holding the kids wanted to risk getting killed too.

Which meant the kids had to have been tied up.

But to what?

Stakes?

Most likely.

Where were those stakes now? Had the Afghans taken the stakes with them when they left?

Possibly.

But I didn't think it likely anyone would throw blood covered stakes in the back seat or trunk of a car and drive around town with them there. I thought it would be pretty damning evidence. Even if the blood had been cleaned off the stakes, modern forensic technology would find traces. There was no such thing as a perfect cleaning solution.

I was willing to bet that the stakes were somewhere in the field. The killers probably wouldn't worry much about the stakes being found, since they seemed pretty confident the FBI was buying their terrorist story. If anything, confident might have been too weak a word to describe how the killers felt. Cocky would have been better, as the FBI appeared to have fallen for their terrorist story hook, line, and sinker.

Hell, if I were the killers, and I knew Burnette was the agent pursuing me, cocky is the only way I *could* feel. And, if for whatever reason that cockiness waned even a scintilla, all the killers would have had to do to raise it back to sky high levels, would have been to witness what I myself was witnessing right then and there. Nearly all the forensic techs were packing up their equipment and lugging it back to their vans. The techs had defined their crime scene, they had investigated it, and now they were preparing to head home.

It was fine with me if the techs headed home. I wasn't going to leave until I found the stakes. I didn't need to find the stakes to prove anything more - I was already convinced my theory about the Afghans playing baseball with Sam's and Lizzy's heads was correct. But something inside me felt as if I wouldn't have done my duty to Sam and Lizzy unless I had borne full witness to their murders by finding the stakes.

So, I asked myself, where was the most likely place the stakes would be?

I scanned the entire field and tried to put myself in the Afghans' place.

I didn't think the Afghans would leave the stakes anywhere near the path they had taken from the house to the grave, or in a direct line extension of that path through the grave and beyond, or anywhere near the path that the kids had made when they had attempted their getaway. Leaving the stakes in any of those locations would have made it much more likely the stakes would be found.

Which meant if the stakes were still in the field, the stakes were probably on the same side of the grave as I was at that moment. If I was right, it wouldn't be too hard for me to find them. For whatever reason, the field had not yet been turned into a makeshift dump - as was the fate of many similar abandoned fields - and the only debris in field I had come across, if you could even call it debris, was all the equipment, bags, and other miscellaneous items the techs had carried onto the site. In fact, the only signs of life in the field I had seen other than those made by the techs, the killers, and the kids, were two sets of bicycle tracks in the sand. The bicycle tracks weren't in straight lines, but looped around in figure-eight patterns, the kind of patterns you would expect children to make if they were riding in the field. I was sure then, that if the stakes were out there, it was likely they would stick out like a sore thumb amid the sage and sand.

I began to walk again, this time just back and forth on the side of the grave on which I'd found the pitcher's mound. I moved in quarter circles of ever increasing distance from the grave, my path almost identical to what I would have done if I was walking back and forth along the rows of seats of an empty amphitheatre, moving up the rows one by one, with each subsequent row farther from the amphitheatre's stage than the one before it.

I found the stakes on my tenth circuit.

There were two of them and they were about forty yards from the grave.

I made my fake wiping sweat move with my sleeve again while I peeked out from under my forearm and took a closer look at the stakes.

The stakes were the kind ranchers used when they wanted to quickly put up a barbed wire fence. The kind one could just hammer into the ground, clip barbed wire to, and move on to the next post. The stakes were officially known as studded T posts. They had a green and white enamel coating, were about eight feet long, and had large anchor plates, blades really, at one end so they could be quickly placed in the ground.

The stakes had not been carried to where I was looking at them, but thrown.

I could tell the stakes had been thrown because there wasn't any evidence of covered up footprints near them and because there were skid marks from where the stakes had initially hit the ground to where they were then lying - just like the stones I had found on the other side of the grave. The two stakes were so clean they almost sparkled - probably a lot cleaner than when they had been sitting in some hardware store bin.

I had no doubt the stakes were the ones I was looking for. The fact they were clean almost certainly meant that the Afghans has tried to wipe away any evidence that they had been used in the murders of Sam and Lizzy. It appeared the Afghans needn't have taken the extra effort the cleaning would have entailed, as I felt there was little chance the FBI techs would find the stakes, let alone understand their significance.

I thought for a moment about what would happen, however, if the techs actually did find the stakes and the FBI's forensic lab determined there were traces of Sam's and Lizzy's blood on them. Wouldn't Burnette have to go through all sorts mental gyrations to explain the use of T posts in ritual Islamic stonings? Would he wind up brazenly quoting a passage he had bowdlerized from the Koran in order to support his theory? Would such bowdlerization be so outrageous that it led to a fatwa being declared against him? I found myself momentarily amused by the prospect of a Burnette fatwa.

I surreptitiously took some photos of the stakes with my iPhone. I left the stakes where they lay and walked back toward the grave. The tech of indeterminate gender was climbing out of the grave and hauling their camera with them. The other techs who had not finished earlier were all packing up their equipment.

The techs' site work was over and it wasn't only I who understood that. The food trucks had already driven away and most of the gawkers were headed for their own vehicles. The sheriff's helicopter was no longer anywhere to be seen. Even the news teams had packed up and were ready to go in search of the next incident of unbearable human suffering to share with their viewers.

I walked back towards the grave. When I reached the grave, I stood beside it and tried to picture what Sam and Lizzy had gone through.

In my mind's eye, I saw Sam and Lizzy and the Afghans heading out to the grave from the house on the edge of the field. I wondered about whether Sam and Lizzy had been allowed to walk on their own or if the Afghans shoved them along. I wondered if Sam and Lizzy had carried their shovels or the Afghans had carried the shovels for them. And I also wondered how long it had taken Sam to figure out what was happening, what he thought his odds of escape were - if a mind so young even thought in odds - and what had finally made Sam make the decision to grab Lizzy and make a run for it.

I hoped that when the Afghans caught Sam at the end of his run, he hurt them a little bit. Maybe Sam whacked them with his shovel, bit their hand, or tried to gouge their eyes out. I had an instinct Sam would have. Lizzy too. I also had an instinct they were the kind of kids who would not go out without a fight, that they were like their dad, Kate's dead husband, the hero Captain Paul Lennon.

I was suddenly overcome with sadness, because it had hit home for me just then that the children, their father, and their grandfather, Milt Feynman, shared something in common - they had all probably been murdered by the same evil entity. That entity was also probably the same entity that had murdered all the NASAD drone sub engineers as well.

I don't know if there's a heaven, but I hoped if there was, that Sam and Lizzy were up there with their dad Paul, that Paul had told them how proud he was of them, and that they were all living happily together ever after.

I hoped too, that in heaven, Sam and Lizzy's last moments had been wiped from their memory. Because those moments could not have been good. I was sure Sam and Lizzy had been tied to the green and white T posts and watched in horror as the Afghans had competed to see who could throw hard high ones at their little heads. I hoped the first stones had knocked the kids unconscious. I didn't want to deal with the idea that Sam and Lizzy had been awake when the stones had ripped apart their eyes, ears, teeth, and finally, their skulls.

It also came to me then why Sam and Lizzy had probably been forced to dig the grave despite the fact the killers had not intended to, nor did they, bury them. True, the grave was necessary to paint the picture of an Islamic stoning, but I felt deep in my soul there was another reason for it. That reason was most likely to terrorize Sam and Lizzy. Someone had wanted Sam and Lizzy to know they were going to die and that their deaths were coming soon. Someone had wanted Sam and Lizzy to experience not just physical torture, but horrific mental anguish as well.

If I was right about my idea that the terrorizing of Sam and Lizzy had been an intentional component of the killers' plan, that would mean I might have badly miscalculated earlier about the killers' motives. It would mean everything that had happened to Sam and Lizzy could have been about more than just making Kate fear for the safety of her own children, and thus trying to scare Kate off from pursuing whatever the Afghans' and Kazakhs' employers didn't want Kate pursuing, or coercing Kate into doing the employers' bidding.

Something else would be in play.

Something that felt...

Personal.

Personal against who though?

Kate?

Paul Lennon?

Milt Feynman?

Someone else?

I didn't yet know or understand.

My instincts told me, however, that without a full understanding of that potential personal component, I would never completely solve the riddle of Nemo, NASAD, and the insurmountable edge.

By then, all the techs were at the vans and finishing up their final loading. The rest of the site was nearly deserted. MacKay had gone off without me noticing.

It was almost time for me to go, but I had one more thing to check on before I left. I walked to the backyard of the abandoned home that was contained within one of the techs' ribboned rectangles.

There were tire tracks in the home's backyard. From the size of the tracks, it appeared to me there had been two fairly large vehicles in the yard, probably vans. I took some photos with my cell phone of the tire tracks and also of all the footprints that were near the tire tracks. The footprints seemed to be the same ones I had found near the grave - those of Sam and Lizzy, the three presumed Afghans, and the mystery person with the dress shoes.

I took one last look around, then turned to head toward the Toyota Corolla 'Mijtrah'/Hart had arranged for me. As I did, however, something caught my eye. That something was about twenty yards to my left, and also fifty yards away from where the techs' vans were still parked in the backyard of one of the abandoned homes on my right.

I realized the reason I hadn't seen the thing before was because the sun had been more or less overhead and the brightness of the sun's light had obscured it. But, then with the sun lower in the sky, it stood out. Faintly, but definitely visible. It was a string strung between the second stories of two of the abandoned homes on the edge of the fairway. It looked like kite string, and I had an idea what the string meant. I decided to come back later that night and check that idea out.

CHAPTER 46

I was one of only a few people left at the stoning site by the time I got to the Corolla at about 6:30 p.m. Nearly all the gawkers were gone. Other than that one last gender unknown FBI forensic tech bagging up stones from inside the grave, all the techs were gone. The news crews had all packed up and departed. The only people left, other than the tech and me, were a few sheriff's motorcycle deputies on the site's perimeter. I assumed the deputies would depart once the tech was done with his or her work.

The Corolla was a four door sedan that seemed to be at least thirty years old. It looked to have once been a deep arctic blue, but then was a mixture of rust and a washed-out indeterminate gray. There were dents on all four fenders, the passenger side rearview mirror was missing, the upper half of the hood radio antenna was broken off, and the tires were nearly bald. Its body radiated heat waves from having baked in the desert sun all day, and I had no doubt that I'd get a nasty burn if I touched it.

I took the keys MacKay had given me out of my pocket, inserted them into the driver's door lock, unlocked the door, gingerly stuck my right index finger under the handle, lifted the handle, opened the door to the accompaniment of a loud metallic screeching noise, and was instantly greeted by a blast of furnace-like air from the car's interior. The Corolla's interior was a match for its exterior and then some. It had a stick shift with a cracked plastic knob, the radio was missing, the windows had old-fashioned cranks to open them, and foam padding showed yellow through holes in the rotting fabric covering the seats. The interior smelled of cigarettes, rancid fried food, and sour wine.

I slipped into the driver's seat and pulled the door shut, its hinges once again loudly screeching. I started the engine and looked for the air conditioning. There wasn't any. Did General Hart have a budgetary problem, or was this Hart's unsubtle attempt at reminding me of the importance of austerity in keeping a soldier's mind focused on his mission? Hart had access to a lot of money, so it had to be the latter.

Which is why, since I saw no reason to sweat for sweat's sake, and knew Hart had lifted his austerity notions from the writings of the ever annoying Sun Tzu, I found myself cussing out both of them when I painfully wrenched my back reaching behind me to crank down the rear seat windows.

My iPhone rang.

Agent Ray Carpenter's number was on the screen.

I put the phone to my ear with my left hand while I cranked open the Corolla's front windows with my right.

"I hope you're calling me to tell me you got Dr. Lennon to Malibu safe and sound," I said into the phone.

"We did," Carpenter's voice said. "Both kids are here too. Alive and well."

I turned the car's fan up high. With the fan blowing and all four windows open, I think the inside temperature dropped half a degree.

"Good," I said. "I doubt you care, but right now I'm sitting in a circa 1980's death trap masquerading as a car."

"Hart's idea," Carpenter said.

"I never thought I'd say this, but it makes me miss the Maybach," I said. "Maybe you can send Manu and Mosi to pick me up."

"You serious?" Carpenter said.

"No," I said. "You get a crew out to Sarah Lennon's house yet?"

"That's what I called about," Carpenter said.

"You don't sound very cheery," I said.

"I'm not," Carpenter said.

"Dead, huh?" I said.

"Found her in the kitchen," Carpenter said. "She'd been decapitated. Someone had broken in through a door that led in from the backyard. House was ransacked. A complete mess."

"I'm liking the guys who are doing all this less and less, Ray," I said.

"You and me both," Carpenter said. "Do me a favor please, General."

"What kind of favor?" I said.

"Don't bring 'em in alive," Carpenter said.

"Clearly you don't know me very well," I said.

"I figured that was the way it was," Carpenter said. "I just didn't want to appear presumptuous."

"That's very polite of you," I said. "I should be pulling into Malibu around midnight. Make sure your guys know I'm coming."

"You don't want to get shot?" Carpenter said.

"Something like that," I said.

"They know you're coming," Carpenter said.

"Bye," I said.

I hung up.

I suddenly realized I was very hungry. I hadn't eaten anything, other than the snacks in the Maybach and the beef jerky Vandross had given me at the jail, since I had left the ranch that morning. I knew I had at least a couple of hours before the sun went down and I could come back to the stoning site to investigate my hunch about the string between the two abandoned houses, so I had plenty of time to eat. I remembered we had passed an IHOP earlier in the day. I thought chocolate chip pancakes, bacon, eggs, orange juice, and coffee made a lot of sense.

I took the Corolla south down to Avenue I, turned right, and headed west. I once again rolled by the Power of Praise Ministry, the pawn shop, and the McDonald's. The IHOP parking lot was next to the AutoZone. I pulled into the lot. The IHOP's blue roof was already making my mouth water.

I entered the IHOP, a welcoming world of yellow walls, wooden tables, copper colored coffee carafes, ceiling fans, bright lights, and air so cold it made my teeth rattle. A television was mounted on a wall near the front door. The television was tuned to a cable news channel. Two newscasters were speculating on the chances of going to war with China while a satellite photo of Chinese troop deployments in Iraq was displayed on the screen behind them.

A man and a woman in their late forties, both of whom were well dressed and height-challenged - they couldn't have been more than three and a half feet tall - were being led to a table by the hostess. When the hostess returned to her stand I asked her for a booth in the rear corner of the restaurant. A rear booth would give me views of both the IHOP's front and rear entrances and also allow me to sit with my back against a solid wall.

Choosing a rear booth was probably a bit of overkill, but I didn't want to risk displeasing my ancestors. Some of the most ancient scribblings in my tattered copy of Winfield Scott's book had been made by my great-great-grandfather and were admonishments to his descendants not to meet the same fate as Wild Bill Hickok. My great-great-grandfather had known Wild Bill and, apparently, Bill was quite scrupulous about always taking seats facing the front door in any of the Old West establishments within which he may have found himself. Bill did this in order to be sure none of his many enemies ever took him by surprise. Bill was also an avid poker aficionado, his favorite game being five card draw. One hot summer day in 1876, Wild Bill found himself waiting an inordinate amount of time for a seat to open up at the draw table in his favorite saloon. When a seat finally did open up, it was one that placed Bill's back to the front door. The impatient Mr. Hickok took the seat anyway. My hope has always been that Wild Bill won a few hands that day, since he was dead a short time later, his killer having snuck in behind him through the front door and put a slug in the back of Bill's head.

The hostess led me over to a booth in the back of the IHOP and I sat down. Once seated, I found I also liked the booth for more prosaic reasons. It was next to a window and I was able to watch the sunset, which was already a pretty spectacular show of purples, reds, and oranges.

My waitress, a sixty-ish woman with auburn hair and wearing a starched white shirt, blue apron, and sensible shoes, took my order and returned quickly with my coffee. She poured me a cup and put the carafe on the table. I lifted the cup to my lips. The coffee was steaming hot and had a smoky nut-like aroma. I took a sip. The coffee scalded my tongue, but it was good and strong.

The table was set for two. The empty setting made me miss Grace. Grace had loved chocolate chip pancakes and made the best ones in the world. Grace didn't like IHOP's chocolate chip pancakes much, but that was just another example of a situation where her taste had been much better than mine. Grace was better than me in many other ways as well, and I had learned a lot from her during the course of our years together. I wished those lessons had never stopped.

I took out my iPhone, started up my web browser, and logged onto the site that tracked Adelaide's ankle monitor. The site showed Adelaide was in the kitchen on the ranch. She appeared to be moving about the kitchen cooking. Which, since it was dinner time, was just what I would have expected to see.

I decided to try to contact Jeff one more time. I called his iPhone. Jeff answered on the first ring.

"Whatever you sellin'," Jeff's voice said over the phone, "I ain't buyin'."

I was, of course, still pissed off at Jeff for not calling me back. I also very much wanted to hear what was behind Jeff's cryptic messages about Adelaide. But I knew if I came on too strong there was a good chance Jeff would just hang up on me. And there really wasn't any rush was there? After all, how bad could the situation with Adelaide have been if she was puttering around the kitchen at that moment?

"What's for dinner?" I said into the phone.

"New York steak and a baked potato," Jeff said. "Ashley having the filet."

"How did Ashley want the filet?" I said.

"Rare," Jeff said. "Like always."

"I'm having chocolate chip pancakes at an IHOP in Lancaster," I said.

"Won't be good as Grace's," Jeff said.

"No, they won't be," I said.

"Bad guys dead yet?" Jeff said.

"Some of them," I said.

"Quick work, Kemosabe," Jeff said.

"Can't take too much credit," I said. "I just happened to be there when they came after Kate."

"Lucky for Kate you with her," Jeff said. "They intending on kidnapping her or killing her?"

"Kidnap to start," I said. "Probably kill later."

"How many?" Jeff said.

"Three," I said.

"Bad bad guys?" Jeff said.

"Pretty bad," I said. "Kazakhstani special forces."

"Tough dudes," Jeff said. "Long way from home."

"Kazakhs also had high-tech tracking equipment in their van," I said. "I'm sure they were using a spotter plane too."

"Expensive operation," Jeff said.

"Seems that way," I said. "Paul Lennon's kids were killed today, too.

Here in Lancaster."

"Kate's kids were killed?!" Jeff said incredulously.

"Sorry, didn't put that as well as I might have," I said. "They weren't Kate's. They were Paul's from a previous marriage."

"So they were Paul's but not Kate's?" Jeff said.

"Yeah," I said.

"How old the kids?" Jeff said.

"Seven and eight," I said.

"We don't like child killers," Jeff said.

"No we don't," I said.

"Someone gonna pay," Jeff said. "Did the Kazakhs do it?"

"Afghans," I said. "Pretty sure they're commandos our boys trained."

"Man, it be old home week in the Mojave," Jeff said.

"Certainly seems like it," I said.

"How did the Afghans take down the kids?" Jeff said.

"Tried to make it look like an Islamic stoning," I said. "But they were actually playing baseball with the kids' heads."

"Maybe special ops needs to cut back on the sports instruction," Jeff said.

"Maybe," I said. "Kids were forced to dig their own grave, so they knew what was coming. FBI found the kids' mom in her home. Her name was Sarah. She'd been decapitated. Don't have any proof yet, but I can't see her being killed by anyone other than the same group that killed her kids."

"I agree," Jeff said. "Whole thing sounds personal, dude."

"That's what I was thinking," I said.

"I didn't get the impression you were working on something personal when you left here today," Jeff said.

"I didn't think I was working on something personal either," I said. "I think we have to assume there's more than one thing going on."

"Things usually one thing," Jeff said.

"I know," I said.

There was silence on Jeff's end of the call. I assumed Jeff was thinking things over. The silence ended after about thirty seconds.

"I gotta hunch," Jeff said.

"What is it?" I said.

"I think NASAD's problems and some dude's personal vendetta all going to tie together in the end," Jeff said.

"Certainly does look that way, doesn't it?" I said.

Two girls came into the IHOP and took the booth next to me. They looked to be about nineteen, were very pretty, and wore lots of eye makeup. They both had bright red gloss lipstick on their full lips and silky brunette hair that fell to the middle of their backs. They had on blue work-shirts, the tops open to show abundant cleavage, and the tails tied up to reveal very toned midriffs above the waistlines of their low-cut jeans. The girl facing me smiled. I smiled back.

Jeff said, "I were you, I'd be looking for whoever imported the Afghans and Kazakhs. Then when you find them, you can make them tell you why it was necessary to be killing little kids and their mom, and NASAD drone sub engineers too."

"You don't think maybe a disgruntled employee is behind it all?" I said.

"You're not serious, are you?" Jeff said.

"It wasn't my idea," I said. "It was the FBI's. At least one of their agent's, anyway."

"That agent got a name?" Jeff said.

"Burnette," I said. "And he's got more than a name. He's also got a gold-plated, pearl handled Glock and a porkpie hat."

"Really?" Jeff said. "A gold-plated, pearl handled Glock?"

"Uh huh, " I said.

"You best stay away from that Burnette boy," Jeff said. "Because whatever else he is, he's definitely a fool."

"Fool's an understatement," I said.

"Moron?" Jeff said.

"Better," I said. "Anyway, disgruntled employee is actually off the table now. The moron is currently convinced Islamic terrorists are behind everything."

"Kazakh special forces mainly Christian dudes," Jeff said.

"Especially the ones I met up with today," I said. "They had cobra and crucifix tattoos behind their ears."

"I seen those tattoos in the Sudan," Jeff said.

"Indeed you did," I said.

I took the iPhone away from my ear and checked on Adelaide's position on the tracking website. The site showed she was still in the ranch's kitchen. Adelaide seemed to be cooking something fairly complicated, as she kept moving back and forth between the refrigerator and the stove.

"Want my honest opinion?" Jeff said.

I put the phone back to my ear.

"Always," I said.

"Guy behind all this got eagle, panther, and tiger statues parked outside the front door of the big old mansion he own," Jeff said.

"Greedy guy with an advanced case of conscience deficiency syndrome?" I said.

"Uh huh," Jeff said. "Full blown psychopath. You got a line on how you gonna find him?"

"Got a notion," I said. "Hart's working on it for me."

"Hart's in this?" Jeff said.

"Yep," I said.

"Told you when I first saw that Maybach that it had something to do with China, bitch," Jeff said. "When you gonna learn to trust my magical eighth sense?"

"Eighth sense, huh?" I said. "Most people would call it a magical *sixth* sense."

"Mine so magical, I got two more than anyone else got," Jeff said.

The waitress brought my chocolate chip pancakes, scrambled eggs, crispy bacon, and orange juice. I poured some maple syrup on the pancakes, cut a big three stack high wedge, and put it in my mouth. I chewed.

"Yeah, well you were right," I said. "Right now, I don't see how Kate's and NASAD's problems can be anything but China."

"Has to do with that Chinese insurmountable edge too, don't it?" Jeff said.

I didn't say anything.

"Cat got your tongue?" Jeff said.

"No," I said.

"You wanna be safe you should apologize right now," Jeff said.

"Safe from what?" I said.

"From having to apologize even more," Jeff said.

"The longer I wait to apologize the more apologizing I have to do?" I said.

"You got it," Jeff said.

"Alright," I said. "You win. Hart and MOM believe the whole NASAD mess is most likely related not just to China, but to the Chinese insurmountable edge as well. From what I've seen, I'd have to agree with them. Sorry I ever doubted you."

"You feel a lot better now, don't you?" Jeff said.

"Yes," I said.

"Apology good for the soul," Jeff said.

I grabbed a strip of bacon, bit off a piece, and washed it down with a swallow of coffee.

"Hart thinks there are Ohio class drone subs involved," I said. "NASAD designed them."

"There's such a thing as drone subs now, huh?" Jeff said.

"Yep," I said.

"Ohios have nukes," Jeff said.

"They do," I said. "And there's someone named Dr. Nemo running around."

"Jules Verne and me goes way back," Jeff said. "But Nemo wasn't a doctor. Nemo was a captain."

"True," I said.

"And China has its own nukes," Jeff said. "Hart be wrong. You best be looking elsewhere."

"That's what I think," I said. "But I'm also thinking I still gotta check it out."

"Check it out all you want," Jeff said. "Ain't it."

I drank some orange juice, ate a forkful of eggs, and put another wedge of pancakes in my mouth. The two girls in the other booth carefully watched me eat. They slid out of their booth and into the seat across from me in mine. They both smiled. Beautiful smiles.

"Hi," I said to the girls.

"Important call?" the girl sitting to my right said.

"You're cute," the girl on the left said.

"I'll be off in a minute," I said to them. "Do you want some bacon?"

The girls both took a piece of bacon. They had very pretty fingers. They put the bacon in their pretty mouths and chewed with their pretty teeth.

"Who you talking to?" Jeff said.

"Two girls think I'm you," I said.

"Put them on the phone," Jeff said.

"My friend wants to talk to you," I said.

I handed the girls the phone. They put it between their pretty heads. I could hear Jeff's muffled voice. The girls laughed.

"No way," said the girl on my left. The girls laughed some more, then gave me back the phone.

"What'd you say to them?" I said to Jeff.

"Told them you were gay," Jeff said. "They didn't believe me."

"That's because they're smart," I said.

I smiled at the girls.

The girls laughed again.

"So you got a plan?" Jeff said.

"I'm looking for a couple of witnesses tonight," I said.

The girl on the right said, "We can be witnesses."

"Have some more bacon," I said.

Jeff said, "To the killings of Paul Lennon's kids?"

"Yes," I said. "I also got Hart working on an empty foil snack bag I took off the Kazakhs."

The girl on the right said, "What's a Kazakh?"

The girl on the left said, "It's a bird you idiot."

Jeff said, "Empty foil snack bag?"

I said, "Eighth sense broken?"

Jeff didn't reply.

"I'll tell you if it pans out," I said.

"You do that," Jeff said.

The girls cut some of my pancakes for themselves.

"Can I speak to Adelaide now, please?" I said to Jeff.

"Adelaide's not here," Jeff said.

"My iPhone shows she's standing right next to you," I said.

There was a pause.

It was a long pause.

A very long pause.

It was so long, in fact, that it made me nervous.

Because such a pause could mean only one thing.

I said, "Adelaide's not there is she, Jeff?"

"She left," Jeff said.

"She took her ankle monitor off?" I said.

"No," Jeff said. "She's got her monitor on."

"I don't understand," I said.

"Adelaide has some program on her computer," Jeff said. "Makes it look like she is where she ain't. I tried to stop her, but she wouldn't listen."

"Where'd she go?" I said.

"She's enlisting," Jeff said.

"In the Army?" I said.

"Uh huh," Jeff said.

"She's only seventeen," I said.

"Found some dude on the internet," Jeff said. "Makes fake birth certificates."

"Goddamnit!" I said.

"It not my fault," Jeff said. "I tried to stop her. Thought I did too."

I sucked in my breath and let it out, trying to calm myself.

"I'm sure you did," I finally said. "I'm not blaming you."

Which actually was the truth. I never could, or would, blame Jeff for what Adelaide had done. I had no doubt Jeff had tried to stop Adelaide - and probably truly thought he had when he texted me he'd fixed the problem and everything was under control - but I didn't see any way Jeff could have succeeded if Adelaide had really wanted to leave. Because Adelaide was as bull-headed as humans come. At that moment, there was also absolutely, positively, nothing to be gained by getting Jeff riled up. If Jeff had a bad PTSD relapse while I was gone, then Jeff and I would both be in trouble.

"Good," Jeff said. "For a minute there I thought you were confused on that point."

"I'm not confused," I said. "You know which recruiting office she went to?"

"Carson City," Jeff said.

That made sense since Carson City was the closest Army recruiting office to the ranch. Since it was after 5:00 p.m., I knew the recruiting office would be closed so there wasn't much I could do about Adelaide just then. I figured I would call the recruiting office in the morning and get everything straightened out.

I didn't understand what Adelaide was thinking, however. Even if Adelaide believed her computer program could fool her parole officer, how could she expect to get through an Army boot camp without anyone noticing she was wearing an ankle monitor? Maybe she was planning on taking the monitor off? But if that was the case, why hadn't she done it already? Did she need to be wearing it for the computer program to work? Did Adelaide know how to override the monitor's GPS software, but not how to trick it into believing it was still attached to her leg?

I realized my thoughts were getting pretty far afield. The only thing I really should have been worrying about was, that Adelaide, by being off the ranch unsupervised by Jeff or me, was in violation of her parole. If some cop picked Adelaide up before she got back to the ranch there would be nothing I could do about it. She'd go straight to prison.

"Okay, don't you worry about any of this," I said to Jeff. "I'll keep trying to reach Adelaide. I'll tell you if I do."

"Au revoir, o filos mou," Jeff said. "Til ci incontriamo di nuovo, muda mrefu."

"I think I'm going to be ill," I said.

"Because you confused?" Jeff said.

"No," I said. "The 'muda mrefu'. It sounds so much better in the original Spanish than in Swahili."

"You just jealous you didn't think of it first," Jeff said.

"True," I said.

Jeff hung up. I put my iPhone back in my pocket and turned to look out the window. The sun was getting very low on the horizon. It was time to get back to the stoning site to see if I was right about the string. I took a twenty out of my wallet, left it on the table, and slid out of the booth.

"Hey, where you going?" the girl on the right said. "Don't you want to party?"

"Have to meet my wife," I said. "Finish the pancakes if you want."

"The guy on the phone said you weren't married," the girl on the left said.

"Yeah, well he also said I was gay," I said.

I dashed out.

ł

CHAPTER 47

Outside the IHOP the sinking sun shone orange above the purple foothills to the west, and a light breeze blew sand and a tumbleweed across my feet. The air was still hot. Most days the desert air will cool a good bit as night approaches, but that wasn't one of those days.

My plan was to get back to the stoning site as close to the onset of darkness as possible. I didn't want to be too early or too late. If I was too early, and there was still enough light to see clearly, the witnesses to the stoning I hoped to find might see me and take off. If I got to the site too far past nightfall, there was a chance the witnesses would have already left and headed home. My hunch was the witnesses belonged to that section of humanity that wasn't allowed to be out too late.

I pulled the Corolla out of the lot, said goodbye to the AutoZone and the IHOP, and headed back east on Avenue I. I passed the McDonald's, the pawn shop, and the Power of Praise Ministry for the third time that day and watched them fade behind me in my rearview mirror.

I didn't know why, but as soon as I turned north on 85th Street, I suddenly felt homesick. The farther I moved away from the IHOP, the more the feeling of homesickness grew. I tried to shake the feeling, but that only intensified it even more.

I thought about what had happened in the IHOP, wondering if something I had said or done while I was there was making me feel the way I did. I had talked to Jeff and found out about Adelaide, but I didn't think that was it. Then I remembered about the empty seats, the chocolate chip pancakes, and what I had said to the two girls. I was pretty sure the emptiness inside me probably had something to do with Grace.

Most people would probably say I had lied when I had told the girls in the IHOP I was married. But I didn't feel like what I had said was a lie. Death had not ended my marriage with Grace. I was separated from her physically, but mentally and spiritually, during both my waking hours and in my dreams, I spent much of my time with Grace. When I went for walks on the ranch she was, more often than not, by my side. When I lay in bed at night, I felt her presence. When I woke from a nightmare, I often heard Grace say, "Don't worry my darling, go back to sleep, it was only a dream," just as she had when she was alive.

That day, the anniversary of Grace's death, had been meant to be a special day, a day of heightened devotion. I had planned to relive a number of cherished moments from my life with her. One of those moments was the moment I fell in love with Grace. It happened on the first day I met her, which was the first day of our sophomore year in high school. We were in English class and I had been sitting behind Grace, spending most of my time staring at the back of her beautiful blond head and marveling at how her bare, tanned shoulders - covered only by the thin strap of her light yellow cotton dress - could appear so delicate and yet so strong at the same time. At some point about halfway through the class, I made a wisecrack that had caused the class to laugh and the teacher to glower. Grace had turned around in her seat to look at me with her gorgeous big blue eyes, a huge smile on her face.

Our eyes had met and that had been it.

For life.

Grace and I had been married two years later, and our wedding was another moment I had planned to relive. The wedding had taken place in a large church with wooden pews and multicolored stained glass windows. Sunlight had streamed through the windows in golden shafts. As Grace had walked towards me, resplendent in her white wedding dress and veil, there seemed to be a glow around her even brighter than those shafts of sunlight. There were a hundred wedding guests in the church, but the only person I saw was Grace. For a moment that seemed to last an eternity, I thought I was in heaven and Grace was an angel.

I knew, however, that if today's anniversary of Grace's death had gone as planned, and I had relived as many wonderful moments with Grace as I could, there would also be bittersweet moments. I knew at some point I would hear Grace's voice telling me I would be okay after she was gone, that I'd miss her but I'd be okay, her words and intonation exactly as they had been on the day we had found out her fight was over, her cancer had won. Grace telling me I would be okay wouldn't be words I'd consciously conjure up, but would come on their own, as if Grace had somehow implanted them in my mind so that I would always hear them whenever my grief became overwhelming - and my grief was always at its most overwhelming on the anniversary of her passing.

I had tried to stop Grace from talking about me and my needs on that day we had found out her death was near. I told her to stop thinking about me, that it was her we needed to focus on. But Grace would have none of that, and had continued to spend her time worrying about me and not herself.

Grace had been right to worry about me of course, just as she had always been right in so many other things. During the last few years, when there was many a time I had found myself in the deepest and darkest of despairs, those times had only been made bearable by the hearing once again of Grace's soothing voice.

But I hadn't been able to relive any of those special moments with Grace today, had I?

And I wasn't going to, was I?

Because, instead, I had been sucked into this nightmare by Kate and Hart. I was sure the two of them had believed they had done the right thing by getting me involved with NASAD, China, and Nemo. But, at that moment, I was sure they hadn't done the right thing at all. Not by me. Not by a long shot. I needed to be back at my ranch. I needed to be back with Adelaide and Jeff. How would I be able to live with myself if Adelaide went to prison or Jeff hurt himself?

And I really, really needed to be with Grace.

I pulled the Corolla over to the side of the road and parked on the shoulder. The heaviness in my body grew until I could barely move. I wondered if what I was feeling was what catatonics felt like when those poor souls had come to the end of the road of whatever mental anguish they had been forced to bear, and just refused to ever move again.

My head sank against the steering wheel and I began to sob, my body wracked with uncontrollable heavings, and tears streaming down my face.

And then I heard a voice.

"Jack, please don't cry, honey," the voice said.

The voice sounded like Grace's voice.

How could that be?

"Grace?" I said.

"Jack, you're going to be okay, my darling," Grace's voice said.

I lifted my head off the steering wheel, turned it from side to side, looking for her.

"You are not going to be able to see me, sweetheart," Grace's voice said.

Despite what Grace's voice had just said, I kept looking for her. I didn't find her.

"You're actually talking to me, Grace?" I said.

"Yes, my love," Grace said.

I tried to control my sobbing, wiped the tears off my face with the sleeve of my shirt.

"But you never actually talk to me Grace," I said. "Not since you died. I mean, I hear your voice, but you've never actually talked back."

"That's true," Grace said. "And you're afraid you're going crazy, aren't you?"

"Yeah, well, kinda," I said.

"You aren't, honey," Grace said.

"I'm not?" I said.

"I think you've got what General Hart and that nice man from the Justice Department said you had," Grace said.

"By nice man, you mean Vandross?" I said.

"Yes," Grace said. "Hart and Vandross called it a stress reaction, didn't they?"

"Yes," I said. "Will it go away?"

"Sweetie, I'm not a doctor," Grace said. "But I think it will."

"How long will it take?" I said.

Grace did not reply.

"Sorry," I said. "I shouldn't have asked you that."

"It's okay," Grace said. "Jack, I think Kate is a very nice woman. I think she'd be good for you."

A large chartreuse Lancaster city bus with big windows stopped across the street from me. I must have parked opposite a bus stop. The bus looked like it was an electric bus. Some of the passengers disembarked. As they did, I noticed many of the occupants on the side of the bus closest to me staring at me through the windows. I gave them a little fake smile. They turned away.

"Kate's on my shit list," I said. "Hart too."

"I know," Grace said. "They manipulated you. But doesn't everyone do a little manipulation from time to time?"

"I suppose," I said.

"You know their cause is noble," Grace said.

"Well, they don't need me," I said.

"That's not true, Jack," Grace said. "They need the best. And that's you, darling."

I didn't say anything. A moment passed. I knew my wife well enough to know she was carefully considering what to say next, looking for the best angle to take to sway me to her line of thinking. It didn't take her long to decide upon it.

"Wasn't Kate's father, Milt Feynman, a great friend of yours?" Grace said.

"Yes, he was," I said.

"You loved him, didn't you?" Grace said.

"Yeah, I did," I said.

"You believe Milt was murdered, don't you?" Grace said.

"Yeah," I said. "I do."

"And those poor little children, Sam and Lizzy, that were stoned to death," Grace said.

I sighed.

Grace was winning.

"What about them, Grace?" I said.

"They were Paul Lennon's, weren't they?" Grace said. "He was a fellow soldier, wasn't he?"

"Yes," I said.

"I've never known you to sit by and not deliver some kind of reckoning for those kinds of things, Jack," Grace said.

"I never have," I said.

"And what about our men and women in Saudi Arabia?" Grace said.

"What about them?" I said.

"Please don't be petulant with me," Grace said.

"Sorry," I said.

"If Hart is right about what's going on, a lot of them are going to die, aren't they?" Grace said.

I sighed again.

"Yes," I said. "But there's plenty of other men who can do this, Grace. Hart doesn't need me. And what about Adelaide and Jeff? Adelaide already screwed up, and I've only been gone less than a day. Hell, she's your niece for chrissake. And God knows what will happen to Jeff if I stay away too long."

Another chartreuse electric bus stopped across the street. It sure seemed like there were a lot of buses in Lancaster for such a small town. More passengers disembarked. More passengers gawked at me.

"I think you know what to do about Adelaide and Jeff," Grace said.

"I do?" I said.

"Yes, you do," Grace said.

Grace seemed pretty convinced, and Grace was rarely wrong when she was convinced. So I thought about it. A plan slowly formulated in my mind. It was a little wild, but it could work. Still...

"You're not serious, are you, Grace?" I said.

"Dead serious," Grace said.

I winced.

"Sorry, dear," Grace said. "There was a little too much irony in that, wasn't there?"

"Uh huh," I said.

"Can I trust you do to whatever it takes to make sure those men and women in the Middle East make it home alive?" Grace said.

I sighed once more.

"Yes," I said.

"Promise?" Grace said.

"I promise," I said.

"I love you, Jack," Grace said.

"I love you, Grace," I said.

"I miss you, darling," Grace said.

"I miss you, too, Grace," I said.

"I have to go now, sweetheart," Grace said.

"Please don't," I said.

"It's not in my control," Grace said.

"What do you mean it's not in your control?" I said.

There was no response.

"Grace?" I said. "Grace? Come on, don't do this to me."

She did not answer.

"Grace," I shouted.

Nothing.

She was gone.

I felt myself about to cry, but I forced myself not to. Grace wouldn't have wanted that. I took a deep breath and leaned back in the Corolla's seat, my head against the headrest. Out of the corner of my eye, I noticed the bus passengers still staring at me. What? They'd never seen a guy talking to himself before? And how did they know I wasn't speaking to someone on a cell phone? I flipped them the finger. They turned away.

I closed my eyes and took a few deep breaths. I slowly began to regain my composure. After a few moments, I opened my eyes again.

Outside, the blue twilight was engulfing the mountains to the west, and all around me it was dark.

"Okay, Grace," I said to myself. "I can do this. I'll do it for you, my love."

I started the car and sped away. I was late, but I thought I could still get to the stoning site in time.

CHAPTER 48

I parked the Corolla on a street that ran perpendicular to the eastern border of the abandoned housing development where Sam and Lizzy had been stoned to death. The spot I chose was about two hundred yards from the development. There was no trace of sunlight behind the western mountain ranges and only the glow from a half moon illuminated the development's decaying homes. The temperature had dropped less than five degrees and the air was hot and dry. To the south and below me, the lights of Palmdale and Lancaster sprawled out across the Antelope Valley.

I exited the Corolla and advanced toward the killing site on foot. Since I believed my quarry, if it was indeed present, would be hidden in the homes along the northern edge of the barren golf course, I approached the site from the south, using the line of homes on the course's southern edge to shield my approach. A soft breeze stirred up the scent of sage and rattled the crime scene tape, the tape making shrill trilling noises in protest. It was so silent that the only other thing I could hear besides the sound of the tape was the gentle pounding of my own heartbeat echoing within my ears.

I had come back to the site because of what I had seen earlier in the day - the bicycle tracks in the sand near Sam and Lizzy's grave and the string suspended between the second floors of two of the houses on the northern border of the golf course. The bicycle tracks had looked like they had been made by kids, and my hunch was the same kids would have installed the string. I thought that maybe those same kids might also have been using the abandoned homes as clubhouses, and that they had attached cups to both ends of the string so that they could use the cups and string combination to talk to each other. The cups and string were a lot less sophisticated than a cell phone, but also probably more fun.

I hoped, that since the schools were out for summer vacation, those kids might have been talking over the string when the Afghans had used Sam and Lizzy's heads for pitching practice. I also hoped that kids who liked to talk with cups and string rather than cell phones might be a little more adventurous than the average child, and that they might risk returning to the site that night, if only to satisfy their curiosity about how death may have changed the landscape of their private little world.

I thought it best to first do a bit of surveillance before heading for the homes that had the string connecting their second floors. The goal of my surveillance would be to determine whether or not the kids had already arrived at the clubhouses that night. If they had, I was confident I could approach them unseen. If, however, I moved on the houses before the kids were already situated within them, it was possible the kids and I might cross paths during their arrival. If that happened, it could cause them to turn tail and head for home before we had a chance to chat.

I chose as my hide one of the development's unfinished houses on the southern border of the golf course. The house looked like all its neighboring houses, except it had a rooster weathervane on its roof. The weathervane made a frail creaking sound as it oscillated in the breeze. I had chosen the house since it was directly across the barren field from the houses with the suspended string. My hide house's front entrance had no door to contend with, so I entered, and passed through a foyer which opened onto a living room, which in turn opened onto a kitchen. I found a set of rickety wooden stairs that led to the second floor. I climbed the stairs and arrived at the doorway of what had probably been planned to be the master bedroom. On my way up, I had passed two tiny, nearly invisible, pinhole video surveillance cameras overlooking the stairs, and there was an additional camera mounted above the frame of the bedroom door. I assumed the home's construction plans had contemplated a high level of security.

No matter what the ultimate goals of the house's security system had been, there was no need for advanced protection at that moment. The only items that required guarding were the crushed beer cans, stained food wrappers, cigarette stubs, and empty condom packages that littered the bedroom floor. I thought maybe the home was also a clubhouse, but a clubhouse for kids a bit older than the ones I was looking for, kids who used it for less childlike purposes. The room also had a high arched ceiling with a wooden beam across it that had some

Nordic-looking carvings. Perhaps the builder thought an alpine look would contrast nicely with the surrounding desert.

I took a position behind the broken glass panes of the bedroom's huge window. The window had a north facing panoramic view. I looked out. I found no sign of life. All I saw was the rustling yellow crime tape, the black silhouettes of the homes across from me, the mountains behind those homes, and a dark night full of shimmering, shining stars.

I settled in to wait. I was an experienced waiter. I had waited on every continent in the world - sometimes for friends, sometimes for foes, sometimes under blistering suns, sometimes in bone chilling blizzards, sometimes for only a few moments, sometimes for days on end.

That night my expert waiting talent went for naught, however. I had been at the window only a little more than five minutes when I saw a flash of metal at the northern edge of the golf course. Two bicycles were moving across the sand toward Sam and Lizzy's grave. The bicycles were being ridden by two small people. The two small people stopped at the yellow crime scene tape. They dismounted their bikes, laid the bikes down gently on the sand, slipped under the tape, then walked towards the grave.

I was better able to determine the riders' size once they were off the bikes. One of them was larger than the other, but even the bigger one seemed at most ten years old. Two tiny lights flicked on - small flashlights I assumed - and danced like fireflies in the children's hands. I watched as the light beams illuminated the interior of the grave, the yellow crime scene tape, and the surrounding earth.

The children's soft voices carried across the parched field towards me, but strain as I might, I could not make out what they were saying. My intensified hearing did, however, pick up the distant sounds of cars traveling on the interstate and, seemingly even farther off, the roar of motorcycles.

Then, just as suddenly as the kid's flashlights had flicked on, they flicked off. The two children dashed back under the crime scene tape, remounted their bikes, and quickly rode toward the houses with the string. I assumed their rapid departure was due to a case of the heebie-jeebies. I know I would have come down with one, if at their age, I had just seen what they had seen.

When the kids reached the houses with the string, they rode through the breezeway between the houses and disappeared. I hustled my way out of the bedroom, back down the stairs, out the front doorway, and onto the street. I jogged east, again using the southern row of houses as a shield, and then turned north at the eastern edge of the barren golf course.

A minute later, I arrived outside the front entrances of the houses with the string.

The kids' bikes were nowhere in sight.

For a moment, I worried the kids had fled, but then I made out two rumpled shapes beneath a tarp a few feet from the front steps of one of the houses. I lifted the tarp. Both bikes were under it.

I knew the kids could be in either of the houses, but I figured it was most likely they would be in the house outside which the bikes lay. I climbed the steps to that house's front entrance. Just like the house I had just come from, there was no door present, and I entered the house. The house's interior, thanks to the miracle of tract home design, looked exactly the same as my hide house. Same foyer. Same living room. Same stairs. And I'd have been willing to bet, same master bedroom.

I stood in the foyer and called in the direction of the second floor landing, "Anybody home?"

I heard some scurrying upstairs, but no answer.

"I'm coming up," I said. "Don't shoot. I'm unarmed."

The moon's glow and the hazy city lights of Lancaster and Palmdale together sifted in through the living room windows and gave me enough light to see where I was headed. I crossed the foyer, climbed the stairs, and came to the master bedroom entranceway.

Just as I had in the hide house.

Only this master bedroom entranceway had a door and the door was closed.

I knocked.

No answer.

I tested the doorknob.

It was locked.

"Knock, knock," I said, loud enough to be heard through the door.

Nothing.

"Aw come on," I said. "Don't make me play knock knock by myself."
Still nothing.

"Okay," I said. "I'll do both parts. Who's there? Water. Water who?
Water you doing? Open the door!"

Utter silence. I guess the kids didn't like it. I admit is was pretty lame
as knock knock jokes go. Jeff would have done a lot better.

I studied the door. Both the door and its frame had significantly
rotted away from long exposure to the desert elements. I thought I
could kick it in, but I didn't want to.

"I really need to speak to the two of you," I said. "I'm not going to
hurt you."

Of course, just as I heard myself saying those words, I realized I
sounded exactly like the kind of person parents warned their children
to stay away from. I knew I would scare the bejesus out of the kids if I
kicked down the door, but I didn't see any other option. I decided to give
them one last chance.

"I'm going to count down from ten," I said. "If you don't open the
door, I'm going to have to open it myself. Ready?"

No response.

"Okay," I said. "10,9,8,7,6,5,4,3,2,1..."

I knew I'd hate myself in the morning for what I was about to do,
but I felt I had no other choice if I was going to speak to the kids. And
I needed to speak to the kids. I leaned back, raised my right leg, and
bracing off my left leg, kicked in the door. The door fell off its hinges,
crashed to the floor, and sent a cloud of dust into the air. My left knee
seared in pain from the effort. Doing my best to ignore the pain, I
stepped onto the doorway's threshold, but did not enter the room.

I scanned the room. I saw a cup tied to a string that came in through
the window, but no living things. I quieted my breathing and listened. I
again heard the breeze outside rolling across the desert, the faint trill of
the crime scene tape, and the distant rumble of traffic and motorcycle
engines - I couldn't be sure, but the motorcycles sounded louder than
when I heard them earlier. I also heard minute cracking sounds as the
house settled slightly and the breathing of two small people. Without
moving my head, I slowly rolled my eyes to the ceiling. The ceiling had
the same high arch and beam as its twin across the field. The two little

kids who I had seen on the bicycles were clinging to the ceiling beam, chest and bellies facing down. They were both boys, and there was a rope tied to the beam and coiled between them. Both boys wore night vision goggles.

Little kids with night vision goggles?

What was the world coming to?

"Whoever is in here must be really good at hiding," I said. "An Army Ranger would be proud."

I put my arms up over my head.

"I'm going to come in now," I said. "I am keeping my hands where you can see them."

Keeping my arms above my head, I walked to the window and bent down over the cup.

"I used to have one of these," I said. "Very effective communication device."

I stood up.

"I'm going to slowly reach into my pocket and bring out my identification," I said.

I took out my wallet and opened it to the same Defense Department identification I had shown Burnette earlier in the day. I held it facing outwards where the kids could see it.

"My name is Jack Wilder," I said. "I'm here investigating what happened in the field this morning. I had a hunch there might be some witnesses who we haven't heard from yet, but who might have seen something."

I waited. Again careful to keep my head facing forward, I slowly tilted my eyes upward. I watched the kids focusing their goggles on my identification. I saw some kind of silent communication pass between them.

"I'm only interested in information," I said. "I promise not to reveal your names to anyone."

"Are you really a general?" One of the boys said.

I kept my arms up, but tilted my head to look at them.

"I haven't been a general for long," I said. "But, yes I am. Wow, nice night vision goggles."

"Our dad was a Marine," the boy said. "He was killed in Iraq."

"I am sorry to hear that," I said. "What was his name?"

"Matt Fenton," the boy said. "He was a sergeant."

"I want to look him up if that is okay with you," I said.

I put my wallet back in my pocket and took out my iPhone. The phone had access to the names of all current and past military personnel records going back fifty years. I typed in their father's name and rank. Matt Fenton's profile came up.

"Your father was a hero," I said. "He won the Medal of Honor. He must have been very brave."

"He was," the other boy said. "We're brave too."

"I can see that," I said. "What are your names?"

"I'm Timmy, and my brother is Bobby," the first boy said.

"Nice to meet you Timmy and Bobby," I said. "Do either of you know how to drive?"

They shook their heads.

"Want to learn?" I said.

CHAPTER 49

We departed Bobby and Timmy's clubhouse and made our way along the eastern edge of the housing development towards the spot where I had parked the Corolla. The Corolla was at that moment about four hundred yards south of us. I was walking, and Bobby and Timmy were riding their bicycles on either side of me. It was by then around 9:45 p.m. and the breeze had completely died. The air, if anything, felt hotter than it had earlier in the night. The moon was higher, and its moonlight, though brighter, was still soft and diffuse. The moon rays caused the cactus and sagebrush to cast shadows on the desert sand.

Up close, and with the moonlight to help me, I was then able to see the boys' features more clearly. They could have been twins, except that Bobby was larger than Timmy. Both boys were rail thin, had closely cropped red hair, blue eyes, pale skin, freckles on their faces, wore matching olive green t-shirts with 'Army' stenciled in black letters across the chest, baggy blue Levi's jeans, and old model black Converse athletic shoes with white laces and white soles. The night goggles were around their necks and the bikes they were riding were Schwinn Stingrays with thick tires. All of which would have added up to normal All American kids, except their clothes and shoes were tattered and threadbare, their pale, freckled skin was grimy and looked like it hadn't been washed for weeks, and the bikes were at least thirty years old and nearly rusted out. The kids were obviously neglected, but then again what should I have expected if they were out here in a killing zone so late into the night?

I had started out wanting to know what, if anything, the kids knew about Sam and Lizzy's killings, but at that point I also wanted to know why the sons of a dead war hero looked the way they did. I also felt like I needed to do something about their neglected state, but I wasn't sure yet what that would be. In any event, I thought it best to get Bobby and Timmy talking about things that were unlikely to make them nervous or self-conscious at the start of our conversation. Beginning by asking them about Sam and Lizzy, or their home life, didn't seem to be the way to build a solid rapport.

"So how long you guys been brothers?" I said.

"Since I was born," Timmy said.

"Aha," I said. "That must mean Bobby is the older one."

"Uh huh," Timmy said.

"How old are you Bobby?" I said.

"Nine," Bobby said.

"How about you, Timmy?" I said.

"Seven and a half," Timmy said.

"Exactly a half?" I said.

"Almost a half," Timmy said.

"Good," I said. "Want to make sure I got that right."

Bobby said, "You need it for your report?"

"Nah," I said. "All this is top secret. Just between the three of us."

Damn. 'Just between the three of us,' huh? There I was sounding like a pervert again. I even felt like a pervert. By the looks on their faces, the boys didn't seem bothered, however.

Bobby said, "Should we call you 'General'?"

"Jack is fine," I said.

Timmy said, "General Jack!"

"That's fine too," I said.

"Cool," Timmy said.

Just then, the distinctive, ferocious rumble of motorcycles traveling in a pack that I had first become aware of about twenty minutes earlier - a rumble that had ever since been waxing and waning, sometimes audible, sometimes not - became incredibly loud. It was as if the cycles, though unseen, were somehow right on top of us.

Bobby and Timmy suddenly looked worried.

They turned to each other.

Some kind of secret communication again appeared to pass between them.

I got the impression the boys knew the sounds - that, for them, the rumbling sounds were emanating not from nameless motorcycles that just happened to be passing nearby that night, but that they knew the motorcycles making the sounds, and, by extension, the cycles' riders. Because of my rapport building goal, however, I hesitated to pry at that moment, and, as the high-pitched whine of the bike's engines suddenly changed to a lower register and rapidly died down to an almost imperceptible hum - as if the bikes' had gotten close to us and then turned away - I was inclined not to push Bobby and Timmy about what I thought I may have descried from the looks on their faces.

That inclination not to push the boys was strengthened by the fact I had what I considered a plausible alternative explanation for the unusual ebbing and flowing nature of the bikes' engines. I had heard similar sound distortions along the slopes of the Bekaa Valley a decade earlier while Jeff and I were hunting - and ultimately killing - a Hezbollah squadron that had killed three of our CIA officers in Lebanon.

At that time Jeff and I had heard what sounded like motorcycles riding right on top of us, but it had turned out the bikes were miles away on the Bekaa Valley floor. The geography of my then present location in that valley surrounding Lancaster, California, was closely analogous to the terrain I had encountered in the Lebanese valley. Both valleys were bowl-shaped, desert valleys, high in elevation, dry in climate, and in both valleys I had been situated so that sprawling cities spread out below me. I assumed then that both valleys could have easily shared the same unusual acoustics. That assumption, along with my hesitation to pry, and the fact I had not actually been able to see the motorcycles making the sounds, led me to move forward without giving the situation any further thought. In retrospect, further thought would have been a wise course of action.

In any event, with the disappearance of the motorcycles' sounds, Bobby and Timmy's tense expressions disappeared as well.

Timmy said, "How many men you killed General Jack?"

"What makes you think I killed anyone, Timmy?" I said.

"'Cause you're a general!" Timmy said.

He had me there. I normally would have tempered my response to kids so young, but I wanted to be honest with them in the hopes they would be honest with me. And they were, after all, the sons of a decorated combat hero.

I said, "I only killed when I had to, Timmy."

"One hundred?" Timmy said. "Two hundred?"

I sighed. In for a penny, in for a pound.

"Close enough," I said.

"Wow!" Timmy said.

"And I only killed very, very bad people," I said.

Bobby said, "My dad said there are good people and bad people. You gotta keep the bad people from hurting the good people."

Timmy said, "Yeah. You especially gotta keep the bad people from hurting other soldiers 'cause they're your brothers."

"Your dad was a very smart man," I said.

Bobby, Timmy, and I came to the east-west street that bordered the southern edge of the housing development. Down that street, to the west and my right, was the house I had used to conduct my stakeout earlier that night. Straight ahead of us, and about a hundred yards away, was the Corolla. The Corolla was still parked where I had left it by the side of the road. I was tempted then to begin questioning the two boys about whether or not they had witnessed Sam's and Lizzy's murders, but decided against it. We would soon reach the car and I thought things might go better inside it. One, the barrier provided by the Corolla's metal shell would probably make them feel comfortable that the outside world couldn't hear any secrets they revealed to me, and two, that shell might also help them feel protected from the killing field and any ghosts they might imagine as still lingering there.

We crossed the intersection of the two streets and continued toward the Corolla. Overhead, a bird passed directly in front of the moon. The bird appeared to be a great horned owl on a night hunt. A jackrabbit suddenly scampered across the intersection in front of us and quickly disappeared into the scrub.

Bobby said, "That rabbit's dead meat."

I said, "You've seen that owl hunting at night before?"

"Uh huh," Bobby said.

We closed in on the Corolla, all of us keeping a watch on the owl as it circled beneath the moon. The owl seemed to glide effortlessly in the still night air, the beating of its giant wings almost imperceptible. We had watched the owl for perhaps twenty or thirty seconds, when, with a single, great thrust of its wings and a barely audible swoosh, it dove to the desert floor. A moment later, there was a brief, wild thrashing in the scrub brush and then a flash of white fur. The underside of the jackrabbit's throat appeared in the owl's curved beak, and the jackrabbit uttered one last, desperate wail.

Bobby said, "What'd I tell you?"

Just then there was another sound. An unmistakable sound I no longer believed was an acoustical illusion. The sound was close by. Very close by. It was the roar of huge Harley Davidson motorcycle engines revving to life, maybe a half dozen them. The roar was coming from directly behind us.

Bobby, Timmy, and I froze in the middle of the street, then slowly turned around to look for the source of the bellowing din. Six bright headlamps flashed on from the breezeways between seven of the houses on the southern edge of abandoned development. The headlamps' beams shot out like searchlights into the night, blinding us, and making it impossible to see who was atop the big machines.

Timmy, stuttering slightly, said, "General Jack, you di...di...didn't go into the h...h...house with the rooster di...di...did you?"

I was so shaken by the motorcycles' sudden, unexpected appearance, I almost didn't comprehend what Timmy had said.

"Rooster?" I said. And then it came back to me. The house I had used for surveillance had had a rooster weathervane on its roof. "Yes, I did Timmy. Why?"

"I...I...It's the dr...dr...drug dealers' house," Timmy said.

Drug dealers?

Bobby, his voice quavering, said, "They have cameras."

Those security cameras were live?

Screw me.

The engines revved again, and the Harleys rolled slowly forward. I had to think fast. My first priority was the kids' safety. If I could hustle Bobby and Timmy into one of the houses and get them upstairs, I could probably keep them out of harm's way. I felt I could keep them safe in the house even if the Harleys' owners had guns, because unless I had somehow run into a hell-bent U.S. special forces squad gone bad smack dab in the middle of the California desert, I was pretty sure I could disarm at least one of the bikers if they came in the house after us. Once I had a gun, it would be game over for the rest of their crew.

But the houses were too far away.

Almost a hundred yards away.

I could send Bobby and Timmy into the desert, but the Harleys' wide tires would chew up the sand as easily as if it were asphalt.

The Harleys' engines all simultaneously revved to full throttle, the engines' deep-throated roar followed instantly by the screech of tires searching for purchase. The six Harleys shot out together from the breezeways, raced across the homes' barren front yards, made skidding left turns onto the street that bordered the development's southern edge, and headed towards the intersection we had just crossed.

I was out of time.

The Harleys would be upon us in less than twenty seconds.

There was only one option.

The Corolla.

But it was still thirty yards away.

I didn't think I could get to the car in time, but the kids were on bikes.

I said, "My hunch is you boys are good soldiers."

They nodded, their bodies trembling slightly.

"And good soldiers take orders from their commanding officers without questioning, right?" I said.

Two more nods.

I took the Corolla's keys out of my pocket. I tossed them to Bobby.

"Ride as fast as you can to that car over there," I said, pointing at the Corolla. "Open the door with the keys, leave your bikes outside, jump in, and lock the doors. Don't come out until I say so. If you do that everything will be fine. Now go!"

They each gave a little salute and started furiously pedaling.

Then keeping my voice far more calm and confident than I actually felt, I yelled after them, "And keep a close eye on what I do. I might have to teach these guys a lesson. In which case you can learn something too."

I hoped my words might keep Bobby and Timmy from increased worry or even panic. And unlike all the other times I'd said words that night I thought would help to calm the two brothers, that time I at least didn't feel like a pervert. A small victory - not quite Virgil's 'Go forth a conqueror and win great victories' - but a victory nonetheless. Unfortunately, while Virgil's inspiring exhortation was still echoing within my head, Sun Tzu's dumbass proclamation, 'The supreme art of war is to subdue the enemy without fighting,' rose up from somewhere within the deep recesses of my grey matter and tried to push Virgil aside.

I had six half-ton Harleys bearing down upon me and I had to listen to that crap?

The hell with you Sun Tzu.

I didn't take my eyes off Bobby and Timmy until they reached the Corolla, scrambled in the driver's side door, and shut it behind them. I figured they'd be safe there because I figured it was me the bikers were after - it was me who they'd seen on their cameras wasn't it? - and that they would want to finish with me before they paid the kids any attention.

I turned to face the Harleys. Their headlamps once again blinded me. Their thundering rumble was deafening, its deep reverb shaking the earth beneath my feet and making my whole body vibrate.

I felt I had three choices at that moment.

One, I could run into the desert and have the bikers chase me.

But that would probably just lead to me stepping in a hole and breaking an ankle or getting ripped up by a cactus.

Two, I could sprint right at the bikers while waving my arms and snarling to try to scare them away.

But that tactic would probably wind up just enraging them further.

Three, I could sit down in the middle of the street, lean back on my hands, and start whistling 'Dock of the Bay' - it would have been nice if Jeff was with me since he whistled it a hell of a lot better than I did - in the hopes of making the bikers wonder what kind of idiot would do such a thing, wonder so strongly they might stop to ask a few questions before attacking me, or doing whatever it was they planned to do.

I had never before tried sitting down and whistling in the middle of the street in the face of an enemy attack. But I thought I remembered it had worked for Indiana Jones when he used it while he was being threatened by a swordsman in an Egyptian bazaar. Only maybe Indiana didn't whistle? Or sit down? Actually, that was probably the scene where Indiana Jones just pulled a gun and shot the guy with the sword.

I didn't have a gun though.

I sat down.

Before I could whistle my first note, however, the Harleys blew right past me, their hot exhaust gases stinging my eyes and nose, my clothes and hair whipped by the air churned up in their wake.

Damn.

That meant they were after Bobby and Timmy.

I jumped to my feet, which, after sitting even for so short a time, sent daggers through my left knee. Shoving aside the pain, I sprinted for the Corolla.

The bikers lined up their motorcycles in a semicircle about fifteen feet from the left side of the Corolla. The bikes' headlamps pointed at the car. Each cycle had two riders. A guy driving in front, and a girl in back with her arms wrapped around the guy's waist. The drivers revved the engines in an obvious attempt to scare Bobby and Timmy. The attempt was working. I could see Bobby and Timmy's terrified faces through the back window of the Corolla.

I really only had one option.

I had to take the high ground.

I kept sprinting, gaining speed with every step, and by the time I was within a few feet of the Corolla I was moving very fast. I leapt off my left foot, extended my right leg, landed my right foot on the trunk of the Corolla, buckling its metal lid with a loud crumpling sound, then pushed off with my right leg, and landed both feet on the Corolla's roof, buckling it as well, and sending another jolt of searing pain through my knee. I quickly laid down on the roof, hung my head over the roof's edge so that I could look in the driver's side window, gave Bobby and Timmy a wink and a thumbs up - which both boys acknowledged with tiny, seemingly forced smiles - then jumped to my feet and faced the bikers.

"Howdy," I said.

The bikers revved their engines even more loudly. It was so loud I may as well have been standing on a runway with a squadron of F15's taking off over my head.

My perch on the Corolla's roof was high enough above the cycles' headlamps so that their light wasn't blinding me. That same light, however, was reflecting back off the side of the Corolla and illuminating the faces and bodies of the Harleys' drivers and their passengers.

I studied those faces and bodies. No one was brandishing a weapon and I didn't see any telltale gun or knife bulges under their clothes. The guys were big enough so that maybe they figured they didn't need any weapons other than their fists. If any weapon had appeared my plan was to launch myself off the roof and take it. If more than one weapon appeared then I'd take the biggest, nastiest one. That plan, like sitting down in the middle of the street and whistling, was not much of a plan, but it was the best plan I had at the moment.

All of the bikers, men and women, looked like they were between eighteen and twenty years old. The men looked tough and athletic and probably were anywhere from 6' to 6' 4" in height, and two hundred to two-fifty in weight. The men also appeared to have stepped off the pages of an Ed Hardy catalogue. They had on alligator leather cowboy boots in shades of either aquamarine, green, or red, embroidered jeans, wide belts, rhinestone caps, and gold necklaces. Their caps and shirts had John Deere, MGM Lion, and Ferrari logos on them, which were of the types of logos also favored by Mexican drug cartels, specifically the Zetas or the Gulf Cartel.

But these guys, even though they were drug dealers according to Bobby and Timmy, weren't cartel members. They were cartel wannabes. Cartel members were Latinos, and these guys were all Caucasian with close-cropped blond or sandy brown hair.

The women were also Caucasian. They had long black or blond hair falling down their backs and their clothes looked like they had come out of the same Ed Hardy catalogue the men had used. All the women had shapely bodies with big breasts bulging out of colorful, skimpy bikini tops, flat stomachs rising above tight leather pants, and pink or white embroidered caps. Ed Hardy must have had a pretty good selection of sizes in the boot department as each of the women wore cowboy boots that exactly matched the pair their man was wearing. The women seemed like ornaments for the men, however, not real people.

The motorcycles were all the same model Harleys with fat tires, big chrome handlebars, and chrome forks. Each bike had been customized with unique paint jobs - mainly flame patterns in different hues of fiery reds, oranges, and yellows - on their gas tanks and rear fenders.

One of the cycles had a felt banner mounted on its rear fender. The banner had a maroon background with a picture of a buccaneer wearing a football helmet drawn on it in silver. Above the buccaneer were the words 'Antelope Valley Marauders', also in silver. I remembered having seen a billboard earlier in the day advertising Antelope Valley College which was the local community college.

I took a stab.

"You guys are football players, aren't you?" I yelled. "Play for Antelope Valley JC, I bet."

The biggest guy in the group was on the Harley in the middle of the semicircle. He looked like a linebacker and had on an Ed Hardy cap embroidered with a human skull wearing a top hat. The guy appeared to say something, but I couldn't hear what it was over the engine noise.

I put my hands open-palmed behind my ears in the universal gesture that meant 'I can't hear you,' and screamed, "What'd you say?"

The Skull Guy held up his hand and made a slicing gesture in the air. All the engines instantly shut down. The headlights stayed on.

"Whether or not we play football is none of your business, dickwad," Skull Guy said.

"I played some ball," I said.

The male on the right side of the semicircle said, "Who with, Abe Lincoln?"

His cohorts laughed hysterically.

"That's pretty funny," I said. "I guess it's a reference to my age, huh? I am old. How's it lookin' for your team next season?"

Skull Guy said, "Why don't you shut your goddamn mouth, dude. We don't give a shit whether you played football or not."

"Okay," I said. "You know I played some basketball too. Any of you guys or gals ballers?"

"Shut the hell up!" Skull Guy said.

My attempts to ingratiate myself with the crowd weren't going very well.

"Alright, I get it," I said. "I can take a hint. You want me to shut up."

"Goddamnit!" Skull Guy said. "Now you listen and listen good, 'cause here's what's going down. First we're gonna beat the crap out of Bobby and Timmy. Then we're gonna beat the crap out of you."

"Hmm," I said. "Sorry, but I don't think that's a good idea."

"Well, there's nothing you can do about it, is there?" Skull Guy said.

"That's not quite true," I said. "I let the revving the engines and scaring the kid shit kinda slide, but a beating? That won't fly."

"That won't fly, huh?" Skull Guy said sarcastically.

"No, it won't," I said. "Why don't all of you just head home. It will save you a lot of grief."

"We ain't leaving 'til we teach those snitches a lesson," Skull Guy said.

"If you're referring to the fact I went into your house," I said, "Bobby and Timmy had nothing to do with that. In case you didn't notice, you don't have a front door."

"I guess that means you can just walk right in and trespass on our property rights?" Skull Guy said.

"You've got cameras," I said. "You saw I didn't take anything."

"That's not the point," Skull Guy said.

"Okay," I said. "What is the point?"

Skull Guy turned to face his compadres and said, "He wants to know the point."

His compadres rolled their eyes and snickered.

Skull Guy turned back to look at me.

"You wanna know the point, huh?" Skull Guy said.

"Well, not if you don't want to tell me," I said.

For a moment Skull Guy seemed confused. Then he narrowed his eyes and crinkled his nose in an apparent attempt to appear menacing.

"What'd you say?" Skull Guy hissed.

"If you want to tell me the point," I said, "please tell me the point."

Skull Guy studied me. I have no idea what he was thinking, but if I had to guess, I would have said he thought I was breaking his balls. But I wasn't. I was just being polite. It appeared our encounter was heading for a violent confrontation and I was still hoping it might end peacefully. A peaceful outcome, however, required that Skull Guy also be polite. It soon became clear politeness was not part of Skull Guy's skill set.

"The point is," Skull Guy said, "those two little bitches been plotting to take our stash for a long time."

"They're seven and nine years old," I said.

"You coulda' walked into any of fifty houses, but you just happened to choose ours, huh?" Skull Guy sneered. "Bullshit. You think I'm an idiot? You were after our drugs and it was Bobby and Timmy who told you where to look for them."

Suddenly a rock flew out of the crowd and hit the Corolla's left rear passenger window, shattering its top few inches. I was so focused on

Skull Guy, I hadn't seen who threw it. I bent down, leaned over the roof again, and looked inside the car. Bobby and Timmy were huddled in the front seat, looking more terrified than ever, but unhurt.

"Everything's gonna be fine, boys," I said to them. "These guys will be leaving very soon. You have my word as a general in the U.S. Army."

They both gave me little nods. Not very confident nods, but nods nonetheless.

I hopped back up and addressed the bikers.

"That was out of line," I said. "Do it again, and you'll all be going home in the back of an ambulance."

Skull Guy turned to his troops.

"This geezer's not only old but he's so stupid he can't count," Skull Guy said.

His biker pals guffawed.

Skull Guy turned back to face me.

"'Case you hadn't noticed," Skull Guy said, "there's six of us and one of you."

"I know," I said. "And it is unfair. But I really don't have time to wait around for you to call up some more of your buds. Now just go on home and we'll forget any of this ever happened."

Skull Guy looked like he might explode. He raised both arms and twirled his index fingers in some kind of signal. All the male bikers dismounted and sidled up next to him. I still didn't see any weapons. The girls had stayed put on the Harleys' seats.

I said, "One last time, boys. Go home. I don't want to hurt you."

"I was going to let you live," Skull Guy said. "But now you've made me so mad, I'm gonna kill you. And Bobby. And Timmy. And you know what? I'm gonna enjoy it."

Skull Guy gave a little twitch of his head. He and the other five bikers moved towards me.

Which was a bad move.

The tighter their pack, the easier it was going to be for me to take them down.

The bikers still hadn't drawn any weapons, which meant there weren't any weapons I could take and use against them. I needed a new action plan.

I took about half a second to come up with one.

I thought it was a pretty good plan considering how little time it had taken me to come up with it.

If all went well, the whole thing would be over in five seconds.

Ten seconds tops.

When the bikers were within five feet of me, they hunched up their shoulders and clenched and unclenched their fists. They appeared to be snarling.

I waited until they got within three feet.

Then I jumped high off the Corolla's roof, somersaulted in midair - it was a pretty good somersault because of the practice I'd gotten in earlier that morning - came down in front of Skull Guy, and utilizing all the momentum created by the somersault, sprang forward and head butted him, using my forehead to smash the top of his nose and the space between his eyes.

Skull Guy went down like a sack of potatoes.

Which opened a gap between the two bikers on either side of him.

I spread my arms, grabbed the bikers' heads, and smashed them together.

Two more down for the count.

The two bikers on the left end of the six man formation seemed unsure what was going on. I didn't give them a chance to find out. I spun off my left knee and, with both my hands, delivered violent straight-fingered jabs to their Adam's apples. They both clutched their necks and appeared unable to breathe. Their knees buckled and they collapsed to the ground.

I turned to the lone biker still standing, the biker who had been on the formation's right end.

Understanding appeared to be dawning in his eyes, but it was dawning much too late.

I kicked him in the balls and, as he fell forward, kneed him in the chin. He went out like a light.

I hadn't timed it, but it felt like seven seconds.

More than five.

But less than ten.

Good enough.

I surveyed the six bodies slumped on the ground, then I turned to the bikers' girlfriends.

"Get off the bikes and get over here," I said.

They hesitated.

"I'm not going to hurt you," I said. "I've just got a job for you."

They still didn't move.

"Don't make me go over there and get you," I said.

The women dismounted the Harleys and walked warily towards me. I held up my hand and stopped them when they were about five feet from me.

I said, "Harleys are pretty expensive, aren't they? These look like they gotta be maybe, what, thirty grand each?"

They all nodded sheepishly.

"Drug business out here must be pretty good," I said.

They shrugged.

"You girls like your guys well enough to keep them alive?" I said.

No answer.

"Well, if you do, each of you better start grabbing arms and legs and haul these boys back up the road," I said. I pointed north towards the housing development. "Fifty feet that way should do it."

They stood there. Like they hadn't understood what I'd said.

"You heard me," I said. "Get goin'!"

This time they did what I asked. The six of them went to the last guy I had downed, four of them grabbing an arm or leg, the other two a belt loop, and started dragging the guy where I had pointed. The girls were moving a little too slow for my taste however.

"Faster," I yelled.

They moved it up to double time.

I removed Skull Guy's cap from his head, turned around, and walked back to the Corolla. I opened the front driver's side door and leaned in. Both Bobby and Timmy had smiles a mile wide.

"You boys learn anything?" I said.

Timmy said, "Wow, General Jack, that was cool!"

Bobby said, "Better'n Chuck Norris!"

I said, "Not sure it was better than Chuck. I mean, that's a *very* high bar. But it is a hell of a compliment, so thank you. Alright, then. I got two more things to do and then we'll be on our way."

"Okay, General Jack," Timmy said.

I opened the left rear passenger door, leaned over, and picked the window glass off the back seat and floor. I used Skull Guy's cap as a trash receptacle.

"Keep your eyes on the girls," I said. "Tell me if they start slackin' off."

Bobby and Timmy glued their eyes on the girls. I picked up more glass shards. There were a lot of them. It took a while.

"How the girls doin'?" I said to Bobby and Timmy.

Timmy said, "They just dropped the last guy off. They're coming back."

"Good," I said.

I walked to where I had last talked to the girls and waited for them to get back to me. When they did, making sure I spoke loud enough for Bobby and Timmy to hear me, I said, "Your boyfriends come to, I want you to deliver a message. You tell them they ever even look at Bobby and Timmy cross-eyed again that I'll be back. And I'll kill them. Then I'll kill all of you as well. Any of you think I won't do that?"

The girls all shook their heads.

"Good," I said. "Now go stand by those jackasses and don't move until I'm gone."

I gave a little nod with my chin towards the heap of unconscious bikers. The girls hustled off.

I realized there was one more loose end that needed tying.

"Wait!" I called after the girls.

They stopped and turned around.

"Your boyfriends," I said. "They all play football for Antelope Valley?"

The girls nodded.

"The big guy who did all the talking," I said. "He a middle linebacker?"

They nodded again.

"Thanks," I said. "You can continue on now."

The girls turned and headed for their sleeping lotharios.

I walked over to the Harleys, pushed them into a nice tight grouping so that they were all side by side. Then one by one, I laid each Harley on the ground, unscrewing their gas caps as I did. Fuel spilled onto the desert floor, filling the air with the slightly sweet aroma of gasoline.

I went back to the Corolla, opened the trunk, and put the boys' stingray bikes inside. The bikes were a tight fit, so tight, in fact, that I wasn't able to close the trunk lid and had to leave it open. I jogged around to the driver's side door and leaned into the car.

"Why don't you two jump in the back seat and buckle up?" I said.

Bobby and Timmy did as I said. I slipped in behind the steering wheel, turned the Corolla's ignition key, and the engine started right up. I wasn't ready to go yet, but since I planned to leave in a hurry, I wanted to make sure the car would be ready when it was time to take off. I pushed in the Corolla's electric cigarette lighter that was under the dash. I waited. After a moment the lighter popped out and I removed it. The lighter's metal coil had a nice orange glow to it.

"I'll be right back, boys," I said.

I returned to the pile of motorcycles. I threw Skull Guy's cap with the glass shards on his Harley. Then I threw the Corolla's cigarette lighter in the puddle of gasoline that had formed beneath Skull Guy's Harley's tank. The puddle instantly caught fire and almost as instantly spread to each of the puddles beneath all the other Harleys.

Pretty soon I had a nice bonfire going.

In a few moments the bonfire would be even bigger as the flames spread to the fuel remaining inside the tanks and the tanks started to explode.

I ran back to the Corolla, jumped in the driver's seat, and put the car in gear.

"Hold on boys," I said.

I floored the gas pedal and we rocketed out of there.

A moment later the first explosion occurred, sending flames twenty feet in the air. I continued down the street, accelerating all the way, the trunk lid flapping violently up and down in the wind. Bobby and Timmy had twisted around in their seats and were watching the show. I kept my own watch in the rearview mirror. Two more towers of flame shot into the night sky, followed by the sounds of two more explosions.

"Cool!" Timmy said.

We kept going.

CHAPTER 50

Bobby, Timmy, and I spent the next few minutes racing south and then west through Lancaster, the whine of the Corolla's straining engine vibrating through our bodies. We were headed in the general direction of where the boys had told me they lived. The streets were dark and empty and lined only by vast acres of sand and an occasional cactus. I had the windows open to quell the heat. The furnace-like air blew across our faces, whistled in our ears, and brought with it the smell of hot sage and fevered asphalt. My eyes were on the road, but my mind was on the two scruffy kids in the back seat. My primary duty was to find out what Bobby and Timmy knew about Sam and Lizzy's murders, but at that moment I was having a hard time focusing on so narrow a definition of duty. I was more concerned with the boys themselves. Why did they look the way they did? And why, even though it was ten o'clock at night, did a seven and nine-year-old seem completely unconcerned with getting home at any specified time? Who the hell was taking care of them? And what was I going to do about the fact I'd had no other choice but to make Bobby and Timmy some potentially deadly enemies in the form of that moronic gang of football playing, drug dealing, biker, cartel wannabes? Enemies that would be around long after I was gone.

I promised myself I was not going to leave Lancaster until I had the answers to those questions.

I turned the Corolla onto what looked like an especially deserted side road and parked. I left the motor running. We were then at least two miles from the stoning site, but the flames from the burning Harley pyre were still visible as they torched the night sky.

I twisted around in my seat to face Bobby and Timmy.

"You boys sure it's okay to be out this late?" I said. "No one's gonna be worried about you?"

They both shook their heads.

"Okay, then," I said. "Time for your driving lesson. Who wants to go first?"

Both boys wildly waved their hands and simultaneously said, "Me!"

"Alright," I said. "I'm going to choose a number between one and ten in my head and whoever gets closest goes first. Bobby?"

"Eight," Bobby said.

"Timmy?" I said.

"Fifteen!" Timmy said.

Timmy, apparently realizing his mistake, looked mortified.

"Oops," Timmy said.

"Don't worry," I said. "Try again."

"Three!" Timmy said.

"The number was seven," I said. "Bobby is first."

I slid into the passenger seat, leaned back over the driver's seat, pulled on the seat positioning control lever, shoved the driver's seat as far forward as it would go, and sat back up.

"Jump on in Bobby," I said.

Bobby clambered over the top of the driver's seat, sat down behind the steering wheel, and buckled his seat belt. With the seat pulled all the way forward Bobby could reach the pedals, and I was close enough to him to reach them as well if I needed to in an emergency. I gave Bobby a little instruction. He put the Corolla in gear and off we went. Bobby drove slowly and did a remarkable job of keeping the car rolling down the center of the street.

"Try the brake," I said.

Bobby stepped on the brake. He pushed a little too hard and the car came to a sudden stop, throwing all of us forward against our seat belts. Timmy's seat belt apparently broke at the end of its run - which, I suppose, was not that surprising given the Corolla's overall condition - and Timmy bounced off Bobby's seat and wound up sprawled on the floor of the car. I thought Timmy might have hurt himself, but he started giggling hysterically as if it was the funniest thing that ever happened to him.

Timmy said, "Do that again, Bobby."

I said, "Be fun, but let's not. Timmy, why don't you get into the other seat and use its seat belt instead, please."

Timmy scrambled up off the floor, took the other seat, and buckled his belt. Bobby let up on the brake. The Corolla moved down the street.

"Let's give it another go, Bobby," I said. "This time push in the brake a little more slowly."

Bobby did as instructed. We came to a nice, safe stop.

"Great," I said. "I think you've got it now. Keep driving. Every hundred yards or so, practice another nice slow stop."

Bobby nodded and got us on our way again.

I figured we'd run the lesson for a while, hoping that it would at least partially distract Bobby and Timmy from any painful emotions that might be lingering from having experienced the murders of Sam and Lizzy and the bikers' aborted attack. I planned to start asking them my questions about Sam and Lizzy's stoning once I sensed they were relaxed enough. As I was worried it might be hard on the boys to relive the murders, I was also pondering the best way to conduct my interrogation without causing them undue trauma. It turned out, however, that my pondering and worrying was for naught, because Timmy, God bless his soul, started the ball rolling on his own.

Timmy said, "The little man wore a tuxedo with shiny black shoes, General Jack!"

I assumed he was talking about the fourth, smaller person who had been at the stoning site, the one who had worn the flat-soled dress shoes and had had a shorter stride than the Afghans.

"He did, did he?" I said.

Bobby, keeping his eyes on the road, and his hands firmly on the wheel, said, "Timmy we don't know for sure it was a man."

"Do too," Timmy said. "It was a man's tuxedo."

I said, "You couldn't tell by their face whether the person was more likely a man or a woman?"

"Uh uh," Timmy said.

Bobby said, "They were wearing a mask."

"A dragon mask!" Timmy blurted out. "Like in the restaurant."

I was confused by that one. What kind of restaurant had people in dragon masks?

"Is it a restaurant near your house?" I said.

Bobby said, "Timmy's favorite restaurant is Great Wall of China."

Timmy said, "Fried shrimp, sweet and sour spareribs, fortune cookies. Yummy!"

I said, "I see. And they have a statue of a Chinese dragon there?"

Timmy nodded vigorously.

There was a stop sign up ahead. Bobby, unbidden by me, stopped cleanly behind the limit line.

"Well done, Bobby," I said.

Bobby smiled and stepped on the gas.

"The dragon man had a deep voice like a man," Timmy said.

Bobby said, "He could have been faking the voice."

"He sounded like Wan Loo," Timmy said.

I said, "Wan Loo?"

Bobby said, "That's Timmy's favorite waiter at Great Wall of China."

"Wan Loo tells good jokes," Timmy said. "You know what happened at the party at the Chinese zoo, General Jack?"

I said, "No. What happened?"

"Pandemonium!" Timmy said cackling.

I rolled my eyes.

"Very funny, Timmy," I said. "To keep it simple, let's just assume the person in the tuxedo was a man for now. You're saying he spoke with a Chinese accent?"

"Yep," Timmy said. "He wore big white gloves like Mickey Mouse and he drank champagne from a glass and he threw the blocks on the little girl's head and then the boy's head."

What had FBI Agent MacKay said at the stoning site?

Wasn't it, *"Then cinder blocks to finish 'em off"*?

Bobby said, "The boy was very brave, General. He tried to save the girl. He hit the men with his shovel and grabbed the girl and tried to run away."

Timmy said, "We would have shot the men but we didn't have a gun."

I said, "I'm sure you would have. How many men were there?"

Bobby said, "Four. The man in the tuxedo, and the three men who built the pitcher's mound and threw stones at the little boy and girl after they tied them to stakes."

Timmy said, "They left the stakes in the field. That's why we bought this."

Timmy took a small 35 millimeter film camera out of his pocket and showed it to me.

"Four dollars and thirty-two cents including tax," Timmy said. "We still have two dollars and twenty-five cents."

I took that to mean the boys had used their savings to buy the camera. I doubted the boys would have the money to actually get their photos out of the camera, however, as my guess too was that the camera was pretty much a scam. Lure people into buying the camera cheaply, and then charge a fortune to develop and print the film.

I said, "You were going to take pictures of the stakes?"

"Criminals return to the scene of the crime, General Jack," Timmy said.

Bobby said, "We thought maybe they would come back tonight to get the stakes. We bought the camera this afternoon. I wish we had it this morning."

I said, "I take it you don't have a cell phone?"

Timmy said, "We would have called 911 if we did!"

"Of course you would have," I said. "I spoke too soon, didn't I?"

I looked at the camera more closely. It had a built-in flash. Were the boys really going to risk using it at night and being seen? I didn't think they would. I got an idea.

"If the men came back tonight, you were going to film them through the night goggles, weren't you?" I said.

Both boys nodded.

I wasn't sure that would have worked, but I said, "That's a pretty smart idea."

Timmy said, "We're smart, General Jack. Just like our dad!"

"He would have been proud," I said. "What did the three men look like who threw the stones?"

Bobby said, "They were tall and skinny and had black beards. They had on the same boots."

Timmy said, "And they weren't Americans."

I said, "Why do you say that, Timmy?"

"Their clothes were really, really baggy and they had bad teeth and they looked like they smelled bad," Timmy said.

Bobby said, "They spoke English sometimes and a foreign language sometimes."

The boot prints and the pitcher's mound I had seen at the stoning site had led me to conclude that Afghans had killed Sam and Lizzy. The boys' descriptions added further weight to that conclusion. I thought about whether or not I should show Bobby and Timmy a photo of some Afghan men from the region in which U.S. special forces had been most active in their recruitment and training of local Afghan talent. If Bobby and Timmy identified those Afghan men as looking like the killers, that would pretty much seal the deal for me. But there was also the risk I could contaminate Bobby's and Timmy's recollections. I decided showing them the pictures was worth the risk.

I took out my iPhone and brought up a photo I had of myself, Jeff, and five Afghan soldiers. It had been taken ten years ago in the Arghandab River Valley. I showed the photo to Timmy.

Timmy said, "That's them!"

Bobby turned around to look and the Corolla swerved towards the opposite side of the road.

I said, "Eyes back on the road please, Bobby."

He did as I requested and the car straightened out.

"Good," I said. "Now, please pull to the side of the road, Bobby, and stop."

Bobby slowly turned the wheel until we were on the shoulder and brought the Corolla to a gentle stop. I leaned over, put the car's transmission into park, and showed Bobby the photos on the iPhone.

"Take a look," I said.

"That's them, alright," Bobby said. "Who are they?"

"Well, it's not really them," I said. "But these men live in a section of Afghanistan where I think the men you saw came from."

"Our dad was in Afghanistan once," Bobby said.

Timmy said, "Afghanistan is very, very dangerous. I'm not going there unless I have a gun. Two guns!"

I said, "If it were me, I'd take at least three."

"And grenades!" Timmy said. "And a knife!"

"Those too," I said.

I put the iPhone back in my pocket. I turned off the Corolla's headlights and ignition. With the car's engine off, I became aware of the sound of a jet passing overhead. I craned my head out the window and recognized the twinkling lights of a C17 cargo plane dancing in the night sky. I thought it had probably come from Edwards, and maybe even was on its way to Saudi Arabia. I pulled my head back in.

I said, "Was anyone else there this morning other than the little boy and girl, the three Afghans, and the dragon man?"

Timmy said, "They wouldn't come out of the bus."

"The Afghans and the dragon man came in a bus?" I said.

"Party bus!" Timmy said.

Bobby said, "Timmy didn't even know what a party bus was until I told him."

I said, "I'm not sure I know what a party bus is myself."

"You know," Bobby said. "It's one of those little black buses people rent when they have a party. They can hold twenty of your friends."

Timmy said, "Show General Jack the paper!"

Bobby said, "You didn't have to tell me to do that, Timmy. I was just going to."

Bobby reached into his back pocket, brought out a crumpled piece of white school paper with blue lines, and handed it to me. I uncrumpled the paper and read what was on it. There were two license plate numbers scrawled in childlike writing.

"You have two license plate numbers here," I said. "Does that mean there were two vehicles?

"Yes," Bobby said. "There was a white van with no windows. The men from Afghanistan drove it."

Timmy said, "They took the boy and girl out of the back!"

I immediately thought of the Kazakhs and their white van at the Coso Junction rest stop.

"No other men in the van?" I said.

"In the bus!" Timmy said.

"But not in the van?" I said.

Bobby said, "Not in the van. The windows were blacked out in the bus, but sometimes we could see two men moving around in it through the gap in an open window."

"Two, not three?" I said.

"Yes," Bobby said.

"Did they look like they were from Afghanistan too?" I said.

After a moment, Timmy said, "They were American."

Bobby said, "I was just going to tell him that too, Timmy."

I said, "How did you know they were American?"

"They didn't have an accent," Bobby said.

"So you heard them talking, and you're saying they both spoke English, but didn't have an accent?" I said.

"Yes," Bobby said.

Timmy added, "They both had white skin and the driver had a racing watch. I saw his arm in the window."

I said, "Just his arm?"

Timmy said, "The dragon man wanted the Americans to come out, but they wouldn't. He poured them champagne through the window."

I said, "The dragon man had the champagne, or the men had the champagne?"

Bobby said, "The man with the dragon mask had the champagne."

Timmy said, "Bobby, it was my turn!"

Bobby rolled his eyes.

I said, "What do you mean by a racing watch, Timmy?"

"Big dials," Timmy said. "Lots of dials."

"Anything else you remember about the watch?" I said.

"Gold!" Timmy said.

"It was a gold watch?" I said.

"Yes, sir!" Timmy said.

"Did you see the watch too, Bobby?" I said.

Bobby said, "No. Timmy had the binoculars. He wouldn't give them to me."

Timmy reached into his back pocket and pulled out a very small pair of folding binoculars. They were made of blue and white plastic, looked more like a toy than a useful tool, and could not have cost more than five dollars. Timmy handed the binoculars to me. I unfolded them, put them to my eyes, and looked out at the city lights in the distance. The magnification was actually pretty good. I handed the binoculars back to Timmy. He refolded them and shoved them in his pocket.

"Could you read the name on the watch?" I said.

Timmy said, "It was too far away."

"What kind of band?" I said.

"Black," Timmy said.

"Nothing else?" I said. "No rings, other jewelry, tattoos?"

Timmy shook his head.

"Okay," I said, "just to make sure I understand, the dragon man was outside the bus, and the two men, one of whom was the driver, were inside the bus?"

"Yep," Timmy said.

Bobby said, "One man moving around in the bus. The bus driver stayed in his seat."

If the boys were right about everything they had told me so far, it probably meant the Kazakhs at the rest stop, and the Afghans at the stoning site, each had their own white van. Which could mean the two mercenary teams were completely unrelated. Which I thought very unlikely. What was more likely was that whoever was running the mercenaries' teams simply favored anonymous white vans for their teams, but didn't mind using a party bus for themselves.

Outside, I heard a coyote howl. When his howl ended, it was replaced by the sound of approaching sirens. I assumed the sirens were coming from fire engines heading for the flames of the bikers' burning Harleys.

I said, "You're saying the dragon man wanted the bus driver to come out, but he wouldn't, so the dragon man gave the bus driver the champagne through the window?"

"Yes, sir," Bobby said.

"Did the dragon man offer the champagne to anyone else?" I said.

"No, sir," Bobby said.

"Did the dragon man drink the champagne before or after he went to the grave?" I said.

Timmy said, "Both!"

Bobby said, "He asked me."

"You've been answering too many questions in a row," Timmy said.

Bobby ignored him and said, "The dragon man was drinking champagne while the Afghans were throwing the stones. When the Afghans were almost done, they waved the dragon man to come over, and he brought the bottle and the glass with him to the grave."

"Did he give the Afghans any champagne?" I said.

Bobby shook his head. Which was the answer I had expected, as I had assumed the Afghans were probably Muslims, and Muslims, at least religious ones, generally don't drink alcohol.

Timmy said, "The dragon man filmed them taking the boy and girl off the stakes with his cell phone."

I thought that was a good time to cut off my then current line of questioning and skip forward in time. If we kept going along that line, I was sure we would soon come to the point where the dragon man smashed Sam and Lizzy's heads in with the cinder blocks. Since Timmy had already said the dragon man had thrown the cinder blocks on Sam and Lizzy, and the pattern of the footprints I had seen pretty much corroborated what both Bobby and Timmy had told me, I saw no need to ask about the blocks again, especially as my asking might cause Bobby and Timmy to relive what must have been the most horrific portion of what had happened out in the field.

From the boys' report, I also had started to form a picture of the dragon man's personality. I had a pretty strong hunch that when the dragon man got to the grave, he had turned over the cell phone filming duties to the Afghans so they could record him finishing off Sam and Lizzy with the cinder blocks. But confirming that hunch wasn't essential in order for me to do my job, so I didn't pursue it. Besides, I figured I could always ask the dragon man about it when I found him. I thought there was a good chance he would be only too happy to tell me about it, maybe even show me the video.

I took out my iPhone again and used it to take a picture of the boys' paper with the license plate numbers on it. I was fairly certain the license plates, as well as perhaps the party bus and van, were stolen, but it was worth a shot researching the plates nonetheless. I texted the picture of the plates, along with the photos I'd taken at the site earlier that day, to General Hart. I handed the piece of paper back to Bobby.

"I'm very impressed with everything you did," I said. "These license plate numbers are especially valuable."

Both boys beamed.

"So, after the dragon man was done at the grave, what happened next?" I said.

Bobby said, "Everyone got in the party bus and the van and they both left."

"What did you and Timmy do after they left?" I said.

"We waited until we were sure they were gone," Bobby said.

Timmy said, "But then we couldn't go!"

This time it was Bobby's turn to scowl.

I said, "Why couldn't you go?"

The boys looked at each other. They said nothing, but it appeared as if another bit of silent communication passed between them. I didn't want to push them, so I thought about what might keep them there even though the killers had left. I couldn't immediately come up with anything, so I reviewed what I knew about the stoning timeline from Carpenter and MacKay. The first thing that had happened that Carpenter and MacKay could absolutely verify was that Sam and Lizzy had been found by a sheriff's deputy who had seen vultures circling overhead and gone to investigate the site. As soon as I visualized the deputy marching out to the grave, I thought I knew the answer to why Bobby and Timmy hadn't left their clubhouse. I figured the boys didn't want to tell me their little secret, but if I guessed at it myself...

"Was it the sheriff's deputy?" I said.

Their eyes opened wide.

"Hey, don't worry," I said. "I ain't no fink."

Bobby said, "How'd you know?"

"You guys hang out here," I said. "Just figured the deputy and you might have crossed paths at the housing development, and he ran you off, told you not to come back."

They both nodded.

"Deputy probably isn't a bad guy, though," I said. "It's his job. Probably just doesn't want you to get hurt."

Timmy said, "We're careful."

"Careful not to get hurt," I said, "or careful not to let him see you?"

I could almost see the wheels spinning in Timmy's head as he wondered how to answer that one.

"I'm just teasing," I said. "You don't have to answer."

Timmy gave a huge sigh of relief.

I thought about what would have happened after the sheriff arrived. I thought I had a pretty good idea about that too.

"So let me throw this at you," I said. "Sheriff's deputy arrives and goes to the gravesite. You see him using his radio and, a little while later, more deputies join him. Then the FBI shows up with a huge crew, and the original deputy leaves, and the two of you figure you can get home without being noticed in the crowd. So the two of you split..."

As I said this, both of the boys' faces fell.

"Wait, wait," I said. "That's not it. You wouldn't want to leave without telling someone what happened."

The boys nodded vigorously.

"With the deputy gone, you figured you could tell the FBI," I said. "So you went up to whoever you thought was in charge of the FBI, but then something happened, and you couldn't. The question is what happened...Oh no! Damn!"

The boys gave me identical questioning looks.

"Burnette was there," I said.

Timmy said, "Is he the big fat guy with the sweaty red face and the pearl handled gun and the dumb looking hat who yells really loud?"

"Yeah, that's Burnette," I said. "He scared you off, didn't he?"

Both boys nodded.

Bobby said, "Burnette was really angry and ordering everyone around. And some of the FBI agents asked him questions and he would just scream and tell them they were stupid."

Timmy said, "And he looked really worried too."

I said, "That's a very astute observation Timmy. I'm sure he was. So what did you guys do?"

Bobby said, "We decided to go home, since we figured even if we told anyone what happened, they wouldn't believe us anyway, and Burnette would just yell at us."

"And maybe just a little bit that the sheriff's deputy might come back and also get you in trouble, too?" I said.

They both nodded sheepishly.

"But you still wanted to do your duty," I said.

Timmy's face brightened instantly, and he said, "We made a plan!"

I said, "To come back tonight and when the criminals returned to the scene of the crime, take pictures of them and send in the pictures..."

"A not a mouse!" Timmy said.

"A not a mouse?" I said.

Bobby said, "Anonymous."

"Of course," I said. "But I don't think the criminals are coming back. However, I do think you both did an incredible job, and I'm sure I can catch them from what you told me."

Both boys beamed.

Timmy said, "And bring them to justice!"

'Bring' wasn't quite what I had in mind. I was thinking more along the lines of 'dispensing' or 'meting out'. Actually, 'inflicting' was probably closest. But that was not something I wanted to share with young ears.

"Yes," I said. "I have one last question. The cameras in the rooster house..."

Timmy said, "Satellite and solar cells! On the roof!"

"Got it," I said. "Timmy, your turn to drive."

The boys crawled over each other to change positions and then buckled up. I gave Timmy the same instructions I had given to Bobby.

"Ready to go Timmy?" I said.

"Yes, sir, General Jack," Timmy said.

"Let's roll then," I said.

I turned on the ignition and then reached for the headlight switch. Timmy, however, slapped my hand away from the switch.

"No lights!" Timmy said.

"We gotta see where we're going," I said.

Timmy lifted his night goggles from around his neck and fastened them around his head and over his eyes.

"Timmy, I don't think that's a good idea," I said.

"No lights!" Timmy said.

He started giggling and put the car in gear. Teaching a seven-year-old how to drive was a risky enough proposition on its own, but teaching a seven-year-old how to drive at night with only those goggles to help him see where to go was more than risky.

It bordered on insane.

But sometimes you just gotta say 'what the hell.'

That was one of those times.

We headed off toward Bobby and Timmy's home, whatever that turned out to be.

CHAPTER 51

Timmy parked the Corolla in front of his and Bobby's house at about 10:30 p.m. The house occupied an otherwise empty patch of desert with nary even a cactus in sight. Its exterior was illumined by a solitary streetlamp mounted on a wooden telephone pole stationed by the side of the road. The closest neighbors to the boys' house appeared to be at least a quarter mile away. The only car then visible didn't have any doors, seats, wheels, or windows, and was up on blocks in the boys' front yard.

A three foot high chain link fence surrounded the quarter acre of dead, brown weeds on which the house sat. The fence and the car appeared to be having a competition as to which of them could rust out faster.

A cracked concrete pathway led to the house's front door. The pathway at the street passed through an opening in the fence, then crossed about twenty feet of front yard until it ended at the porch steps at the front of the house. The pathway lay atop the dead roots of a long vanished tree, and the roots had forced the pathway's thick, disarticulated concrete sections to jut upward at odd angles. The opening in the fence appeared to have once been guarded by a gate, but the gate was then long gone, and all that remained to signal the gate's previous presence were two gateposts and the rusty hinges attached to the gateposts.

The house itself was a one story ranch style that extended about fifteen feet on either side of its front door and maybe forty feet into the backyard. Its exterior walls were made of stucco that was chipped and colored a sun-bleached, ashen pink. A brand new satellite dish sat on the house's shingled roof. The dish was kept company on the roof by a collapsed brick chimney and an air conditioning unit that was rattling badly and making loud, high-pitched compressor noises.

Soft, multicolored lights from a television flickered through the grimy, torn yellow lace curtains that hung in the house's front windows. The lights were accompanied by the muffled voices of what I assumed to be the actors in whatever program was playing on the television.

A smell that seemed to be a combination of rotting food, human sewage, and a dead skunk wafted into the Corolla. I doubted there was a breeze anywhere within fifty miles of us, and it had remained unbearably hot.

"Looks like someone's still up watching TV," I said. "Guess we won't have to worry about waking them up."

"Foster Mom's asleep," Bobby said.

Timmy said, "Foster Mom wouldn't wake up even if you set off a cherry bomb in her ear."

"She gets drunk around five o'clock and then she takes a nap," Bobby said.

"She won't get up until ten tomorrow morning," Timmy said.

I said, "Long nap."

Both boys nodded.

"What's Foster Mom's real name?" I said.

Timmy said, "Foster Mom."

Bobby said, "She doesn't want us to call her mom 'cause she says she doesn't want us to forget she's not our real mom."

"She doesn't have to worry, though," Timmy said, "'cause we'd never forget."

"I'm sure you wouldn't," I said. "Where's your real mom?"

Bobby said, "She died."

"I'm sorry," I said. "I guess I should have realized you wouldn't be living with Foster Mom if your real mom was alive."

Timmy said, "Our real mom loved us."

"She had a lot to love," I said.

The boys nodded again.

"Shall we go inside?" I said

Bobby and Timmy looked at each other. They both looked uncomfortable.

Bobby said, "You don't have to do that, General Jack. We're fine now."

'You two are fine, huh?', I thought to myself. You live in a house that barely seems to be able to stay upright, and Foster Mom not only probably has no idea where you are, or when you're coming home, but she probably doesn't care either.

"I insist," I said. "I want to meet Foster Mom."

I could see their young minds spinning, most likely trying to figure out a way to keep me from entering the house.

"Let's go," I said. "Time's a wastin."

I exited the Corolla, walked around to the trunk, took their bikes out, put the bikes on the ground, and, with one hand on each of the bikes' handlebars, started rolling them to the house's front door. For a moment, I thought Bobby and Timmy were going to stay in the car, but I heard the sounds of two doors opening and closing behind me. Those sounds were quickly followed by the pounding of the boys' feet as they raced to join me.

I climbed the house's cement front steps, tugging the bicycles by my side. I felt a jolt every time the bicycle tires clunked over the edge of each successive step. I reached the porch, put down the kickstands, and rested the bikes to the left side of the front door. Bobby and Timmy caught up to me, but neither of them made a move to open the door.

"I'm getting the sense you don't want to invite me in," I said.

The boys didn't say anything.

"Resistance is futile," I said. "I'm going in whether you let me in or not."

Bobby sighed. He yanked open the aluminum screen door which guarded the front door. The screen door had so many tears in its metal wire mesh that the screen could not possibly have been of any use. The screen door's spring closure mechanism was apparently miraculously still functioning, however, so Bobby held the screen door open with his hip as he grasped the front doorknob. The front door was made of two one-eighth inch thick sheets of plywood, the sheets held together by a two-by-four frame. The space between the plywood sheets was hollow. I could tell all about the door's construction because someone had kicked a ragged, through-and-through hole in the bottom half of the door. Bobby jiggled the front doorknob a few times before it finally turned in his hand and he was able to open the door.

Timmy trudged inside the house. Bobby followed him, and I followed Bobby. We entered a small foyer. The boys kept on going farther into the house, but I stopped in my tracks.

I'm not going to say I've never been scared, but it usually takes a lot to scare me.

Walking into an ambush.

A parachute failing to open.

Stepping on a bouncing betty.

Those are the kinds of things that scare me.

I can honestly say, however, that I was as scared at that moment as I had ever been in my life.

Not for myself.

But for Bobby and Timmy.

Because, there before me, in the living room of that isolated house in the middle of the Lancaster desert, was one of the oddest tableaus I had ever seen.

Part, a small part, of what disturbed me was the room itself. Its walls were plastered with lime green wallpaper that was spotted with multi-colored stains. Most of the stains seemed to be comprised of either food, vomit, or human feces. The ceiling was made of asbestos tiles that had once been white, but were then varying shades of brown. The pine wood floor was buckled and warped, and, in many places, worn down to its supporting joists. The floor was covered in fast food wrappers, empty super-size paper soft drink cups, beer bottles, soda cans, cigarette butts, and used Kleenex. Six couches, an empty baby crib whose rails were down, and a brown Naugahyde Barcalounger surrounded a spanking new, giant flat screen television. White balls of kapok stuffing and metal springs poked through rips in the couches' fabric. All six couches faced the television, which was then the only source of illumination in the room. The Barcalounger, which was smack dab in the center of the room, had by far the best television viewing location. The smell in the room seemed to be a combination of odors from the wall stains mixed with beer, cigarettes, and urine.

What was most disturbing about the living room, however, were its occupants. I counted fourteen kids, seven boys and seven girls, along with a creature I assumed had to be 'Foster Mom'. The children all appeared to be under ten years old, the youngest a baby, sans diapers, crawling around amidst the filth on the floor. There was not a child among them who didn't appear to need a bath or whose clothes didn't need washing. All of the children, except the baby, were sprawled on the couches. All but one of the children on the couches were watching 'Nightmare on Elm Street'.

The scene from the movie playing at that moment was the one in which, Tina, splattered with blood, flops up the walls of her bedroom until she finally reaches the ceiling, then falls dead onto her bed. Tina's screams filled the living room. The television's dancing, flashing images reflected on the children's mesmerized faces.

A pajama-wearing boy, who looked to be about six years old, fiddled with two huge hearing aids in his ears, but I couldn't tell if he was adjusting the volume up or down. The only kid that was not watching the horror movie was a girl in a dirty red flannel nightgown whose age I guessed to be about seven. She wasn't watching the movie since she was blind, and she was reading a book in Braille on her lap.

Besides the baby, the deaf boy, and the blind girl, the children that attracted my attention the most were a set of twin girls. The girls were rocking identical Raggedy Ann dolls in their arms. The dolls had red yarn hair, triangle noses, black button eyes, and wore blue checkered shirts, white aprons, and red and white striped socks. The twins wore outfits nearly identical to the dolls' clothes, only the twins' clothes were much more frazzled and frayed than the dolls'.

Foster Mom was asleep and snoring in the Barcalounger, the lounger's settings at maximum incline. She appeared to be about sixty-five years old, five feet, four inches tall, and three hundred pounds. Her orange hair was in curlers, and she wore a dirt encrusted blue muumuu with yellow and red flowers on it, support hose, and soiled white sneakers. The sneakers had had holes cut in them through which the big and little toes on each of her feet protruded. Most of the room's cigarette butts and empty beer cans were congregated on the floor around Foster Mom's Barcalounger, and both the floor and the lounger bore blackened burn marks too numerous to count.

I had been held so spellbound by the scene in front of me, that I think a full minute must have passed before I realized that Bobby and Timmy had probably been staring at me the whole time I had been anchored in place. They both looked worried.

"Sorry boys, I don't think I've ever quite seen...," I said, before catching myself and changing course. "Nice place."

Bobby's and Timmy's eyes narrowed. I guess they hadn't bought my lie.

"Then again," I said, "maybe it's not so nice."

I pretty much knew right then and there what I needed to do about Bobby and Timmy's situation - their home life, their witnessing of the stoning of Sam and Lizzy, and the fact I'd made them mortal enemies of the drug dealing biker football players - and how I was going to do it. There was always the chance, a small chance, but a chance nonetheless, that the boys might consider my plan to be overstepping. I decided it would be best to check on a few things with them, and if need be, sell them on my plan before I set the plan in motion.

"Is there someplace we can talk in private?" I said.

"Everyone but them," Bobby said, pointing with his chin towards the right side of the living room, "is out here watching television. We can go to our room."

I turned my head to see what Bobby was pointing at. It was the house's kitchen. Inside the kitchen were two boys and two girls sitting around a table smoking cigarettes and drinking beer. The boys and girls couldn't have been more than twelve years old. A dalmatian sat at their feet. The dog was so scrawny and mangy I could hardly make out its spots.

"Lead the way," I said.

Bobby and Timmy started off towards a hallway that extended off the left end of the living room. I followed them, but before I left the living room, I detoured, picked up the baby, put it in the crib, and raised the crib's rails. The baby started wailing. I found a pacifier on the crib's mattress and gently stuck it in the infant's mouth. The baby seemed to think the pacifier a good trade for the loss of mobility and contentedly sucked on the pacifier.

We entered Bobby and Timmy's bedroom. It was about fifteen by fifteen feet. A threadbare throw carpet was in the middle of the room, and on it lay a single ancient sleeping bag. The room's lone pane glass window had spots for twelve panes. Ten of the panes were either missing or broken. A lacerated Tom Brady poster was mounted on a section of wall next to the window. The rest of the wall was covered in graffiti that appeared to have been written with crayons. One slogan said, 'Foster Mom is the best'. It didn't say what she was best at.

Three triple decker bunk bed units - consisting of nine beds in all - were stacked against the room's three non-windowed walls. Seven of the beds were covered by messy jumbles of well worn sheets, blankets, and pillows. The middle and top beds of one of the triple decker bunks were neatly made, however. Those beds had sharply tucked hospital corners, blankets pulled so tight one could have bounced a quarter off of them, and would have fit right in in a Marine barracks.

The bedroom had no shelves or dressers, but scattered on the floor were nine piles of clothes. The clothes were boy's clothes and mixed in with the piles were a kite, a slingshot, comic books, sports magazines, four baseball gloves, and a basketball. Two of the piles were neat and orderly with all the clothes carefully folded, but the other seven piles were untidy shambles of clutter and confusion. I had counted seven boys in the living room and kitchen. I assumed each boy, along with Bobby and Timmy, had his own clothes pile.

It was obvious to me which beds - and clothes piles -were Bobby's and Timmy's, but not wanting to appear presumptuous, I said, "Which beds are yours?"

Timmy pointed to the two beds that conformed to Army regulations.

"I was never able to get my bed to look like yours," I said. "You're going to have to show me how to do that one day."

Timmy smiled and nodded.

"Mind if I close the door?" I said.

Both boys shook their head. I shut the bedroom door. For a moment I felt like a pervert again, but the feeling passed.

"So," I said, "you related to any of those kids out there?"

Bobby said, "No, sir."

"You especially close any of them?" I said. "I mean, if you had to move, would you miss them?"

Both boys looked uncomfortable.

"Don't worry," I said. "I'm not going to tell anyone what you say."

Bobby said, "We get along with everyone, General Jack..."

Timmy interrupted, "It's me and Bobby against the world!"

"That's what I thought," I said. "I assume Foster Mom isn't related to you?"

Bobby said, "No sir, General Jack."

"Do you have any grandparents still alive?" I said.

"No, sir," Bobby said.

"Aunts or uncles?" I said.

Timmy said, "We have an aunt. But she's in an institute."

"An institute?" I said.

Bobby said, "He means an institution."

"I understand," I said. How could I not have understood? The way things had been going that day, I had figured I'd wind up in an institution soon myself. "No cousins, older brothers, or sisters?"

"No, sir," Bobby said.

"Well," I said, "I'm not sure there's any easy way to put this, but given what you two saw today, we may be better off moving you for a while."

A long, long while, I thought. Forever would be perfect.

Timmy said, "Witness protection! Like the mafia!"

I think I would have been shocked if any other seven-year-old had just uttered those words, but given the television fare being aired in their living room, I didn't find it shocking at all. Then again, considering the fact I was so out of touch with kids Timmy's age, it was entirely possible every one of them knew what witness protection was.

"That's what I was thinking, Timmy," I said. "Both of you okay with that?"

The brothers looked at each other. A bit of secret communication seemed to pass between them again.

Bobby said, "It's a matter of duty, isn't it, General Jack?"

"I'm afraid it is," I said.

Timmy said, "We'll do it!"

"Let me make a phone call," I said.

I pulled my iPhone out of my pocket, but before I could dial it, it rang. I looked at the screen. It was Adelaide.

"Sorry, boys," I said. "I gotta take this."

I pushed the call button, moved over to a corner of the bedroom, put the phone up close to my mouth, cupping the phone with my free hand as I did, and spoke in hushed tones.

"Where the hell are you, Adelaide?" I said into the phone.

"Home," Adelaide's voice said. "Where else would I be, Uncle Jack?"

"Hold on," I said.

I quickly navigated my way around the iPhone screen until the tracking app I had for Adelaide's ankle monitor displayed her location.

According to the app, Adelaide was still moving around in the ranch's kitchen, just as she had appeared to have been doing earlier when I had checked the app during my call with Jeff.

"You cookin' a pretty fancy dinner, are you?" I said.

"Dinner?" Adelaide said.

"According to my tracking app, you've been in the kitchen for the last four hours," I said.

"Damn, Uncle Jack, it was supposed to be a surprise!" Adelaide said.

"What was supposed to be a surprise?" I said.

"I'm baking a cake for when you get back," Adelaide said.

"Cut the crap, Adelaide," I said.

"It's not crap," Adelaide said. "It's chocolate."

"Adelaide, I know you're in Carson City," I said. "I know you have a fake ID, and I know you have an appointment at the Army recruiting office tomorrow morning."

There was dead silence on the other end of the line.

"Whatever you're thinking," I said, "it can't possibly work. You really believe you'll get through basic training without anyone noticing your ankle monitor?"

More silence.

"Well, it doesn't matter anyway," I said. "There's no way the recruiting office is going to let you enlist."

"You don't know that," Adelaide said.

"I do know that," I said. "Because I'm going to call them and tell them not to."

"What makes you think they're going to listen to you?" Adelaide said.

"Good question," I said. "Maybe, just maybe, because I'm a goddamned general in the goddamned U.S. Army? And maybe since I am a goddamned general in the goddamned U.S. Army, the staff sergeant in charge of the Carson City office will believe me when I tell him or her that if he or she signs you up I'll have him or her busted down to buck private before the sun sets on his or her goddamn, sorry ass. How does that sound to you, Adelaide? Because it sounds pretty damn good to me."

"That asshole Jeff," Adelaide said. "He told you about the letter, didn't he?"

"Jeff is looking out for your best interests," I said.

"Yeah, right," Adelaide said.

"I'm also looking out for your best interests," I said. "Which is why I've come up with a plan."

Adelaide said nothing.

"You're going to like the plan," I said.

"Wanna bet?" Adelaide said.

"How much?" I said.

"A hundred bucks," Adelaide said.

"You're on," I said.

"Fine," Adelaide said. "What's your stinky plan?"

I told her the plan.

Adelaide said, "You serious?"

"Yes," I said.

"You promise?" Adelaide said.

"Yes," I said. "Now get yourself home. As soon as you get there, I want you and Jeff together to give me a call."

"What, you won't believe I'm really home unless Mr. Rat Fink verifies it?" Adelaide said.

"Correct," I said.

"That's insulting," Adelaide said.

"Take it any way you want," I said.

"Hmphhh," Adelaide said.

"Just get home, Adelaide," I said. "And make sure the next time I see you, you've got my hundred bucks."

Adelaide hung up on me.

I walked back over to Bobby and Timmy.

"Witness protection still sound good to both of you?" I said.

The boys nodded.

Before Adelaide called, I had been about to dial Agent Ray Carpenter and ask him to get someone to come to Bobby and Timmy's house to pick them up. But at that moment, I thought better of it. Ray was with MOM, but he was also with the FBI. I didn't see any way Ray could help me get Bobby and Timmy into some form of witness protection without the FBI finding out about it. Which meant Burnette would find out about it. If Burnette found out about it, his special blend of incompetence, stupidity, and arrogance would make it highly unlikely Bobby and Timmy would stay safe for long. I set Ray aside, and decided to go with a different option.

"I got a buddy who was a special forces major who should be able to help us out," I said. "Okay to call him?"

Timmy said, "Delta?"

"As a matter of fact, yes," I said.

Timmy pumped his fist.

"Delta, Delta, Delta!" Timmy said.

Bobby looked pleased as well.

I dialed a number I had been given earlier in the day. My call was answered on the first ring.

"General Wilder," the voice on the other end said. "Good to hear from you. Have you already got the whole NASAD thing figured out?"

"Just about," I said. "I've got two boys whose father won the Medal of Honor in Iraq that want to speak to you. I'm going to put you on speaker."

I put the iPhone on speaker and pointed its microphone at Bobby and Timmy.

"Bobby and Timmy, say hello to Major Vandross," I said.

Timmy said, "Major Vandross, Major Vandross, Major Vandross!"

Bobby said, "Hi, Major Vandross."

Vandross said, "Hello Bobby and Timmy. Nice to meet you."

I took the phone off speaker and put it to my ear.

Vandross said, "You told them I was retired, right?"

"Of course," I said into the phone.

"They sound kinda young to be up so late," Vandross said. "Their dad okay with that?"

"Well...," I said.

"Sorry, I shouldn't have asked," Vandross said. "He was KIA, yes?"

"Uh huh," I said.

"Damn," Vandross said. "No mom either?"

"Roger that, Major," I said.

"What do you need me to do?" Vandross said.

I told him. After I was finished telling him, I hung up the phone and turned my attention back to Bobby and Timmy.

"Vandross says we got forty-five minutes until departure," I said.

"So, let's get your stuff packed up and get ready to go."

I walked over to one of the two neatly folded piles of kid's clothes lying on the floor, picked the pile up, and shoved it under my arm. I then picked up the other neatly folded pile and shoved it under my other arm. I turned to face Bobby and Timmy. They both looked puzzled.

"What's up?" I said.

Bobby said, "General Jack, how did you know that was our stuff?"

Oops.

"Uh, it is, isn't it?" I said.

Bobby and Timmy both nodded.

"Lucky guess," I said.

The brothers seemed to buy it.

"You guys have anything else you want to take with you?" I said.

They shook their heads.

"Let's get out of here, then," I said.

I led them out of the room, back down the hallway, across the living room, out the front door, and onto the porch. As I had expected, no one, not the preteen drinkers in the kitchen, the children watching 'Nightmare On Elm Street,' or the snoring Foster Mom, had paid any attention to us.

"Why don't you guys grab your bikes," I said.

Bobby said, "We get to take them to witness protection?"

"You're going to need something to get around on, aren't you?" I said.

The boys rolled their bikes at their sides as we walked to the Corolla. They set the bikes on their kickstands next to the car, and I laid the brothers' clothes down on the back seat. We had some time to kill before Vandross's people arrived, so all of us sat on the Corolla's trunk, and I told them a story about how Jeff and I had been stuck in the hinterlands of Zimbabwe for a week and had learned how to catch trout with our bare hands.

Forty minutes later, two olive green, four door, mid-size Dodge sedans with government-issue plates pulled up behind us and parked. A gorgeous woman with long brown hair, who looked to be about five foot ten and in her early thirties, got out of the first sedan. She was wearing an expensive, professional-looking, woman's blue suit whose skirt ended just above her exceptional knees, and a white silk blouse.

A second woman, plump, in her late fifties, with carefully permed bleached blond hair and wearing a well-tailored light brown tweed jacket and skirt, got out of the other car.

The women approached us.

"General Wilder, I presume," the younger woman said. "I am assistant U.S. Attorney Audrey Delahoussaye. This is Kathy Gustafson. Kathy is a federal social worker."

Federal social worker? I hadn't even known there was such a thing.

I shook both their hands.

"These two fine gentlemen are Bobby and Timmy Fenton," I said. "I assume Vandross brought you up to speed?"

"He certainly did," Audrey said.

"Bobby and Timmy are invaluable to the security interests of the United States," I said. "You promise to take good care of them?"

"I promise with all my heart," Audrey said, putting a lot of emphasis on 'heart'.

Could it be? I had believed Vandross would send me someone good. But this good?

"MOM?" I silently mouthed to her.

She nodded.

Would wonders never cease in the land of Hart? Probably not. And despite some lingering, mild annoyance with my commanding officer and substitute dad, my own heart warmed immediately. Bobby and Timmy would be safe. No question about it.

About a hundred yards away from us, a large vehicle turned from a cross street onto the street we were on and headed toward us. Its big headlamps shot brilliant, wide swaths of light through the darkness. As the vehicle got closer, I was able to see it was a big yellow school bus. The bus pulled to the side of the street and parked behind Kathy's sedan.

Kathy said, "I guess that's my cue. Nice meeting you, General."

She turned, marched up the house's cracked walkway, and entered the front door without knocking, just as if she owned the place.

Audrey said, "I don't envy her."

I said, "She looks like she can handle herself. She going to take all those kids away tonight?"

"Do we have any other choice?" Audrey said.

"Absolutely not," I said. "They'll get good homes?"

"Without a doubt," Audrey said.

"And the dog?" I said.

"The dog too," Audrey said.

Bobby and Timmy seemed concerned about what they had overheard us say.

"That nice lady is going to get Foster Mom some help," I said. "It's just too hard for one person to take care of so many kids at once."

Bobby said, "Yeah, that's what Timmy and I have been thinking."

"Like I said, you two are smart," I said. "Okay, time to begin your new adventure with Audrey."

I grabbed Bobby and Timmy's clothes and loaded them in Audrey's car. The boys brought their bicycles over and we put them in the trunk.

I knelt down in front of the brothers.

"It's been great meeting you, and I thank you for your service to your country," I said. "I've got to finish my mission, but I promise to check up on you when I'm done."

I opened my arms. Bobby and Timmy walked into them and I gave the boys a big hug.

I didn't feel like a pervert at all.

CHAPTER 52

It was just after midnight when I said goodbye to Lancaster and turned south onto Highway 14. I drove as fast as the Corolla would allow. Which wasn't very fast since the car started to violently shake and shimmy as soon as it got above seventy miles an hour. At that speed, semi-tractor trailers blew right past me, and I had to tightly grip the steering wheel to keep the Corolla from fishtailing in the trucks' wakes. The only sounds I could hear were the wind blowing through the newly broken back passenger window and the whine of the car's engine. A night-blooming desert plant permeated the air with its scent. The scent irritated my lungs and breathing was hard for a while.

I had calculated it would take me about two hours to get to Kate's home in Malibu. My route would take me from Highway 14 to Highway 5, down the San Diego Freeway, then north and west along the Ventura Freeway to the Kanan Dume Road exit. Kanan Dume would carry me over the coastal foothills of Malibu to the Pacific Coast Highway.

I thought about what I knew and didn't know.

I knew that Milt Feynman, Paul Lennon, and twelve NASAD drone sub engineers were dead. Their deaths had been deemed accidental, but I was nearly certain they'd all been murdered.

I knew the Chinese were going to start a war in Saudi Arabia, that General Hart thought that war would start in less than eleven days, and that the Chinese believed they had some kind of insurmountable edge.

I knew there was some guy running around named Dr. Nemo who had sent Kate a coded message. Nemo also seemed to know what the Chinese edge was and eagerly wanted to tell Kate about it. The problem was that until I either found Nemo, Nemo gave us the key to his encryption, or MOM's code breakers cracked his code, whatever Nemo had to tell was going to remain a mystery.

I also knew someone had gone to a lot of trouble to make it look like the Chinese insurmountable edge was related to drone submarines and that Hart had bought what that someone was selling. I, however, hadn't bought it. I believed the drones to be a diversion from the real threat.

What the real threat was, I didn't know.

When I got to what I knew and didn't know about the strange man in the dragon mask that Bobby and Timmy had described as going around celebrating while Sam and Lizzy had been stoned to death, I also started to think about what Jeff had said about things being one thing. Just starting to think about things being one thing made my mind nearly spin out of control. I realized I needed some help.

I called Jeff. He answered on the first ring.

"I found some witnesses," I said. "Two fine young boys named Bobby and Timmy. Dad was a Medal of Honor winner."

"Was?" Jeff said.

"He's dead," I said. "Mother too. Boys were living with some evil troll named Foster Mom, but a U.S. Attorney working for Hart named Vandross got them into witness protection."

"What Bobby and Timmy see?" Jeff said.

I told Jeff about Dragon Man and his mask, the party bus, the white van, my forwarding of the vehicles' license plates to Hart, the Caucasian bus driver with the big sports watch, the unidentified person that was also in the bus with the driver, the absolute confirmation that the 'baseball' players had been Afghans, the fact Dragon Man had used his cell phone to video the stoning, and Dragon Man's champagne.

"Party bus, champagne, video," Jeff said. "Sound like there was a big celebration going on."

"It does," I said.

"Would have been helpful if Bobby and Timmy had gotten a good look at the other two guys in the bus, though," Jeff said.

"It would have," I said.

"But at least we know we searching for three guys traveling together who like to party," Jeff said.

"That's one way to look at it," I said.

"Whole thing play into what we said about it being personal too," Jeff said.

"Which is the real reason I called," I said. "I'm trying to make the whole problem at NASAD and the killing of Paul Lennon's kids into one thing, not two, but I can't quite get there yet."

"I'm there," Jeff said.

"You are?" I said.

"Way I look at it, it's a pretty expensive take down," Jeff said. "Have to get Afghans and Kazakhs into the country. Afghans and Kazakhs also have their own vans and Dragon Man has a party bus."

"Too expensive just to kill the relatives?" I said.

"What you think?" Jeff said.

"I got a pretty good line on what I think," I said. "But I need to know what you think."

"I'm probably thinking what you thinking," Jeff said. "If NASAD is the source of the Chinese insurmountable edge..."

"Which we have to go with, since it's our best option at this point," I said. "Especially with time running out and war about to commence."

"You just interrupted me," Jeff said. "You want to hear what I got to say or not?"

"Sorry," I said.

"As I was saying," Jeff said. "If NASAD is the source of the Chinese insurmountable edge, then whatever plan was formulated to put the edge in play now got a fly in the ointment. That fly be in the form of a NASAD employee."

"Dr. Nemo," I said.

"Um-hmm," Jeff said. "All those Afghans and Kazakhs here to find Nemo, but whoever brought them over also figure it be a good time to settle a personal vendetta with Paul Lennon. Whoever brought them over is, in effect, killing two birds with one stone. Sorry. No pun intended."

"No need to apologize, since I'm sure that wasn't your intent," I said. "However, what you said does fill a hole."

"There's no hole to fill," Jeff said.

"There was in my mind," I said. "I wasn't sure why the Kazakhs' plan was to kidnap Kate from the Coso Junction rest area, rather than kill her. But now it seems likely the bad guys must have figured out Dr. Nemo had contacted her, and they wanted to know what he told her."

"I agree," Jeff said. "Which means whoever killed Sam and Lizzy probably also behind the insurmountable edge. Which gets us back to my original hunch that NASAD's problems and some dude's personal vendetta are all going to tie together. Now, however, we also know who that dude most likely is."

"Dragon Man," I said.

"Yep," Jeff said.

I thought for a moment.

"Maybe I should get MOM to start looking for people with a grudge against Paul Lennon," I said.

"Good a place to start as any," Jeff said. "There's another thing we need to know too, though."

"What's that?" I said.

"How many claws Dragon Man mask got?" Jeff said.

"Claws?" I said.

"I take it you don't be asking Bobby and Timmy that question?" Jeff said.

"What have claws got to do with anything?" I said.

"I'll tell you after you ask Bobby and Timmy," Jeff said. "Don't want you influencing them when you ask."

"Fine," I said.

"Are we done here?" Jeff said. "I need to sleep."

"We're almost done," I said. "I just have one more thing to talk to you about. I spoke to Adelaide. We have a plan."

Jeff said nothing.

"Don't you want to know what the plan is?" I said.

"If the two of you come up with a plan," Jeff said, "odds are it ain't any good. I prefer not to be implicated."

"How about you hear me out and then decide?" I said.

"If it means that much to you, be my guest," Jeff said.

I told Jeff the plan. When I was done, Jeff said, "That wasn't as stupid as I thought it'd be."

"You in?" I said.

"I'm in," Jeff said.

"Good," I said.

"Now may I go to sleep?" Jeff said.

"You may," I said.

CHAPTER 53

The Corolla and I kept pushing towards Malibu along Highway 14. I had texted Hart to request that he tell MOM to begin looking for anyone with a grudge against Paul Lennon as soon as I had gotten off the phone with Jeff. Something continued to nag at the corners of my consciousness, however. Something I felt I had missed, something my gut told me was really bad. I couldn't figure out what that something was, and my failed attempt at doing so had made my head spin.

I decided I needed to distract myself and regroup. I looked at the passing landscape. The landscape was no longer barren desert, but was instead occupied by a giant mall. There was a Macy's, an El Torito, an Olive Garden, a Red Lobster, and a Dillard's. I had a pretty good idea what everything was other than the Dillard's. Was it a restaurant? A drug store? A shoe store? A bar?

Thinking about what Dillard's might be only made my head spin more, so I took a deep breath. The breath didn't clear my head, but it was lucky I had taken it.

Because it made me aware of the uniquely pungent smell of gasoline exhaust and that the smell was much stronger than it should have been. Which meant the Corolla was leaking exhaust gases, including carbon monoxide, into its cabin, gases that were apparently accumulating despite the ventilation provided by the gaping new wound at the top of the back passenger window.

I quickly rolled down my window and the front passenger window. Just when I had finished getting the windows down, a big eighteen-wheeler going at least ninety miles an hour roared past me in the left lane. The truck's wake nearly sent the Corolla sideways and the truck's tires kicked up sand and dirt that sprayed through the open window, stung my face, and blurred my vision. I struggled to see and keep the Corolla steady. I zigzagged across the lanes to my left and right. I narrowly avoided a car that had 'Just Married' written across its back window and was also trailing dozens of small cans that had been tied to its rear bumper. I heard a few angry horns but never saw who was doing the honking. Finally, my vision sharpened, and I regained control of the car and straightened it out.

My fight with the car, the pain of the sand and dirt, along with the falling carbon monoxide levels, worked wonders to clear my mind. Clear enough anyway to get back to focusing on that nagging feeling that I had missed something important. I became convinced that if the meaning of that nagging feeling eluded me, something might be lost, maybe forever.

But the harder I tried to comprehend the feeling's meaning, the more that meaning seemed to slip away.

Not one to give up easily, however, I tried harder still.

Yet, the source of the nagging feeling only continued to elude me. Until it didn't.

"Aw shit," I said to myself.

Keeping one hand on the wheel, I dug my iPhone out of my pocket with the other, and, looking at the phone's screen out of the corner of my eye, found Agent Ray Carpenter's number and pushed call. Carpenter answered almost immediately.

"Figured you'd have joined us in Malibu by now, General," Carpenter's voice said.

"I would have if I had a better ride," I said.

"Ouch," Carpenter said. "Sorry about that. Must be a budgetary issue."

"If I pass out from all the carbon monoxide in the cabin and kill someone, it's gonna wind up being a hell of a lot more expensive for MOM than getting me something a little nicer would have been," I said.

"Exhaust leak, huh?" Carpenter said.

"I've got the windows open," I said. "I'll survive. I'm more worried about something else, though."

"Something I can help with?" Carpenter said.

"Hope so," I said. "Since Paul Lennon's ex-wife Sarah, and the kids they had together, Sam and Lizzy, are all dead, I'm wondering if Paul Lennon has any living relatives other than Kate and her kids?"

"I don't know, but I can find out," Carpenter said.

"If there are any," I said, "let's get them some protection."

"You believe they're in danger?" Carpenter said.

"Might be," I said.

"You think the murders were personal and not NASAD related?" Carpenter said.

Jeff's and my conversation a few minutes earlier had of course convinced me that it was both personal *and* NASAD related, but I didn't tell Carpenter that. I didn't tell Carpenter that for two reasons. One, it's always best if information is only shared on a need to know basis, and I didn't feel Carpenter needed to know anything about Bobby and Timmy and what they had relayed to me about Dragon Man and his celebratory participation in Sam's and Lizzy's murders in order for Carpenter to arrange protection for any remaining living relatives of Paul Lennon. Two, Carpenter was MOM, and completely trustworthy, but even the most trustworthy person can accidentally leak something they shouldn't, and I still believed it would be safer for Bobby and Timmy if the FBI never learned of their existence.

"I don't know what I think," I said. "But I'd rather be safe than sorry."

"Understood," Carpenter said. "I'll get right on it, General."

"Thanks," I said. "You happy with your security at the Lennon compound?"

"Yes," Carpenter said. "I think you will be too."

"I'm sure I will," I said. "Please tell your men, that despite all appearances to the contrary, the guy who will be pulling up in the ancient Corolla in about ninety minutes is a friendly."

"Don't want to get shot, huh?" Carpenter said.

"Exactly," I said. "Bye."

I hung up.

The Corolla was then climbing the hill at Palmdale's southern end. I had the gas pedal to the floor, but the straining engine was having a hard time maintaining the car's speed. I was being passed by other southbound cars, their taillights moving rapidly away from me, and it made me feel lonely. But the slower speed meant I didn't have to focus as hard on keeping the Corolla under control. Which meant I could devote more mental energy to thinking about my mission.

Which I never got around to doing. Because just then the Corolla reached the top of the incline where the road leveled off and began to fall towards the canyon floor that held the Santa Clara River, and the car picked up speed again, shimmying and shaking as it did so, a shimmying and shaking followed by my brain doing its own version of shimmying and shaking.

My brain's shimmying and shaking was an uncomfortable feeling. It felt like someone was simultaneously blowing a loud, out of tune trumpet and clashing cymbals inside my head. I wanted the cacophony to stop, but the trumpet playing and cymbal clashing grew even more loud and callithumpian.

"What the hell do you want from me?" I said to myself.

As soon as I said that, I knew what it was. I was wasting time. I needed help. I had plenty of theory about Nemo, NASAD, the insurmountable edge, Paul Lennon's relatives, and Dragon Man, but I needed facts. MOM was the only one who could help me get those facts, and just texting Hart to ask MOM for help wasn't going to cut it. I needed to make a call I hadn't made in over two years.

It was then 12:30 a.m. my time. The person at MOM I wanted to talk to was probably in a later time zone. That person was also probably asleep. But if I was up, wasn't it only fair they should be up too?

CHAPTER 54

For reasons that will soon become clear, a simple phone call to MOM would not suffice. No, the only way my communications with MOM would make me truly happy would be if I conducted them using video chat. I pulled the Corolla off the highway at the Agua Dulce Road exit, turned right onto Agua Dulce itself, and drove about twenty yards north of the freeway overpass. At that point the street was bordered on both sides by high, steeply sloped, scrub brush covered walls of rock and sand. I backed the rear of the Corolla up against the slope on the street's eastern side, so that the car's nose faced out. From there I could watch the road, but my back was protected, my parking job thus a variation on my Wild Bill Hickok theme.

Kinda like what Brahms did to Haydn.

Or maybe not.

I shut off the Corolla's engine. It made popping noises as it ran on for a while. The engine hadn't done that any other time I had turned it off. Maybe I'd broken it. Maybe MOM would charge my account. I wasn't going to worry about it. The only other sounds I heard were the whoosh of a rare car traveling above me on the overpass or the rarer howl of a lone coyote. The only smells came from the Corolla's burning engine oil and the desert sage. The sky was full of stars.

I took out my iPhone and tapped on the FaceTime icon. My phone's version of FaceTime was not your average, everyday FaceTime. It had artillery strength encryption designed by some of MOM's computer geeks. I put in my password, chose 'Edith Bunker' from the contacts, and tapped again.

It rang twice.

An automated voice answered. The iPhone's screen remained dark.

"This number is out of service," the automated voice said. "Please check the number and dial again."

I punched in another twelve digit code. The line was filled with electronic hisses and clicks. This time the voice of a live human female operator answered. The screen still remained dark.

"Please speak your name clearly," the operator's voice said.

"General Jack Wilder," I said.

There was silence for a moment. I knew that the operator was watching her terminal as the computer performed voice recognition.

"Please send me an image," the operator said.

I had passed the first test and it was time for the second. The lens in my iPhone had been specially modified to be able to take a picture of my retina. I put the lens up to my left eye and snapped a photo that was automatically sent to the operator.

There was more silence as the operator's computer checked my retinal scan against the MOM's database. If I didn't pass this next test, the line would have been cut immediately.

It had always seemed to me that just cutting the line wasn't enough.

That maybe something should be done to the intruder.

I once asked a tech at MOM about that.

The tech had said, "Of course we don't just cut the line."

I said, "We don't?"

"Missile lock," the tech had said, and sweeping his arms up and out, added, "Pow!"

I hadn't been sure if the tech was kidding or not. Before I could ask him anything further, however, he winked at me and walked away. When I told Jeff about it, Jeff had just said, "Don't worry about it dude. Your retina ain't gonna change."

A moment later it appeared that Jeff had been right about my retina, since the operator put me through to MOM's routing desk. The face of the night routing officer, Captain Leah Van Zant - a gorgeous young woman with fine high cheekbones, green eyes, a wide, inviting smile, and shoulder length blond hair tucked under a white crowned, black brimmed female naval officer's hat with a gold USN anchor medallion on its front - popped up on my screen. Behind Van Zant was a wall covered in government issue lime green paint. An American flag was draped on the wall.

"Good evening, General," Van Zant said. "Heard you were back in the saddle. What can we do for you?"

"A martini would be nice, Captain Van Zant," I said. "Shaken, not stirred."

"You must have me confused with Miss Moneypenny," Van Zant said. "Which would be disappointing."

"Disappointing?" I said.

"As I remember it," Van Zant said, "Bond and Moneypenny's relationship never went beyond the purely professional."

"How sad," I said.

"Indeed," Van Zant said.

"Where are you tonight, Captain?" I said.

"A bunker in Wyoming," Van Zant said.

"Wyoming nice this time of year?" I said.

"If you like cold and cloudy," Van Zant said.

"I was hoping to wake you," I said. "But you look positively chipper."

"I couldn't sleep," Van Zant said. "I was told you might call."

"That's very sweet," I said. "Alas, I have some business to conduct."

"Of course you do," Van Zant said.

"Would you please put me through to Haley in Operations Support?" I said.

"You're making me jealous," Van Zant said.

"Can't be helped," I said.

"May I make a request before I put you through, sir?" Van Zant said.

"Yes, Captain?" I said.

"I don't like child killers," Van Zant said.

"News travels fast," I said.

"It does," Van Zant said. "I hope you won't think me out of line, but please, don't bring the scumbags back alive."

"Wasn't planning on it," I said.

"And if the scumbags should happen to suffer before dying...," Van Zant said.

"Understood," I said.

"Thank you, sir," Van Zant said. "Goodnight, General."

Van Zant's face disappeared and the screen went dark. There were more hisses and clicks. Seconds, then minutes, went by. I drummed my fingers on the steering wheel and waited impatiently. What was taking Haley so long? A wave of exhaustion came over me and I struggled to stay awake.

Suddenly the hisses and clicks on the video line were drowned out by the trumpeting of an eighteen-wheeler's air brakes coming from the overpass. The air brakes sounded like a wounded elephant and they were joined by the screech of skidding tires. I looked up. A coyote dashed over the side of the highway closest to me, ran down the embankment, and stopped outside my window. His green eyes stared into mine. For a moment I thought it was the same coyote I had seen the day before in Lancaster. But no, this one had a scar on his left brow.

"We come from such different sets of circumstance," I said to the coyote.

I got no response.

"Were you a prisoner of the white lines of the freeway?" I said.

Still nothing.

"Peeking through through keyholes in numbered doors?" I said.

The coyote seemed to smile.

"I like Joni Mitchell, too," the coyote said.

I was about to continue my conversation with the coyote, when a female voice said, "What the hell, Jack? I'm up all night slaving away and you're sleeping?"

The voice was husky, sensuous. Haley's voice. But sleeping? Not me. I tried to tell her so, but my mouth didn't move.

"Ah, come on," Haley's voice said. "Snoring too? Get up, or I'm outta here. I got work to do."

"Keyholes in numbered doors," I heard myself mumble, my eyes locked on the coyote.

"Keyholes in numbered doors?" Haley said. "Isn't Joni Mitchell a little old school even for you?"

Old school? Who is she calling old school? And then just like that, the coyote was gone. I realized that Haley had been right. I *had* been asleep. Jeez, I thought to myself, that stress reaction must be really getting to me.

I stared down at my iPhone. A large bank of electronic equipment with hundreds of tiny flashing orange and yellow lights was on the screen. Major Marian Haley was in front of the equipment.

Haley.

Van Zant had been excuse enough to use video chat. But Haley was a goddess. She was in her early thirties and had long, silky brown hair, and huge, beautiful, brown eyes that seemed to invite you into endless depths of intelligence and humor. Her tanned skin was flawless and her teeth sparkled between her full red lips. Her neck was long and graceful. I knew Haley would not have purposely done it, but almost too painful to bear was the fact that somehow Haley's computer's camera was focused too low on Haley's chest and her large breasts were evident beneath her starched khaki uniform shirt.

Haley smiled.

It was a smile that was sexy, but not consciously so - it just couldn't help itself.

I said, "It took you long enough to answer."

"You don't call me for two years," Haley said, "and now you can't wait for five minutes?"

"Has it really been two years?" I said.

"You know it has," Haley said.

"Where are you tonight, my love?" I said.

"Inside a mountain," Haley said.

"NORAD?" I said.

"Um-hmm," Haley said. "I was working on an assignment with the Air Force until Hart pulled me off yesterday morning to work full time on what he termed, 'The Insurmountable Edge Problem.'"

"Lucky you," I said.

"Lucky me, lucky you," Haley said. "How's Jeff?"

"Better," I said.

"Why don't I believe you?" Haley said.

"Why don't you believe me, Haley?" I said to myself. "Well, maybe because neither I, nor anyone else, can get anything by you."

Haley was the best mission planner the Army had, which is why she was with MOM. She also was the head of MOM's cyber warfare division - offensive, not defensive - and was a wizard at gathering intel from all of MOM's sources, from which she sifted the wheat from the chaff, the truth from the bullshit.

"Because I lied," I said out loud. "What I meant to say was, I *think* he's better."

Something passed behind Haley's eyes. It looked like sadness. Haley didn't like to admit she had a heart - probably thought all of MOM's stone cold killer types would think less of her, even though she was as stone cold as anyone when she had to be - so I didn't say anything about what I thought I'd seen. I knew Haley truly cared about Jeff. I also knew that the reason we hadn't heard from Haley for the last two years was that she was smart enough to know there was nothing she could do for him, and that she was deeply pained by that reality.

"That, I'll buy," Haley said. "How about your wildcat niece?"

"Long story," I said.

"Later, then," Haley said. "Shall we get down to business? I assume you called since you have questions for me. How about I cut straight to the answers? It'll save a lot of time."

"How do you know what the questions are?" I said.

Haley rolled her eyes.

"Please," Haley said.

"Sorry," I said. "I don't know what got into me."

"That's better," Haley said. "First, yes, I have personally reviewed the autopsies and accident scene reports of the NASAD drone sub engineering project managers. While it certainly is impossible to believe the engineers all died of accidents, it is equally impossible to find anything in the autopsies or reports that would support any other conclusion. There were also no witnesses to any of the deaths."

"Which means that if all the drone sub engineers were actually murdered, then the murders were committed by highly skilled professionals," I said.

"Highly," Haley said. "Two. We ran the license plates of the van the Kazakhs used at the rest stop that you texted to Hart. The plates were stolen from a car in Dallas, Texas. The FBI took a look at the Kazakhs' van too. Their initial forensic reports show the van's vehicle identification number also had been filed off."

"The FBI shared their reports with you?" I said.

"No," Haley said. "We hacked into their computers."

"Of course you did," I said. "No vehicle ID and stolen plates means that, as far as we know, the van could have come from anywhere."

"Correct," Haley said. "The van did have some useable fingerprints, however. We're checking those fingerprints now."

"Don't think that's going to do much good," I said. "I doubt the

Kazakhs will show up in any databases, Interpol, or otherwise."

"Really?" Haley said.

I knew by the way she had said 'Really' that I was in trouble.

"Uh oh," I said. "I know that tone."

"Really?" Haley said.

"Don't rub it in," I said.

"I'm not trying to identify the Kazakhs' prints," Haley said.

"You're not?" I said.

Haley raised her eyebrows, smiled, and shook her head, but said nothing.

I thought about where I'd gone wrong.

Damn.

I'm so stupid sometimes.

"You're looking for the owner of the car," I said.

Haley licked her lips.

I wished she hadn't done that.

"Bingo," Haley said. "Or anyone else that might have been in it."

"No matches yet?" I said.

"We're close on one," Haley said. "The FBI, since they're the ones who gathered the fingerprints at the rest stop crime scene, were in position to have the first shot at identifying the prints. But we got the jump on them."

"You got the jump on the FBI?" I said.

"They were quick to examine the van and check on the vehicle ID number, but the prints were uploaded to a different FBI forensic lab's computers," Haley said. "The techs there didn't look at them right away."

"But you hacked right into that lab as well, and took a look yourself?" I said.

"It would have been wrong not to have, wouldn't it?" Haley said.

"Very wrong," I said.

"Anyway, we found a set of prints with a potential match, and then deleted that set from the FBI's files," Haley said. "The FBI will be clueless about the lead we're tracking down."

"So you know about Burnette," I said.

"Flaming asshole," Haley said. "Hart told me. I'll be damned if I let a clown like that screw up this mission."

"You and me both, babe," I said.

"Sonny and Cher reference?" Haley said.

"Hadn't meant it to be," I said, "but I can see that."

"I think it is," Haley said. "Everyone says you're a bit out of it, darling. I'm sure it was your unconscious speaking."

"Unconscious is the only conscious I got right now," I said.

"I'll pretend I didn't hear that," Haley said. "We'll continue to hack the FBI files, and, after taking any evidence they found at the crime scene that we deem of potential value for ourselves, we'll delete the FBI's copy. That'll continue to keep the FBI out of our hair as we conduct our own investigations into that evidence."

"Sounds like a plan," I said. "Did you find anything on those plates from the vehicles at the stoning site that I also texted?"

"Nothing other than that they were stolen too," Haley said.

"That's not surprising," I said. "How about the photos of the stoning site I sent to Hart? Were they of any use?"

"Not yet," Haley said. "But we're working on them."

"Okay," I said. "What else you got?"

"As you surmised, the would-be kidnappers/killers at the rest stop were not just Kazakhs, but Kazakh mercenaries," Haley said. "The cobra and crucifix tattoos in the photos you texted Hart were authentic, and the FBI found traces of dust on their boots consistent with an area of Kazakhstan that is used as a mercenary training camp."

"The FBI thinks they're Islamic terrorists," I said.

"Which is why I didn't delete anything about the dust or tattoos from their files," Haley said. "That stuff isn't going to help them if they've already jumped to the wrong conclusions."

I took the pork rind snack food wrapper I'd taken off the dead Kazakh at the rest stop out of my pocket and showed it to Haley.

"Hart told me about your pork rind snack," Haley said. "Said you think it's the Kazakh equivalent of airline peanuts, and it means they've only been in country a short time."

"You sound skeptical," I said.

"I'm always skeptical," Haley said.

"But not so skeptical you're not going to check it out?" I said.

"We're checking everything out," Haley said. "There are a thousand ways the Kazakhs might have come into the U.S."

"We only have eleven days until war breaks out," I said.

"I'll have an answer well before then," Haley said.

"I'm sure you will," I said. "What else you got for me?"

"We're working on a profile of Dr. Nemo from the tape of his message you texted to Hart," Haley said. "We don't have anything yet, but we're close. We're also working on your request for a list of people who might have a grudge against Paul Lennon. Nothing there yet, either. Other than those two items, I can't think of anything else right now."

Outside, another truck's air brakes brayed, accompanied by the sound of more skidding tires. I looked for the coyote. He didn't show that time. I heard the truck climb through its gears as it moved off.

"You didn't mention my theory that it wasn't just the twelve NASAD drone sub engineers that were murdered, but Milt Feynman and Paul Lennon as well," I said. "Hart must have told you what I said."

"Hart did," Haley said. "Feynman's and Lennon's deaths come under the same heading as the dead engineers."

"Meaning their deaths weren't accidents, but it's impossible to prove they weren't?" I said.

"Yes," Haley said. "MOM's forensic team and I poured over the entire search and rescue record and there's nothing there."

"Really?" I said.

Haley's eyes narrowed ever so slightly. It made her look even more beautiful.

"I recognize that tone," Haley said.

"Really?" I said.

"Don't screw with me, Jack," Haley said. "Tell me what you're thinking."

"Someone near and dear to me, who shall remain nameless, wears an ankle monitor," I said.

"I'm supposed to pretend I don't know who you're talking about?" Haley said.

"Yes," I said. "That way I won't feel like I'm breaking any confidences."

"I thought you said you weren't capable of any conscious thought," Haley said.

"I would never ask you to part with your illusions," I said.

"Twain," Haley said. "A bit mangled, but Twain nevertheless."

"I believe so," I said. "In any event, last night this nameless person, according to her ankle monitor tracking app, was making dinner in the kitchen at my ranch, but..."

I paused.

"But...?" Haley said

"She was actually in Carson City," I said.

"Aha," Haley said.

The 'Aha' appeared to have been close to a knee-jerk reaction on Haley's part, but then almost immediately her eyes slightly narrowed again, and something dark seemed to cross her mind. I hoped her narrowed eyes and that seeming crossing of the dark thing might mean my mentioning of Adelaide's ankle bracelet had had its intended effect - that Haley might be starting to see Milt Feynman's and Paul Lennon's 'accidental' deaths in a new light.

Haley's right hand went up to her mouth and she gently rubbed her lower lip between her thumb and forefinger. I knew that rubbing meant she was thinking. I wished I was that lip. Or the thumb and forefinger. Either would have rocketed me to heaven.

Haley said, "I think I might have missed something."

"That's okay," I said. "So did Hart."

"I'm not supposed to miss anything," Haley said.

"Everybody misses something sometime," I said. "And, anyway, my theory could be wrong. Since I don't want to put my foot in my mouth any further than I have to, how about we go over what I think I know, and you point out any errors before I actually say out loud what I believe might have happened?"

Haley's face told me she had fallen into a deep funk over the fact she thought she had messed up. But Haley was nothing if not game.

"Go ahead," Haley said.

"Two years ago a plane carrying Milt Feynman and Paul Lennon left Homer on its way to Kodiak for a fishing expedition," I said. "The plane went down in the Gulf of Alaska. I was told there was an EPIRB on board, but that neither it, the plane, nor the passengers were ever found."

"There was an EPIRB aboard," Haley said. "The search teams tracked right to it, but you're correct, they never found it. Goddamnit, Jack, how did I miss it?"

"Chill," I said. "I assume they also had a radar trace on the plane?"

"Yes," Haley said, "they had a radar trace. Nothing was at the end of it either."

Haley looked disgusted with herself. I felt bad for her.

"By your reaction, I'm pretty sure I know the answer to my next question," I said. "But I'm going to ask it anyway."

Haley nodded.

"Here goes," I said. "Does the technology exist to fake a flight path on FAA radar and mislocate an EPIRB signal?"

"NASAD built it for MOM a little over three years ago," Haley said. "No other agency or service branch knows it exists."

"Interesting," I said.

"I drank the Kool-Aid, Jack," Haley said. "'Weather up there can get real rough,' the reports said. 'Currents are strong...Small planes can sink fast and don't leave much of a trace...EPIRB stops working, the rescue crews could miss the crash site by miles,' and on and on and on..."

Haley looked like she wanted to punch someone. I had never seen her quite so worked up before. It was a surprisingly attractive look for her, however.

"In the grand scheme of things, you didn't do anything so terrible," I said. "Been three years. Not like if you'd seen it earlier you could have saved Feynman and Lennon's lives."

Haley didn't say anything.

"We've had satellites monitoring the Alaskan coast for over half a century, haven't we?" I said.

"Yes," Haley said.

"United States has been saving all the satellite surveillance imagery in its data banks since at least 9/11 hasn't it?" I said.

"That and every other defense-related communication or surveillance - be it digital, oral, visual, or written - involving the U.S., our friends, and our not so friends," Haley said. She sighed. "The search and rescue team didn't ask for any of the satellite images."

On the overpass above me, another set of airbrakes fired off and there was the sound of more skidding tires. I looked. Again no coyote. After a moment, I heard the truck's engine rev and the truck's transmission grind up through its gears, the truck apparently on its way once again.

"I'm sure they didn't even think about it," I said. "In their minds, the EPIRB and radar trace told them exactly where to look."

"You mean exactly where *not* to look," Haley said.

"That's what I've been thinking ever since Ms. Nameless turned out to be in Carson City," I said. "I think that plane may have actually traveled in the opposite direction from where the radar trace said it was traveling."

Haley sighed.

"Alright, Jack," Haley said. "Here's what I'm going to do. I've got the wing numbers. We know the plane went down on August 14th. I'll pull the satellite images from that day and follow the plane from Homer until it goes down."

"You'll call me as soon as you find anything?" I said.

"Of course," Haley said.

"And if you ID the owner of the van the Kazakhs used at the rest stop?" I said.

"Yes, Jack," Haley said. "That and anything else you can use."

"I'll be getting off to Malibu, then," I said.

"Hold on," Haley said. "You had Vandross pick up two brothers today and put them in witness protection. You didn't tell Vandross much about why you needed them protected. I want to know the full why."

"Actually, I meant to tell you about the brothers because I need your help with them too," I said. "But my brain, Haley, my brain."

"You have a brain?" Haley said. "I'm shocked."

"Thank you," I said. "Your compassion overwhelms me."

"Tell me about the brothers," Haley said.

"They're young, and their names are Bobby and Timmy," I began.

And then I told Haley everything about what Bobby and Timmy had said, and also what I had found at the stoning site on my own - the pitcher's mound, the pattern of the stones on the ground, that Sam's and Lizzy's footprints showed they had attempted to escape from the grave only to be dragged back to it, the stakes, the party bus, Dragon Man and his mask, the man with the big gold racing watch, the unseen third man in bus, and the Afghans and their bootprints. I left nothing out, even things I assumed Haley may have already discovered from her hack of the FBI's computers.

When I was done, Haley said, "FBI can't make heads or tails about the bootprints, but I had figured they were Afghans from what I saw. Still would have been nice if you could've gotten the message through to me a little earlier. Would have saved me some time."

"My brain," I said.

"No comment," Haley said. "I'll send someone out to get the stakes you said the Afghans left in the field. We'll see if we can get any useable fingerprints or DNA off of the stakes. So far none of the stones the FBI found at the gravesite have produced any good prints or DNA."

"You would know," I said. "I don't think the Afghans are any more likely to show up in any databases than the Kazakhs are, though."

"Really?" Haley said.

"Not again," I said.

Haley laughed.

"I'm teasing you," Haley said. "And I agree with you there's no reason to believe that 'Dragon Man' is Chinese just because of the mask. It could easily go either way - yes he is, or no he isn't. I also agree there seems to be a personal aspect behind yesterday's murders. We'll continue to look at Paul Lennon's life since the day he popped out of the womb."

"Sounds like a plan," I said. "Can I go now?"

"Not yet," Haley said. "Captain Lennon won a Bronze Star, didn't he?"

"Yes," I said.

"We've got a lot of innocent dead at NASAD, and a lot of relatives of those dead whose lives will never be the same, not to mention Feynman and Lennon themselves," Haley said. "But killing the kids of a certified U.S. war hero is beyond the pale. Whoever did this needs to die a very unpleasant death, Jack."

"You'll get no argument from me on that," I said.

"If you need any input on the actual methods to employ when the time comes, make sure you give me a jingle," Haley said.

"I'm sure you'll have some doozies," I said.

"I will," Haley said.

"Goodnight, Major," I said.

"Goodnight, General," Haley said.

I clicked off my iPhone screen.

Boy, Haley and Van Zant are tough, I thought to myself. Both women wanted the perps to die badly, even horribly. It was nice of Haley to offer her help on how I might ultimately dispose of the bad guys, but, truthfully, her imagination was no match for mine. Not even close.

I started the Corolla. I turned around and gave one last look for the coyote. He was nowhere in sight. I looked both ways, crossed the road, pulled onto the on-ramp, and accelerated up its slope. As soon as I merged onto the freeway, I looked back behind me. I saw what the trucks had been stopping for. A big box spring mattress lay sideways on the roadbed, imprisoned between the fine white lines of the freeway.

PART IV

MALIBU

CHAPTER 55

The Corolla and I rolled swiftly south and west across the deserted nighttime Los Angeles freeways and rapidly ate up the miles that lay between us and Kate's Malibu home. The freeways could only take us as far as Agoura Hills, however, and it was there that we exited onto Kanan Dume Road.

Kanan Dume was a byway of hairpin curves that wound through the Santa Monica Mountains. A car went by on the other side of the road as I began Kanan's uphill climb out of Agoura. The car's license plate said 'STGSTAR'. "Shooting star," I silently mouthed. I thought about Dr. Nemo and what Kate and I had said about Dr. Nemo's name possibly being an anagram. I remembered we had come up with 'Omen Road', 'Ned Mor', and 'M Drone'. Were there other combinations Kate and I hadn't thought of? It seemed to me there must be, but I was unable to think of any at that moment.

When the Corolla and I passed through the tunnel that is at a spot just before Kanan reaches its highest elevation, the lights within the tunnel suddenly flickered on and off. A chill ran down my spine. Was the flickering a warning? Perhaps. But wasn't it just as likely a greeting as a warning? Or, far more likely than either of those, just a glitch in the lights' circuits? In any event, I gave the flickering not another moment's thought, and, a little after 2:00 a.m., the Corolla and I reached Kanan's western end where we turned right onto the Pacific Coast Highway.

I was actually feeling pretty fond of the ancient Toyota by then. It had, after all, protected Bobby and Timmy while I dealt with the biker-drug dealer-football players, and performed at least some small role in delivering the boys from the grips of Foster Mom. Also, once we had left the freeway, the Toyota had persevered mightily during our uphill climb through the Santa Monica Mountains and then willingly sacrificed its precious last bits of brake linings on the downhill run on the mountains' other side.

Yes, I was very fond of the little bugger.

But sad too.

Sad, because my brave comrade had thrown a rod when I accelerated northwards on the Pacific Coast Highway. Black smoke was billowing out from under his hood and his engine was making loud clacking noises that sounded like the treads of an M1 tank clattering along an asphalt road. I knew then that the Corolla didn't have long to live. But Kate's home was just past Broad Beach, only about five miles away, and I thought we might perhaps reach our goal before the bitter end.

The Pacific Coast Highway itself was dark and I saw no other cars. The only way to tell the land was inhabited at all was the presence of a few scattered lights from homes in the hills to the east, homes that seemed far, far away from the road. I left the Corolla's windows open, having decided breathing the small amounts of black smoke eddying in through them was probably less dangerous than sucking carbon monoxide in an enclosed compartment.

The Pacific Ocean was close by. I heard it and smelled it before I saw it. Waves were crashing in the distance, and the scent of seaweed and salt water filled my nostrils. A breeze came in from the ocean, and the air - at least the air that permeated between the smoke eddies - was cool and pleasant and provided a welcome contrast with the desert furnace from which I had come. When I finally did see the ocean, it lay beyond the wide, white sandy beaches of Zuma Beach. The moon hung halfway up the cloudless sky and laid down a shimmering path of moonlight across the surface of the sea.

There was also another light in the sky besides the moonlight.

A few miles ahead, beyond a small hill the Corolla and I still had to climb, the night was lit up like the Fourth of July. Giant beacons of white light emanated from the earth's surface, the beacons' lights so intense they made my eyes momentarily sting. I was unable to determine the beacons' exact point of origin, but their harsh rays ascended well into the night sky, creating cone-shaped luminescences that dissipated only when they were perhaps a quarter mile high.

A helicopter, its searchlight ablaze, circled above the earth. The copter crossed back and forth between the brilliant cones of light and the darkness of the night. Whenever the helicopter traversed the cones, the cones' fiery light made the helicopter's searchlight beam nearly invisible. The helicopter itself almost completely disappeared whenever it flew into the obsidian-like blackness of the night zone, the helicopter's location marked only by the downward arc of its searchlight and the blinking of its taillights.

Where else could the light show be taking place other than over Kate's home? And what else could the light mean other than that Carpenter's FBI security team was hard at work?

In front of me, Trancas Canyon Road intersected the highway. The stoplight there turned red just as I approached. I didn't stop, however, afraid if I did, the Corolla would never get going again. Barreling through the intersection, the two of us then chugged up the small hill. I hoped, with only a few more miles to go to get to Kate's house, we might just make it.

Those few more miles along the Pacific Coast Highway were agonizing as I dealt with the impending death of my little car friend.

In the end we did make it to Kate's house, though.

Barely.

But we did.

The only thing I could be sure of upon our initial arrival at her house, however, was that we'd made it to the address Kate had given me. I had to take it on faith the house was Kate's house, as when I arrived, all I could see of her property was a ten foot high, sand-colored, concrete wall that stretched for what looked to be close to a quarter mile along the left, or western side, of the highway. An opening in the wall that clearly served as the entrance to the house's grounds was spanned by a massive gate. The gate was as tall as the wall and made of thick sheets of weathered steel plate set on giant hinges. The gate also had an entry keypad mounted on a metal post. One would have had to have been very brave or very stupid to try to get at the keypad, however, as it was then blocked by two FBI SWAT agents swathed in body armor and holding Heckler and Koch submachine guns.

A half dozen news vans with satellite dishes mounted on their roofs were parked on the eastern side of the Pacific Coast Highway. The vans were positioned almost directly opposite the gate and were accompanied by an equivalent number of luxury RVs like the kind one would find on movie sets. There were, however, no newscasters in view. Perhaps they were getting their beauty sleep, something of which I was fairly certain they could never get enough.

I turned left across the southbound highway lanes and headed toward the gate in the estate's concrete wall. The helicopter, apparently having laid in wait for just such a move, buzzed the Corolla and me, seemingly missing the Corolla's rooftop by inches. The roar of the helicopter's engines was momentarily deafening, and the backwash of its rotors sent more of my poor little friend's ominously darkening and ever expanding smoke clouds into my face. The Corolla, despite being close to death, ignored the chopper's rude greeting and kept clacking away. Together we safely negotiated our highway crossing and came to a halt in front of the gate.

The two FBI SWAT agents who had been standing in front of the keypad approached us. They both looked to be in their late twenties. Their faces were intelligent and their eyes sharp, despite the fact it was the middle of the night. They were over six feet tall and beefy, their bodies straining the seams of their uniforms. It was a strong beefy, and both men were far bigger than most mortals, but the thought crossed my mind that either of them could easily be tossed aside by Manu or Mosi. I found myself momentarily missing the Samoan twins and wondered if they were somewhere inside the concrete walls.

One of the FBI agents stopped a few feet from the car. The other agent continued up to my window. He fanned the engine's smoke away with his left hand while his right hand pointed his submachine gun at the ground.

"With all due respect, sir," the agent at my window said, "these wheels look better suited for a buck private than a United States Army general."

"Be careful what you say, agent," I said. "This car's a very good friend of mine."

The Corolla made a loud noise that sounded like a huge chunk of brittle metal being snapped in two. Its engine rattled one last time and abruptly died. The smoke billowed for a few more seconds, then stopped.

I almost cried.

"Looks like your friend just gave its life for its country," the FBI agent at my window said.

"Indeed," I said. "And it is a far, far better thing than I have ever done, and he will go to a far, far better rest than I will ever know."

"If you say so, sir," the agent at my window said.

"I'm going to make sure he gets a nice medal too," I said.

The other agent stepped forward.

"Evening, General," the second agent said. "That was from 'A Tale of Two Cities', wasn't it?"

"Mostly," I said. "I'm glad to see the FBI is still employing educated men."

The second agent smiled, then turned to the agent at my window.

"Pay up, buddy," the second agent said.

The agent at my window said, "I ain't paying you nothing. Corolla didn't even make it through the gate."

What? They'd bet on whether the Corolla and I would make it? That seemed a bit coarse, didn't it? I gently patted my deceased comrade's dash. "We showed them, didn't we," I said quietly to him alone.

The second agent said, "Nobody said anything about the gate. Bet was the general and the car would make it here."

"Exactly," the agent at my window said. "Here. But 'here' meant the house."

"'Here' did not mean the house," the second agent said. "'Here' meant here, which is right where we are."

"We're on the street," the agent at my window said. "House is inside the wall."

"I know where the goddamned house is," the second agent said.

I got out of the car and stood with the agents on the estate's driveway.

"Boys," I said, "I really appreciate you providing such good security for Dr. Lennon, but I've been on the road for quite a while now and could use a nice warm shower. How about you open the gate and continue this discussion without me?"

They looked at each other and nodded, as if to say, 'he has a point'.

The agent who had been at my window said, "Sure, General," and opened the gate.

With the gate open, I could see that the compound behind the walls was at least fifteen acres in size. A crushed granite driveway led from the gate into the compound. The driveway split into two separate paths about fifty yards from the gate. Each path led to its own large house on the compound, one to the compound's north and one to the south.

The houses were separated by about one hundred yards of open area. I assumed one of the houses was Kate's house, but I didn't know which one.

"You'll be wanting Dr. Lennon's house, sir?" the agent who had been at my window said.

The constant din created by the continually circling helicopter had garbled his voice a bit. I wasn't sure I'd heard him correctly. I turned to face him.

"Sorry, agent," I said. "What was that?"

The agent who had been at my window winked at me and said, "Dr. Lennon's house. It's the one on the right."

The second agent then gave me a knowing smile.

I suspected the FBI snipers on the roof of the building that housed the morgue in Lancaster had probably told their cohorts about Kate's and my behavior in the morgue parking lot, so I thought I had a pretty good idea what was behind the wink and the smile. But I certainly wasn't going to engage the agents in a conversation that might allow me to confirm my suspicions. Especially since the agents were making me feel like I was an adolescent back in high school. I'd faced similar situations in high school, and the lesson I'd learned during those somewhat painful teenage years was it was vital not to let the taunting party, or parties, get a rise out of you.

"Thank you, agents," I said, my face a mask that revealed nothing. Or so I hoped.

Both agents appeared to study me. I thought they looked a bit disappointed. Disappointed or not, the first agent pressed on.

"No problem, sir," the agent who had been at my window said. "Dr. Lennon said she was going to take a nap, but asked us to wake her up just before you got here. We called her when we saw you coming down the highway, so don't be surprised if she's waiting for you when you get to the house."

The agent who had been at my window elbowed the second agent in the ribs and they both stifled a grin.

"How nice of her," I said. "Thank you again."

I turned on my heel and strode off towards the house on the right.

"Oh, and sir," the agent who had been at my window called after me, "Agent Carpenter is waiting for you as well. He's in the mobile unit."

"Don't forget to close the gate, boys," I said without turning around or breaking stride. "And be sure the tow truck operator treats my friend with the dignity he deserves."

An FBI mobile command center was parked well off the granite driveway and about halfway between Kate's house and me. The command center was painted blue and grey and looked like a giant RV that had fallen from the sky and landed atop a hook and ladder fire truck. I headed for it and took a closer look at the compound as I did.

The entire compound, other than its seaward side, was surrounded by the high wall through whose gate I had just passed. I assumed there was a cliff at the seaward edge since the land seemed to end abruptly there, the line of its ending cutting like a knife blade across the moonlit sea. The huge cones of light I had seen from the highway emanated from giant portable diesel light towers with halide lamps that were scattered throughout the landscape. The hard-packed crushed granite driveway was lined by palm trees and traversed through acres of well-manicured green grass, red and yellow hibiscus, and spiked cordylines. Two man FBI teams armed with Heckler and Koch submachine guns - some accompanied by one or two leashed German shepherd guard dogs - roamed the property.

At the end of the driveway's left fork was a multileveled home of Mediterranean design with large blocky pink plaster walls and lots of balconies and arches. The home on the right appeared to be of a more modern design and was built of glass, steel, and wood.

A flash of light caught my eye. I turned to find that the flash had been created by the opening of the FBI mobile command center's door. Agent Ray Carpenter, helmeted and body armored, exited the door, walked down the steel stairway that had been installed beneath it, and approached me.

"General," Carpenter said, "glad you made it."

"What were the odds?" I said.

"Odds?" Carpenter said.

"Yes, Carpenter, the odds the Corolla and I would make it here," I said.

"Three to five, sir," Carpenter said.

"For or against?" I said.

"Against, sir," Carpenter said.

"So little respect," I said. "What side did you take? Wait, don't answer that."

"Thank you, sir," Carpenter said.

"And next time, let me in on the action," I said. "I can always use some extra dough."

"Will do, sir," Carpenter said. "I was just about to call you, sir."

"By the sound of your voice," I said, "I take it you don't have glad tidings."

"I'm afraid not, sir," Carpenter said.

"Lennon's relatives?" I said.

"Yes, sir," Carpenter said. "We sent a team to Lennon's parents' house. We found both Lennon's mother and father dead. Their hands were tied behind their backs and it looked like they had been killed while they were on their knees."

I heard the sound of a loud motorcycle coming from somewhere out on the Pacific Coast Highway. The FBI sentry dogs must have heard it too, as they began barking. The sound quickly raised in pitch, then just as quickly dropped in pitch. The motorcycle must have raced past the compound going at high speed.

"Killed how?" I said.

"Their heads were cut off, just like Sarah Lennon," Carpenter said.

"Clearly the work of Islamic terrorists," I said.

"Burnette thinks so," Carpenter said.

"Burnette can think what he wants," I said. "When were they killed?"

"Best guess is about 7:00 a.m. yesterday morning," Carpenter said. "Even if we thought to check on them earlier, it wouldn't have helped."

I said nothing.

"I do have some good news, however," Carpenter said.

"Give it to me," I said.

"Lennon has a sister," Carpenter said. "Her name is Margaret Lennon. As far as we know, she's still alive."

"'As far as we know' now qualifies as good news?" I said. "How the mighty have fallen."

"Sorry, sir," Carpenter said, "There's been so much bad news lately I guess I'm just looking for any silver lining I can find."

"That's understandable," I said.

"How about I just give you the facts," Carpenter said.

"Facts are good," I said. "Then we can distort them as we please."

"Sir?" Carpenter said.

"Twain," I said.

I knew that wasn't the first time I'd quoted Twain in the last twenty-four hours, but, as far as I was concerned, the more Twain the merrier. Jeff, if he'd been there, would have agreed.

"Of course, sir," Carpenter said. "The facts then. Lennon's sister is a poetry professor at Pomona College. We haven't been able to find her, but we obtained a list of her colleagues in the poetry department. One of them saw her having dinner in a local cafe at about 7:00 p.m. tonight."

"What makes you think the bad guys haven't killed her in the last seven hours?" I said.

"We believe her house in Claremont had been broken into this morning," Carpenter said. "The evidence was subtle - just a few scratches around the rear door lock. But there were no signs of violence inside. We think the most likely scenario is the killers expected her to be at home and she was not. Since she was alive at 7:00 p.m., we're hopeful the killers, like us, haven't been able to locate her as of yet."

"Hope, as deceitful as it is, serves at least to lead us to the end of our lives by an agreeable route," I said.

"La Rochefoucauld?" Carpenter said.

"None other," I said.

"You always this quote happy, sir?" Carpenter said.

The FBI helicopter buzzed low and fast over our heads. Two FBI agents and their sentry dog were momentarily illuminated in the chopper's spotlight.

"The lateness of hour may be taking its toll," I said. "I can see your point, however. In theory, you should have more resources for finding her than the killers do."

"In theory, yes," Carpenter said.

"I take it the professor doesn't have a cell phone?" I said.

"She does not," Carpenter said. "According to her colleagues she prefers a simpler life."

"Good for her," I said. "I assume you have a watch on her house?"

"Yes, sir," Carpenter said.

"I suppose we'll just keep our fingers crossed and hope we find Professor Margaret Lennon alive then," I said. "Fingers crossed professional enough for you, Carpenter?"

"Yes, sir," Carpenter said. He seemed to be about to say something else, but hesitated.

"What's on your mind?" I said.

"I know we talked about this before," Carpenter said. "But have you given any more thought to the idea that this thing is feeling kind of personal?"

"It does appear that there's at least a personal component, doesn't it?" I said.

"But it's not completely personal though, is it?" Carpenter said. "I mean it's not just Lennon's relatives who are dead. There's also the matter of NASAD's twelve dead drone sub engineers. And as far as we know, none of them were related to Lennon."

Carpenter was right about the dead engineers. Their deaths didn't appear to have a personal connection to Paul Lennon. Dr. Nemo also had to be considered, as Dr. Nemo's involvement in the hellish situation at NASAD didn't seem to be personally connected to Lennon either, at least not at that moment.

There was also Jeff's and my notion that things were usually one thing, not two. If that notion was correct, the murders of Lennon's relatives, the NASAD engineers, and Feynman and Lennon would turn out to be the work not of two separate evil entities, but one - one solitary enemy pursuing two goals on seemingly parallel tracks. My hope, of course, was that those tracks would intersect at some point, and that intersection would reveal our enemy's identity.

However, at that moment, I didn't see how there was anything to be gained in talking to Carpenter about Dr. Nemo, or Jeff's and my 'one thing, not two' notion, so I didn't say a word to him about either subject.

"As far as we know, yes, none of them seem related to Lennon," I said.

"It's a very strange situation, isn't it?" Carpenter said.

"It is," I said.

Carpenter again seemed to have something on his mind he was reluctant to share.

"Carpenter," I said, "haven't you learned by now you're always welcome to share any of your thoughts with me?"

"I believe I have, sir," Carpenter said. "But this is still a bit uncomfortable for me to mention."

"I think I know what it is," I said.

"You do, sir?" Carpenter said.

The low-throated rumble of large, rapidly revving, diesel engines came from below the seaward side of the cliff. I assumed the engines powered the Coast Guard cutter Carpenter had earlier told me was patrolling the area of the ocean near Kate's compound. I wondered if the cutter was off in pursuit of a specific threat, or simply moving to a better spot from which to observe the sea below the compound.

"Does it have anything to do with the natural curiosity and highly trained observational skills of your team?" I said.

"Hmm," Carpenter said, thinking it over. "I suppose it does."

"And does it also have to do with the fact that snipers on the rooftop of a building housing a morgue in Lancaster, and/or that men behind the tinted glass of SUV's in the parking lot of that same morgue building, might have witnessed things that had gone on between a man and a woman in said parking lot?" I said.

"You're referring to the situation yesterday afternoon outside the morgue in Lancaster, sir?" Carpenter said.

"Yes," I said. "And the sequelae. Such sequelae being that the aforesaid witnesses, having witnessed those things between the man and the woman - namely, Dr. Lennon and myself - perhaps leapt to certain conclusions and, having made those conclusions, then, for lack of a better word, 'spread' those conclusions around?"

"You're good, sir," Carpenter said.

"A lady's reputation is at stake, Carpenter," I said. "I trust you will deal with the situation appropriately."

"Aye aye, sir," Carpenter said.

Another flash of light caught my eye. This time it came from the direction of Kate's house. The front door had just opened. Someone stepped out of the door and walked onto the house's front landing. I was still so far away from the house that I couldn't be sure who it was.

"Yonder, the lady awaits," Carpenter said.

"Carpenter...," I said.

"Sorry, sir," Carpenter said.

"Please inform me immediately if you find Paul Lennon's sister," I said.

I turned and walked toward the house. The figure on the landing didn't move toward me, but stood in a way that seemed to say it would wait patiently for me. As I got closer to the house, I could see that the house was constructed almost completely of glass. Thick, dark tropical hardwoods, copper, granite, and steel had been used only as necessary to keep the glass in place. The house looked to be twenty thousand square feet and two stories tall, with each story at least fifteen feet high. Golden light emanated from the windows and I could see brightly colored works of modern art and marble sculptures inside. If not for the presence of black clad FBI snipers in helmets and bulletproof vests on its roof, the house could easily have qualified as a home for the gods of Mt. Olympus.

I gave the snipers a wave.

They waved back.

I took that as a good sign.

I got close enough to the house to be able to confirm that the person on the landing was Kate. She stood in front of a pair of twelve foot high, three foot wide, wood and steel doors. The landing itself was made of gleaming black marble that spanned over a dozen feet from back to front and twenty feet from side to side.

"You didn't have to go through all this trouble for me," I called out to Kate. "I would have been happy to stay at the Motel 6 I saw on my way in."

"Could still be arranged," Kate said.

"Well, I probably should at least give this place a try," I said. "Be rude to do otherwise, wouldn't it?"

"I'm happy you're here Jack," Kate said.

I hadn't realized I needed any soothing, but that's just what Kate's voice did to me. Soothed me. Her voice was warm and soft and gentle. If anything, Kate looked more beautiful than before. She wore a tight, sequin covered, designer t-shirt that did nothing to hide her large breasts. Her jeans outlined her perfect backside and clung to her beautiful long legs. She wore sandals that showed off her strong yet delicate feet. Her flaxen hair was tied back with a ribbon that revealed the exquisite line where her jaw met her neck. Her cornflower blue eyes and wide mouth both seemed to smile just for me.

And, of course, she looked more like Grace than ever before.

"Come inside," Kate said. "I'll show you around."

CHAPTER 56

Kate led me into the house's atrium through the huge steel swinging doors. I enjoyed Kate's body being close to mine. I could feel her warmth. She smelled differently than she had the day before. Her perfume was gone, replaced by the scent of lavender soap. The atrium itself was two stories high and its floor was polished black and silver granite. To my right, a ten foot wide curved staircase that was lined by dark mahogany rails, and whose stairs were also made of silver and black granite, swept up to the second floor.

Beyond the atrium was the home's first floor. The entire floor was a giant, unobstructed space of perhaps ten thousand square feet surrounded by windows. There were vistas out to the sea in three directions. It must have taken some miracle of engineering to suspend the room's ceiling with no interior support beams or pillars.

The placement of furniture, sculptures, chandeliers, and intricately woven rugs marked out areas that, if they truly were separate rooms, would have been named den, dining, entertainment, library, and living. The only thing I couldn't see was a kitchen. I assumed it was behind the wall next to the staircase.

Paintings hung on the few upright steel columns that lay between the windows. The paintings were expertly lit to show them off, and were by Kandinsky, Rothko, and Lucien Freud. The sculptures were by Moore and Giacometti. I recognized the artists since Grace loved modern art and used to drag me into museums. Among those museums were the Musée d'Orsay in Paris and the Guggenheim Museum in Bilbao, both places I would never have stepped into if not for her.

"Nice house," I said.

"It's a little embarrassing," Kate said. "My father built both of the houses on the estate for Freddy and me. Paul and I always planned to move out. I never had the strength to do it after my father and Paul died."

The lights of a boat suddenly appeared on the portion of the sea that was visible through the house's western windows. The lights moved erratically as the boat tossed about on the waves. I assumed the lights belonged to the Coast Guard cutter patrolling the shore below the compound. I guessed the reason I hadn't seen the lights before was that the cutter had been closer to the shore and the lights had been blocked out by the high seaside cliffs.

Kate noticed where I was looking.

"Coast Guard," Kate said.

"That's what I thought," I said. "Carpenter's got you well protected, except..."

"Except?" Kate said.

"Well," I said. "He's got the helicopter. He's got the dog patrols. And he's got the cutter. But what if someone tunnels under the house?"

"You aren't serious are you?" Kate said.

"No," I said.

"Don't scare me like that," Kate said.

"Okay, I'll stop," I said. "What keeps the ceiling up?"

"You'd know more about that than me," Kate said.

"I would?" I said.

"It's made from the same material they build Stealth Bombers with," Kate said.

"Your dad's idea?" I said.

Kate nodded.

I looked over at the other house on the estate.

"That's the pink palace," Kate said.

"Aptly named," I said. "As I remember it, your father was not big on pink, however."

"Freddy designed it," Kate said. "It's his dream house. Traditional California Spanish Mission."

"Freddy's got something against Stealth Bombers?" I said.

"Only in regard to his house," Kate said.

"What about swallows?" I said. "Has he got swallows?"

"No swallows," Kate said.

She took my hand. Her hand felt warm and soft and strong. I felt a tingle all the way up my arm.

"I'll take you to your room," Kate said.

We climbed the staircase. I heard loud snoring above me. When we reached the large landing that was at the top of the stairs, I saw what the snoring was about. Manu and Mosi, in identical sets of giant blue cotton pajamas, were asleep on love seats that were positioned on opposite sides of a tall oak door that lay on the left side of the landing. The landing was made of dark oak planks. The love seats were upholstered in red velvet and looked like they could have come from Napoleon's apartments in the Louvre. Which I only knew since Grace had taken me to the Louvre as well.

"Manu and Mosi wanted to stay up for you," Kate said.

"They had a long day," I said.

Kate smiled. She put a finger to her lips, gently squeezed my hand, and led me over to the door between the Samoan twins. Kate very carefully and quietly opened the door and we stood in the doorway. There was the sound of breathing in the room, but unlike the snoring of the twins, this breathing was gentle and soft. The only light came from a night light. It was a big room. It was also a little boy's room. There were Marvel Comics action figures littered on the floor, posters of baseball and football players on the walls, and bookshelves filled with hundreds of sports books. Baseballs, baseball bats, basketballs, footballs, and a few skateboards were jammed into wire mesh baskets.

A bed was against the center of the wall on the far side of the room. A boy, who looked to be about six years old, was sleeping under a blue and white Dodgers blanket on the bed. On the night table next to the bed was a photograph of Paul Lennon standing waist deep in a swimming pool with a little boy on his shoulders. I assumed the sleeping boy and the little boy on Paul's shoulders were one and the same, just separated by the years that had passed since the photo had been taken. During those intervening years the little boy's features had changed, and while he was cute when the picture had been taken, the boy sleeping before me could more accurately be described as handsome. He looked just like Paul.

At the foot of the boy's bed were two sleeping bags. A little girl who seemed slightly younger than the boy was asleep in one of the sleeping bags and a young woman was in the other. The woman had a very pretty and kind face and long brown hair that spread out over the sleeping bag. I assumed the woman was the nanny, Elizabeth Wells.

The little girl was beautiful and looked just like Kate. Which meant she also looked like Grace. I had a hard time coping with the idea of a young, still living Grace.

And then, my mind being what it was that day, the faces of Kate's children slowly morphed into the mutilated visages of Sam and Lizzy in the morgue. I shut my eyes to try to clear the vision. Which worked. But with my eyes shut, my mind wandered, and I began to think about how close Kate's little boy and girl and their nanny had come to meeting a fate similar to Sam and Lizzy's. Which discomforted me nearly as much as my original vision of the dead Sam and Lizzy. And then, focusing on the disaster that almost befell Kate's son and daughter somehow led me back to Grace, and I thought, 'What if Grace had been killed as a little girl? What would have become of me?'

My throat tightened.

I struggled to breathe for a moment. I felt disoriented and dizzy. My eyes opened almost on their own, seeking to get my body its bearings once again. With my eyes opened, I realized Kate was looking at me. Unsurprisingly, she seemed more than a little concerned.

"You okay Jack?" Kate said softly.

Somehow I managed to eke out a hoarse whisper.

"Me?" I said. "Of course. Why do you ask?"

"You looked like you were about to faint," Kate said.

"No, no," I said. "My throat was just a little constricted. Must be some kind of allergy to one of the plants around here."

"You sure it wasn't a bee?" Kate asked.

I stared at her for a moment.

"That's a joke, right?" I said.

"It would be if I wasn't so worried about you," Kate said.

"You don't have to worry about me," I said. "I've had a rough day, but I've had much, much rougher ones and I'll be fine. I will admit, however, that staring down the barrel of a sniper rifle pointed at you by your best friend, who just happens to be a bit crazy..."

"Jeff?" Kate said.

"Yeah," I said. "It happened right before you showed up at the range."

"I didn't know that," Kate said.

"He was trying to get me to take a shot I didn't want to take," I said.

"The pancaked bullets?" Kate said.

"The pancaked bullets," I said. "Then the Kazakhs, Burnette's elephant tranquilizer, and the biker gang..."

"Biker gang?" Kate said.

"It's a long story," I said. "I'll tell you later." I gestured with my head at Kate's sleeping children. "Your children are beautiful."

"Thank you," Kate said. "My daughter has her own room, but the three of them had such a scary day they wanted to stay together tonight."

Kate gently tugged me from the doorway and quietly closed the door. My throat relaxed and my breathing came easier. Manu and Mosi were still snoring away on the love seats.

"I thought Manu and Mosi worked for Freddy," I said.

"Freddy insisted they stay with me until this whole thing is over," Kate said.

"You okay with that?" I said.

"I actually feel safer with them around," Kate said.

"Maybach come with the deal?" I said.

"Uh huh," Kate said. "You're welcome to use it. I heard you might need a ride."

I sighed.

"Not you too," I said.

"Sorry," Kate said.

"You didn't bet did you?" I said.

"Do you really want to know?" Kate said.

"Uh...no," I said.

Past the children's door were two thirty foot long, twelve foot wide corridors, one stretching to the west, and the other north. The carpet along the corridors was lush, deeply piled, and patterned in subdued colors and repeating rectangles that were reminiscent of the modern paintings downstairs. Big picture windows were at the end of both corridors. Through the windows I could see the FBI dog teams moving around the estate under the harsh glare of the halide lamps.

Kate took us down the north running corridor, which meant we were paralleling the ocean. There were six doors lining the corridor, three on each side. When we got to the last door on the left, we stopped.

"As you can probably tell, I'm doing my best to soldier on," Kate said. "Coming back home to find Carolyn and Dylan safe and sound and getting some rest helped, but inside I'm still pretty shattered. Thank you again for saving my life, Jack."

"No thanks necessary," I said. "It was all pretty much instinct."

"You know how to make a girl feel special," Kate said.

"I suppose I could have said that better," I said.

"Yes," Kate said. "You could have."

Kate opened the door and led me in. The room was as luxuriously furnished as the rest of the house. Directly in front of me, a fifteen foot wide window looked out on the ocean. The Coast Guard boat was still bobbing out at sea. The helicopter streaked along the cliff line and then banked sharply upwards and disappeared from view. There must have been excellent soundproofing in the room, as I heard nothing but the sound of Kate's and my breathing and the low level hum of air conditioning. The air conditioning was obviously working well - the room was the coldest spot I'd been in since I'd left the snow on my ranch the previous morning.

A king-sized bed with a gold and maroon silk bedspread and ten matching decorative pillows was against the wall to the right of the window. Night tables were on both sides of the head of the bed. An antique writing desk with a rattan-backed chair and two large easy chairs upholstered in blue velvet were arranged in the center of the room. The wall to the left of the window had a large, open walk-in closet. Next to the closet was a big flat screen television, and next to the television was a door that led to the bathroom. The bathroom's floors, walls, and counter were white marble.

My rucksack, which I'd last seen in the trunk of the Maybach, was on the bed.

"I told them not to put away your things," Kate said. "I thought you might not want anyone going through your stuff."

"Thanks," I said. "How'd you know?"

"Do I really have to say?" Kate said.

"Not if you don't want to," I said.

Kate hesitated, then said, "I don't want you reading too much into this. But I think we're alike in a lot of ways. And I wouldn't want anyone going through my stuff, so..."

"I get it," I said. "What will happen if I read too much into that, though?"

Kate smiled.

"Not sure," Kate said. "But it could be very dangerous."

Kate went to the room's entry door and closed and locked it. She turned around to face me and leaned her back against the door. Her body seemed to have tensed up, and she was standing in such a way that she appeared to be guarding the door.

"Have a seat," Kate said, gesturing to the bed.

"Am I in trouble?" I said.

"You?" Kate said. "No."

"Phew," I said. "For a moment there I thought I was going to be imprisoned again for the second time since I left home."

"Funny," Kate said.

"Since it's not me that's in trouble," I said, "then who is?"

"Sit," Kate said.

Generally, when I'm alone with a beautiful woman and she twice tells me to sit down on the bed, I don't argue with her. That time was no exception.

Kate reached her hand behind her and took a cell phone out of her back pocket. The phone looked like one of those disposable phones that can be bought without a contract at a convenience store. They usually cost about twenty-five dollars. The police call them 'burners'.

"I found this under my pillow before I took a nap this evening," Kate said.

"Let me guess," I said. "It's not yours, and you didn't expect to find it there?"

Kate nodded.

"Does it belong to the person who's in trouble?" I said.

"I don't who know it belongs to," Kate said. "But..."

"But..," I said.

"The phone has a message on it," Kate said.

"Dr. Nemo?" I said.

Kate nodded again.

"And since you don't trust anyone but me to know about the message," I said, "that's why we're alone together in a locked room?"

Kate smiled.

"You were thinking something else?" Kate said.

"Hoping might be a better word," I said.

"Jack, we talked about that," Kate said.

"Talk is cheap," I said. "Tell me about the phone."

"The phone was off when I found it," Kate said. "Before I turned it on, I made sure no one else was around and closed and locked my bedroom door."

"Like now?" I said.

"Like now," Kate said. "When I turned on the phone a recorded voice message instantly downloaded into the text message section."

"Is the text still there?" I said.

"Yes," Kate said.

Kate handed me the phone. I tapped on the text message icon and played the message. The voice was the same deep, electronically altered, Darth Vader-like voice I'd heard yesterday morning. Dr. Nemo.

"I'm so sorry, Dr. Lennon," Nemo's voice said. "I think I really messed up. I hope you are safe. Time is running out. I'm afraid they might be on to me. I have to be sure I can trust the person you found. Is he the same one that was on television in the Mojave Desert? All three of us need to talk. I believe I have a plan that will allow us to meet, but will not know for sure until tomorrow. Keep this phone. I will message you again soon."

I said, "Television in the desert?"

"You didn't see yourself?" Kate said.

"No," I said. "Do I want to?"

"The news stations are playing a clip of you when you sat down in the middle of the stoning site in Lancaster," Kate said. "The commentators are all speculating as to who you were and what you were doing."

I didn't say anything.

"By the way," Kate said. "What were you doing?"

"Resting," I said.

"Resting, like you needed rest because of Jeff and the sniper gun, the Kazakhs, Burnette, and the biker gang?" Kate said.

"You catch on quick," I said.

Kate appeared to study me for a moment.

"Actually, it didn't look like you were resting to me," Kate said.

"What did it look like?" I said.

"I don't know," Kate said. "Maybe hallucinating?"

Outside, the helicopter flew low across the treetops. The Coast Guard ship still circled out at sea. The ship varied its path, never taking the same one twice.

"It's not something I really want to talk about," I said.

"You don't have to then," Kate said.

Despite her words, Kate seemed hurt I hadn't been more forthcoming. I felt bad about hurting her. I felt even worse, since I could see Grace in Kate's beautiful face and I felt I had hurt Grace too. Which is why, even though I really, really didn't want to talk about what had happened to me at the stoning site, my resistance to talking about it melted away, and I did.

"I was so angry at what I saw out at the stoning site," I said, "that I think my blood actually boiled. Which made me dizzy. I felt like I was going to faint. I sat down so I wouldn't collapse down. That's what a tough guy I am."

Kate gave me a long appraising look. She walked over to the bed, sat down next to me, leaned in very close, and spoke into my ear. Her breath was soft and warm, but in a different way than her hand had been. A better way.

"If I had been there," Kate said, "I would have felt exactly the same way you did. I'm not sure I would have had the courage, however, to risk embarrassing myself and sit down in front of all those people like you did, before I fainted and crashed to the ground."

I turned to face her. We looked into each other's eyes for a moment. Something passed between us that made me feel as if I had known Kate forever. And it had nothing to do with the fact that Kate looked like Grace. It was different. I liked it very much.

Kate pulled away.

"You can't do that," Kate said.

"What?" I said.

"Look at me like that," Kate said.

"You were looking too, though," I said.

"I know," Kate said. "But..."

"Yes, I know," I said. "The mission. Nothing can take precedence over the mission."

"Correct," Kate said.

"Anyway," I said, "embarrassing is exactly the right word for my performance in the desert, and thank you for being so kind about it. Now, do you have any idea how Nemo's phone got under your pillow?"

"No," Kate said. "But I think it had to be put there before the FBI showed up this afternoon. I don't see how anyone could get through their security cordon."

The FBI helicopter buzzed very close to the bedroom windows. The windows' panes vibrated, and the chopper's spotlight momentarily illuminated the wall behind me with its harsh, white light.

"No, I don't think anyone could either," I said. "Your regular staff didn't see anybody?"

"I just have a housekeeper," Kate said. "I didn't say anything to her about the phone directly, but just asked her if there were any deliveries, or if anyone had come by."

"And there weren't any, and no one had?" I said.

"No," Kate said.

"I didn't see any security cameras outside," I said.

"We don't have any," Kate said. "I hate them."

"So either Nemo, or someone Nemo sent, somehow got up to your room without being seen," I said. "But we don't know how."

"It's important we find out, isn't it?" Kate said.

"Yes," I said. "Because it raises the possibility Dr. Nemo is someone you know, or perhaps has access to someone you know. Or he could even be just someone who once visited or worked here and knows the layout of the compound and your house reasonably well."

"Otherwise, how would he know which room was mine," Kate said.

"That's what I was thinking," I said.

"I've lived in this house, in the same room, for years," Kate said.

"Which means the list of people who could know which room is yours is most likely a very long one," I said.

"Yes," Kate said.

Kate appeared to think this over, and as she did, a look of growing frustration played upon her face.

"Let's not worry about the list for now," I said.

"You're sure?" Kate said.

"We can revisit it in the morning when we've had a chance to sleep on it," I said. "What's important now is the message on the phone. Did you try to call the number of the cell phone that Nemo sent the text from?"

"I did," Kate said. "But it didn't work. I didn't expect it to, though. Look at the number."

I pushed the info icon next to the message on the phone.

"I see your point," I said.

The number was '404046809104414919070'. Way too long for a phone number.

"What kind of number is it?" Kate said.

"I don't know," I said. "It's too long for any kind of normal phone number. It's probably just some number string Nemo used to hide the real number of the phone he used to text you."

"Maybe the number is the key to Nemo's code," Kate said.

"Could be," I said. "But it's pretty doubtful."

"Why doubtful?" Kate said.

"Well, while it's too long for a phone number, it's also much too short for a code key," I said. "It would be extremely easy to crack. I'm pretty sure Dr. Nemo would use something more sophisticated. Probably something that is even self-regenerating."

"Self-regenerating?" Kate said.

"The key automatically constantly changes itself," I said.

"How could anyone crack something like that?" Kate said.

"The technical details are beyond my pay grade," I said. "But I know people at MOM who can, and they're working on it right now."

I tapped some numbers into the burner phone and pushed send.

"What are you doing?" Kate said.

"I forwarded the voice message Nemo left on this phone to my iPhone," I said. "I'll then send Nemo's message, along with the burner's long phone number, on to MOM. We'll see what MOM can do with both the message and the long number."

"Good idea," Kate said.

I gave Kate back the phone.

"Keep it safe," I said.

"I will," Kate said. "But Jack..."

"Yes," I said.

"What if Dr. Nemo doesn't get back to us?" Kate said.

"We'll have to find another way to figure out what national security issues Nemo's so concerned about, and then deal with them somehow," I said.

"How can we figure it out without him?" Kate said.

"For one, we might be able to determine who Nemo actually is," I said. "Then we could either track him down without the need for him to come to us, or we might be able to find something that clues us into what he knows, or at least what he was working on at NASAD."

"What makes you believe we can determine who he is?" Kate said.

"MOM is working on a profile of Nemo from the voice message you showed me yesterday," I said. "This new voice message should help too."

"They can profile Nemo just from the messages?" Kate said. "It seems to me like the messages don't contain enough information to do that. And Nemo's voice is disguised, too."

"I'm no expert in how they do it," I said. "But in the past, MOM's linguistic team has told me they look at things like the content the message is conveying, sentence construction, the range of vocabulary used, timing between the words, pronunciation of vowels versus consonants, and relative empathy levels. Knowing MOM's technicians, they've probably found a lot more things they can study since the last time I asked them about it."

"They can really tell how empathic someone is?" Kate said.

"I've seen them do it," I said. "Of course, usually the empathy level of the people I'm targeting is zero, or so infinitesimally small, it might as well be zero."

"That doesn't surprise me," Kate said.

"Anyway, as I said, I'm sure there's a lot more stuff the techs study than I've ever been told about, and I'm also sure I've forgotten most of the things they did tell me about," I said. "But once the experts have got it all parsed, they'll use their computers to run the components of Nemo's voice against their database of hundreds of millions of voices, and a profile will pop out."

"There's no way they'll know exactly who Nemo is though, right?" Kate said.

"Correct," I said. "That's very unlikely. It should really whittle down the list of possibilities, however. And I'm hoping, that once we get the profile, your people at NASAD can help us whittle it down even further."

"Human Resources should be able to help," Kate said.

"That would be a good place to start," I said.

"You'll like the woman in charge of HR," Kate said.

"Why is that?" I said.

"She's smart, gorgeous, and funny," Kate said.

"Not my type," I said.

Kate rolled her eyes.

"Now, please," I said, "I'm fading fast. I better take a shower and get to bed."

"I guess we both could use some sleep," Kate said. "We'll get going again when you wake up."

Kate patted my knee. I found it hard to believe she didn't know what that did to me, but her face looked so innocent and sweet, I decided to give her the benefit of the doubt.

Kate stood up and walked to the door. She stopped before she got there, however, and turned around.

"Did the FBI ever get ahold of Sarah?" Kate said.

"Carpenter didn't tell you?" I said.

"Tell me what?" Kate said.

"Maybe you better sit back down," I said.

She didn't move.

"Please, Kate," I said. "Sit back down."

"What?" Kate said. "Is something wrong with Sarah?"

I gestured to the spot on the bed on which she had just been sitting. "Please," I said.

Kate came back and sat back down next to me.

"Sarah's dead," I said.

Kate looked horrified.

"How?" Kate said.

"Murdered," I said. "Probably the same people who killed Sam and Lizzy."

"Oh God," Kate said.

Kate burst into tears. I put my arm around her shoulders. I held her as she cried. After a few moments, I said, "There's no easy way to put this. But there are other relatives of Paul who were also murdered yesterday."

Kate didn't seem to immediately comprehend what I had said. A few seconds passed, and then she turned to look at me, tears streaming down her face.

"Other relatives?" Kate said. "Besides Sam, Lizzy, and Sarah?"

I nodded.

"Paul's parents," I said. "They were murdered too."

"That can't be, Jack!" Kate said.

"I'm sorry, but it's true," I said.

"What am I going to tell my children?" Kate said.

"You don't have to tell them, do you?" I said. "I mean, why do they have to know?"

"Paul's parents are my children's grandparents, Jack," Kate said.

Had my mind really been so dense and slow that day that I hadn't realized that Paul's parents were also Kate's children's grandparents? The answer was obviously a very pathetic 'yes'.

"I'm sorry, Kate," I said. "I have no idea how I could be so stupid."

"You're not stupid," Kate said. "It's just been a nightmarish day."

"It has, but that's no excuse," I said.

"It's plenty of excuse, Jack," Kate said. "Plenty of excuse."

Kate suddenly began to sob uncontrollably. She leaned her head against my chest, and I let her cry herself out. When Kate was done crying, with her guiding the way, I helped her to her bedroom.

The bedroom was dark when we entered, and I thought it best to leave the lights off and get her into her bed as quickly as I could. Because it was dark, I couldn't see many of the details of the room, but it was large, and, from what I was able to see, appeared to be as lavishly decorated as the rest of the house. It had expensive, deeply hued carpet and drapes and rich woods. I could smell just the slightest hint of Kate's lilac perfume. I have no idea why, but being there with Kate made me feel as if something had taken hold of me and was comforting me. As if, just for that moment, all was well, and the realities of the outside world had fallen far, far away.

Kate and I made our way in the darkness to her bed. I pulled back the satin covers, she laid down, and I tucked her in. She fell almost instantly to sleep.

I went back to my own room. I forwarded Nemo's voice message that had been on the burner phone, and the long, strange phone number that the burner showed Nemo had called from, to Haley at MOM. I then took a quick shower. After I was done toweling off, I closed the bedroom's curtains. My iPhone said it was 3:00 a.m. I put the phone on the night table next to the bed. I lay down on the bed and was asleep almost before my head hit the pillow.

CHAPTER 57

I was sound asleep and dreaming when my iPhone rang sometime later that morning. I had a hard time getting out of the dream. My eyes wouldn't open and my body wouldn't move. The dream kept running in my mind even though I knew it was a dream. In the dream, the coyote that had talked to me when the Corolla was still alive and the Corolla and I were parked on Agua Dulce Road, had returned.

"Too bad you don't know how to spell," the coyote said in the dream.

"What don't I know how to spell?" I said.

The coyote laughed a high-pitched laugh like a hyena's laugh and shook his head.

"You can't count, either," the coyote said.

"I can count just fine," I said.

"Oh yeah, asshole?" the coyote said. "How many claws does it have then?"

"What's 'it'?" I said.

The coyote just laughed like a hyena again.

"What kind of coyote laughs like a hyena?" I said.

"It's *your* dream, dickwad," the coyote said and disappeared.

I finally escaped the dream, but still couldn't move for a moment. I realized the 'it' the coyote was talking about was the dragon mask the Asian man at the stoning site had been wearing, and that the coyote, like Jeff, knew the number of claws was important. I made a mental note to remember to ask Vandross for help in contacting Bobby and Timmy so that I could ask the brothers about the claws.

It was pitch black since I had closed the bedroom curtains earlier. The only thing I could hear was the ringing of my iPhone on the night table by my side and the hum of the air conditioner. When I was finally able to move, I took my iPhone off the night table. The phone showed the time to be 4:02 a.m. I'd been asleep for all of an hour. The number on the phone was Haley's and she was requesting me to FaceTime with her.

I pushed the FaceTime icon and Haley appeared on the screen. The lights from the bank of NORAD equipment still blinked behind her.

Haley's brown eyes sparkled with vibrant energy, her brown hair was as luminous as it was before, her lips were red and inviting, and her breasts still strained at the seams of her uniform. She looked fresh as a daisy.

"You better not have been asleep again," Haley said. "Not when I've been up all night working for you."

"I wasn't sleeping," I said. "I was dreaming."

"That's the Jack Wilder I know," Haley said. "When it comes to bullshit, go big or don't go at all."

"I can see you've never tried to wake up from a dream," I said. "It's a lot harder than just waking up."

"Do I really have to listen to this?" Haley said.

"I assume you called for a reason," I said.

"Green Day," Haley said.

"Green Day?" I said

"Um-hmm," Haley said.

"Is this some kind of test?" I said.

"I don't know," Haley said. "You tell me."

I thought it over. The only 'Green Day' I knew was a band.

"Billie Joe Armstrong, Mike Dirnt, and Tre Cool," I said.

"You're good," Haley said. "Why didn't you mention them?"

I had no idea what she was talking about.

"I wanted to see if you could figure it out on your own," I said.

"Bullshit," Haley said.

I could see by Haley's expression she thought she was going to win this round. Not if I could help it. Alright. Green Day is a band. What do bands do? They make music. Music is a form of sound. And sound...

"Hold on," I said.

I muted my FaceTime and tapped on my message icon. I replayed the first voice message that Nemo had sent to Kate, the one that Kate had played for me on my ranch. I listened very, very hard. I'd missed it before, but it was there. A song had been playing very softly in the background as Nemo spoke. I unmuted the iPhone.

"'Time Of Your Life,'" I said.

"You idiot," Haley said.

"What now?" I said.

"You muted your phone," Haley said, "but we're on FaceTime. I could still see what you were doing."

"Fine," I said. "I missed it the first time. Shoot me."

"You think it means something?" Haley said.

"I think everything this guy does means something," I said.

"So do I," Haley said. "What do you think it means?"

"I don't know," I said. "Maybe it's something in the lyrics. Maybe the title. Could even have something to do with when the song was originally recorded."

"It was recorded at Conway Studios in Los Angeles in 1997," Haley said. "The band stayed at the Sunset Marquis Hotel while they were recording. The sessions took a lot longer than they expected since they spent more time playing foosball and pool than their instruments."

"That's an interesting bit of knowledge to have at your fingertips," I said.

"I looked it up," Haley said.

"Of course you did," I said.

"I vote for the lyrics," Haley said.

"Good a guess as any," I said. "Let's both give it some more thought and reconvene later. What else you got for me?"

"What makes you think I have anything else?" Haley said.

"Alright, fine," I said. "I'm going back to sleep."

"Wait, wait," Haley said. "Don't do that. I do have something else. Two something elses in fact."

"I knew it," I said.

"How'd you know?" Haley said.

"You have the Haley look," I said.

"What's that?" Haley said.

"Your ears and your shoulders do kind of a wiggly thing," I said. "Like some kindergarten kid."

"A kindergarten kid?" Haley said.

The FBI helicopter made another close flyby. The bedroom's windows rattled once more and the helicopter's spotlight flashed between a gap in the curtains.

"You know," I said. "The kid in every class who's been told repeatedly not to raise their hand until the teacher at least finishes the question, but anyone can see it's always a life and death struggle for the kid to comply."

"And I'm that kid?" Haley said.

"You said it, not me," I said.

Haley didn't say anything.

"So," I said. "What you got?"

Haley looked like she wanted to reach through the screen and punch me. But, being the professional she was, she just took a few deep breaths and calmed herself. I sensed she was also trying to determine whether or not her ears and shoulders were wiggling. Apparently, Haley convinced herself they weren't, because she then continued on as if she had never been even the slightest bit nonplussed.

"We've got a profile on Nemo," Haley said.

"Reliable?" I said.

"Ninety-nine percent," Haley said. "But that's because it's so broad."

"How broad?" I said.

"NASAD computer programmer, male, between the ages of eighteen and thirty-two," Haley said.

"Is Nemo empathic?" I said.

"The profilers are neutral on that subject," Haley said.

"Huh," I said. "I thought they could figure that kind of stuff out."

"Not this time," Haley said. "Why do you want to know?"

"I told Dr. Lennon the profile could determine relative empathy levels," I said.

"Well, for your sake, I hope she's not too disappointed," Haley said.

"If I thought for a moment you were being sincere, I'd thank you," I said. "How many male programmers between the ages of eighteen and thirty-two does NASAD have?"

"About fifteen hundred," Haley said.

"Huh," I said. "So we've eliminated the other 75,000 or so NASAD employees?"

"Yes," Haley said. "Fifteen hundred is still a lot. I thought you'd be upset."

"I'm thinking," I said.

Thankfully, Haley was quiet for a moment and let me think.

Finally, I said, "Get them to run a cross-check of those fifteen hundred looking for anyone who personally knows Dr. Lennon, anyone in her family, or anyone who has ever worked in the Malibu house."

"You think there's some kind of personal connection?" Haley said.

"Yeah, well, I forgot to tell you something," I said.

"I'll be a monkey's uncle," Haley said.

"It's been a very, very long day, Haley," I said.

"Maybe you need to repeat kindergarten," Haley said.

I said nothing.

"What did you forget?" Haley said.

"I forgot to tell you where Dr. Lennon found the phone that had Nemo's voice message on it," I said.

"What does that mean?" Haley said. "It wasn't Dr. Lennon's phone?"

"No, it was a burner," I said. "And it was left under the pillow of her bed."

"It's a big house, isn't it?" Haley said.

"Yeah," I said.

"So most likely only someone who has been in the house or knew Paul or knows her would know which bedroom was hers," Haley said.

"Something like that," I said. "How come you're being so nice?"

"Pity," Haley said.

"Pity's good," I said.

"I'll get the cross-check started," Haley said.

"Any luck with the number I sent you that Nemo called from?" I said.

"Not yet," Haley said. "If it turns out to be anything special I'll tell you, but right now we're pretty convinced it was just a number Nemo used to disguise where he sent the message from."

"That's what I figured it was," I said.

"Do you have access to a computer?" Haley said.

"Is that for the other else?" I said.

"Yes," Haley said.

"I can't just use my iPhone?" I said.

"I want to show you something," Haley said. "And trust me, you'll want to see this in all its full screen glory."

"I'll go look for a computer," I said.

CHAPTER 58

I kept Haley on the line as I threw on my shirt and pants, exited the bedroom door, and went in search of a computer. I was working on the assumption there must be an office tucked away somewhere on the huge first floor space. I walked down the second floor corridor past the still snoring Manu and Mosi. Through the picture window I could see the FBI dog teams and the moving searchlight beam of the helicopter. I tiptoed down the granite staircase. I threaded my way through the sofas, coffee tables, and lamps of the first floor area that most resembled a living room, then continued on past the den and library.

Haley said, "Where are you?"

"Shh," I said. "Downstairs."

"What's taking so long?" Haley said.

I took the iPhone from my ear and pointed its camera at the room.

"Wow," Haley said. "That's a big room."

I zigged and zagged around some more sofas and tables and finally found a cozy office along the north side of the first floor. The window there looked out at seaside cliffs, the cliffs' limestone scalloped in the moonlight. I could also see the lights of the Coast Guard ship bouncing on the waves.

The office was done in light green and yellow pastels. Glass bookshelves held silver framed pictures of Paul Lennon and Kate, their children, and Kate's father, Milt Feynman. There was also a photo of the children standing in front of a smiling, older, gray-haired couple. The man and woman had their hands on the children's shoulders. I noticed a resemblance between the man and woman and Paul Lennon. I suddenly felt very hollow inside. Who else could the couple be but Paul's parents - the children's grandparents - who had been murdered the day before?

The office had a desk made of a thick sheet of glass atop two gold and silver granite pillars. A high-backed chair in magenta-hued leather was behind the desk. A computer, its screen dancing with a flaring rainbow screensaver, was on the desk. I pulled out the chair, sat down, and tapped on the keyboard. The screensaver disappeared. I started up the browser.

"What's going on now?" Haley said.

"I'm sitting at a computer," I said.

"Thanks for being so forthcoming with updates," Haley said. "I swear, working with you is like pulling teeth sometimes."

"You do realize you're talking to a general," I said.

"Least likely general in the history of the Armed Forces," Haley said.

"Thank you," I said. "Where am I going?"

Haley gave me a web address and a password. I punched them in. An overhead picture of a large ocean bay and a seaside town came on screen. There appeared to be a storm front moving in along one side of the bay.

"What am I looking at?" I said.

"Homer, Alaska," Haley said. "The bay is Kachemak Bay. The gathering clouds are in the direction of Katmai."

"This is from the satellite pictures from three years ago?" I said.

"Roger that," Haley said. "August sixteenth, the day Feynman and Lennon's plane went down."

"The image you've got here is incredibly sharp Haley," I said.

"It's like you said," Haley said. "Ever since 9/11 our satellites have been tasked to provide detailed coverage of the Alaska coastline. The technology they use has improved exponentially every year since then."

"Even so," I said. "You had to have done something to the original satellite footage didn't you?"

"We've got a bunch of new young hotshots in MOM's digital video enhancement division," Haley said. "They did a lot of pixel massaging."

"Uh huh," I said.

"You know," Haley said, "things like Fourier transformations, logarithmic transformations, and threshold transformations."

"Obviously," I said.

"Right," Haley said. "You have no idea what I'm talking about, do you?"

"Of course not," I said.

"Trust me, it works," Haley said. "We've also got access to a new custom Titan that blows the socks off even the most powerful Tianhe."

The Titans are a series of supercomputers designed at the Oak Ridge National Laboratory in Oak Ridge, Tennessee. The Tianhe are supercomputers made by the Chinese. As far I knew the Tianhe were at one time faster than the Titans, but I had no reason to doubt Haley's statement that the newest Titans were faster.

"Lots of petaflops, huh?" I said.

"Yeah, a lot of petaflops," Haley said. "By the way..."

"Yes?" I said.

"What is a petaflop, Jack?" Haley said.

"Just because I don't know what a Fournier transformation is...," I said.

"That's Fourier with an 'r,'" Haley said. "No 'n.'"

"Whatever," I said. "But just because I don't know what that is, doesn't mean I don't know what a petaflop is."

"Okay," Haley said. "I repeat. What's a petaflop?"

"It is a measure of a computer's processing speed," I said. "A petaflop is one quadrillion floating point operations per second."

Haley raised her hands up closer to her face where I could see them on the iPhone screen. She gave me a few tiny claps. Her hands were exquisite.

"Bravo," Haley said.

"I assume you used all those petaflops not only to process the pixels," I said, "but also to search through what must have been a staggeringly vast quantity of satellite images to find the ones you needed to track the plane?"

"Wait and see," Haley said. "We're going to zoom in now."

The picture of Kachemak Bay was still frozen, but the earth grew larger and closer as the view became magnified, and the area of focus narrowed to a small section. A peninsula jutting into the bay came into view.

"The road running through the peninsula is Homer Spit Road," Haley said. "On the seaside end is a harbor. Airport is on the inland side."

The view continued to zoom in.

"We're over the airport now," Haley said. "It sits between Mud Bay and Beluga Lake."

The picture zoomed until it hovered over a plane sitting on the runway waiting to take off. The plane was a de Havilland Otter seaplane. The picture was so clear I could read the wing number: N83198.

"I waited and I saw," I said. "That's the plane Feynman and Lennon took that day, correct?"

"Yep," Haley said. "We verified it's the right one by the wing number. Okay, we're going to start moving now."

Up until then, the picture had been still other than for the zoom. But now the frame of the picture began to move with the plane, as if a camera was outside the plane and following it. I assumed Haley's experts had somehow created the camera-like effect by manipulating the satellites' digital video data with their own special brand of technological wizardry.

The plane picked up speed along the runway. As the plane left the ground I thought I heard movement behind me. I turned to look, but there was nothing there. I returned to the screen. The plane climbed away from Homer and the camera followed it, zooming out as it did.

Haley said, "The accident report says that Paul Lennon and Milt Feynman were originally going to Kodiak Island to go fishing, but changed their minds that morning and decided to go grizzly viewing in Katmai."

"That's what Kate told me," I said.

"Radar trace confirmed that the plane was headed to Katmai as well," Haley said. "Radar further confirmed the plane passed through some gathering clouds that lay directly in its flight path. Everyone assumed back then that the clouds represented a much worse pattern than expected, and that the plane encountered severe turbulence that somehow caused it to ultimately plunge into the bay below."

The plane on the screen was now out over Kachemak Bay and continuing to climb.

"What's that they say about Alaska weather?" I said.

"If you don't like it, wait five minutes and it will change," Haley said.

"Yeah," I said. "Worse pattern than expected seems like it would have been a plausible assumption."

"Plausible enough anyway so that that assumption became part of the official story," Haley said. "The official story also says that the plane hit the water and the EPIRB went off."

"Kate told me that too," I said.

"Let me finish," Haley said. "Official story also says search and rescue was alerted and followed the EPIRB signal to the crash site. The would-be rescuers used the radar trace for additional backup to pinpoint the site. The clouds that didn't look so bad at the time of the crash grew into big thunderheads. A violent storm erupted that lasted for days. The sea was rocked with twenty foot waves. Rescue teams did their best, but nothing was ever found of the Otter or its passengers. The search was called off after three days."

"What actually happened?" I said.

"Who said that's not what actually happened?" Haley said.

"My gut," I said. "Also since you said 'official story' three times."

"Watch," Haley said.

The picture zoomed out some more. The plane became smaller. It's direction relative to Homer and the clouds became evident.

"Am I seeing what I think I'm seeing?" I said.

"What do you think you're seeing?" Haley said.

"The plane is heading nowhere near the direction of the clouds," I said.

"That's correct," Haley said.

"Where is it headed?" I said.

"Katmai is west of Homer," Haley said. "The plane is heading south. As I remember it, you said your hunch was that the plane might have actually traveled in the opposite direction from which the search and rescue teams were led to believe it had traveled?"

"That was my hunch," I said. "But it was just a hunch."

"Well, the true direction was more perpendicular than opposite," Haley said. "But from a practical point of view, it worked just as well."

"You mean it worked just as well if someone wanted to be sure the plane was never found?" I said.

"Uh huh," Haley said.

"Let me guess," I said. "Kodiak Island lies to the south of Homer?"

"Correct," Haley said.

"So they didn't change their plans after all," I said.

"Looks that way," Haley said.

"Why did people believe they'd changed them?" I said.

"The seaplane charter company received an in-flight radio message from the pilot," Haley said.

"Which had to have been faked," I said.

"One would think so," Haley said. "Keep watching. It gets worse."

The picture sped up. The plane continued on its southward path.

"Distance to Kodiak Island from Homer is 118 miles," Haley said. "We are now about 70 miles into our journey, 70 miles away from the mainland and 48 miles from Kodiak. Effectively in the middle of the ocean."

The camera began to zoom in again. The plane got bigger and bigger until it was as if we were only a hundred feet above it.

"You watching?" Haley said.

"What else would I be doing?" I said.

"I don't know," Haley said. "Sleeping, maybe. You've been doing that a lot lately."

The plane continued over a calm blue sea, its wings rolling slightly with the gentle winds it was encountering. Sunlight glittered off the fuselage. The waves glistened below. It looked like a commercial for an investment fund. Give us your money, and we will make sure you enjoy your golden years in exotic, far off locales. I half expected to see a breaching whale leap out of the water.

"Looks peaceful, Haley," I said.

"Couple more seconds," Haley said. "There. See that?"

I saw it, but I didn't believe it.

"Is this the original film?" I said. "Not doctored in any way?"

"As I said, we enhanced it..." Haley said.

"With the Fourier," I said.

"With the Fourier," Haley said. "We also added the zoom ins and zoom outs and messed around with cutting it all together, but, no, it wasn't doctored, Jack. What do you think?"

What I thought was that it was worse than I had expected. On the computer screen in front of me three orange explosions had suddenly appeared, one emanating from each wing and one from just in front of the tail. The explosions were violent, massive, and catastrophic. The tail separated from the fuselage and fell away from the plane. The wings flew end over end and out of the picture. The fuselage moved forward on its own momentum, its propeller spinning uselessly, then exploded in a massive fireball as the Otter's fuel tanks ignited. The mass of fire and steel plunged to the sea below.

"One explosion could be due to some mechanical failure," I said. "Leaking fuel line, whatever. Two simultaneous explosions are nearly impossible to imagine as accidental. Three are impossible."

"What'd they use?" Haley said.

I felt a rustle of air behind me. I turned. Again, nothing. I assumed I was just jittery from being overtired. "C4, PETN, maybe Semtex," I said. "Can't tell just by looking."

"Sophisticated timers," Haley said. "Seemed like they all went off exactly at the same time."

"Or someone pushed a button," I said.

"From a hundred and fifty miles away?" Haley said.

"Could be done," I said. "Satellite relay. I've done it."

"Less room for error?" Haley said.

"They can be confident the plane goes down where they want it to," I said. "Would help them make sure there weren't any planes or boats in the area carrying potential witnesses."

"Abort and wait for another day if there were?" Haley said.

"Yes," I said. "You told me NASAD had the technology to alter the radar trace and make the EPIRB signal look like it was coming from somewhere else. Any other country able to do the same thing?"

"We don't know of any," Haley said. "Also hard to imagine any other country could get into our radar system without us detecting it."

"Yeah," I said. "I can see that."

"Why didn't the killers just dismantle the EPIRB?" Haley said.

"Looks better," I said.

"Looks better how?" Haley said

"No plane crash is ever routine, but the EPIRB going off would make Feynman and Lennon's crash appear to be within the realm of a routine crash, at least in regard to the EPIRB," I said. "If the EPIRB doesn't go off, the crash is well outside that routine realm. Maybe someone starts thinking, digs a little deeper."

"Sees what we just saw," Haley said.

"Let's run the tape back," I said. "I want to look at the explosions again."

Haley rolled the tape back and the scene ran in reverse. The fireball sucked into itself and became a fuselage. The wings reattached themselves and the three orange explosions shrunk back into the wings and the area in front of the tail. The plane floated serenely backwards in the Alaskan sky. Kate's husband and father were alive again.

"Freeze it there, please," I said.

The Otter froze in place, its wing numbers clearly visible.

"Run it forward frame by frame now, please," I said.

The film ran again. The plane resumed its journey. Three little white puffs simultaneously appeared in one frame, three little white puffs that were to become three orange explosions in the next few frames.

"Freeze it again, please," I said.

The picture froze again.

"They all go off at the same time," Haley said.

"Hard to believe three timers would be so exact," I said. "I don't see them wiring all three bombs to one timer either. Much easier to plant each one alone than thread wires through the plane's interior and connect them together. Roll it forward slowly again, please."

The orange explosions appeared. I heard a creak in the floor behind me. I felt the rustle of air again, this time with a bit of warmth in it. I turned. Kate stood behind me. She was barefoot in a white bathrobe. Her hair was no longer tied with a ribbon and it flowed down onto her shoulders. Her beautiful blue eyes were fixed on the screen. Her expression was uncomprehending.

"What is that, Jack?" Kate said.

I didn't say anything. My throat was so tight, I couldn't have said anything even if I had known what to say.

"I recognize the wing numbers," Kate said. "It's Paul and my father's plane, isn't it?"

I still couldn't say anything. I should have told Haley to stop the film but I was too shocked to think of it. The film rolled on. Kate watched in horror as the wings and tail separated from the fuselage and the fuselage became a ball of fire.

"Is someone there with you, Jack?" Haley said.

Haley's words jolted me out of my trance.

"Shut it down," I said. "Turn off the damn film, Haley."

"Someone killed Paul and my father didn't they?" Kate said. "They were murdered, weren't they?"

Continued in Book Two of *THE INSURMOUNTABLE EDGE...*